THE MAN WHO DISAPPEARED
(AMERICA)

RITCHIE ROBERTSON is Taylor Professor of German at Oxford and a Fellow of the Queen's College. He is the author of *Kafka: A Very Short Introduction* (2004) and has written the introductions and notes to *The Trial* (trans. Mike Mitchell), *The Metamorphosis and Other Stories* (trans. Joyce Crick), and *The Castle* (trans. Anthea Bell) for Oxford World's Classics. He has also translated Hoffmann's *The Golden Pot and Other Stories* for the series, and introduced editions of Freud and Schnitzler. He is the editor of *The Cambridge Companion to Thomas Mann* (2002), and his most recent work is *Mock-Epic Poetry from Pope to Heine* (2009).

OXFORD WORLD'S CLASSICS

For over 100 years Oxford World's Classics have brought readers closer to the world's great literature. Now with over 700 titles—from the 4,000-year-old myths of Mesopotamia to the twentieth century's greatest novels—the series makes available lesser-known as well as celebrated writing.

The pocket-sized hardbacks of the early years contained introductions by Virginia Woolf, T. S. Eliot, Graham Greene, and other literary figures which enriched the experience of reading. Today the series is recognized for its fine scholarship and reliability in texts that span world literature, drama and poetry, religion, philosophy, and politics. Each edition includes perceptive commentary and essential background information to meet the changing needs of readers.

OXFORD WORLD'S CLASSICS

FRANZ KAFKA

The Man who Disappeared (America)

Translated with an Introduction and Notes by
RITCHIE ROBERTSON

OXFORD
UNIVERSITY PRESS

OXFORD
UNIVERSITY PRESS

Great Clarendon Street, Oxford OX2 6DP

Oxford University Press is a department of the University of Oxford.
It furthers the University's objective of excellence in research, scholarship,
and education by publishing worldwide in

Oxford New York

Auckland Cape Town Dar es Salaam Hong Kong Karachi
Kuala Lumpur Madrid Melbourne Mexico City Nairobi
New Delhi Shanghai Taipei Toronto

With offices in

Argentina Austria Brazil Chile Czech Republic France Greece
Guatemala Hungary Italy Japan Poland Portugal Singapore
South Korea Switzerland Thailand Turkey Ukraine Vietnam

Oxford is a registered trade mark of Oxford University Press
in the UK and in certain other countries

Published in the United States
by Oxford University Press Inc., New York

© Ritchie Robertson 2012

The moral rights of the author have been asserted
Database right Oxford University Press (maker)

First published as an Oxford World's Classics paperback 2012

British Library Cataloguing in Publication Data

Data available

Library of Congress Cataloging in Publication Data

Data available

Typeset by Cenveo, Bangalore, India
Printed in Great Britain
on acid-free paper by
Clays Ltd, Elcograf S.p.A.

ISBN 978-0-19-960112-7

10

CONTENTS

BIOGRAPHICAL PREFACE

FRANZ KAFKA is one of the iconic figures of modern world literature. His biography is still obscured by myth and misinformation, yet the plain facts of his life are very ordinary. He was born on 3 July 1883 in Prague, where his parents, Hermann and Julie Kafka, kept a small shop selling fancy goods, umbrellas, and the like. He was the eldest of six children, including two brothers who died in infancy and three sisters who all outlived him. He studied law at university, and after a year of practice started work, first for his local branch of an insurance firm based in Trieste, then after a year for the state-run Workers' Accident Insurance Institute, where his job was not only to handle claims for injury at work but to forestall such accidents by visiting factories and examining their equipment and their safety precautions. In his spare time he was writing prose sketches and stories, which were published in magazines and as small books, beginning with *Meditation* in 1912.

In August 1912 Kafka met Felice Bauer, four years his junior, who was visiting from Berlin, where she worked in a firm making office equipment. Their relationship, including two engagements, was carried on largely by letter (they met only on seventeen occasions, far the longest being a ten-day stay in a hotel in July 1916), and finally ended when in August 1917 Kafka had a haemorrhage which proved tubercular; he had to convalesce in the country, uncertain how much longer he could expect to live. Thereafter brief returns to work alternated with stays in sanatoria until he took early retirement in 1922. In 1919 he was briefly engaged to Julie Wohryzek, a twenty-eight-year-old clerk, but that relationship dissolved after Kafka met the married Milena Polak (née Jesenská), a spirited journalist, unhappy with her neglectful husband. Milena translated some of Kafka's work into Czech. As she lived in Vienna, their meetings were few, and the relationship ended early in 1921. Two years later Kafka at last left Prague and settled in Berlin with Dora Diamant, a young woman who had broken away from her ultra-orthodox Jewish family in Poland (and who later became a noted actress and communist activist). However, the winter of 1923–4, when hyperinflation was at its height, was a bad time to be in Berlin. Kafka's health declined so sharply that, after moving through several clinics and sanatoria around Vienna, he died on 3 June 1924.

The emotional hinterland of these events finds expression in Kafka's letters and diaries, and also—though less directly than is sometimes thought—in his literary work. His difficult relationship with his domineering father has a bearing especially on his early fiction, as well as on the *Letter to his Father*, which should be seen as a literary document rather than a factual record. He suffered also from his mother's emotional remoteness and from the excessive hopes which his parents invested in their only surviving son. His innumerable letters to the highly intelligent, well-read, and capable Felice Bauer bespeak emotional neediness, and a wish to prove himself by marrying, rather than any strong attraction to her as an individual, and he was acutely aware of the conflict between the demands of marriage and the solitude which he required for writing. He records also much self-doubt, feelings of guilt, morbid fantasies of punishment, and concern about his own health. But it is clear from his friends' testimony that he was a charming and witty companion, a sportsman keen on hiking and rowing, and a thoroughly competent and valued colleague at work. He also had a keen social conscience and advanced social views: during the First World War he worked to help refugees and shell-shocked soldiers, and he advocated progressive educational methods which would save children from the stifling influence of their parents.

Kafka's family were Jews with little more than a conventional attachment to Jewish belief and practice. A turning-point in Kafka's life was his encounter with Yiddish-speaking actors from Galicia, from whom he learned about the traditional Jewish culture of Eastern Europe. Gradually he drew closer to the Zionist movement: not to its politics, however, but to its vision of a new social and cultural life for Jews in Palestine. He learnt Hebrew and acquired practical skills such as gardening and carpentry which might be useful if, as they planned, he and Dora Diamant should emigrate to Palestine.

A concern with religious questions runs through Kafka's life and work, but his thought does not correspond closely to any established faith. He had an extensive knowledge of both Judaism and Christianity, and knew also the philosophies of Nietzsche and Schopenhauer. Late in life, especially after the diagnosis of his illness, he read eclectically and often critically in religious classics: the Old and New Testaments, Kierkegaard, St Augustine, Pascal, the late diaries of the convert Tolstoy, works by Martin Buber, and also extracts from the Talmud. His religious thought, which finds expression in concise and profound aphorisms, is highly individual, and the religious allusions which haunt his fiction tend to make it more rather than less enigmatic.

During his lifetime Kafka published seven small books, but he left three unfinished novels and a huge mass of notebooks and diaries, which we only possess because his friend Max Brod ignored Kafka's instructions to burn them. They are all written in German, his native language; his Czech was fluent but not flawless. It used to be claimed that Kafka wrote in a version of German called 'Prague German', but in fact, although he uses some expressions characteristic of the South German language area, his style is modelled on that of such classic German writers as Goethe, Kleist, and Stifter.

Though limpid, Kafka's style is also puzzling. He was sharply conscious of the problems of perception, and of the new forms of attention made possible by media such as the photograph and cinema. When he engages in fantasy, his descriptions are often designed to perplex the reader: thus it is difficult to make out what the insect in *The Metamorphosis* actually looks like. He was also fascinated by ambiguity, and often includes in his fiction long arguments in which various interpretations of some puzzling phenomenon are canvassed, or in which the speaker, by faulty logic, contrives to stand an argument on its head. In such passages he favours elaborate sentences, often in indirect speech. Yet Kafka's German, though often complex, is never clumsy. In his fiction, his letters, and his diaries he writes with unfailing grace and economy.

In his lifetime Kafka was not yet a famous author, but neither was he obscure. His books received many complimentary reviews. Prominent writers, such as Robert Musil and Rainer Maria Rilke, admired his work and sought him out. He was also part of a group of Prague writers, including Max Brod, an extremely prolific novelist and essayist, and Franz Werfel, who first attained fame as avant-garde poet and later became an international celebrity through his best-selling novels. During the Third Reich his work was known mainly in the English-speaking world through translations, and, as little was then known about his life or social context, he was seen as the author of universal parables.

Kafka's novels about individuals confronting a powerful but opaque organization—the court or the castle—seemed in the West to be fables of existential uncertainty. In the Eastern bloc, when they became accessible, they seemed to be prescient explorations of the fate of the individual within a bureaucratic tyranny. Neither approach can be set aside. Both were responding to elements in Kafka's fiction. Kafka worries at universal moral problems of guilt, responsibility, and freedom; and he also examines the mechanisms of power by which authorities can subtly coerce and subjugate the individual, as well as the individual's scope for resisting authority.

Placing Kafka in his historical context brings limited returns. The appeal of his work rests on its universal, parable-like character, and also on its presentation of puzzles without solutions. A narrative presence is generally kept to a minimum. We largely experience what Kafka's protagonist does, without a narrator to guide us. When there is a distinct narrative voice, as sometimes in the later stories, the narrator is himself puzzled by the phenomena he recounts. Kafka's fiction is thus characteristic of modernism in demanding an active reading. The reader is not invited to consume the text passively, but to join actively in the task of puzzling it out, in resisting simple interpretations, and in working, not towards a solution, but towards a fuller experience of the text on each reading.

INTRODUCTION

KAFKA'S first novel will pleasantly surprise readers who expect something gloomy, oppressive, and conventionally 'Kafkaesque'. Instead of the anonymous settings Kafka usually favours, this book is set in America—admittedly, since Kafka had never been there, an America of the imagination. And while *The Trial* and *The Castle* show individuals baffled by inscrutable bureaucratic systems, unable to make headway and oppressed by a feeling of confinement, *The Man who Disappeared* is considerably lighter in tone. Its narrative moves faster, taking its hero through a variety of locales. It has plenty of humour, though the humour is often black, and it even has episodes of slapstick comedy. The ultra-modern civilization of America is depicted throughout with horrified fascination.

The Man who Disappeared belongs to the great creative phase that began with Kafka's literary breakthrough of 22–3 September 1912, when he sat up all night writing the story entitled *The Judgement*, perhaps the only one of his works with which he was thoroughly satisfied. His friend Max Brod recorded in a diary entry of 29 September that Kafka was energetically working on his American novel: 'Kafka is in ecstasy, writes whole nights through. A novel, set in America.'[1] One reason why Kafka could work so fast was that he was rewriting a novel which he had first drafted in the winter of 1911–12. He became dissatisfied with this draft (which is lost), but not with the project, and he returned to it with new confidence. In a letter of 11 November Kafka tells Felice Bauer, soon to become his fiancée, that he has completed five chapters and almost finished a sixth. As he gives their titles, from 'The Stoker' to 'The Robinson Affair', we can see that the bulk of the novel was written with great fluency in about six weeks. Thereafter progress slowed. The untitled chapter set in Brunelda's flat was written with some difficulty. On 17 November Kafka reported that the novel was going badly, and that very night, seized by another idea, he started writing *The Metamorphosis*. He did not return to the novel until his next phase of energetic writing whose main product was *The Trial*, largely written in the second half of 1914. The fragments,

[1] Max Brod, *The Biography of Franz Kafka*, tr. G. Humphreys Roberts (London: Secker & Warburg, 1948), 101.

one headed 'Brunélda's Departure', the other untitled but recounting Karl's admission to the 'Theatre of Oklahama', were produced
between August and October 1914.

   Why should Kafka commit himself so passionately to a novel set in
America, and why should he choose in the first place a setting where
he had never been? His America combines two impulses. On the one
hand, it is an America of the imagination, a space of fantasy defined
less by empirical realities than by cultural myths. Kafka revises one
such myth in the very first paragraph, where the new immigrant Karl
Rossmann sees the Statue of Liberty holding a sword instead of a
torch—a warning that this America will prove to be a place of discipline based ultimately on violence. On the other, Kafka was anxious, as
he told his publisher, to present 'the most up-to-date New York' and
to give so far as possible an accurate picture of modern life. In search
of realism, he makes his American travellers eat steaks and drink
Coca-Cola—though these are defamiliarized, from the viewpoint of a
new immigrant, as 'almost raw meat' and 'a black liquid that burned
your throat' (p. 75). Yet despite its skyscrapers, machinery, endless
traffic, and contrasts of extreme wealth and poverty, Kafka's America
feels unreal or 'hyper-real'.[2] Partly because it is viewed through the
astonished eyes of a teenage immigrant, partly because of its fanciful
geography (New York is next to Boston; other towns are called
Butterford, Ramses, and Clayton; San Francisco is also referred to,
knowingly, as 'Frisco', but Oklahoma becomes 'Oklahama'), it comes
across (to quote Mark Anderson) as 'a mythical rather than a referen-
tially verisimilar landscape'.[3]

   Kafka knew about America from both oral and written sources.
Nineteenth-century Germany and Austria, especially from the
'Hungry Forties' onwards, sent millions of emigrants to the United
States, and many of those, especially the successful ones, revisited the
old country to report on their experiences. Several of Kafka's own
relatives had emigrated to America.[4] His cousin Otto, arriving in
New York in 1906 after some years in South America and South

   [2] Anne Fuchs, 'A Psychoanalytic Reading of *The Man who Disappeared*', in Julian
Preece (ed.), *The Cambridge Companion to Kafka* (Cambridge: Cambridge University
Press, 2002), 25–41 (p. 25).
   [3] Mark Anderson, *Kafka's Clothes: Ornament and Aestheticism in the Habsburg Fin de
Siècle* (Oxford: Clarendon Press, 1992), 107.
   [4] For full details, see Anthony Northey, *Kafka's Relatives: Their Lives and His Writing*
(New Haven and London: Yale University Press, 1991), ch. 6.

Africa, without contacts or knowledge of English, had risen, albeit less spectacularly than Karl's Uncle Jakob, to become export manager in a corset-making company and later to found his own business, the Kafka Export Corporation. He married an American, Alice Stickney, an independent-minded woman with a career as a painter, and brought her back to visit the old country in 1911. Otto's younger brother Franz, known in America as Frank, joined his company as a clerk. Another relative, Emil Kafka, worked for the mail-order business Sears, Roebuck & Co. in Chicago, and may have helped to suggest the student Mendel. Finally, yet another cousin, Otto's and Franz's brother Robert, had been seduced by his parents' forty-year-old cook and fathered her son; instead of emigrating to America, he stayed in Prague and became a successful lawyer, but his misadventure no doubt suggested Karl's experience with Johanna Brummer, especially as the name Robert Kafka could easily be transposed into Karl Rossmann.

Kafka also learnt a great deal from written sources, particularly from the travel book by Arthur Holitscher, *America Today and Tomorrow* (1913), large extracts from which had previously been published in a literary journal Kafka read.[5] Holitscher describes both the gigantic scale of American life and the exploitation of industrial workers. He tells how time-and-motion studies were used to increase their efficiency, and how workers were required to maintain a rapid tempo under the direction of a 'speed-boss', with the prospect, even if they could stand the pace, of being worn out by the age of forty. Holitscher also talks about the fortunes of the various European nations in America, stressing that Irishmen are particularly dangerous and that they dominate the corrupt New York police force. Hence Karl is especially on his guard against the Irishman Robinson, who turns out, however, to be less dangerous than the Frenchman Delamarche. Another informative source was a lecture, afterwards published in book form, by the Czech politician František Soukup, which Kafka attended on 1 June 1912. Soukup talked about the practice of electing local officials, and the frequent eccentricities of American politics: 'Yesterday lecture on America by Dr. Soukup. (The Czechs in Nebraska, all officials are elected, everyone must belong to one of the three parties—Republican,

[5] See Ritchie Robertson, *Kafka: Judaism, Politics, and Literature* (Oxford: Clarendon Press, 1985), 48–9; Wolfgang Jahn, *Kafkas Roman 'Der Verschollene'* (Stuttgart: Metzler, 1965).

Democratic, Socialist—Roosevelt's election meeting, with his glass he threatened a farmer who had made an objection, street speakers who carry a small box with them to serve as a platform.)'[6] This lodged in Kafka's mind and was put to use in the farcical account of a district judge's election meeting.

It was not just discrete items of information, however, that went to compose Kafka's America. Kafka also deploys cultural myths. The myth of rising from rags to riches, from log cabin to White House, is realized in the person of Karl's uncle, who began as a penniless immigrant and is now a millionaire and a Senator. At the same time, Kafka undercuts the myth by showing that to reach his present eminence the Senator has broken his ties with Europe and made himself into an inhuman embodiment of rigid principle. He also satirizes the myth by showing its reversal in the fate of Karl, who descends from riches to rags. The motif of travelling westwards to make one's fortune ('Go west, young man!') features ironically when Karl is given a one-way ticket to San Francisco and when Robinson (surely sixty years out of date?) fantasizes about making a fortune in the California golddiggings. A famous American icon, the Statue of Liberty, is given a sword instead of a torch, intimating the ruthlessness which governs the land of the free. 'For one need not hope for any compassion here', as Karl's uncle says (p. 29). Another icon, the Presidential box in which Abraham Lincoln was assassinated, appears near the end, empty of people and conveying a sense of autocracy (p. 208).

Even in Kafka's time Europeans regarded America ambivalently. 'Americanization' was often envisaged as Europe's future and as meaning the destruction of traditional culture by materialism and technology.[7] In keeping with this discourse, Kafka's America represents the pinnacle of modernity. All activities are organized on a massive scale. Karl's millionaire uncle has a nine-storey house containing a lift specially for furniture. The Hotel Occidental is variously said to have five or seven storeys, up to thirty or thirty-one lifts, and five thousand guests. Dwarfed by such gigantic settings, humanity is

---

[6] *The Diaries of Franz Kafka, 1910–1913*, ed. Max Brod, tr. Joseph Kresh (London: Secker & Warburg, 1948), 263. 'Roosevelt' is Theodore Roosevelt, President of the United States from 1901 to 1909.

[7] The first of many such warnings against the Americanization of German culture was issued by the prominent Berlin physiologist Emil Du Bois-Reymond in 1877: see Dieter Heimböckel, ' "Amerika im Kopf". Franz Kafkas Roman *Der Verschollene* und der Amerika-Diskurs seiner Zeit', *Deutsche Vierteljahresschrift*, 77 (2002), 130–47 (p. 133).

helplessly subjected to the demands of efficiency. In the business premises of Karl's uncle, even such an acknowledgement of shared humanity as greeting people has been abolished as unproductive:

Through the middle of the room people were constantly coming and going at a frantic pace. Nobody said good day, that had been abolished, each person followed in the footsteps of the one preceding him and looked at the floor, on which he wanted to advance as fast as possible, or picked up single words or figures by glancing at the papers that he was holding in his hand and that fluttered as he strode along. (p. 35)

Similar frantic haste governs the actions of the employees taking telephone messages, as it does the machine-like work of the assistant porters in the Hotel Occidental who dispense information in an unbroken flow without looking at their questioners. It is significant that the business that Uncle Jakob has built up from modest beginnings is a nationwide delivery service. Everything in Kafka's America centres on the transmission of goods and messages, not on their production or their reception. Kafka, as Anderson notes, and as his diaries confirm, was 'fascinated by the movement of traffic in the modern city'.[8] 'Verkehr' (a multivalent word meaning both 'traffic' and social or sexual 'intercourse') is the final word of *The Judgement*. Accordingly, the highway between New York and the city of Ramses carries an uninterrupted flow of traffic, seeming almost to move without human agency:

Karl sat upright and looked at the road a few metres below, where automobiles, as they had done all day, were rushing past one another, as though a precise number of them were continually being sent from a distant point and awaited at another distant point in the opposite direction. All day, ever since early in the morning, Karl had not seen a single automobile stop nor a single passenger get out. (pp. 77–8)

For most people, leisure is just as frenetic as work. New York theatregoers rush to the theatres in terror of being late. In the dining-room of the Hotel Occidental, diners jostle at the buffet for bad food and devour it in cramped spaces. Rather than increasing people's comfort, American life is often, as here, absurdly inconvenient. Perhaps the most ludicrous example concerns the traffic outside the Hotel Occidental. The movement of cars there is so uninterrupted that to

---

[8] Anderson, *Kafka's Clothes*, 98.

get to the street people have to scramble through the vehicles, ignoring their occupants.

The pace of American life precludes rest, and so lack of sleep is a recurrent motif in the novel. Staying with his uncle, Karl suffers from perpetual sleepiness. On the way to Mr Pollunder's house Karl is already sleepy, and throughout his misadventures there he feels so tired that he would like to snatch at least a few minutes' slumber. The Head Cook in the Hotel Occidental is a bad sleeper because of her worries while establishing herself in America: she counts herself lucky if she falls asleep by three, and she has to get up at five. The lift-boys' dormitory is so noisy that Karl usually gets only a few hours' sleep. Running away from the policeman, Karl is 'distracted by lack of sleep'. On arriving at Brunelda's flat, he remarks: 'I haven't slept for a good twenty-four hours' (p. 149). There his neighbour, the student Josef Mendel, works during the day in Montly's department store and studies at night, sustaining himself with black coffee and postponing sleep until he has finished his studies.

People are kept at work by terror of poverty. Karl has heard about 'the eastern districts of New York, which his uncle had promised to show him, where several families were said to live in a single room and a family's home consisted of the corner of a room in which the children crowded round their parents' (p. 50). Therese, the Head Cook's secretary at the Hotel Occidental, tells how as a child she lived with her mother in these very districts and how her mother, after a frantic search for a place to stay the night, died in an accident on a building site. We hear much about the difficulty of getting a job. Working as Delamarche's servant is said to be the best that Karl can hope for. Josef Mendel considers it the greatest achievement of his life to get a lowly job as a salesman.

Not everyone accepts these conditions. On their way to Mr Pollunder's country house Karl and his host are held up by a demonstration by metalworkers who are on strike. The renovations to Mr Pollunder's house have been delayed by a strike by building workers, which is also proving very expensive for the father of Karl's friend Mack, owner of the biggest building firm in New York. On the road with Delamarche and Robinson, Karl has a further glimpse of the underside of American capitalism when he learns that his uncle's firm is notorious for its underhand methods of recruiting labour.

Kafka shows no confidence that these conditions can be improved through democratic politics. We see democracy in action through the chaotic campaign for the election of a district judge which Karl witnesses from the balcony of Brunelda's flat. His neighbour Josef Mendel informs him that although the candidate, improbably named Lobter, is a competent man, he stands not the slightest chance of being elected. Late in the novel Karl sees a photograph of the box at the Theatre of Oklahoma reserved for the President of the United States: it looks inhumanly autocratic. What seems like popular democracy merely disguises the authoritarian rule of the political and economic elite.

Technology is here another way of oppressing human beings. It has become an autonomous, elemental power, free from human control, and restoring on a higher level man's former subjection to the forces of nature. This becomes especially clear from the description of passengers being rowed through New York harbour, where the ceaseless movement of technology combines with that of nature to render human beings powerless:

Boats belonging to ocean liners were rowed forwards by furiously toiling sailors and were full of passengers who sat in them just as they had been squeezed in, quietly and expectantly, though many could not refrain from turning their heads to observe the changing scenery. An incessant motion, an unrest transferred from the restless elements to the helpless humans and their works. (p. 15)

Moreover, the freedom of movement apparently offered by modern technology keeps being restricted. The novel offers repeated examples of long straight roads, like the highway between New York and Ramses, the road running almost straight from Karl's uncle's house to the riding-school, and the suburban street along which Karl is chased by the policeman. Alongside them, however, we find virtual labyrinths. Mr Pollunder's car has to take a roundabout route through a maze of side-streets because the main street is blocked by a demonstration. Delamarche saves Karl from the police by guiding him through a labyrinth of courtyards and corridors. Therese and her mother spend a desperate night in a similar labyrinth. And even Mr Pollunder's country house, allegedly in process of renovation, turns out to contain a Gothic labyrinth of corridors in which Karl gets almost hopelessly lost. In Kafka's America the potential for freedom is defeated by social conflict, poverty, and, in Pollunder's house, the lingering power of the past.

America, however, is only the setting for *The Man who Disappeared*. What kind of novel is it? Affinities have been suggested with the German 'Bildungsroman'. In this genre, whose classic representative is Goethe's novel *Wilhelm Meister's Apprenticeship* (1795–6), a young man is supposed, through a series of adventures and misadventures, to escape from his youthful self-centredness and become a responsible member of society. However, while Goethe's book certainly provided a model for several subsequent novels, the term 'Bildungsroman' did not become current till after 1870. Most of the novels claimed as 'Bildungsromane' depart from their model by showing their protagonist attaining, at best, a marginal place in society. And since Karl's career takes him ever downwards into the underworld, one can at most claim that *The Man who Disappeared* is an inversion or 'contrafacture' of the 'Bildungsroman'.[9] Similarly, the term 'picaresque', implying an episodic novel set amid low life, hardly fits *The Man who Disappeared*, for although Karl certainly descends into low-life, he is far from being the resourceful and unscrupulous rogue who would normally provide the hero of a picaresque narrative.

Kafka himself described *The Man who Disappeared* as an imitation of Dickens. He wrote in his diary:

Dickens's *Copperfield* ('The Stoker' a sheer imitation of Dickens, the projected novel even more so. The story of the trunk, the boy who delights and charms everyone, the menial labor, his sweetheart in the country house, the dirty houses, *et al.*, but above all the method. It was my intention, as I now see, to write a Dickens novel, but enhanced by the sharper lights I should have taken from the times and the duller ones I should have got from myself. [...]).[10]

The items from Dickens listed here have been transformed in Kafka's version: the charming boy, presumably alluding to Steerforth, reappears partly as Mack, partly as Renell, and the aggressive, highly sexed Klara is a very different person from Emily, the 'sweetheart' mentioned. Both novels also share the motifs of expulsion from a secure home; of severe quasi-paternal discipline (Mr Murdstone, Uncle Jakob); of a succession of father-substitutes; a kind mother-substitute (Peggotty, the Head Cook); and a dangerous journey on foot—Karl's

    [9] Peter-André Alt, *Franz Kafka: Der ewige Sohn. Eine Biographie* (Munich: Beck, 2005), 357.
    [10] *The Diaries of Franz Kafka, 1914–1923*, ed. Max Brod, tr. Martin Greenberg (London: Secker & Warburg, 1949), 188.

march to Ramses in the company of the untrustworthy Delamarche and Robinson, David's escape from the blacking factory and his walk to Dover in search of refuge with his aunt Betsey Trotwood.[11]

Alongside these shared motifs, however, the affinity between *David Copperfield* and *The Man who Disappeared* lies in the theme of childlike innocence adrift in a wicked world. Although his parents have unjustly punished him for an offence in which he was the passive victim, Karl remains loyal to them, wishes they could be proud of him, and is distressed when his photograph of them disappears. Throughout the novel Karl follows his conscience. He tries ineffectually to help the stoker secure justice from the ship's captain against the machinations of the Chief Engineer. Having accepted Mr Pollunder's invitation despite his uncle's evident disapproval, Karl thinks only of returning to his uncle's house and being reconciled. In the company of Delamarche and Robinson he behaves frankly and scrupulously, even offering them the entire contents of his suitcase if they will restore the photograph. At the Hotel Occidental he is the most conscientious of all the lift-boys. When Robinson shows up drunk, Karl copes with an impossible situation as best he can. Even in the chaotic flat occupied by Brunelda and Delamarche he does his best to tidy up, and when sent to fetch breakfast he is resourceful in putting together an acceptable meal from leftovers.

However, Karl is expelled from each refuge by a combination of bad luck and arbitrary power. When he mildly defies his uncle's inexplicable disapproval and pays a visit to Pollunder's house (without enjoying it at all), he loses his uncle's favour and is dismissed with only a ticket to San Francisco. At the Hotel Occidental, his efforts to handle the drunken Robinson require him briefly to desert his lift, and after he is called to account for this breach of order, evidence mounts to suggest that Karl is a liar and debauchee who spends every night on the town. The trial scene in the Head Waiter's office is a black comedy in which Karl's efforts to explain are either ignored or get him into a still deeper mess.

Karl's original fall was sexual. Far from being to blame, however, he was clearly the victim of abuse, amounting to rape, at the hands of the much older Johanna Brummer. Apart from feeling disgusted and

[11] See E. W. Tedlock, 'Kafka's Imitation of *David Copperfield*', *Comparative Literature*, 7 (1955), 52–62; Mark Spilka, *Dickens and Kafka: A Mutual Interpretation* (Bloomington, Ind.: Indiana University Press, 1963).

helpless, he seems still too naive to understand exactly what has happened, and though he is told he has a son, the fact does not seem to register with him. In America he is subjected to repeated homosexual fondlings, first from the stoker and then from Mr Pollunder, which resemble his original seduction insofar as he is forced into contact with an adult's body, felt to be oppressively large, within a confined space. His innocence is confirmed when he fails to understand why Klara sighs when he has his arms round her, and the sexual relationship is largely lost on him. He is pardonably embarrassed when, hearing Brunelda scream, he sees her 'sitting upright on the sofa, spreading her arms wide and embracing Delamarche as he knelt before her' (p. 150), but he is also fascinated: Brunelda is alarmed by the intensity with which he stares at her. Karl suffers under a series of mother-figures: the opening paragraph juxtaposes the seductress, who was old enough to be his mother, with the phallic female authority-figure of the sword-bearing Statue of Liberty; the motherly Head Cook turns out to be sexually involved with the authoritarian Head Waiter; and Karl and Robinson are treated like children by the sexually active couple Brunelda and Delamarche.[12]

Sexuality is often close to sadism. Klara tussles with Karl, throws him to the ground by ju-jitsu, and threatens to slap his face. The Head Porter holds Karl's arm so tightly as to cause him severe pain, and later resolves to 'enjoy' him in unspecified ways, which Karl fortunately avoids by his quick-witted escape. The relationship between Brunelda and Delamarche has elements of masochism. Brunelda is so infatuated with Delamarche that she left her luxurious apartment to live with him in comparative squalor, yet he is so much in thrall to her that he struggles to obey all her whims. Robinson meanwhile spends most of his time on the balcony trying to obtain voyeuristic glimpses of Brunelda's body. We can see here traces of the defining text of masochism, Leopold von Sacher-Masoch's *Venus in Furs* (1870), where the hero's thraldom to Wanda von Dunajew not only obliges him to serve her, like Delamarche, but, like Robinson, to lurk in a neighbouring room while she enjoys herself with her lovers.[13]

---

[12] See Elizabeth Boa, 'Karl Rossmann, or The Boy who Wouldn't Grow Up: The Flight from Manhood in Kafka's *Der Verschollene*', in Mary Orr and Lesley Sharpe (eds.), *From Goethe to Gide: Feminism, Aesthetics and the French and German Literary Canon* (Exeter: University of Exeter Press, 2005), 168–83.

[13] See Robertson, *Kafka*, 72.

The novel's atmosphere becomes more sinister after Delamarche and Robinson appear. Initially they seem only dirty and unkempt, but soon Robinson reveals his self-pity and dishonesty, Delamarche his potential for violence. It turns out that, having once met Karl, they are intent on drawing him into their power by making him Brunelda's servant. Robinson's visit to the Hotel Occidental may be part of this plot, intended to provoke a scandal and ensure Karl's dismissal. Hence, though Delamarche saves Karl from the policeman, he defames him so much that Karl will never dare to seek help from the police against Delamarche's tyranny. In the Delamarche household there is an intense atmosphere of seamy sexuality, concentrated in Brunelda's massive body, and a complex mechanism of power and degradation. Robinson has been reduced from Delamarche's partner to his servant: 'And if you keep being treated like a dog you end up thinking you are one', he says, thereby anticipating Kafka's use of the dog as an image of humiliation in *In the Penal Colony* and *The Trial*.[14] The ultimate support of power, namely violence, is revealed here, more nakedly even than by the sadistic Head Porter, when Delamarche, finding Karl trying to pick the lock of the apartment door, beats him up and leaves him unconscious.

If Kafka had completed the story, what else would have happened to Karl? The surviving fragments seem to show him descending further into the underworld. In 'Brunelda's Departure', where nothing is heard of Delamarche or Robinson, Karl seems to be doing a moonlight flit. He gets Brunelda downstairs with the help of Josef Mendel, then transports her in an invalid carriage to 'Enterprise No. 25', which sounds like a brothel. Reporting to the recruiters for the Theatre of Oklahoma, Karl recalls several recent but unspecified jobs, in the last of which he bore the name 'Negro'. This has led some interpreters to surmise a terrible fate for him.[15] Holitscher's *America Today and Tomorrow* not only includes a chapter on the maltreatment of American blacks but gives an illustration of one being lynched. The picture bears the sarcastic caption 'Idyll from Oklahoma', using the incorrect spelling which Kafka adopted. So perhaps the 'Theatre

[14] See *The Metamorphosis and Other Stories*, tr. Joyce Crick, Oxford World's Classics (Oxford: Oxford University Press, 2009), 75; *The Trial*, tr. Mike Mitchell, Oxford World's Classics (Oxford: Oxford University Press, 2009), 61, 139, 165.

[15] Alfred Wirkner, *Kafka und die Außenwelt: Quellenstudien zum 'Amerika'-Fragment* (Stuttgart: Klett, 1976), 81.

of Oklahama' is a device to decoy Karl into near-slavery and eventually a violent death. On the other hand, as John Zilcosky tells us, early in the twentieth century, as Kafka may have known, Oklahoma was 'viewed as a kind of "promised land" for American blacks', with many black landowners, businessmen, and financiers; this state of affairs ended in 1921 (long after the composition of Kafka's novel) when a race riot in the city of Tulsa killed as many as 300 blacks in a single night.[16] In any case, Kafka's own comments suggest a much milder end. We may not entirely credit Max Brod's recollection of his friend's words, since Brod always sought an upbeat interpretation of Kafka:

> From what he told me I know that the incomplete chapter about the Nature Theatre of Oklahoma (a chapter the beginning of which particularly delighted Kafka, so that he used to read it aloud with great effect) was intended to be the concluding chapter of the work and should end on a note of reconciliation. In enigmatic language Kafka used to hint smilingly, that within this 'almost limitless' theatre his young hero was going to find again a profession, a standby, his freedom, even his old home and his parents, as if by some celestial witchery.[17]

A diary entry by Kafka himself, comparing Karl to the protagonist of *The Trial*, suggests that Karl would also have died, but gently: 'Rossmann and K., the innocent and the guilty, both executed without distinction in the end, the guilty one with a gentler hand, more pushed aside than struck down.'[18]

The 'Theatre of Oklahoma' fragment has especially puzzled interpreters, one of whom has summed it up as 'a strange scenario of demagogic fakery, eschatological promise, and egalitarian social policy'.[19] In many ways it reads like a vision, however qualified, of redemption. It may even invite an allegorical reading, but to offer one might risk making too much of the hints that Kafka provides then partially withdraws. An institution that has a place for everyone, including—perhaps especially—the unfortunate and destitute; that advertises itself with

---

[16] John Zilcosky, *Kafka's Travels: Exoticism, Colonialism, and the Traffic of Writing* (Basingstoke and New York: Palgrave Macmillan, 2003), 67–9.

[17] Max Brod, 'Afterword', in *America*, tr. Willa and Edwin Muir (London: Routledge, 1938), 299–300.

[18] *The Diaries of Franz Kafka, 1914–1923*, 132.

[19] Rolf J. Goebel, 'Kafka and Postcolonial Critique: *Der Verschollene*, "In der Strafkolonie", "Beim Bau der chinesischen Mauer"', in James Rolleston (ed.), *A Companion to the Works of Franz Kafka* (Rochester, NY: Camden House, 2002), 187–212 (p. 196).

trumpets blown alternately by women dressed as angels and men dressed as devils; that most people are afraid to approach—all this may suggest that Karl has found a kind of religious salvation. If so, however, the devils disturb the picture; is this a conception of religion that, instead of sharply distinguishing good from evil, comprehends both? Moreover, the combination of vulgar razzmatazz and faulty organization—the trumpets are blown incompetently and discordantly, the pedestals on which the trumpeters stand seem to put them in danger, the new recruits have to run to catch their train—puts the entire undertaking in an ironic light. Kafka wrote this chapter in October 1914, at the same time as *In the Penal Colony*. The latter story also has hints of religious allegory, with the Old and New Commandants suggesting the Old and New Testaments, and the punishment-machine, whose victims are said to experience transfiguration, making one think of religious practices which, as Nietzsche maintains in *The Genealogy of Morals*, compel believers to suffer and recompenses them by offering a meaning for their sufferings. The malfunctioning and collapse of the punishment-machine, however, implies that religion is no longer tenable in the modern world, and the ramshackle character of the Theatre's organization may convey a similar message.

However, it is not likely that the Theatre is entirely fraudulent. It does fulfil its promise by offering employment to everyone who has the courage to cross the stage with the angels and devils. Its various booths seem to fit every possible category of person, including former European secondary-school pupils, and it takes Karl on even though he has no personal papers, no qualifications, no possessions, and a false name. Its invitation runs: 'If you want to be an artist, come along!' When Karl tries out the trumpet, Fanny remarks: 'You're an artist.' And Karl's admission is decided in the last and smallest office, on the edge of the set-up, where the manager is reluctantly obliged to accept the decision made by the clerk ('Schreiber', literally 'scribe' or 'writer'). It is as though the writer of the novel has consciously intervened to provide Karl with a happy ending that goes against the logic of the narrative. In all these ways, the Theatre of Oklahoma stands for art as a means of salvation that may continue to be valid after traditional religion has ceased to be credible.

Commentators have looked hard in the novel for a further layer of meaning related to Kafka's gradual exploration of his identity as a

Jew. Initially detached from his parents' residual attachment to Jewish traditions, and repelled by their half-heartedness, he found another access to Jewish culture when he attended the performances given in Prague by a small Yiddish theatre troupe. One of the actors, Yitzkhok Löwy, became a close friend and told Kafka much about the traditional Jewish culture of Eastern Europe. It is notable, however, that the immigrants to Kafka's America include Germans, Irishmen, Slovaks, a Frenchman, but no Jews, and that both Europe and America in this novel are conspicuously Christian. The stoker has an image of the Virgin Mary (p. 10), after which we hear of Johanna Brummer's 'wooden cross' (p. 23), the 'cathedral' in New York (p. 29), Karl's recollection of toy cribs at the Christmas market (p. 30), the disused chapel in Pollunder's house (p. 52), Karl's pocket bible (p. 67), which he leafs through but does not read, and the angel- and devil-disguises of the recruiters for the Theatre of Oklahoma (pp. 196, 198). Christianity does nothing to temper the inhumanity of either Europeans or Americans. These references form part of Kafka's satire and are connected with the hostile critique of Christianity that can be discerned in two contemporaneous texts, *The Judgement* and *The Metamorphosis*.[20] However, though Kafka's America lacks Jews, it is dominated by the quintessentially Jewish theme of exile. The Theatre of Oklahoma, which promises Karl integration into a society, may have been suggested by the Yiddish theatre where Kafka attended so many performances. And the name 'Negro' which Karl adopts may be linked, by a lengthy chain of associations, to his friend Yitzkhok Löwy.[21] Although a sustained 'Jewish' reading of the novel does not seem possible without strain, it shares with his other fiction of this period an intermittently 'Jewish' subtext.

If the logic of Kafka's story allows more hope here than in his later novels, his narrative method is also more relaxed. It is a commonplace of Kafka criticism that in his novels the narrative viewpoint is identical with the hero's, so that the narrator, and therefore the reader, can perceive only what the hero perceives and must therefore be just as perplexed as the hero by the unfamiliar realities that are encountered.

[20] See Ritchie Robertson, 'Kafka as anti-Christian: "Das Urteil", "Die Verwandlung" and the Aphorisms', in Rolleston (ed.), *A Companion to the Works of Franz Kafka*, 101–22.
[21] See Joseph Metz, 'Zion in the West: Cultural Zionism, Diasporic Doubles, and the "Direction" of Jewish Literary Identity in Kafka's *Der Verschollene*', *Deutsche Vierteljahresschrift*, 78 (2004), 646–71.

This account has subsequently been qualified. There are several passages in the novels that show us things that the hero cannot see (for instance, the civilities that K.'s executioners in *The Trial* exchange outside the entrance to his flat), and it is often possible to tell that the hero's reaction to events is inappropriate, even if one cannot confidently say what he should have done. In *The Man who Disappeared*, however, the narrator, while showing us America through Karl's eyes, often adds comments which do not sound like Karl's voice: e.g. the sentence that sums up the description of New York harbour: 'An incessant motion, an unrest transferred from the restless elements to the helpless humans and their works' (p. 15). Occasionally, too, the narrator tells us about things that Karl cannot see, as when Karl's uncle says: 'The stoker seems to have cast a spell on you', while 'casting a glance of understanding over Karl's head towards the Captain' (p. 27). Sometimes the narrative voice addresses Karl rhetorically: 'So hurry, Karl, make the most of the time that is left before the witnesses appear and swamp everything' (p. 19).

In many other parts of the novel the narrative method reveals Kafka's fascination with the cinema.[22] Kafka was particularly struck, and disturbed, by the restlessness of cinematic images. 'The cinema communicates the restlessness of its motion to the things pictured in it', he noted in his diary in 1911.[23] Hence the American scenes that Karl observes are almost always in rapid motion. Attention is also given to the effects of light. In the very first paragraph, the Statue of Liberty is seen 'in a sudden blaze of sunlight' (p. 5). When Karl looks down at the street from his uncle's house, the traffic seems to be 'grasped and permeated by a powerful light that kept being diffused, dispersed, and eagerly restored by the innumerable objects, and that seemed to the bedazzled eye physically palpable, as though a glass pane covering the entire street were being repeatedly smashed every moment with the utmost force' (p. 29). Here and in similar passages

---

[22] See esp. Jahn, *Kafkas Roman*, 53–67; Anderson, *Kafka's Clothes*, 117–21; Hanns Zischler, *Kafka Goes to the Movies*, tr. Susan H. Gillespie (Chicago and London: University of Chicago Press, 2003), which identifies all the films Kafka saw; and Peter-André Alt, *Kafka und der Film: Über kinematographisches Erzählen* (Munich: Beck, 2009), an important study on which the following paragraphs are mainly based.

[23] *The Diaries of Franz Kafka, 1914–1923*, 241. Despite its title, this volume also contains Kafka's early travel diaries, including the notes kept on an official trip to the provincial towns of Friedland and Reichenberg in January–February 1911, from which this quotation comes.

Kafka has found a verbal counterpart to the flickering light that was so conspicuous in early cinema.

Cinematic methods are especially prominent in slapstick scenes such as Karl's pursuit by the policeman and the knockabout comedy in Brunelda's flat when Karl and Robinson search vainly for her perfume. The films produced by Mack Sennett for the Keystone Film Company specialized in speeded-up chases, in which the person fleeing would be rescued at the last moment. We have just such a chase when Karl runs away from the policeman and is saved in the nick of time by Delamarche. And we have a cinematic model for it in the five-minute film *Nick Winter et le vol de la Joconde* ('Nick Winter and the Theft of the Mona Lisa') which Kafka saw in Paris on 10 September 1911 and which involves a farcical chase through Parisian cafés.

In addition, there is something cinematic about the occasional panoramas of American cityscapes and landscapes. There is the famous view of New York harbour and beyond it the city, 'looking at Karl with the hundred thousand windows of its skyscrapers' (p. 11); Karl's distant prospect of New York and Boston, impossibly connected by the Hudson; and the enormous racetrack at Clayton where the Theatre of Oklahoma recruits employees and 'which on all sides stretched as far as the distant forests' (p. 204). These broad visual perspectives are not found in Kafka's later novels.

Although several films—by Orson Welles and Michael Haneke, among others—have been based on *The Trial* and *The Castle*, film-makers have shown less interest in *The Man who Disappeared*.[24] It was filmed in 1984 as *Klassenverhältnisse* ('Class Relations') by the French husband-and-wife team of film-makers Jean-Marie Straub and Danièle Huillet. Their version, as the title suggests, concentrates on relations of power and oppression, expressed especially by dark interiors in which intimidating authority-figures deliver monologues; the movement is slow and stiff, and the sense of space evoked by Kafka's panoramic descriptions is largely lost.[25] It is surely time for a director

[24] A handy list of films based on Kafka's texts is provided in Oliver Jahraus, 'Kafka und der Film', in Bettina von Jagow and Oliver Jahraus (eds.), *Kafka-Handbuch* (Göttingen: Vandenhoeck & Ruprecht, 2008), 224–36 (pp. 228–9).

[25] On this film, see Martin Brady and Helen Hughes, 'Kafka Adapted to Film', in Preece (ed.), *The Cambridge Companion to Kafka*, 226–41 (pp. 234–7); Marino Guida, 'Resisting Performance: Straub/Huillet's Filming of Kafka's *Der Verschollene*', in Carolin Duttlinger, Lucia Ruprecht, and Andrew Webber (eds.), *Performance and Performativity in German Cultural Studies* (Oxford and Bern: Peter Lang, 2003), 131–5.

to appreciate Kafka's cinematic effects and retranslate them to the screen. In the meantime, however, readers of *The Man who Disappeared* can enjoy a novel which refreshingly breaks free from the cliché of the 'Kafkaesque'.

NOTE ON THE TEXT

THE only part of this novel published in Kafka's lifetime was the first chapter, which appeared as a self-contained book, entitled *Der Heizer. Ein Fragment* ('The Stoker: A Fragment'), in May 1913. It was number 3 in the series of modernist texts published by the Kurt Wolff Verlag under the title 'Der jüngste Tag' ('The Day of Judgement'). Kafka also considered publishing it, together with *The Metamorphosis* and *The Judgement* (in that order), in a book to be entitled *Die Söhne* ('The Sons'): see his letter to Kurt Wolff of 11 April 1913. Although this project was never realized, it was based on a number of affinities among the three stories: all concern sons who are treated badly, even murderously, by their families, and contain motifs of degradation, especially the image of vermin ('Ungeziefer').

The novel as a whole was edited by Kafka's friend Max Brod and published, again by the Kurt Wolff Verlag, in 1927, three years after Kafka's death. Brod gave the novel the title *Amerika*, though it is now apparent from Kafka's diary that his own title for it was *Der Verschollene*. This is not easy to translate: *The Man who Disappeared*, like the French title *Le Disparu*, conveys only part of the meaning, since 'verschollen' implies 'lost without trace' or 'missing, presumed dead'.

Brod's edition contains eight chapters. The present chapters 1–6 are given with the titles Kafka intended for them and are followed by the chapter recounting Kafka's arrival at Brunelda's flat and his unsuccessful attempt to escape, which Brod called 'A Refuge', and by the incomplete account of Karl's admission to the Theatre of Oklahama, which Brod entitled 'The Nature Theatre of Oklahoma'. 'Nature Theatre' implies a large open-air theatre, such as Kafka could have found depicted in Holitscher's *America Today and Tomorrow*. The term 'nature theatre' does not occur in Kafka's text, however, and from the description of the President's box, the theatre would appear to be a building. The episode beginning ' "Get up! Get up!" cried Robinson' and the one which Kafka entitled 'Brunelda's Departure' are classified by Brod as fragments and given in an appendix. In addition, Brod corrected some of Kafka's mistakes, changing pounds to dollars, Boston to Brooklyn, the Hudson to the East River, and 'Oklahama' to Oklahoma, and tidied up his inconsistencies of spelling (Mak/Mack, Rennel/Renell).

The present translation is based not on Brod's version but on the text as critically edited by Jost Schillemeit and published as *Der Verschollene* by the S. Fischer Verlag in 1983. Schillemeit judges that the episode beginning ' "Get up! Get up!" cried Robinson' is a separate chapter following on from the chapter about Karl's arrival at the flat. He therefore removes it from the appendix and puts it in its proper place in the main body of the text. 'Brunelda's Departure' and the theatre episode strike him as too incomplete to be integrated with the main text, and hence they appear as fragments.

I have preserved most of Kafka's apparent mistakes. Some commentators in any case now think that they are deliberate mistakes designed to make America into a fantastic rather than realistic landscape. However, although Kafka alternates between the spellings 'New York' and 'Newyork', I have consistently written 'New York', since this particular inconsistency would have been too conspicuous.

NOTE ON THE TRANSLATION

A TRANSLATOR has to find a compromise between the extremes of 'domestication'—making a text read as though it had originally been written in English—and 'foreignization'—preserving its alien character at the risk of making the text difficult to approach. I have tried to provide a congenial reading experience, especially since this is the most relaxed and informal of Kafka's major works, but without entirely losing the distinctiveness of his style.

Kafka's style is simple, and I have sought to retain its simplicity. Where English has such alternatives for everyday words as 'big, large, great', 'small, little', 'pull, draw, tug', and so on, German has only one common word—*groß, klein, ziehen*—and one creates a false impression if one artificially enlarges Kafka's vocabulary. If the text repeats commonplace words, therefore, that is because the original does so.

The Critical Edition preserves the punctuation of Kafka's manuscripts. Both for the sake of authenticity, and to convey the flavour of Kafka's text, I have, despite some compromises, retained his punctuation in one important respect. Kafka favours long sentences in which main clauses are linked only by commas. The translator is tempted either to make them into separate sentences or to link them by means of conjunctions, but either decision would seriously slow the pace of Kafka's narrative. It is particularly important to keep his pace in such breathless passages as Therese's account of her mother's death.

Kafka's sentences are often linked by particles such as 'aber', 'zwar', 'übrigens', 'überdies', 'allerdings', and his verbs are qualified by intensifiers such as 'ja' and 'doch'. If one translates all these, the sentences become cluttered, but if one leaves them out, the style becomes barer and sparer than Kafka's. I have compromised, translating these expressions whenever possible ('but', 'however', 'indeed', 'after all', 'moreover', 'anyway', 'all the same', 'to be sure') but trying not to overload the sentences with insertions which are more obtrusive in English than in German.

Forms of address are another problem. Karl calls the Head Cook and the Head Porter 'Frau Oberköchin' and 'Herr Oberportier', but

I could not bring myself to translate these as 'Mrs Cook' and 'Mr Porter', and not just because of the irritating echoes of a music-hall song. Instead I have opted for 'ma'am' and 'sir', which, by being incongruously old-fashioned, underline the incongruity of the hierarchical rules which Kafka shows to operate in supposedly democratic America.

Since the novel is set in America, there is an obvious temptation to use American English, especially as we are meant to assume that the characters are all speaking American English, except for the conversation between Karl and the stoker in the first chapter and a brief exchange between Karl and the Head Cook. The distinction between American and British English has of course no counterpart in German. I have used the form of English that comes naturally to me, namely British English, except that I have used 'elevator' alongside 'lift', corresponding to Kafka's variation between 'Aufzug' and 'Lift', and 'automobile' alongside 'car', corresponding to Kafka's 'Automobil' and 'Wagen'. At certain points it also seemed natural to make Mak say 'Hi' and Delamarche say 'You sure are'. Otherwise, the characters speak an English which, I hope, is not strongly flavoured or dated.

I have benefited from occasionally consulting the previous translations by Michael Hofmann (*The Man who Disappeared (Amerika)*, London: Penguin, 1996) and Mark Harman (*Amerika: The Missing Person*, New York: Schocken, 2008), and am grateful to Mark Harman for giving me a copy of his translation. I have tried, however, to make my version as far as possible independent of theirs. I also thank Joyce Crick for her detailed comments on a sample chapter, and David Horton (Saarbrücken) for a valuable conversation about translation and for sharing with me his reflections on translating Thomas Mann and on translating between German and English generally.

SELECT BIBLIOGRAPHY
(CONFINED TO WORKS IN ENGLISH)

Translations of Kafka's Non-Fictional Works

The Collected Aphorisms, tr. Malcolm Pasley (London: Penguin, 1994).

The Diaries of Franz Kafka, 1910–1913, ed. Max Brod, tr. Joseph Kresh (London: Secker & Warburg, 1948).

The Diaries of Franz Kafka, 1914–1923, ed. Max Brod, tr. Martin Greenberg (London: Secker & Warburg, 1949).

Letters to Friends, Family and Editors, tr. Richard and Clara Winston (New York: Schocken, 1988).

Letters to Felice, tr. James Stern and Elizabeth Duckworth (London: Vintage, 1992).

Letters to Milena, expanded edn., tr. Philip Boehm (New York: Schocken, 1990).

Letters to Ottla and the Family, tr. Richard and Clara Winston (New York: Schocken, 1988).

Biographies

Adler, Jeremy, *Franz Kafka* (London: Penguin, 2001).

Brod, Max, *The Biography of Franz Kafka*, tr. G. Humphreys Roberts (London: Secker & Warburg, 1948).

Diamant, Kathi, *Kafka's Last Love: The Mystery of Dora Diamant* (London: Secker & Warburg, 2003).

Hayman, Ronald, *K: A Biography of Kafka* (London: Weidenfeld & Nicolson, 1981).

Hockaday, Mary, *Kafka, Love and Courage: The Life of Milena Jesenská* (London: Deutsch, 1995).

Murray, Nicholas, *Kafka* (London: Little, Brown, 2004).

Northey, Anthony, *Kafka's Relatives: Their Lives and His Writing* (New Haven and London: Yale University Press, 1991).

Stach, Reiner, *Kafka: The Decisive Years*, tr. Shelley Frisch (San Diego and London: Harcourt, 2005).

Storr, Anthony, 'Kafka's Sense of Identity', in his *Churchill's Black Dog and Other Phenomena of the Human Mind* (London: Collins, 1989), 52–82.

Unseld, Joachim, *Franz Kafka: A Writer's Life*, tr. Paul F. Dvorak (Riverside, Calif.: Ariadne Press, 1997).

Introductions

Gray, Richard T., Ruth V. Gross, Rolf J. Goebel, and Clayton Koelb, *A Franz Kafka Encyclopedia* (Westport, Conn.: Greenwood Press, 2005).

Preece, Julian (ed.), *The Cambridge Companion to Kafka* (Cambridge: Cambridge University Press, 2002).

Robertson, Ritchie, *Kafka: A Very Short Introduction* (Oxford: Oxford University Press, 2004).

Rolleston, James (ed.), *A Companion to the Works of Franz Kafka* (Rochester, NY: Camden House, 2002).

Speirs, Ronald, and Beatrice Sandberg, *Franz Kafka*, Macmillan Modern Novelists (London: Macmillan, 1997).

Critical Studies

Alter, Robert, *Necessary Angels: Tradition and Modernity in Kafka, Benjamin and Scholem* (Cambridge, Mass.: Harvard University Press, 1991).

Anderson, Mark, *Kafka's Clothes: Ornament and Aestheticism in the Habsburg Fin de Siècle* (Oxford: Clarendon Press, 1992).

——'Kafka, Homosexuality and the Aesthetics of "Male Culture"', *Austrian Studies*, 7 (1996), 79–99.

Boa, Elizabeth, *Kafka: Gender, Class and Race in the Letters and Fictions* (Oxford: Clarendon Press, 1996).

Corngold, Stanley, *Lambent Traces: Franz Kafka* (Princeton: Princeton University Press, 2004).

Dodd, W. J., *Kafka and Dostoyevsky: The Shaping of Influence* (London: Macmillan, 1992).

——(ed.), *Kafka: The Metamorphosis, The Trial and The Castle*, Modern Literatures in Perspective (London and New York: Longman, 1995).

Duttlinger, Carolin, *Kafka and Photography* (Oxford: Oxford University Press, 2007).

Flores, Angel (ed.), *The Kafka Debate* (New York: Gordian Press, 1977).

Gilman, Sander L., *Franz Kafka, the Jewish Patient* (London and New York: Routledge, 1995).

Goebel, Rolf J., *Constructing China: Kafka's Orientalist Discourse* (Columbia, SC: Camden House, 1997).

Heidsieck, Arnold, *The Intellectual Contexts of Kafka's Fiction: Philosophy, Law, Religion* (Columbia, SC: Camden House, 1994).

Koelb, Clayton, *Kafka's Rhetoric: The Passion of Reading* (Ithaca and London: Cornell University Press, 1989).

Politzer, Heinz, *Franz Kafka: Parable and Paradox* (Ithaca, NY: Cornell University Press, 1962).

Robertson, Ritchie, *Kafka: Judaism, Politics and Literature* (Oxford: Clarendon Press, 1985).

Sokel, Walter H., *The Myth of Power and the Self: Essays on Franz Kafka* (Detroit: Wayne State University Press, 2002).

Spilka, Mark, *Dickens and Kafka: A Mutual Interpretation* (Bloomington, Ind.: Indiana University Press, 1963).

Zilcosky, John, *Kafka's Travels: Exoticism, Colonialism, and the Traffic of Writing* (Basingstoke and New York: Palgrave Macmillan, 2003).

Zischler, Hanns, *Kafka Goes to the Movies*, tr. Susan H. Gillespie (Chicago and London: University of Chicago Press, 2003).

Historical Context

Anderson, Mark (ed.), *Reading Kafka: Prague, Politics, and the Fin de Siècle* (New York: Schocken, 1989).

Beck, Evelyn Torton, *Kafka and the Yiddish Theater* (Madison, Wisc.: University of Wisconsin Press, 1971).

Bruce, Iris, *Kafka and Cultural Zionism: Dates in Palestine* (Madison, Wisc.: University of Wisconsin Press, 2007).

Gelber, Mark H. (ed.,), *Kafka, Zionism, and Beyond* (Tübingen: Niemeyer, 2004).

Kieval, Hillel, J., *The Making of Czech Jewry: National Conflict and Jewish Society in Bohemia, 1870–1918* (New York: Oxford University Press, 1988).

Robertson, Ritchie, *The 'Jewish Question' in German Literature, 1749–1939* (Oxford: Oxford University Press, 1999).

Spector, Scott, *Prague Territories: National Conflict and Cultural Innovation in Franz Kafka's Fin de Siècle* (Berkeley, Los Angeles, and London: University of California Press, 2000).

The Man who Disappeared

Boa, Elizabeth, 'Karl Rossmann, or The Boy who Wouldn't Grow Up: The Flight from Manhood in Kafka's *Der Verschollene*', in Mary Orr and Lesley Sharpe (eds.), *From Goethe to Gide: Feminism, Aesthetics and the French and German Literary Canon* (Exeter: University of Exeter Press, 2005), 168–83.

Fuchs, Anne, 'A Psychoanalytic Reading of *The Man who Disappeared*', in Julian Preece (ed.), *The Cambridge Companion to Kafka* (Cambridge: Cambridge University Press, 2002), 25–41.

Goebel, Rolf J., 'Kafka and Postcolonial Critique: *Der Verschollene*, "In der Strafkolonie", "Beim Bau der chinesischen Mauer" ', in James Rolleston (ed.), *A Companion to the Works of Franz Kafka* (Rochester, NY: Camden House, 2002), 187–212.

Metz, Joseph, 'Zion in the West: Cultural Zionism, Diasporic Doubles, and the "Direction" of Jewish Literary Identity in Kafka's *Der Verschollene*', *Deutsche Vierteljahresschrift*, 78 (2004), 646–71.

Robertson, Ritchie, 'Mothers and Lovers in Some Novels by Kafka and Brod', *German Life and Letters*, 50 (1997), 475–90.

Ryan, Michael P., 'Kafka's *Die Söhne*: the Range and Scope of Metaphor', *Monatshefte*, 93 (2001), 73–86.

Tedlock, E. W., 'Kafka's Imitation of *David Copperfield*', *Comparative Literature*, 7 (1955), 52–62.

Further Reading in Oxford World's Classics

Kafka, Franz, *The Castle*, tr. Anthea Bell, ed. Ritchie Robertson.

——*A Hunger Artist and Other Stories*, tr. Joyce Crick, ed. Ritchie Robertson.

——*The Metamorphosis and Other Stories*, tr. Joyce Crick, ed. Ritchie Robertson.

——*The Trial*, tr. Mike Mitchell, ed. Ritchie Robertson.

A CHRONOLOGY OF FRANZ KAFKA

1883 3 July: Franz Kafka born in Prague, son of Hermann Kafka (1852–1931) and his wife Julie, née Löwy (1856–1934).

1885 Birth of FK's brother Georg, who died at the age of fifteen months.

1887 Birth of FK's brother Heinrich, who died at the age of six months.

1889 Birth of FK's sister Gabriele ('Elli') (d. 1941).

1890 Birth of FK's sister Valerie ('Valli') (d. 1942).

1892 Birth of FK's sister Ottilie ('Ottla') (d. 1943).

1901 FK begins studying law in the German-language section of the Charles University, Prague.

1906 Gains his doctorate in law and begins a year of professional experience in the Prague courts.

1907 Begins working for the Prague branch of the insurance company Assicurazioni Generali, based in Trieste.

1908 Moves to the state-run Workers' Accident Insurance Company for the Kingdom of Bohemia. First publication: eight prose pieces (later included in the volume *Meditation*) appear in the Munich journal *Hyperion*.

1909 Holiday with Max and Otto Brod at Riva on Lake Garda; they attend a display of aircraft, about which FK writes 'The Aeroplanes at Brescia'.

1910 Holiday with Max and Otto Brod in Paris.

1911 Holiday with Max Brod in Northern Italy, Switzerland, and Paris. Attends many performances by Yiddish actors visiting Prague, and becomes friendly with the actor Isaak Löwy (Jitzkhok Levi).

1912 Holiday with Max Brod in Weimar, after which FK spends three weeks in the nudist sanatorium 'Jungborn' in the Harz Mountains. Works on *The Man who Disappeared*. 13 August: first meeting with Felice Bauer (1887–1960) from Berlin. 22–3 September: writes *The Judgement* in a single night. November–December: works on *The Metamorphosis*. December: *Meditation*, a collection of short prose pieces, published by Kurt Wolff in Leipzig.

1913 Visits Felice Bauer three times in Berlin. September: attends a conference on accident prevention in Vienna, where he also looks in on the Eleventh Zionist Congress. Stays in a sanatorium in Riva. Publishes *The Stoker* (= the first chapter of *The Man who Disappeared*) in Wolff's series of avant-garde prose texts 'The Last Judgement'.

1914 1 June: officially engaged to Felice Bauer in Berlin. 12 July: engagement dissolved. Holiday with the Prague novelist Ernst Weiss in the Danish resort of Marielyst. August–December: writes most of *The Trial*; October: *In the Penal Colony*.

1915 The dramatist Carl Sternheim, awarded the Fontane Prize for literature, transfers the prize money to Kafka. *The Metamorphosis* published by Wolff.

1916 Reconciliation with Felice Bauer; they spend ten days together in the Bohemian resort of Marienbad (Mariánské Lázně). *The Judgement* published by Wolff. FK works on the stories later collected in *A Country Doctor*.

1917 July: FK and Felice visit the latter's sister in Budapest, and become engaged again. 9–10 August: FK suffers a haemorrhage which is diagnosed as tubercular. To convalesce, he stays with his sister Ottla on a farm at Zürau (Siřem) in the Bohemian countryside. December: visit from Felice Bauer; engagement dissolved.

1918 March: FK resumes work. November: given health leave, stays till March 1919 in a hotel in Schelesen (Železná).

1919 Back in Prague, briefly engaged to Julie Wohryzek (1891–1944). *In the Penal Colony* published by Wolff.

1920 Intense relationship with his Czech translator Milena Polak, née Jesenská (1896–1944). July: ends relationship with Julie Wohryzek. Publication of *A Country Doctor: Little Stories*. December: again granted health leave, FK stays in a sanatorium in Matliary, in the Tatra Mountains, till August 1921.

1921 September: returns to work, but his worsening health requires him to take three months' further leave from October.

1922 January: has his leave extended till April; stays in mountain hotel in Spindlermühle (Špindlerův Mlýn). January–August: writes most of *The Castle*. 1 July: retires from the Insurance Company on a pension.

1923 July: visits Müritz on the Baltic and meets Dora Diamant (1898–1952). September: moves to Berlin and lives with Dora.

1924 March: his declining health obliges FK to return to Prague and in April to enter a sanatorium outside Vienna. Writes and publishes 'Josefine, the Singer or The Mouse-People'. 3 June: dies. August: *A Hunger Artist: Four Stories* published by Die Schmiede.

1925 *The Trial*, edited by Max Brod, published by Die Schmiede.

1926 *The Castle*, edited by Max Brod, published by Wolff.

1927 *Amerika* (now known by Kafka's title, *The Man who Disappeared*), edited by Max Brod, published by Wolff.

1930 *The Castle*, translated by Willa and Edwin Muir, published by Martin Secker (London), the first English translation of Kafka.

1939 Max Brod leaves Prague just before the German invasion, taking Kafka's manuscripts in a suitcase, and reaches Palestine.

1956 Brod transfers the manuscripts (except that of *The Trial*) to Switzerland for safe keeping.

1961 The Oxford scholar Malcolm Pasley, with the permission of Kafka's heirs, transports the manuscripts to the Bodleian Library.

THE MAN WHO DISAPPEARED
(AMERICA)

CONTENTS

I

The Stoker

As the seventeen-year-old* Karl Rossmann, who had been sent to America by his poor parents because a servant-girl had seduced him and had a child by him, entered New York harbour in the already slowing ship, he saw the statue of the Goddess of Liberty,* which he had been observing for some time, as though in a sudden blaze of sunlight. Her arm with the sword stretched upward as though newly raised and the free breezes wafted around her.

'So high,' he said to himself, never thinking of leaving the ship, and gradually getting pushed over to the railings by the ever-growing crowd of porters streaming past him.

A young man whom he had got to know slightly during the voyage said in passing: 'What, aren't you keen to get off the ship?' 'I'm quite ready,' said Karl, smiling at him, and, from high spirits and because he was a strong lad, he lifted his suitcase onto his shoulder. But as he looked past his acquaintance, who, twirling his stick a little, was already moving away with the rest, he noticed that he had left his umbrella down below in the ship. He asked his acquaintance, who did not seem much gratified, to be kind enough to wait for a moment beside his suitcase, surveyed the location quickly so that he could find his way back, and hurried off. Below, to his disappointment, he found a passage that would have shortened his journey a good deal closed for the first time, probably because all the passengers were disembarking, and had to make his way laboriously through innumerable small rooms, corridors constantly branching off, short flights of stairs always followed by others, an empty room with an abandoned desk, until, since he had been this way only once or twice and always in a large group, he really was completely lost. Being utterly perplexed, and since he encountered nobody else and only kept hearing the trampling of thousands of people's feet above his head and noticed, like a distant breath, the last throbbings of the engine which had already been switched off, he began, without reflecting, to hammer on a randomly chosen small door, at which he had paused amid his wanderings. 'It's open,' called someone inside, and Karl, breathing a heartfelt sigh of relief, opened the door. 'Why are you hammering on the door like a madman?' asked a huge man, barely glancing at Karl. Through some shaft in the ceiling a dim light, long since used up on the upper decks, penetrated the miserable cabin, in which a bed, a cupboard, a chair, and the man were standing side by side as though they had been packed away. 'I've lost my way,' said Karl, 'I didn't notice it so much during the voyage, but it's a dreadfully large ship.' 'Yes, you're right there,' said the man with a touch of pride, as he fiddled incessantly with the lock of a small suitcase, repeatedly pressing it shut with both hands in order to hear the bolt snapping into place. 'But come on in,' went on the man, 'you can't just stand outside.' 'Aren't I disturbing you?' asked Karl. 'Oh, how can you disturb me.' 'Are you a German?' said Karl, seeking reassurance, as he had heard much about the dangers, especially from Irishmen, which threaten newcomers to America. 'That's right, that's right,' said the man. Karl was still hesitating. Then the man unexpectedly seized the latch, quickly pulled the door shut, and pulled Karl inside with it. 'I can't stand people looking in at me from the corridor,' said the man, again busy with his suitcase. 'Everyone who runs past looks in, it's past enduring.' 'But the corridor's completely empty,' said Karl, standing uncomfortably squashed against the bedpost. 'Yes, it is now,' said the man. 'I meant now,' thought Karl, 'this man isn't easy to talk to.' 'Lie down on the bed, you'll have more room there,' said the man. Karl crept in as best he could, laughing loudly at his first unsuccessful attempt to swing himself onto it. But he was no sooner in the bed than he cried: 'Goodness, I forgot all about my suitcase.' 'Where is it?' 'Up on deck, an acquaintance is keeping an eye on it. What on earth is his name?' And from a secret pocket that his mother had sewn into the lining of his coat for his journey, he took out a visiting-card. 'Butterbaum, Franz Butterbaum.' 'Do you really need the suitcase?' 'Of course.' 'Well, why did you give it to a stranger?' 'I'd forgotten my umbrella down below and ran to fetch it, but I didn't want to drag the suitcase with me. Then I got lost as well.' 'Are you alone? Nobody with you?' 'Yes, alone.' Perhaps I should hold on to this man, it occurred to Karl, where am I going to find a better friend. 'And now you've lost your suitcase too. I say nothing about the umbrella,' and the man sat down on the chair, as though Karl's affair had begun to interest him. 'But I don't think the suitcase is lost yet.' 'Thought is free,' said the man, scratching hard at his dark, short, thick hair. 'On the ship, manners change along with ports. In Hamburg your Butterbaum might have guarded the suitcase, but here they've very likely both vanished without trace.' 'Then I must go up at once and take a look,' said Karl, looking round to see how he could get out. 'Stay where you are,' said the man, shoving him quite roughly back into the bed with one hand. 'Why?' asked Karl crossly. 'Because there's no point,' said the man. 'In a short while I'll be going too, then we can go together. Either the suitcase is stolen, in which case there's nothing to be done and you can mourn its loss till the end of your days, or the fellow is still guarding it, in which case he's a fool and can go on guarding it, or he's simply an honest man and has left the suitcase where it was, in which case we'll find it more easily once the ship is completely empty. The same goes for your umbrella.' 'Do you know your way round the ship?' asked Karl distrustfully, feeling that the idea, convincing in itself, that his things could be found most easily when the ship was empty, had some hidden catch. 'Of course, I'm a ship's stoker,' said the man. 'You're a ship's stoker,' cried Karl joyfully, as though this surpassed his expectations, and propped himself on his elbow to look at the man more closely. 'Just in front of the cabin where I slept alongside the Slovaks there was a hatch through which you could see into the engine-room.' 'Yes, that's where I worked,' said the stoker. 'I've always been so interested in technology,' said Karl, pursuing his train of thought, 'and I'm sure I'd have ended up as an engineer, if I hadn't had to go to America.' 'Why did you have to go?' 'Never mind!' said Karl, dismissing the whole story with a wave of his hand. As he did so, he smiled at the stoker, as though asking him to look indulgently on what he hadn't confessed. 'There must have been some reason,' said the stoker, and it wasn't clear whether he was asking Karl to tell him the reason or not. 'Now I could become a stoker too,' said Karl, 'my parents don't care any more what job I do.' 'My job's vacant,' said the stoker, and in full consciousness of this he put his hands in his trouser pockets and swung his legs, in crumpled, leather-like, iron-grey trousers, onto the bed, in order to stretch them out. Karl had to edge closer to the wall. 'You're leaving the ship?' 'That's right, we're off today.' 'But why? Don't you like it?' 'Well, it's the way things are, it doesn't always matter whether you like it or not. Anyway you're right, I don't like it. You probably aren't really resolved to become a stoker, but that's the easiest way for it to happen. So I strongly advise you against it. If you wanted to study in Europe, why don't you want to here? The American universities are incomparably better.' 'That may be true,' said Karl, 'but I've hardly any money for studying. I did read about somebody who worked in a shop by day and studied at night till he became a doctor and, I think, a mayor. But for that you need a lot of stamina, don't you? I'm afraid I lack it. Besides, I wasn't a specially good pupil, I really didn't mind leaving school. And the schools here may be even stricter. I hardly know any English. Altogether, people here are so prejudiced against foreigners, I believe.' 'You've already found that out, have you? Well, that's good. You're the man for me. Look here, we're on a German ship, it belongs to the Hamburg–America Line, why aren't all of us here Germans? Why is the Chief Engineer a Romanian? His name is Schubal. It's incredible. And this bastard treats us Germans on a German ship like dirt. You mustn't think'— he ran out of breath and waved his hand—'that I'm complaining for the sake of complaining. I know you haven't any influence and are a poor boy yourself. But it's too bad.' And he pounded the table several times with his fist, which he never took his eye off as he pounded. 'I've already served on so many ships'—and he uttered twenty names in succession as though it were a single word, Karl felt quite confused— 'and I did a first-rate job, I was praised, I was a worker just to my captains' taste, I even spent several years on the same merchant ship'—he rose as though that had been the high point of his life— 'and here on this old tub, where everything is done by the rules, where no wit is required—here I count for nothing, I'm always in Schubal's way, I'm a lazybones, I deserve to be thrown out, and get my wages as a favour. Do you understand that? I don't.' 'You mustn't put up with that,' said Karl excitedly. He had almost lost the feeling that he was on the insecure footing of a ship beside the coast of an unknown continent, for he felt so at home here on the stoker's bed. 'Have you been to see the Captain? Have you asked him for your rights?' 'Oh, get lost. I don't want you here. You don't listen to what I say and you give me advice. How am I supposed to go to see the Captain.' And the stoker sat down again wearily, covering his face with both hands. 'I can't give him any better advice,' said Karl to himself. And he decided that he should have gone to fetch his suitcase, instead of giving advice that was dismissed as stupid. When his father had handed over the suitcase to him for ever, he had asked jokingly: 'How long will you keep it?' and now this expensive suitcase might be lost in all seriousness.

The only consolation was that his father could not find out the slightest thing about his present position, even if he were to make enquiries. All the shipping line could say was that he had got as far as New York. But Karl was sorry that he had hardly used the things in the suitcase, although, for example, it was high time he changed his shirt. He had economized in the wrong way, and now, at the beginning of his career, when he would need to present himself cleanly dressed, he would have to appear in a dirty shirt. These were fine prospects. Otherwise the loss of the suitcase wouldn't have been so bad, for the suit he had on was actually better than the one in the case, which was really only a suit for emergencies which his mother had had to patch up just before his departure. He now remembered too that the suitcase also contained a piece of Veronese salami which his mother had packed as an extra present, but of which he had only been able to eat a tiny portion, since during the voyage he had had no appetite and the soup doled out to steerage passengers had been ample for him. Now, however, he would have been glad to have the sausage to hand in order to present it to the stoker. For such people are easily won over if you give them some trifle or other, Karl knew that from his father, who won over all the lower-ranking employees he dealt with by handing out cigars. The only thing Karl still had that he could give away was his money and he didn't want to touch that, especially if he might have lost his suitcase. His thoughts returned to the suitcase, and he really could not grasp why he had guarded the suitcase so carefully during the voyage that he hardly got any sleep, if he had now surrendered the suitcase so easily. He recalled the five nights during which he had continually suspected a little Slovak, who slept two places to his left, of planning to steal his suitcase. This Slovak had only been waiting for Karl, finally overcome by weakness, to nod off for a minute, so that he could draw the suitcase over to himself by means of a long pole with which he kept playing or practising during the day. By day this Slovak looked innocent enough, but no sooner had night come than he would rise from his bed from time to time and gaze sadly across at Karl's suitcase. Karl could make this out quite clearly, for someone with the restlessness of the emigrant had always struck a light, even though this was forbidden by the ship's rules, and was trying to decipher the unintelligible prospectuses issued by the emigration agencies. If there were such a light close by, then Karl could drowse a bit, but if it were distant or if it was dark, then he had to keep his eyes open. This effort had left him quite exhausted. And now it might all have been in vain. That Butterbaum, if he were ever to run into him again—

At that moment the complete calm which had prevailed hitherto was disturbed by short small tappings, like children's footsteps, far away; they came closer, increasing in volume, and now it was the sound of men marching steadily. They were obviously walking in single file, as was natural in the narrow corridor, a clanging as though of weapons could be heard. Karl, who had been on the point of stretching himself out in the bed to enjoy a sleep free from worries about suitcases and Slovaks, started up and nudged the stoker to arouse his attention, for the head of the procession seemed just to have reached the door. 'That's the ship's band,' said the stoker. 'They've been playing on deck and are going to pack up. Now everything's over and we can go. Come along.' He seized Karl by the hand, took at the last moment a picture of the Virgin Mary from the wall above the bed, stuffed it into his breast pocket, grabbed his suitcase, and hastily left the cabin together with Karl.

'Now I'll go into the office and tell the gentleman what I think. There's nobody left, we've nothing to worry about,' the stoker kept repeating in different words, and as he walked he tried to crush a rat that crossed his path with a sideways kick, but only pushed it more quickly into the hole that it had reached just in time. He was in general slow in his movements, for although he had long legs, they were too heavy.

They went through part of the kitchens, where some girls in dirty aprons—they spilled things on them deliberately—were washing crockery in big tubs. The stoker called a certain Line* to him, put his arm round her waist, and led her a short distance, while she kept pressing herself coquettishly against his arm. 'It's pay-time, are you coming?' he asked. 'Why should I bother, bring me the money yourself,' she answered, slipped under his arm, and ran away. 'Where did you pick up that pretty boy?' she called, without expecting an answer. All the girls, who had paused in their work, could be heard laughing.

They went on, however, and came to a door with a small projecting lintel borne by small gilded caryatids. That looked quite extravagant for the furnishing of a ship. Karl, as he noticed, had never been in this area, which was probably reserved during the voyage for first- and second-class passengers, whereas now the dividing doors had been taken off their hinges in preparation for the great cleaning of the ship. They had in fact met some men who carried brooms over the shoulders and had said hello to the stoker. Karl marvelled at all this activity, in his steerage he had of course noticed little of it. There were also electric cables stretching along the corridors and a small bell could be heard continually.

The stoker knocked respectfully at the door, and when someone called 'Come in', urged Karl with a gesture to enter without fear. He did enter, but stopped beside the door. Outside the room's three windows he saw the waves of the sea, and as he gazed at their cheerful motion his heart pounded as though he hadn't been looking at the sea incessantly for five long days. Big ships crossed one another's paths, yielding to the rising and falling waves only so far as their tonnage permitted. If you screwed up your eyes, the ships seemed to be swaying just because of their heavy tonnage. On their masts they bore narrow but long flags which were stiffened by the ship's motion but still fluttered to and fro. Salutes could be heard, probably from the guns of battleships, the barrels of the cannon, gleaming in their steel casing, on one such ship that was passing not far off seemed to be caressed by its secure, smooth, and yet not horizontal motion. The smaller ships and boats could be seen, at least from the door, only in the distance, darting in large numbers into the openings between the big ships. But behind them all was New York, looking at Karl with the hundred thousand windows of its skyscrapers. Yes, in this room one knew where one was.

At a round table three gentlemen were sitting, one of them a ship's officer in a blue ship's uniform, the two others officials of the port authority, in black American uniforms. On the table lay various documents in great piles, which the officer first glanced through with his pen in his hand and then passed to the two others, who now read, now took notes, now put them in their briefcases, except when one of them, who almost uninterruptedly made a little noise with his teeth, dictated something to his colleague who was taking a memorandum.

At the window there sat at a desk, his back to the door, a smallish gentleman, who was fiddling with large folios placed side by side in front of him on a sturdy bookshelf level with his head. Beside him was a cashbox, open and, at least at the first glance, empty.

The second window was unoccupied and offered the best view. Near the third, however, stood two gentlemen conversing in an undertone.

One of them, leaning beside the window, also wore a ship's uniform and was playing with the handle of his sword. The one he was speaking to was facing the window and occasionally revealed by a movement part of the row of medals on the other man's chest. He was in civilian clothes and had a thin bamboo cane, which, as both his hands were clutching his hips, stood out like another sword.

Karl had not much time to look at everything, for a servant soon came up to them and asked the stoker, looking at him as though he did not belong here, what he was after. The stoker answered, in as low a voice as the question had been put, that he wanted to speak to the Chief Purser. The servant, for his part, rejected this request with a gesture, but yet went on tiptoe, giving a wide berth to the round table, to the gentleman with the folios. This gentleman, as was clearly apparent, practically froze on hearing the servant's words, but finally looked round at the man who wanted to speak to him, and then indicated a firm refusal by gesticulating at the stoker and, for safety's sake, at the servant too. Thereupon the servant went back to the stoker and said in the tone of somebody imparting a confidence: 'Get out of this room at once!'

The stoker, on receiving this answer, looked down at Karl, as though the latter were his master to whom he was silently lamenting his grief. Without further reflection Karl freed himself and ran diagonally across the room, even brushing against the officer's chair, the servant ran stooping with arms ready to catch him, as though chasing some kind of vermin,* but Karl was the first to reach the Purser's table, which he held onto tightly in case the servant should try to pull him away.

Of course the whole room promptly came to life. The ship's officer at the table had leapt to his feet, the gentlemen from the port authority were watching calmly but attentively, the two gentlemen at the window had stepped close together, the servant, thinking he was out of place once the higher-ups were taking an interest, stepped back. The stoker, at the door, was waiting tensely for the moment when his help would be needed. The Chief Purser, finally, turned sharply to the right in his chair.

Karl rummaged in his secret pocket, which he had no scruples about exposing to these people's gaze, for his passport, which, instead of any further introduction, he placed open on the table. The Chief Purser seemed to think the passport unimportant, for he brushed it

aside with two fingers, whereupon Karl, as though this formality had
been satisfactorily completed, put the passport back in his pocket.
'I'm taking the liberty to say', he began, 'that in my opinion this gentleman, the stoker, has suffered injustice. There is here a certain
Schubal, who makes his life a misery. He has already served on many
ships, all of which he can name for you, and has given entire satisfaction, he works hard, tries to do his best, and it is really impossible to
see why he should fit badly into this ship, where the work is not so
extremely hard as, for example, on merchant ships. It can therefore
only be slander that hinders his advancement and denies him the
recognition which otherwise would certainly not be lacking. I have
spoken about this matter only in general terms, he himself can tell
you his specific complaints.' While explaining this matter Karl had
turned to all the gentlemen, because in fact they were all listening,
and it seemed much more likely that a just person was to be found
amid the whole group than that the Chief Purser should be that just
person. Karl had, moreover, been cunning enough to conceal the fact
that he had known the stoker only for such a short time. What is
more, he would have spoken much better still if he had not been distracted by the red face of the gentleman with the bamboo cane, whom
he had not previously been able to see.

'It's all correct, every single word,' said the stoker, before anyone
had asked him, indeed before anyone had so much as looked at him.
The stoker's haste would have been a grave mistake if the gentleman
with decorations, who, as Karl now realized, must be the Captain, had
not obviously already resolved to listen to the stoker. For he stretched
out his hand and called to the stoker: 'Come here!' in a voice so firm
that you could have struck it with a hammer. Now everything
depended on the stoker's behaviour, for Karl had no doubt about the
justice of his cause.

Fortunately it became clear on this occasion that the stoker had
already seen a lot of the world. With exemplary calm he extracted
from his small suitcase, at the first attempt, a small bundle of papers
and a notebook, went with these things, as though it were the obvious
thing to do, completely ignoring the Chief Purser, to the Captain, and
spread his pieces of evidence out on the window-ledge. The Chief
Purser had no choice but to lumber across to it himself. 'This man is
a well-known malcontent,' he said by way of explanation, 'he spends
more time in the purser's office than in the engine-room. He's driven

Schubal, who's a peaceful person, to complete despair. Listen, you!'
he said, turning to the stoker, 'you're really taking your impertinence
too far. How often have you already been thrown out of the accounts
office, as your completely unjustified demands, one and all, deserve!
How often have you gone running from there to the purser's main
office! How often have people told you kindly that Schubal is your
immediate superior and that you as his subordinate have to sort things
out with him alone! And now you actually turn up here, when the
Captain is present, you aren't ashamed to bother even him, but have
the impudence to bring along, as the well-drilled spokesman of your
vile accusations, this boy, whom I've never seen on board this ship
before.'

Karl restrained himself with difficulty from jumping forward. But
the Captain was already there and said: 'Give the man a hearing.
Schubal is anyway getting a bit too independent for my liking, but
you mustn't interpret that to your advantage.' This latter remark was
intended for the stoker, it was only natural that he couldn't immediately take his side, but everything seemed to be going as it should.
The stoker began his explanations and controlled himself at the very
outset by calling Schubal 'Mr'. How pleased Karl was, standing at the
Chief Purser's deserted desk, where he kept pressing down a set of
scales from sheer pleasure. Mr Schubal is unfair. Mr Schubal favours
foreigners. Mr Schubal ordered the stoker to leave the engine-room
and made him clean toilets, which certainly wasn't the stoker's job.
At one point doubt was even cast on Mr Schubal's competence, which
was said to be illusory rather than real. Here Karl stared as hard as he
could at the Captain, affably as though he were his colleague, just so
that the stoker's somewhat clumsy mode of expression should not
have an unfavourable influence on him. Still, the long speeches didn't
reveal anything of substance, and even if the Captain was still staring
straight ahead, his eyes revealing his determination to hear the stoker
out, the other gentlemen were getting impatient and the stoker's voice
no longer dominated the room, which gave grounds for considerable
anxiety. The gentleman in civilian clothes was the first to stir, setting
his bamboo cane in motion and tapping, albeit quietly, on the floor.
The other gentlemen of course looked hither and thither, the gentlemen from the port authority, who were obviously pressed for time,
reached for their documents again and began, though somewhat
absent-mindedly, to glance through them, the ship's officer moved

closer to his table, and the Chief Purser, thinking he had won, gave a deep, ironic sigh. Nobody seemed exempt from the general inattention but the servant, who felt some sympathy for the sufferings of the poor man placed below the higher-ups and nodded gravely to Karl, as though to explain something.

Meanwhile, outside the windows, the life of the port went on, a flat cargo ship piled high with barrels, which must have been stowed away in a wonderful manner in order not to start rolling, passed by and almost completely darkened the room, small motor-boats, which Karl, if he had had time, could have taken a good look at, whirred past in a straight line, guided by the twitching hands of a man standing upright at the helm, peculiar floating objects popped up here and there under their own power from the restless water, were immediately submerged again, and vanished before the astonished gaze. Boats belonging to ocean liners were rowed forwards by furiously toiling sailors and were full of passengers who sat in them just as they had been squeezed in, quietly and expectantly, though many could not refrain from turning their heads to observe the changing scenery. An incessant motion, an unrest, transferred from the restless elements to the helpless humans and their works.

But everything called for haste, clarity, a precise account, yet what was the stoker doing? Certainly he was working himself into a sweat, his trembling hands had long been unable to hold onto the papers on the window-ledge, from every point of the compass complaints about Schubal were streaming into his mind, any of which, in his opinion, would have sufficed to bury this Schubal completely, but what he could show the Captain was only a dismal medley of all of them together. The gentleman with the bamboo cane had long been whistling softly at the ceiling, the gentlemen from the port authority already had the officer at their table and showed no signs of ever letting him go, the Chief Purser was visibly restrained only by the Captain's calm from the intervention he was itching to make. The servant was standing to attention, awaiting at any moment an order from his captain concerning the stoker.

Karl could no longer remain inactive. So he went slowly over to the group, considering, as he went, all the more quickly the most skilful way of addressing the matter. It really was high time, only a little while longer and they might well both be thrown out of the office. The Captain might well be a good man and also have a special reason, as it seemed to Karl, for showing himself a fair employer, but after all he wasn't an instrument that one could play on till it was ruined—and that was how the stoker was treating him, if only because his feelings had been offended beyond all bounds.

So Karl said to the stoker: 'You must explain this more simply, more clearly, the Captain can't appreciate it the way you tell it. Does he know all the engineers and errand-boys by name, let alone by their Christian names, so that you only have to mention a name for him to know who it refers to? Put your complaints in order, state the most important first and then the others in descending order, then perhaps you won't even need to mention most of them. You always described it so clearly to me.' If one can steal suitcases in America then one can also tell the occasional lie, he thought by way of apology.

If only it had done any good! Was it already too late? The stoker did stop immediately on hearing the familiar voice, but with his eyes obscured by tears of injured male honour, terrible memories, and the utmost present desperation, he could no longer recognize Karl clearly. After all—Karl, silent in front of the now silent stoker, saw that all right—how was he suddenly to alter his way of speaking, since he felt that he had put forward all he had to say without the slightest acknowledgement but also that he hadn't yet managed to say anything and couldn't expect the gentlemen to listen to the whole thing all over again. And that's the moment when Karl, his sole supporter, comes along and tries to teach him a lesson, but only shows him that all, all is lost.

If only I'd come along sooner, instead of looking out of the window, said Karl to himself, lowering his face before the stoker and slapping his trouser-seams as a sign that all hope was gone.

But the stoker misunderstood this, probably surmising that Karl intended some covert criticism, and with the good intention of convincing him otherwise he crowned his deeds by beginning to quarrel with Karl. Now, when the gentlemen at the round table had long become indignant at the pointless fuss that disturbed their important business, when the Chief Purser was beginning to find the Captain's patience incomprehensible and was about to burst out in fury, when the servant, back in his masters' domain, was glaring at the stoker, and finally the gentleman with the bamboo cane, to whom even the Captain occasionally threw a friendly glance, by now completely indifferent to the stoker, even disgusted by him, had produced a small notebook and, obviously preoccupied with quite different affairs, was letting his eyes stray between the notebook and Karl.

'I know, I know,' said Karl, who was having difficulty in fending off the tirade which the stoker had now directed at him, but despite their quarrel still had a friendly smile for him, 'you're right, quite right, I never doubted it for a moment.' He would have liked to hold down the stoker's gesticulating hands for fear of being hit, and even more to push him into a corner and whisper a few calming words to him, which nobody else need have heard. But the stoker was completely out of control. Karl was even beginning to draw some comfort from the fact that in an emergency the stoker, with the strength drawn from despair, could overpower all seven men present. Admittedly, there was on the desk, as a glance at it showed, a panel with far too many electric buttons, and one hand, simply pressed on them, could create a rebellion on the entire ship with all its corridors filled with hostile people.

Then the gentleman with the bamboo cane, who seemed so uninterested, stepped over to Karl and asked, not loudly, but audibly above the stoker's bawling: 'What's your name?' At that moment, as though somebody behind the door had been waiting for this utterance by the gentleman, there came a knock. The servant looked at the Captain, who nodded. The servant went to the door and opened it. Outside, wearing an old imperial frock-coat,* stood a man of moderate proportions, who didn't look particularly suitable to work with machinery, yet was—Schubal. If Karl hadn't realized this from observing how everyone's eyes expressed a certain satisfaction from which even the Captain was not free, he would have seen it, to his horror, from the way the stoker stretched out his arms and clenched his fists, as though clenching his fists were the most important thing about him, for which he was ready to sacrifice his whole life. All his strength, even that which kept him upright, was now concentrated there.

And so there was the enemy, free, fresh, and festively clad, a ledger under his arm probably containing the stoker's pay-slips and work records, and looking in turn into everyone's eyes with the undisguised admission that he wanted above all to check each person's mood. All seven, besides, were already his friends, for even if the Captain had previously had, or perhaps only pretended to have, certain reservations about him, after the suffering the stoker had inflicted on him he probably no longer had the slightest fault to find with Schubal. A man like the stoker could not be handled too severely, and if Schubal were to blame for anything, it was because he had failed in the course of time to break down the stoker's obduracy, so that the latter had today even ventured to appear before the Captain.

Now one might think that the confrontation between the stoker and Schubal could not but have the effect even on human beings that it deserved to have before a higher forum, for even if Schubal were good at dissimulation, that did not mean that he could keep it up until the end. A brief flash of his vileness would be enough to reveal it to the gentlemen, Karl would make sure of that. He already had some idea of the acuity, the weak points, the whims of the individual gentlemen, and from that point of view the time spent here had not been wasted. If only the stoker had been in a more aggressive mood, but he seemed completely unfit for a fight. If Schubal had been offered to him, he could doubtless have smashed open his hated skull with his fists, like a thin-shelled nut. But even to take the few steps across to him seemed beyond his powers. Why hadn't Karl foreseen what was so easy to foresee, that Schubal was bound to turn up in the end, if not of his own volition, then summoned by the Captain. Why hadn't he worked out a precise plan of campaign with the stoker on the way here, instead of doing what they had actually done and entering, hopelessly unprepared, as soon as they reached the door? Was the stoker still capable of speaking at all, even of saying yes or no, as would be required for the cross-examination that was the best they could hope for? He was standing there, his legs apart, his knees slightly bent, his head somewhat raised, and the air was passing through his open mouth as though he no longer had any lungs with which to process it.

Karl, to be sure, felt stronger and more alert than he had ever been at home. If only his parents could see him now, fighting for the right in a foreign country before respected personalities, and even if he hadn't yet gained a victory, he was all ready for the final push. Would they revise their opinion of him? Sit on either side of him and praise him? Look him even once, once, in his eyes that were so devoted to them? Uncertain questions, and a most unsuitable moment in which to ask them!

'I've come because I believe the stoker has accused me of some kind of dishonesty. A girl from the kitchens told me she had seen him on the way here. Captain, and all you gentlemen, I am ready to refute any accusation by means of written materials and if necessary by the testimony of unprejudiced and neutral witnesses who are waiting outside the door.' Thus spoke Schubal. That, to be sure, was a clear and manly speech, and the way his listeners' faces changed might have made one think that for the first time for a while they were hearing human sounds again. They of course didn't notice that even this fine speech had some gaps. Why was the first factual word that occurred to him 'dishonesty'? Should the charges against him have begun with this, perhaps, rather than with his national prejudices? A girl from the kitchens had seen the stoker on his way to the office, and Schubal had tumbled to the point immediately? Wasn't it his guilt that was sharpening his intellect? And he had promptly fetched witnesses, and called them unprejudiced and neutral into the bargain? Roguery, mere roguery, and the gentlemen tolerated it and even acknowledged it as proper conduct? Why had he undoubtedly allowed a long time to elapse between the kitchen-maid's report and his own arrival, for no other reason than to let the stoker tire the gentlemen out and deprive them of their clear judgement, from which Schubal had most to fear? He must have been standing outside the door for quite a while, and hadn't he knocked at the very moment when that gentleman's trivial question had allowed him to hope that the stoker's fate was sealed?

Everything was clear, and Schubal was presenting it in that way despite himself, but one had to say that to the gentlemen differently, even more explicitly. They needed to be shaken up. So hurry, Karl, make the most of the time that is left before the witnesses appear and swamp everything.

Just then, however, the Captain gave Schubal a sign to stop talking, whereupon he promptly stepped aside—for his affair seemed to have been deferred for a little—and began talking in an undertone with the servant, who had immediately joined him, casting many sidelong glances at the stoker and Karl and making gestures indicating his certainty. Schubal seemed to be practising for his next big speech.

'Didn't you want to ask this young man a question, Mr Jakob?' said the Captain, amid general silence, to the gentleman with the bamboo cane.

'To be sure,' said the latter, bowing slightly to acknowledge this attention. And then he asked Karl once more: 'What's your name?'

Karl, thinking it would assist the main business to settle this incident with the persistent questioner quickly, answered briefly, without introducing himself, as he usually did, by showing his passport, which he'd have had to look for: 'Karl Rossmann.'

'Well, well!' said the gentleman addressed as Jakob, stepping back with an almost incredulous smile. The Captain, the Chief Purser, the ship's officer, and even the servant also displayed extreme astonishment at Karl's name. Only the gentlemen from the port authority and Schubal appeared unaffected.

'Well, well!' repeated Mr Jakob, coming up to Karl with somewhat stiff steps, 'then I'm your Uncle Jakob and you are my dear nephew. I suspected it all along,' he added to the Captain as he embraced and kissed Karl, who submitted to everything in silence.

'What is your name?' asked Karl on feeling himself released, very politely but quite unmoved, and he struggled to work out the consequences that this new event might have for the stoker. For the moment there was nothing to suggest that Schubal could derive any advantage from this matter.

'Just think how lucky you are, young man,' said the Captain, considering the question injurious to the dignity of Mr Jakob, who was now facing the window, obviously to avoid showing his excited face, which he was dabbing with a handkerchief, to the others. 'It is Senator Edward Jakob who has revealed himself to you as your uncle. A brilliant career, no doubt quite contrary to your earlier expectations, now awaits you. Try to appreciate that as best you can in this first moment, and compose yourself.'

'I have an Uncle Jakob in America, to be sure,' said Karl, facing the Captain, 'but if I understood correctly, only the Senator's surname is Jakob.'

'That's so,' said the Captain expectantly.

'Well, my Uncle Jakob, who is my mother's brother, only has the Christian name Jakob, while his surname must naturally be the same as my mother's, which is Bendelmayer.'

'Gentlemen!' exclaimed the Senator, returning briskly from the spot beside the window where he had been recovering his calm, with reference to Karl's explanation. All except the port officials burst out laughing, some as though moved, others incomprehensibly.

'There was nothing so absurd about what I've just said,' thought Karl.

'Gentlemen,' repeated the Senator, 'against my will and yours, you are involved in a little domestic scene, and therefore I cannot forbear to give you some explanation, since so far as I know only the Captain' (on his title being mentioned, each bowed to the other) 'is fully in the picture.'

'Now I really must pay attention to every word,' thought Karl, pleased to observe on glancing sideways that the stoker seemed to be coming back to life.

'Throughout the long years of my residence in America— "residence", to be sure, is hardly the word for an American citizen such as I am with my whole heart—throughout these long years I have been entirely cut off from my European relatives, for reasons which, for one thing, are not relevant here, and which, for another, I would find too exhausting to recount. I am even afraid of the moment at which I shall be compelled to recount them to my dear nephew, for I fear that it will be impossible to avoid some frank remarks about his parents and their entourage.'

'It's my uncle, no doubt about it,' said Karl to himself, listening intently. 'He probably changed his name.'

'My dear nephew has simply been—let us use the word that actually describes the matter—discarded by his parents, as one ejects an irritating cat. I have no intention of using euphemisms about what my nephew has done to be thus punished—euphemism is not the American way—but his misdemeanour is of the kind that is sufficiently excused by merely naming it.'

'That sounds good,' thought Karl, 'but I don't want him to tell everyone. Besides, he can't know about it. How would he? But we'll see, he probably does know everything.'

'He was, you see,' continued Karl's uncle, leaning on the bamboo cane which he had planted in front of him, giving occasional small bows, and thus managing to reduce the unnecessary solemnity which the matter must otherwise have had—'he was, you see, seduced by a servant-girl called Johanna Brummer, a person of thirty-five or so. I have no wish to offend my nephew by using the word "seduced", but it is hard to find another word that is equally appropriate.'

Here Karl, who had already gone fairly close to his uncle, turned round in order to see from the faces of those present what impression the story was making on them. Nobody was laughing, all were listening patiently and seriously. After all, one doesn't laugh at a Senator's nephew on the first opportunity that offers itself. One might have said that the stoker was smiling at Karl, though only slightly, but for one thing that was pleasing as a renewed sign of life, and secondly it was excusable, since in the cabin Karl had particularly wanted to conceal this matter which was now becoming so public.

'Now this Brummer,' continued Karl's uncle, 'had a child by my nephew, a healthy boy, who was christened Jakob, doubtless in memory of my humble self, since even my nephew's casual references to me must have made a deep impression on the girl. Fortunately, I say. For since his parents, to avoid paying for the child's maintenance or being implicated in any other scandal—I must emphasize that I am unacquainted either with the local laws or with the parents' other circumstances, but am aware only of two begging letters they had previously sent me and which I left unanswered but kept and which form our sole and, moreover, one-sided communication in the entire period—since his parents, to avoid maintenance payments and scandal, have had their son, my dear nephew, transported to America, lamentably ill-equipped, as you can see—the boy, apart from any signs and wonders that may still exist in America, would probably, if left to his own devices, have perished by now in an alleyway near New York harbour, had not this servant-girl, in a letter addressed to me which, after lengthy detours, came into my possession the day before yesterday, told me the entire story, along with a description of my nephew's appearance and, very sensibly, the name of his ship. If I had any design of providing you with entertainment, gentlemen, I could no doubt read aloud some passages from this letter'—he drew two huge, closely written sheets from his pocket and waved them; 'it would certainly make an impression on you, since it is written with rather naive though well-intentioned cunning and considerable affection for the father of her child. But I wish neither to entertain you any more than is required for an explanation, nor to welcome my nephew by injuring the feelings he may still retain, since if he wishes he can read the letter for his own instruction in the room that has been made ready for him.'

But Karl had no feelings for the girl. Amid the thronging memories of a past he was increasingly repressing, she was sitting in her kitchen beside a cupboard, on the top of which she was resting her elbow. She looked at him whenever he came into the kitchen to fetch a glass of water for his father or to pass on a message from his mother. Sometimes she would be writing a letter in an awkward position beside the cupboard and drawing inspiration from Karl's face.

Sometimes she would keep her eyes covered with her hand, and then nothing one said got through to her. Sometimes she would kneel in her tiny room beside the kitchen and pray to a wooden cross, Karl as he passed would then watch her shyly through the slightly open door. Sometimes she would run wildly round the kitchen and jump back, laughing like a witch, when Karl crossed her path. Sometimes she would close the kitchen door when Karl had entered and keep the latch in her hand until he asked to leave. Sometimes she would fetch things that he did not want at all and press them silently into his hands. Once, however, she said to him, 'Karl!', and led him, surprised at this unexpected form of address, with sighs and grimaces into her little room, which she locked. She threw her arms round his neck, almost strangling him, and while she asked him to undress her, in reality she undressed him and put him in her bed, as though she would henceforth entrust him to no one else and would caress and tend him until the end of the world. 'Karl, oh my Karl,' she cried, as though she were gazing at him and confirming that he was her possession, while he could not see the slightest thing and felt uncomfortable in the warm bedclothes which she seemed to have piled up specially for him. Then she got into bed with him and wanted him to reveal some secrets or other, but he could not tell her any and she got annoyed, in jest or earnest, shook him, listened to his heart beating, offered him her breast so that he could listen similarly, which however she could not induce Karl to do, pressed her naked belly against his body, fumbled with her hand between his legs in such a disgusting manner that Karl wriggled his head and neck out of the pillows, then thrust her belly against him several times, he felt as though she were part of himself and perhaps for this reason he was seized by a terrible sense of needing help. Weeping, and after many wishes for their next meeting on her part, he at last got to his own bed. That was all, and yet his uncle managed to turn it into a long story. And so the cook had thought about him and informed his uncle of his arrival. That was nice of her, and he would no doubt pay her back some day.

'And now,' exclaimed the Senator,* 'I want you to tell me openly whether I am your uncle or not.'

'You are my uncle,' said Karl, kissing his hand and receiving a kiss on the forehead in return. 'I'm very glad to have met you, but you're wrong if you think that my parents only say bad things about you. But even apart from that, your speech got some things wrong, that is,

I don't think everything happened quite that way in reality. Still, you can't really judge things so well from here, and anyway I don't think it will do any particular harm if the gentlemen are misinformed in a few details about a matter that can't really concern them much.'

'Well spoken,' said his uncle, and he led Karl up to the visibly sympathetic Captain and said: 'Haven't I got a splendid nephew?'

'I am happy', said the Captain, with the kind of bow that only people with a military training can make, 'to have got to know your nephew. It is a special honour for my ship to have provided the setting for such an encounter. But the crossing by steerage was probably very unpleasant, for who is to know what sort of company one will find there. Once, for example, the first-born son of the principal Hungarian nobleman, his name and the reason for his journey have escaped me, travelled on our steerage deck. I didn't find out about it till much later. Well, we do everything possible to make the crossing easier for the people in steerage, much more, for example, than the American lines, but to make such a crossing into a pleasure is something we have not yet achieved.'

'It did me no harm,' said Karl.

'It did him no harm!' repeated the Senator, laughing loudly.

'Only I'm afraid my suitcase has got—' And with these words he remembered everything that had happened and that remained to be done, looked round, and saw all present, silent with respect and astonishment, in their previous places, their eyes fixed on him. Only the port officials, so far as their severe, self-satisfied faces disclosed any feelings, showed their regret at having come at such an inconvenient time, and the watch they now had lying in front of them probably mattered more to them than anything that was happening and could still happen in the room.

The first person after the Captain to express his pleasure was, surprisingly, the stoker. 'I congratulate you warmly,' he said, shaking Karl's hand and meaning also to express something like appreciation. As he was about to turn to the Senator with the same utterance, the latter stepped back, as though the stoker were overstepping his proper limits; the stoker immediately desisted.

The others, however, saw what ought to be done, and instantly clustered round Karl and the Senator. Hence it came about that Karl even received congratulations from Schubal, and accepted them with thanks. Finally, when calm was restored, the port officials joined the group and said two words in English, which made an absurd impression.

The Senator was in the mood to savour the pleasure to the full and to recall more trivial incidents for his and the others' benefit, which of course they not only put up with but responded to with interest. Thus he drew their attention to the fact that he had entered Karl's distinguishing features mentioned in the cook's letter in his note-book, in case he had to make use of them on the spot. During the stoker's insufferable rantings he had drawn forth the notebook for no other purpose than to divert himself and had tried playfully to compare the cook's observations, which were not quite up to a detective's standard, with Karl's appearance. 'And that's how one finds one's nephew,' he concluded in a tone suggesting he wanted to be congratulated yet again.

'What will happen now to the stoker?' asked Karl, ignoring his uncle's last story. He felt that in his new position he could say whatever he thought.

'What will happen to the stoker is what he deserves,' said the Senator, 'and what the Captain thinks right. I think we have had more than enough of the stoker, and I am sure all the gentlemen present will agree with me.'

'But that isn't the point in a matter of justice,' said Karl. He was standing between his uncle and the Captain and thought, perhaps influenced by this position, that he had the decision in his hands.

And yet the stoker seemed to have given up all hope. His hands were half tucked inside his belt, which had become visible, thanks to his excited movements, along with the striped pattern on his shirt. That did not trouble him in the slightest, he had lamented his woes, now people might as well see the few rags that covered his body, and then they could carry him off. He thought that the servant and Schubal as the two lowest-ranking people here should do him this last favour. Schubal would then be left in peace and no longer driven to despair, as the Chief Purser had put it. The Captain could employ no one but Romanians, Romanian would be spoken everywhere, and per-haps things would then go better. No stoker would rant any longer in the purser's office, but his last rantings would be remembered with some kindness since, as the Senator had expressly declared, they had led indirectly to his recognition of his nephew. Besides, this nephew had often tried to help him and had therefore long before thanked him more than adequately for his part in the recognition; it wouldn't cross the stoker's mind to ask him for anything more. Anyway, he might be the Senator's nephew, that was a long way short of being a captain, but it was from the Captain's lips that the fateful word would come.—In accordance with this opinion, the stoker tried not to look at Karl, but unfortunately in this room full of enemies there was nowhere else for his eyes to rest.

'Don't misunderstand the state of affairs,' said the Senator to Karl, 'it may be a matter of justice, but at the same time it is also a matter of discipline. Both, and especially the latter, are subject to the judgement of the Captain.'

'That's so,' murmured the stoker. Anyone who noticed and understood this gave a puzzled smile.

'But we have kept the Captain for so long from his official duties, which must be unbelievably pressing during his arrival at New York, that it is high time we left the ship, so that we don't add to the confusion by some utterly superfluous intervention which would turn this trifling dispute between two engineers into a major event. I perfectly understand your action, my dear nephew, but for that very reason I have the right to take you away from here with all speed.'

'I'll have a boat launched for you right away,' said the Captain, not making, to Karl's astonishment, the least objection to his uncle's words, which were surely to be seen as his uncle's self-imposed humiliation. The Chief Purser rushed to the desk and telephoned the Captain's order to the boatswain.

'Time is pressing,' said Karl to himself, 'but I can't do anything without offending everybody. I can't leave my uncle now when he's only just found me. The Captain is polite, but that's all. He won't be polite when imposing discipline, and I'm sure my uncle said what he was thinking. I won't talk to Schubal, I even wish I hadn't shaken his hand. And all the other people here are mere chaff.'

And amid such thoughts he went slowly over to the stoker, pulled his right hand out of his belt, and held it playfully in his own. 'Why don't you say anything?' he asked. 'Why do you put up with everything?'

The stoker furrowed his brow as though he were seeking the words for what he had to say. For the rest, he looked down at his and Karl's hands.

'You've suffered more injustice than anyone on the ship, I'm absolutely sure of it.' And Karl drew his fingers in and out of the stoker's fingers, while the latter gazed all round with shining eyes, as though experiencing a delight for which nobody ought to blame him.

'You must defend yourself, say yes and no, otherwise these people will have no inkling of the truth. You must promise to do what I say, for I've every reason to fear that I won't be able to help you any more.' And now Karl was weeping as he kissed the stoker's hand and took the callused, almost lifeless hand and pressed it against his cheeks, like a precious object with which one must part.—But then his uncle the Senator was at his side, pulling him away, albeit very gently. 'The stoker seems to have cast a spell on you,' he said, casting a glance of understanding over Karl's head towards the Captain. 'You felt abandoned, then found the stoker and are now grateful to him, that's entirely praiseworthy. But for my sake, don't take it too far, and learn to appreciate your own position.'

A hubbub arose outside the door, cries were heard, and it even seemed as if someone were being thrust brutally against the door. A sailor entered, looking dishevelled, with a girl's apron round his waist. 'There are people outside,' he cried, shoving with his elbow as though he were still in the throng. Finally he came to his senses, and was about to salute the Captain when he noticed the girl's apron, tore it off, threw it to the ground, and cried: 'That's disgusting, they tied a girl's apron round my waist.' Then, however, he clicked his heels and saluted. Someone tried to laugh, but the Captain said severely: 'That's what I call good humour. Who is outside?' 'It's my witnesses,' said Schubal, stepping forward, 'I humbly apologize for their improper behaviour. When the voyage is over, people sometimes almost go mad.'—'Call them in at once,' ordered the Captain, and turning immediately to the Senator he said, politely but quickly: 'Please have the kindness, respected Senator, to go with your nephew and follow this sailor, who will take you to the boat. I need hardly say what a pleasure and honour it has been for me, sir, to make your personal acquaintance. I hope soon to have the opportunity, sir, to resume our interrupted conversation about the state of the American fleet and then perhaps to be interrupted once more in such a pleasant manner as we were today.' 'One nephew is enough for the time being,' said Karl's uncle, laughing. 'And now please accept my warmest thanks for your kindness. Goodbye! Moreover, it's by no means out of the question that we'—he clasped Karl cordially to him—'might spend considerable time together on our next trip to Europe.' 'I should be delighted,' said the Captain. The two gentlemen shook each other's hands, Karl could give his hand to the Captain only silently and hastily, for the latter was already beleaguered by the fifteen or so people who were streaming in, a little abashed but still very noisily, under Schubal's leadership. The sailor asked the Senator's permission to lead the way and then parted the crowd for him and Karl, who passed easily through the bowing group. It seemed that these normally good-natured people regarded Schubal's dispute with the stoker as a jest which retained its absurdity even in the Captain's presence. Karl noticed among them the kitchen-maid Line, who winked at him merrily as she tied round her waist the apron which the sailor had thrown away, for it was hers.

Following the sailor, they left the office and turned into a small corridor which soon brought them to a little door, whence a short stairway led down into the boat that had been made ready for them. The sailors in the boat, into which their leader promptly took a flying leap, rose and saluted. The Senator was just warning Karl to climb down carefully, when Karl, still on the top step, burst into tears. The Senator put his right hand under Karl's chin, pressed him close, and stroked him with his left hand. Thus they went slowly down, step by step, and, closely entwined, got into the boat, where the Senator found Karl a good seat directly facing him. At a sign from the Senator the sailors pushed off from the ship and were immediately hard at work. When they had moved only a few yards from the ship, Karl made the unexpected discovery that they were on the same side of the ship as the windows of the purser's office. All three windows were filled with Schubal's witnesses, who were calling and waving to them in friendly fashion, even Karl's uncle thanked them, and a sailor performed the trick of kissing his hand to them without interrupting the regular motion of the oars. It really seemed as though the stoker no longer existed. Karl looked more closely at his uncle, whose knees were almost touching his, and began to doubt whether this man could ever replace the stoker for him. His uncle, moreover, avoided his gaze and stared at the waves that were rising and falling around their boat.

2

Karl's Uncle

IN his uncle's house Karl soon got used to his new circumstances. His uncle, moreover, was very helpful in every detail, and Karl never had to learn from unpleasant experiences, such as usually make the beginning of one's life in a new country so bitter.

Karl's room was on the sixth floor of a building whose five lower floors, beneath which were three underground levels, were taken up by his uncle's business premises. The light that poured into his room through two windows and a door giving onto the balcony always astonished Karl when he entered it in the morning from his little bedroom. Where might he have had to live if he had come ashore as a mere poor immigrant? Indeed, he might—and his uncle, being familiar with the laws governing immigration, thought this highly probable—not have been allowed into the United States at all but have been sent home, with no concern given to the fact that he no longer had a home. For one need not hope for any compassion here, and what Karl had read about America in this respect was quite true; only the fortunate seemed truly to enjoy their good fortune here amid the untroubled faces that surrounded them.

A narrow balcony ran the full length of the room. Although in Karl's home town it might have been the loftiest viewpoint, here it permitted little more than the view over a street which ran straight, as though fleeing, between two rows of houses that looked as if they had been chopped into blocks, into the distance where the enormous outlines of a cathedral arose amid a dense haze. And from morning to evening and amid the dreams of the night there passed along this street an incessant bustle of traffic, which looked from above like a confused, constantly self-renewing medley of distorted human shapes and the roofs of all kinds of transport vehicles, from which arose a new, manifold, yet more savage medley of noise, dust, and smells, and all this was grasped and permeated by a powerful light that kept being diffused, dispersed, and eagerly restored by the innumerable objects, and that seemed to the bedazzled eye physically palpable, as though a glass pane covering the entire street were being repeatedly smashed every moment with the utmost force.

Cautious as his uncle was in all things, he advised Karl for the moment not to get seriously involved with anything whatever. He should observe and examine everything, but not let himself be taken captive. A European's first days in America, he said, could be compared to a birth, and although here, not to alarm Karl unnecessarily, one settled in more rapidly than if one had arrived in the human world from the beyond, one must bear in mind that one's initial judgements were always ill-founded and one should not allow them to discompose all the future judgements which one would need in order to continue one's life here. He had himself known newcomers who, instead of following these sound principles, had spent whole days standing on their balconies gazing down into the street like lost sheep. That was bound to confuse them! For a tourist such solitary inactivity, gaping idly at a busy working day in New York, might be permissible and even, though not without reservations, advisable, but for someone who meant to stay here it was pernicious—this word could be used in this case, even if it is exaggerated. And indeed Karl's uncle always frowned with irritation when on one of his visits, which occurred only once a day and at various times, he found Karl on the balcony. Karl soon noticed this and therefore denied himself the pleasure of standing on the balcony, so far as possible.

Besides, it was far from the only pleasure he had. In his room there was an American desk of the best make, such as his father had longed to have for years and had tried to buy at a variety of auctions for a low price within his means, but, because of his poverty, always without success. Of course this desk was not to be compared with the so-called American desks that drift about at European auctions. On its top part, for example, it had a hundred drawers of various sizes, and even the President of the Union could have found a suitable place for every one of his files, but in addition it had a regulator at the side, and by turning the handle one could rearrange and reorganize the drawers in a great variety of ways, according to one's wishes and needs. Thin side partitions slowly descended and formed the base or the top of new drawers that rose up; a single turn of the handle gave the top a quite different appearance, and everything happened slowly or with wild rapidity, depending on how you turned the handle. It was a brand new invention, but it reminded Karl very vividly of the toy cribs that were shown to wondering children at the Christmas market, and Karl too, wrapped up in his winter clothes, had often stood in front of them, continually comparing the movement of the handle, turned by an old man, with the effect on the crib, the halting entry of the three wise men, the shining of the stars, and the confined life in the holy stable. And he always felt that his mother, standing behind him, was not following all the events closely enough, he had pulled her towards him till he could feel her at his back, and spent so long drawing her attention with loud cries to inconspicuous details, perhaps a rabbit in the grass at the front that alternately sat upright and prepared to run away, that finally she put her hand over his mouth and probably relapsed into her previous state of inattention. Of course the desk was not intended to recall such things, but in the history of inventions there was probably some such vague connection as in Karl's memories. His uncle, unlike Karl, did not approve of this desk, but he had wanted to buy Karl a proper desk and all such desks were now equipped with this new feature, which had the advantage that it could be fitted to old desks without much expense. All the same, his uncle did not fail to advise Karl to avoid using the regulator at all if possible; to underline this advice, his uncle maintained that the machinery was very sensitive, easy to damage, and very expensive to repair. It was not hard to see that such remarks were mere excuses, although on the other hand it had to be said that the regulator could easily be rendered immobile, which Karl's uncle, however, did not do.

In his early days, when naturally Karl and his uncle had had frequent conversations, Karl had also recounted how at home he had played the piano, not much, but with enjoyment, albeit only with the basic knowledge that his mother had taught him. Karl was well aware that such a story was also a request for a piano, but he had seen enough to know that his uncle had no need to economize. Nevertheless his request was not fulfilled immediately, but a week or so later his uncle said, almost in the form of a reluctant admission, that the piano had just arrived and Karl, if he wanted, could watch it being transported. That was an easy task, to be sure, but not much easier than transporting the piano itself, for the building contained an elevator specially for furniture* into which a whole furniture van could fit without crowding, and in this elevator the piano floated up to Karl's room. Karl himself could have travelled in the same elevator with the piano and the transport workers, but as an ordinary elevator was available right next to it, he travelled in this, keeping level with the other elevator by means of a lever, and gazing fixedly through the glass partitions at the handsome instrument that was now his property. When he had it in his room and first touched the keys, he was so beside himself with joy that, instead of playing any more, he leapt up and preferred to marvel at the piano from a distance with his hands on his hips. The room also had excellent acoustics which helped to remove the slight unease he had initially felt at living in a building made of iron. In fact, however iron-clad the building might look from outside, the room showed not the slightest trace of iron construction materials, and nobody could have pointed out any detail in the furnishings that could in any way have spoiled its complete comfort. In his early days Karl had great hopes of his piano-playing and was not ashamed, at least before going to sleep, to contemplate the possibility that this piano-playing might have a direct effect on conditions in America. It sounded strange, to be sure, when in front of the windows opening into the noisy air outside he played one of the old military songs from his home that the soldiers sing in the evening, when they lean out of the windows of their barracks and look down into the dark square, one man responding to another from one window to the next—but when he then looked down at the street, it was unchanged and was only a small part of a great circulatory system which one could not stop without understanding all the forces at work throughout its full extent. His uncle tolerated his piano-playing and said nothing against it, especially as Karl, without being admonished, only rarely allowed himself the pleasure of playing, indeed he even brought Karl the scores of American marches and of course the national anthem, but his enjoyment of music could not fully explain why one day, in all seriousness, he asked Karl if he would not like to learn to play the violin or the French horn.

Karl's first and most important task, of course, was to learn English. A young teacher from a business school appeared in Karl's room every morning at seven o'clock and found him already sitting at his desk with his exercise-books, or walking up and down in his room memorizing words. Karl realized that he must acquire English with all haste and that here, moreover, he had the best opportunity to give his uncle extraordinary pleasure by his rapid progress. And in fact, although at first the English in his conversations with his uncle was confined to saying hello and goodbye, he soon managed to conduct more and more of their conversations in English, whereby more intimate themes began to be expressed. The first American poem, an account of a fire,* that Karl managed to recite to his uncle one evening, made the latter deeply serious from sheer contentment. They were both standing at a window in Karl's room, his uncle was looking outside, where all the light had already vanished from the sky, and responded to the verses by clapping his hands slowly in time with the metre, while Karl stood upright beside him with glazed eyes as he struggled to utter the difficult poem.

The better Karl's English became, the more pleasure his uncle took in introducing him to his acquaintances, only requiring, for all eventualities, that at such meetings Karl's English teacher should always hover close by. The very first acquaintance to whom Karl was introduced one morning was a young, slim, incredibly supple man, whom his uncle brought into Karl's room with a special display of politeness. He was obviously the son of a millionaire, one of the many whom their parents consider to have gone off the rails, whose life was such that for an ordinary person to observe a day chosen at random from this young man's life would be a painful experience. And as though he knew or suspected this, and as though he were defying it as best he could, a continual smile of happiness was visible round his lips and eyes, intended apparently for himself, the person he was talking to, and the whole world.

With this young man, a Mr Mak,* the plan was discussed, with unqualified support from Karl's uncle, of going riding together at half-past five in the morning, either in the riding-school or in the country. Karl did at first hesitate to give his consent, since he had never sat on a horse and wanted first to learn a little about riding, but his uncle and Mack urged him so strongly, assuring him that riding was a pure pleasure and a healthy exercise but not at all an art, that he finally agreed. Now, to be sure, he had to get out of bed at half-past four, which he often found very disagreeable, for he was suffering here, doubtless because of the constant concentration required during the day, from perpetual sleepiness, but in his bathroom he soon forgot his regret. The entire length and breadth of the bath was covered by the shower-head—which of his fellow-pupils at home, however rich he might be, possessed anything of the kind, let alone just for himself?—and now Karl lay there at full length, in this bath he could stretch out his arms, letting the lukewarm, hot, again lukewarm, and finally ice-cold water rain on him, just as he pleased, over part or all of the surface. He lay there as though still enjoying the last stages of sleep, and particularly enjoyed letting the last drops fall on his closed eyelids, then, as he opened them, roll over his face.

In the riding-school, where his uncle's towering automobile deposited him, the English teacher would already be waiting for him, while Mak invariably arrived later. He had no need to worry about coming later, however, for the riding only really came to life when he was there. Didn't the horses, previously half asleep, rear up when he entered, didn't the whip crack more loudly through the room, didn't individuals, spectators, stable-men, pupils, or whatever they might be, suddenly appear in the gallery that ran round it? Karl, however, used the time before Mak's arrival to practise, at least a little, the first basic exercises in riding. There was a tall man there who could reach the highest horse's back by barely raising his arm and who gave Karl this instruction, which never lasted more than a quarter of an hour. Karl's success in this was not great, and he was able to learn many English cries of dismay which he uttered breathlessly during his lesson for the benefit of his English teacher, who always leant against the same doorpost, usually very drowsy. But his discontentment with riding ceased almost entirely when Mak came. The tall man was sent away and soon nothing was audible in the semi-darkness of the room but the hooves of the galloping horses and hardly anything was visible but Mak's raised arm giving Karl a command. After half an hour of such enjoyment, which vanished like sleep, a halt was called, Mak was in a great hurry, took his leave of Karl, sometimes patted him on the cheek when he was especially pleased with his riding, and disappeared, in such a hurry that he did not even wait to accompany Karl out of the door. Karl would then give the English teacher a lift in the automobile, and they would drive to their English lesson, usually by a roundabout route, for the journey through the dense traffic on the main street that actually led directly from his uncle's house to the riding-school would have cost too much time. Moreover, the English teacher soon ceased to accompany him, for Karl, who blamed himself for making the weary man come to the riding-school for no purpose, especially as communication with Mak in English was very easy, asked his uncle to relieve the teacher of this obligation. After some reflection his uncle granted this request.

It took a relatively long time for his uncle to decide to let Karl take even a brief look at his business, although Karl had often asked him. It was a kind of commission and delivery service such as was, so far as

Karl could remember, perhaps not to be found in Europe. The business consisted of distribution, which, however, did not transfer goods from producers to consumers or to commercial outlets, but was responsible for the transfer of all goods and primary products to and between the great manufacturing cartels. Hence it was a business that comprehended purchases, storage, transport, and sales on a gigantic scale and had to maintain precise and continuous connections by telephone and telegraph with its clients. The telegraph room was not smaller but bigger than the telegraph office in Karl's home town, which Karl had once gone through in the company of a fellow-pupil who was known there. In the telephone room, wherever you looked, the doors of the telephone booths were opening and closing, and the ringing meant one could not hear oneself think. Karl's uncle opened the nearest of these doors, and they saw in the fizzing electric light an employee, ignoring the sound of the door, his head encased in a steel band that pressed the earpieces against his ears. His right arm was lying on a small table as though it were particularly heavy, and only his fingers, holding the pencil, twitched with inhuman regularity and rapidity. The words he spoke into the speaking-tube were very economical and you could often see that he wanted to criticize something the speaker had said or question him more closely, but certain words he heard compelled him, before he could carry out his intention, to lower his eyes and write. Nor did he need to speak, as his uncle explained to Karl, for the same messages this man was receiving were also being received simultaneously by two other employees and were then compared with one another, so that mistakes were ruled out as far as possible. At the same moment as his uncle and Karl went out of the door, a trainee slipped inside and emerged with the paper on which the message had by now been written. Through the middle of the room people were constantly coming and going at a frantic pace. Nobody said good day, that had been abolished, each person followed in the footsteps of the one preceding him and looked at the floor, on which he wanted to advance as fast as possible, or picked up single words or figures by glancing at the papers that he was holding in his hand and that fluttered as he strode along.

'You really have come a long way,' said Karl once on one of these tours of the offices, which required many days to inspect, even if one did no more than glance at each department.

'And I started it all thirty years ago, let me tell you. At that time

I had a small business near the port, and if five crates were unloaded there in a single day, it was a lot, and I would go home proud of myself. Now I have the third largest warehouses in the port and that shop is the dining-room and tool-room for the sixty-fifth group of my porters.'

'That's almost miraculous,' said Karl.

'Everything develops here as rapidly as that,' said his uncle, ending the conversation.

One day his uncle arrived just before dinner, which Karl expected to eat by himself as usual, and told him immediately to put on a black suit and come to dinner with two of his business colleagues. While Karl changed his clothes in the next room, his uncle sat down at the desk and examined the English exercise he had just finished, slapped the desk with his hand, and exclaimed: 'Really excellent!' No doubt Karl found it easier to get dressed on hearing this commendation, but in fact he was already fairly confident of his English.

In his uncle's dining-room, which he still remembered from the evening of his arrival, two large, fat gentlemen got up to greet him, one called Green, the other called Pollunder, as emerged during conversation at table. For it was his uncle's habit to say barely a casual word about any of his acquaintances and to leave Karl to find out by his own observations what it was necessary or interesting to know about them. After the actual meal, during which only intimate business matters were discussed, which was for Karl a good lesson in commercial vocabulary, and Karl had been allowed to concentrate on his food as though he were a child who must keep up his strength, Mr Green bent over to Karl and asked, clearly trying to speak English as distinctly as possible, what his first general impressions of America were. Karl answered, amid a deathly hush all round, and with some side-glances at his uncle, in considerable detail, trying to make himself agreeable and show gratitude by speaking in a New York accent. At one expression he used all three gentlemen burst out laughing, and Karl feared that he had made a stupid mistake, but no, as Mr Pollunder explained to him, he had said something very witty. This Mr Pollunder seemed altogether to have taken a special liking to Karl, and while his uncle and Mr Green resumed their business discussions, Mr Pollunder made Karl push his chair close to his own, and first asked him many things about his name, his family, and his voyage, then, to give Karl a rest, told him rapidly, laughing and coughing, about himself and his daughter, with whom he lived on a small country estate near New York, but where, to be sure, he was only able to spend his evenings, for he was a banker and his job kept him in New York all day long. Karl was also cordially invited to come out to this estate, for a new-minted American like Karl must surely feel the need for an occasional change from New York. Karl promptly asked his uncle for permission to accept this invitation, and his uncle gave permission with a semblance of pleasure, but without naming or even considering a definite date, as Karl and Mr Pollunder had expected.

But on the very next day Karl was summoned to one of his uncle's offices—his uncle had ten different offices in this building alone—where he found his uncle and Mr Pollunder both lying back in their armchairs and saying very little. 'Mr Pollunder', said Karl's uncle, barely visible in the twilight of the room, 'has come to take you to his country estate, as we discussed yesterday.' 'I didn't know it was to be today,' answered Karl, 'or else I'd have been prepared.' 'If you aren't prepared, then perhaps we should postpone your visit for a while,' remarked his uncle. 'What preparations!' exclaimed Mr Pollunder. 'A young man is always prepared.' 'It's not because of him,' said Karl's uncle, turning to his visitor, 'but he would still have to go up to his room, and you'd be kept waiting.' 'There's plenty of time for that,' said Mr Pollunder, 'I expected some delay and closed my business early.' 'You see', said Karl's uncle, 'what trouble your visit is already causing.' 'I'm sorry,' said Karl, 'but I'll be back in a moment,' and was about to dash off. 'Don't hurry,' said Mr Pollunder, 'you aren't giving me the slightest trouble, while your visit gives me nothing but pleasure.' 'You'll miss your riding lesson tomorrow, have you cancelled it?' 'No,' said Karl, this visit, to which he had been looking forward, was becoming a nuisance, 'I didn't know—' 'And you still want to go?' asked his uncle. Mr Pollunder, that kind person, came to his aid. 'We'll stop at the riding-school on the way and arrange things.' 'That sounds good,' said his uncle. 'But Mak will be expecting you.' 'He won't be expecting me,' said Karl, 'but he will certainly go there.' 'Well then?' asked his uncle, as though Karl's reply had not satisfied him in the slightest. Mr Pollunder again settled the matter: 'But Klara'—that was Mr Pollunder's daughter—'is expecting him too, this very evening, and surely she has priority over Mak?' 'To be sure,' said Karl's uncle. 'Well, run up to your room,' and he slapped the arm of his chair several times, as though unintentionally. Karl was already at the door when his uncle kept him back with the question: 'Will you

be back here tomorrow morning in time for your English lesson?'
'Goodness!' exclaimed Mr Pollunder, turning round in his armchair,
so far as his bulk permitted, with astonishment. 'Can't he stay with us
tomorrow at least? I'd bring him back early the following morning.'
'That's out of the question,' said Karl's uncle. 'I can't allow his studies to be disorganized in such a way. Later on, when he's established
in a professional routine, I'll be happy to allow him, even for a longer
period, to accept such a kind and gratifying invitation.' 'What
contradictions!' thought Karl. Mr Pollunder was downcast. 'But one
evening and one night can hardly matter.' 'That was my view too,'
said Karl's uncle. 'One must take what one can get,' said Mr Pollunder,
laughing again. 'So I'll wait,' he called to Karl, who, as his uncle said
nothing more, hurried away. On coming back, ready for his trip, he
found only Mr Pollunder in the office, his uncle had gone away.
Mr Pollunder shook both Karl's hands with delight, as though he
wanted to make absolutely sure that Karl was coming after all. Karl
was still flushed from hurrying and likewise shook Mr Pollunder's
hands, pleased to be able to make the excursion. 'Wasn't my uncle
annoyed at my going?' 'Goodness, no! He didn't mean it seriously. He
sets great store by your education.' 'Did he tell you himself that he
didn't mean what he said seriously?' 'Oh, yes,' drawled Mr Pollunder,
proving that he could not tell a lie. 'It's strange how reluctant he was
to give me permission to visit you, although you're a friend of his.'
Mr Pollunder, though he did not admit it openly, could not explain
this either, and both of them, as they drove in Mr Pollunder's automobile through the warm evening, pondered it for a long time,
although they immediately began talking about other things.

They were sitting close together, and Mr Pollunder held Karl's
hand in his own while he told stories. Karl wanted to hear much about
Miss Klara, as though the long journey were making him impatient
and he could arrive sooner with the help of stories than in reality.
Although he had never yet driven through the New York streets in the
evening, and the noise raced over the pavement and the roadway,
changing direction each moment as though in a whirlwind, seeming
not like a product of humanity but like an alien element, Karl paid
attention, as he tried to absorb Mr Pollunder's words exactly, only to
Mr Pollunder's dark waistcoat, over which a golden cross hung
quietly. From the streets where the theatre-goers, in undisguised
terror of being late, were rushing to the theatres with rapid strides

and in vehicles driven in the utmost haste, they passed through intermediate areas into the suburbs, where their automobile kept being directed into side-streets by mounted policemen, since the main streets were occupied by a demonstration by metalworkers, who were on strike, and only the most essential traffic could be permitted at the crossroads. If the automobile, emerging from dark echoing alleyways, crossed one of those streets, resembling whole squares, then on both sides, in vistas that nobody could follow to the end, the pavements appeared filled with a mass of people, moving with tiny steps and singing in unison greater than that of a single voice. On the roadway, which was kept free, could be seen here and there a policeman on a motionless horse or people carrying flags or inscribed banners that stretched across the street or a workers' leader surrounded by fellow-workers and stewards or an electric tram that had not taken flight quickly enough and was now empty and dark, while its driver and conductor sat on the platform. Small groups of inquisitive people were standing a long way from the real demonstrators, not moving from the spot although they were not sure what was actually happening. Karl, however, leaned back happily in the arm that Mr Pollunder had put round him, the certainty that he would soon be a welcome guest in a well-lit country house surrounded by walls and guarded by dogs gave him an enormous sense of well-being, and although, as he was getting sleepy, he could no longer take in accurately, or at least continuously, everything that Mr Pollunder was saying, he pulled himself together from time to time and wiped his eyes in order to check whether Mr Pollunder had noticed his sleepiness, for he did not want that to happen at any price.

3

A Country House near New York

'WE'RE there,' said Mr Pollunder at one of the moments when Karl's attention had wandered. The automobile was standing in front of a country house, which, as usual with rich people's country houses in the neighbourhood of New York, was loftier and more extensive than a country house that serves only one family really needs to be. As only the lower part of the house was illuminated, one could not tell quite how high it was. At the front chestnut trees were rustling, and between them—the iron gate was already open—a short drive led to the front steps. His tiredness as he got out suggested to Karl that the journey had taken quite a long time. In the darkness of the chestnut-lined avenue he heard a girl's voice close to him saying: 'Here's Mr Jakob at last.' 'My name's Rossmann,' said Karl, grasping the hand held out to him by a girl whose outlines he could now make out. 'He's only Jakob's nephew,' said Mr Pollunder in explanation, 'and his own name is Karl Rossmann.' 'We're still happy to have him here,' said the girl, who didn't care about names. All the same, Karl asked, as he walked towards the house between Mr Pollunder and the girl: 'You must be Miss Klara?' 'Yes,' she said, and already some light from the house enabled him to make out her face, which was inclined towards him, 'but I didn't want to introduce myself here in the darkness.' 'What, was she waiting for us at the gate?' thought Karl, gradually waking up as he walked. 'We've got another guest this evening as well,' said Klara. 'Impossible!' exclaimed Mr Pollunder in annoyance. 'Mr Green,' said Klara. 'When did he arrive?' asked Karl, as though suspecting something. 'A moment ago. Didn't you hear his automobile in front of yours?' Karl looked up at Pollunder to see what he thought of the matter, but he had put his hands in his trouser pockets and was merely stamping harder as he walked. 'It's no use living just outside New York, one keeps being disturbed. We must definitely move further away. Even if I have to drive half the night before I get home.' They stopped at the foot of the steps. 'But Mr Green hasn't been here for a long time,' said Klara, who evidently agreed with her father, but wanted to calm him down. 'Why does he have to come this evening of all times,' said Pollunder, his words rolling furiously over his bulging lower lip, a loose heavy piece of flesh which was easily agitated. 'To be sure!' said Klara. 'Perhaps he'll soon go away again,' remarked Karl, astonished at the sympathy he already felt with these people who yesterday had been complete strangers. 'Oh, no,' said Klara, 'he has some big piece of business to discuss with Papa, which will probably take a long time, for he threatened me in jest that if I wanted to be a polite hostess I would have to listen until morning.' 'That's all I need. That means he'll stay the night,' cried Pollunder, as though this were worse than anything. 'I would really like,' he said, becoming friendlier as a new idea struck him, 'I would really like, Mr Rossmann, to return to the automobile and take you back to your uncle. This evening is already spoiled and who knows when your uncle will let us have you again. But if I take you back now, at least next time he won't be able to refuse.' And he was already taking Karl's hand in order to carry out his plan. But Karl did not budge and Klara begged her father to leave him there, for at least she and Karl could not be disturbed in the slightest by Mr Green, and finally Pollunder realized that his mind was not firmly made up. Moreover— and this may have been decisive—they suddenly heard Mr Green calling down from the top step into the garden: 'What's taking you so long?' 'Come on,' said Pollunder, beginning to mount the steps. After him went Karl and Klara, now studying each other in the light. 'What red lips she has,' said Karl to himself, thinking of Mr Pollunder's lips and how beautifully they were transformed in his daughter. 'After supper,' she said, 'if it's all right with you, we'll go straight to my room, so that at least we'll be rid of this Mr Green, even if Papa has to spend time with him. And you'll be kind enough to play the piano for me, for Papa has already told me how good you are at it, but I'm afraid I'm quite incapable of playing music and never touch my piano, much as I love music.' Karl was entirely happy with Klara's suggestion, even though he would have liked to draw Mr Pollunder into their company. But on seeing Green's gigantic figure—Karl had just got used to Pollunder's size—which slowly became visible as they mounted the steps, Karl lost all hope that this evening Mr Pollunder might by some means be lured away from this man.

Mr Green received them in a great hurry, as though there were a lot to catch up on, took Mr Pollunder's arm, and pushed Karl and Klara ahead of him into the dining-room, where the flowers on the table, rising from clusters of fresh leaves, looked very festive and made the inconvenient presence of Mr Green doubly regrettable. Karl, who was waiting beside the table until the others had sat down, was just taking pleasure in the fact that the big French windows leading to the garden would stay open, for it admitted a powerful scent and made the room feel like a bower, when Mr Green, puffing and panting, went to shut the French windows, bent down to the lowest bolt, reached up to the highest, and did all this with such youthful rapidity that the servant, hurrying to his aid, found nothing left to do. Mr Green's first words at table were expressions of astonishment that Karl had obtained his uncle's permission for this visit. He raised one spoonful of soup after another to his lips as he explained to Klara on his right and Mr Pollunder on his left why he was so astonished and how his uncle watched over Karl and how his uncle's love for Karl was so great that one could no longer call it merely an uncle's love. 'It's not enough for him to interfere here unnecessarily, he's also got to interfere between my uncle and me,' thought Karl, unable to swallow a single mouthful of the gold-coloured soup. Then, however, not wanting to show how upset he felt, he began silently pouring the soup down his throat. The meal passed as slow as torture. Only Mr Green and to some extent Klara were lively, occasionally finding something to laugh about. Mr Pollunder took part in the conversation only a few times, when Mr Green began talking about business. He moreover emphasized—and it was then that Karl, who had pricked up his ears as though threatened by danger, had to be reminded by Klara that his roast meat was in front of him and he was at supper—that he had not originally intended to pay this unexpected visit. For even if the business they had to discuss was of special urgency, its most important aspects at least could have been dealt with today in town and the more trivial parts saved up until tomorrow or later. And so he had in fact been to see Mr Pollunder long before the close of business, but had not found him, so that he had been compelled to telephone home saying that he would be away overnight and to drive out here. 'Then I must apologize,' said Karl loudly and before anyone had time to answer, 'for it's my fault that Mr Pollunder left his business early today, and I'm very sorry.' Mr Pollunder covered most of his face with his napkin, while Klara smiled at Karl, not sympathetically but in a somehow manipulative way. 'There's no need to apologize,' said Mr Green, carving a pigeon with brisk strokes, 'on the contrary, I'm glad to be spending the evening in such pleasant company, instead of having my supper by myself at home, served by my old housekeeper, who is so old that she even has difficulty walking from the door to my table and I can spend a long time leaning back in my chair and watching her on the way. I managed only recently to arrange that the servant should carry the food as far as the dining-room door, but the way from the door to my table belongs to her, if I understand her rightly.' 'Goodness,' exclaimed Klara, 'how faithful she is!' 'Yes, there is still faithfulness left in the world,' said Mr Green, putting a bite of food in his mouth, where his tongue, as Karl happened to notice, coiled itself round the food in a single movement. Feeling almost sick, he stood up. Mr Pollunder and Klara reached almost simultaneously for his hands. 'You must stay in your seat,' said Klara. And when he had sat down again, she whispered to him: 'Soon we'll disappear together. Be patient.' Mr Green meanwhile had been quietly occupied with eating, as though it were Mr Pollunder's and Klara's natural duty to calm Karl down when he made him feel sick.

The meal lasted a long time, mainly because Mr Green treated each course with great thoroughness, though he was also ready to welcome each new course with undiminished energy, it really seemed as though he wanted a complete change from his old housekeeper. From time to time he praised Miss Klara's skilful running of the household, which visibly flattered her, while Karl felt like resisting him as though he had been attacking her. But Mr Green was not satisfied with talking to her; instead he often regretted, without looking up from his plate, that Karl had so remarkably little appetite. Mr Pollunder defended Karl's appetite, though as host he ought also to have encouraged Karl to eat. And indeed the constraint Karl suffered throughout the supper made him feel so sensitive that against his better judgement he interpreted this remark by Mr Pollunder as a sign of hostility. And it was only to be expected in this state that he would suddenly eat too much too quickly, then wearily put down his knife and fork for long periods and be the most immobile of the company, thus often puzzling the servant who handed out the food.

'Tomorrow I'll tell the Senator how you hurt Miss Klara's feelings by not eating,' said Mr Green, indicating the humorous intention of these words only by the way he toyed with his cutlery. 'Just look how unhappy the girl is,' he continued, seizing Klara under the chin. She put up with it, closing her eyes. 'You little rascal,' he exclaimed, leaning back and laughing, purple in the face, with the strength of one who has eaten his fill. Karl tried vainly to make sense of Mr Pollunder's behaviour. The latter was sitting and staring at his plate as though the really important things were happening there. He did not pull Karl's chair closer to his own, and if he spoke he spoke to everyone, but to Karl he had nothing in particular to say. And yet he tolerated Green, that sly old New York bachelor, touching Klara with unmistakable intentions, insulting Karl, Pollunder's guest, or at least treating him like a child, and fortifying and preparing himself for who knew what actions.

After the end of the meal—when Green noticed the general mood, he was the first to get up, virtually raising everyone else with him—Karl went aside by himself to one of the big windows, divided by narrow white strips of wood, which led to the terrace and were actually, as he saw on stepping closer, proper doors. What remained of the dislike that Mr Pollunder and his daughter had initially felt for Green and that Karl had at that time found hard to understand? Now they were standing beside Green and nodding to him. The smoke from Mr Green's cigar, a present from Pollunder, which was of a thickness that Karl's father at home used now and again to tell of as a fact that he had probably never seen with his own eyes, spread through the room, carrying Green's influence even into corners and crannies that he himself would never enter. However far away Karl was standing, he could still feel the smoke tickling his nose, and Mr Green's behaviour, which he observed only by one quick glance from the place where he was standing, struck him as disgraceful. He now thought it by no means unlikely that his uncle had refused for so long to let him pay this visit simply because he knew Mr Pollunder's weak character and hence, if he did not actually foresee that Karl's feelings would be hurt, at least considered it within the realm of possibility. He didn't like the American girl either, thought he certainly hadn't imagined her as being much more beautiful than she was. Since Mr Green had been paying attention to her, he was even surprised by the beauty of which her face was capable, and especially by the gleam of her restlessly straying eyes. He had never before seen a skirt that clung so close to the body as hers did, small creases in the yellowish, delicate, and strong material showed how it was being stretched. And yet Karl did not care one jot about her and he would gladly have forgone being taken to her room, if he could instead have opened the door, having placed his hands on the latch just in case, and got into the automobile, or, if the chauffeur was already asleep, have been allowed to walk back to New York by himself. The clear night, with the full moon inclined towards him, was free for anyone, and to be frightened out in the open air struck Karl as senseless. He imagined—and for the first time he felt at ease in this room—how in the morning—he could hardly arrive home on foot any earlier—he would surprise his uncle. He had never been in his bedroom, and had no idea where it was, but he would ask the way. Then he would knock, and on hearing the formal 'Come in!' he would run into the room and surprise his dear uncle, whom he had hitherto only seen fully dressed and buttoned up, sitting upright in bed with his eyes turned in astonishment towards the door, in his nightshirt. That might not be much in itself, but one only had to think what it might lead to! Perhaps he would have breakfast together with his uncle for the first time, his uncle in bed, he on a chair, the breakfast on a little table between them, perhaps this shared breakfast would become a regular custom, perhaps as a result of such a breakfast they would, as could hardly be avoided, meet oftener than just once a day, as hitherto, and then of course they'd be able to talk much more frankly. After all, it was simply because they didn't have frank exchanges that today he had been somewhat disobedient, or rather, stubborn towards his uncle. And even if he had to spend tonight here—it looked like it, unfortunately, although he was left to stand at the window and amuse himself as best he could—perhaps this unfortunate visit would mark a change for the better in his relationship with his uncle, perhaps his uncle in his bedroom this evening was having similar thoughts.

Feeling a little comforted, he turned round. Klara was standing in front of him, saying: 'Don't you like it here? Wouldn't you like to feel a little bit at home in this house? Come on, I'll make one final effort.' She led him across the room to the door. At a side table the two gentlemen were sitting with tall glasses containing gently bubbling drinks, which Karl did not recognize and which he would have liked to taste. Mr Green had put one elbow on the table and was holding his entire face as close as possible to Mr Pollunder; if one had not known Mr Pollunder, one might well have supposed that some criminal activity was being discussed instead of business. While Mr Pollunder followed Karl to the door with a friendly gaze, Green, although one usually looks involuntarily in the same direction as the person one is speaking to, did not make the slightest move to look at Karl, who took this behaviour to express Green's conviction that each of them, Karl on his side and Green on his, should try to make the most of his abilities, and the necessary social connection between them would eventually emerge as the victory or the annihilation of one or other of them. 'If that's what he thinks,' said Karl to himself, 'then he's a fool. I honestly don't want anything from him, and I wish he'd leave me alone.' Hardly had he entered the corridor when it occurred to him that he had probably behaved impolitely, for with his eyes fixed on Green he had let Klara almost drag him out of the room. He now walked beside her all the more willingly. Passing through the corridors he at first could not believe his eyes on seeing every twenty steps a liveried servant standing with a candelabrum and holding its thick shaft with both hands. 'The new electric cable has been installed so far only in the dining-room,' explained Klara. 'We bought this house only a short time ago and have had it completely rebuilt, so far as an old house with its odd construction can be rebuilt.' 'So there are old houses in America too,' said Karl. 'Of course,' said Klara, laughing, and pulled him along. 'You mustn't laugh at me,' he said crossly. After all, he knew about Europe and America, but she only knew America.

In passing, Klara pushed open a door with her outstretched hand and said without pausing: 'That's where you'll sleep.' Karl of course wanted to take a look at the room right away, but Klara declared impatiently, almost screaming, that there was plenty of time for that and he should come along. They pulled each other to and fro in the corridor till Karl decided he didn't have to do whatever Klara said, freed himself, and entered the room. The surprising darkness outside the window turned out to be due to the dense foliage of a tree that was swaying there. Birdsong could be heard. In the room itself, which the moonlight had not yet penetrated, practically nothing, to be sure, could be made out. Karl regretted not having brought the electric torch which his uncle had given him as a present. Really, in this house you needed a torch, if they had had a few such torches they could have sent the servants to bed. He sat down on the windowsill and looked outside, listening. A frightened bird seemed to be making its way through the foliage of the old tree. The whistle of a New York suburban train was heard somewhere in the countryside. Otherwise it was quiet.

But not for long, for Klara came rushing in. Visibly cross, she cried: 'What's the meaning of this?' and slapped her skirt. Karl did not want to answer until she was politer. But she advanced towards him with long strides, cried: 'So are you coming with me or aren't you?' and shoved, whether on purpose or from excitement, so hard at his chest that he would have fallen out of the window if at the last moment, as he was slipping from the windowsill, he had not touched the floor with his feet. 'I nearly fell out,' he said reproachfully. 'Pity you didn't. Why are you so rude. I'll shove you out again.' And indeed she put her arms round him and carried him, too astonished at first to make himself heavy, with her sport-toughened body almost as far as the window. But there he recovered his presence of mind, freed himself by a twist of his hips, and put his arms round her. 'Oh, you're hurting me,' she said at once. But now Karl thought he couldn't let her go. He did leave her free to walk as she pleased, but followed her and didn't let her go. Besides, it was so easy to keep his arms round her in her tight-fitting dress. 'Let me go,' she whispered, her flushed face close to his, it was an effort for him to see her, she was so close, 'let me go, I'll give you something nice.' 'Why is she sighing like that,' thought Karl, 'it can't hurt her, I'm not squeezing her,' and he still did not let her go. But suddenly, after standing there in silence for a moment in which he relaxed his attention, he again felt her growing strength on his body, and she had slipped from his grasp, seized him with an expert grip, avoided his legs by adopting the positions of some exotic combat technique, and drove him in front of her, breathing with wonderful evenness, against the wall. There was a sofa there on which she laid Karl, saying without bending down far towards him: 'Now move if you can.' 'You cat, you crazy cat,' Karl just managed to call, engulfed by a confused mixture of fury and shame. 'You're mad, you crazy cat.' 'Mind your language,' she said, sliding one hand towards his throat and beginning to squeeze it so hard that Karl was quite incapable of doing anything but gasp for breath, while with her other hand she approached his cheek, touched it as though experimentally, drew her hand back further and further into the air, and seemed about to slap him at any moment. 'How would it be,' she asked, 'if I punished you for your behaviour to a lady by sending you home with a real good box on the ear. It might be useful for your future life, even though it wouldn't be a nice memory. I'm sorry for you and you're quite a nice-looking boy, and if you'd learnt ju-jitsu you'd probably have beat me up. All the same—I really want to give you a slap, the way you're lying there. I'll probably regret it, but if I do it, I'm telling you right now that I'll be doing it almost against my will. And then of course I won't be content with one slap, but I'll hit you right and left till your cheeks swell up.* And perhaps you're a man of honour—I'd like to think so—and you won't be able to live with the slapping and you'll make an end of yourself. But why were you so hostile to me? Don't you fancy me? Isn't it worth coming to my room? Watch out! I nearly gave you a good slap just now without meaning to. If you get free today, behave better next time. I'm not your uncle; you can't defy me. Anyway, let me tell you that if I let you go without slapping you, you needn't think that, as far as honour is concerned, your present situation amounts to the same thing as really being slapped, if you did think that I'd sooner slap you after all. I wonder what Mack will say when I tell him all this.' On remembering Mack she let Karl go, in his confused thoughts Mack appeared as his liberator. Feeling Klara's hand on his throat for a while longer, he wriggled a little and then lay still.

She told him to get up, he did not answer and did not stir. She lit a candle somewhere, the room acquired some light, a blue zigzag pattern became visible on the ceiling, but Karl lay with his head on the sofa cushions, just as Klara had placed him, and did not turn it an inch. Klara walked around the room, her skirt rustled round her legs, she stopped, probably at the window, for a long while. 'Going to be good, are we?' she could be heard asking. Karl felt it was hard that in this room, where Mr Pollunder after all intended him to spend the night, he could get no peace. There was this girl wandering around, standing and talking, and he was so utterly sick of her. To drop off to sleep and then get away from here was his sole wish. He didn't even want to go to bed any more, just to stay here on the sofa. He watched for her to leave so that he could leap to the door after her, bolt it, and then throw himself back down on the sofa. He had such a need to stretch out and yawn, but he didn't want to do that in front of Klara. And so he lay staring upwards, felt his face becoming more and more immobile, and a fly that was buzzing round him flickered in front of his eyes without his knowing what it was.

Klara came over to him again, bent down in an attempt to meet his gaze, and if he hadn't restrained himself he could not have avoided looking at her. 'I'm going now,' she said. 'Perhaps you'll feel like coming to see me later. The door of my room is the fourth, counting from this door, on this side of the corridor. So you go past three more doors and the one you get to then is the right one. I'm not going downstairs again, I'll stay in my room. I won't exactly wait for you, but if you want to come along, then come. Remember you promised to play the piano for me. But perhaps I've worn you out and you can't stir. In that case, stay and have a good sleep. I won't tell my father a word about our little scrap for the moment; I'm saying that just in case you're worried.' Thereupon, despite claiming to be tired, she took two bounds out of the room.

Karl promptly sat upright, lying down had already become unbearable. To get some exercise, he went to the door and looked out into the corridor. How dark it was! He was glad when he had closed and locked the door and was again standing by his table in the light of the candle. He had resolved not to stay in this house any longer but to go down to Mr Pollunder, to tell him frankly how Klara had treated him—he didn't mind about admitting his defeat—and on these surely sufficient grounds to ask for permission to drive or walk home. If Mr Pollunder raised any objection to this immediate departure, then Karl would at least ask him to get a servant to take him to the nearest hotel. Admittedly, what Karl was planning was not the normal way of treating a kind host, but then it was still more unusual to treat a guest the way Klara had done. She had even implied that her promise to tell Mr Pollunder nothing about their scrap for the present was an act of kindness, that was really shocking. What, had Karl been invited for a wrestling bout, so that it was shameful for him to be thrown by a girl who had probably spent most of her life learning wrestlers' tricks? For all one knew she might have been taught by Mack. Just let her tell him everything, he would understand, Karl knew that, although he had never had the chance actually to establish it. But Karl also knew that if Mack taught him he would be a much quicker learner than Klara, and then he'd come back here one day, most likely uninvited, inspect the premises first, of course, since Klara had had a big advantage from knowing her way around, then he'd grab this same Klara and beat her up on the very same sofa onto which she'd thrown him today.

Now the only thing that mattered was to find his way back to the dining-room, where he had probably, in his absence of mind, left his hat in some unsuitable place. Of course he would take the candle, but even with a light it wasn't easy to find one's way. He didn't even know, for example, whether this room was on the same floor as the dining-room, on the way here Klara had kept pulling at him so that he hadn't

been able to look round, Mr Green and the servants carrying cande-
labra had also filled his mind, in short, he really had no idea whether
they had gone up one flight of stairs, or two, or perhaps none at all.
Judging by the view from the window, his room must be fairly high
up, and he therefore tried to imagine that they had climbed some
stairs, but even at the entrance to the house they had had to go up
some stairs, why couldn't this side of the house be raised as well?
But if only a crack of light from a door had at least been visible in the
corridor, or if a distant voice, however faint, had been audible.

His watch, a present from his uncle, showed eleven o'clock, he took
the candle and went out into the corridor. He left the door open so
that in case his search was in vain he would at least be able to find his
room and thereafter, in an emergency, Klara's room. To be on the safe
side, and so that the door would not shut by itself, he wedged it open
with a chair. In the corridor, unfortunately, there was a draught of air
blowing towards Karl—he was of course going left, away from Klara's
door—which, though very weak, could still have blown out the candle, which meant Karl had to shield the flame with his hand and to
pause frequently so that the flame, reduced to almost nothing, could
flare up again. It was slow progress, which made the way seem twice
as long. Karl had already passed long stretches of wall without a single door, it was impossible to imagine what was behind them. Then
came one door after another, he tried to open several, they were locked
and the rooms obviously unoccupied. It was an unparalleled waste of
space, and Karl thought about the eastern districts of New York,
which his uncle had promised to show him, where several families
were said to live in a single room and a family's home consisted of the
corner of a room in which the children crowded round their parents.
And here there were so many empty rooms with no purpose but to
give a hollow sound when one knocked on the door. Mr Pollunder
seemed to Karl to have been misled by false friends, and infatuated
with his daughter, and thus ruined. Karl's uncle must have judged
him correctly, and only his principle of letting Karl judge people for
himself was to blame for this visit and these wanderings along the corridors. Karl would tell his uncle that tomorrow without any more ado,
for on his own principle his uncle would hear his nephew's judgement
of him willingly and calmly. In addition, this principle was perhaps
the only thing Karl did not like about his uncle, and even this dislike
was not unqualified.

Suddenly the wall on one side of the corridor came to an end and was replaced by an ice-cold marble banister. Karl put down the candle and bent cautiously over. A dark void blew towards him. If that was the house's main hall—in the gleam of the candle part of a vaulted ceiling was visible—why hadn't they entered through this hall? What was the point of this huge, deep space? It was like standing in the gallery of a church. Karl almost regretted that he couldn't stay in this house until the morning, he would have liked Mr Pollunder to show him round by daylight and explain everything to him.

The banister, anyway, was not long and Karl was soon inside another closed corridor. At a sudden turning in the corridor Karl bumped very hard against the wall, and only the continual care with which he was gripping the candle happily prevented it from falling and going out. As the corridor seemed never-ending, and no window anywhere afforded a view, Karl was already thinking that he might be going in a circle round the whole house and was hoping to regain the open door of his room, but neither it nor the banister reappeared. Till now Karl had refrained from calling out, for he did not want to make a noise in a strange house at such a late hour, but he now realized that there was nothing wrong with doing so in this unlit house and was just about to shout 'Hallo!' towards both ends of the corridor, when in the direction he had come he noticed a small light approaching. Only now could he tell how long the straight corridor was, this house was a fortress, not a villa. Karl's joy at being rescued by this light was so great that he threw caution to the winds and ran towards it, at the first bound he took his candle went out. He paid no attention, for he no longer needed it, here was an old servant with a lantern coming towards him, who would show him the right way.

'Who are you?' asked the servant, holding the lantern up to Karl's face and thus at the same time illuminating his own. His face seemed rather stiff because of a long white beard which ended on his chest in silky curls. It must be a loyal servant who is allowed to wear such a beard, thought Karl, staring at the full length and breadth of this beard without feeling inhibited by the fact that he was being observed himself. For the rest, he replied immediately that he was Mr Pollunder's guest and wanted to go from his own room to the dining-room but couldn't find it. 'Oh, I see,' said the servant, 'we haven't installed electric lighting yet.' 'I know,' said Karl. 'Don't you want to light your candle from my lamp?' asked the servant. 'Yes please,' said Karl, and did so. 'There's such a draught in the corridors,' said the servant, 'a candle easily goes out, that's why I've got a lantern.' 'Yes, a lantern is much more useful,' said Karl. 'But you've got candle-grease all over you,' said the servant, examining Karl's suit in the light of the candle. 'I didn't notice,' exclaimed Karl, feeling very sorry, as it was a black suit which his uncle had said fitted him better than any other. The fight with Klara probably hadn't done the suit any good either, he now recalled. The servant was kind enough to clean the suit so far as could be done in a hurry; Karl kept turning round in front of him and showing him here and there a stain which the servant obediently removed. 'Why is there such a draught here?' asked Karl as they were moving on. 'There's a lot of building still to be done,' said the servant, 'the rebuilding has begun, but it's very slow. And now the building workers are on strike, as you may know. A building like this causes a lot of irritation. A couple of large breaches have been made in the walls but not closed up, and the draught goes through the whole house. If I didn't have my ears full of cotton-wool, I couldn't cope.' 'Should I speak louder?' asked Karl. 'No, you have a clear voice,' said the servant. 'But to come back to the building works, especially here near the chapel, which has got to be separated from the rest of the house later on, the draught is quite unendurable.' 'So the banister you pass on this corridor leads to a chapel?' 'Yes.' 'That's what I thought,' said Karl. 'It's well worth seeing,' said the servant, 'if it hadn't been for that, Mr Mack probably wouldn't have bought the house.' 'Mr Mack?' asked Karl, 'I thought the house belonged to Mr Pollunder.' 'To be sure,' said the servant, 'but Mr Mack had the final say when it was bought. Don't you know Mr Mack?' 'Oh yes,' said Karl. 'But what's his connection with Mr Pollunder?' 'He is the young lady's fiancé,' said the servant. 'I certainly didn't know that,' said Karl, stopping. 'Are you so astonished?' asked the servant. 'I'm just thinking it through. If you don't know about such connections, you can make the greatest blunders,' answered Karl. 'I'm only surprised that nobody mentioned it to you,' said the servant. 'Yes indeed,' said Karl in embarrassment. 'They probably thought you knew,' said the servant, 'it isn't news. Anyway, here we are,' and he opened a door behind which a staircase could be seen leading downwards to the back door of the dining-room, which was as brightly lit as on their arrival. Before Karl entered the dining-room, from which the voices of Mr Pollunder and Mr Green could be heard exactly as they had been some two hours earlier, the servant said: 'If you like, I'll wait for you here and then take you to your room. It's quite difficult to find your way around here on your first evening.' 'I won't be going back to my room,' said Karl, wondering why he felt unhappy on saying this. 'It can't be that bad,' said the servant, with a slightly superior smile, patting him on the arm. He had probably taken Karl's words to mean that Karl intended to stay in the dining-room all night, talking and drinking with the two gentlemen. Karl did not feel like making any confessions, and besides he thought that this servant, whom he liked better than any of the other servants here, might point him in the direction of New York, and so he said: 'If you want to wait here, that's certainly very kind of you and I gladly accept. At any rate, I'll be back in a little while and then I'll tell you what I'm going to do next.' 'Good,' said the servant, putting the lantern on the floor and sitting down on a low pedestal, which was empty no doubt because of the rebuilding of the house, 'I'll wait here.' 'You can leave the candle with me,' added the servant, as Karl was about to enter the room with the lighted candle in his hand. 'I really am absent-minded,' said Karl, handing the candle to the servant, who merely nodded at him, one could not tell whether purposely or just because he was stroking his beard.

Karl opened the door, which gave a loud rattling sound that was not his fault, for it consisted of a single sheet of glass which almost bent when the door was opened suddenly and only held by the latch. Karl let go of the door in alarm, for he had wanted to enter very quietly. Without turning round any further, he noticed how behind him the servant, who had obviously got down from his pedestal, was carefully closing the door without the least sound. 'I'm sorry to disturb you,' he said to the two gentlemen, who were staring at him with astonished expressions. At the same time, however, he cast a look round the room in case he could see his hat anywhere. But it was nowhere to be seen, the dinner-table had been completely cleared, perhaps the hat, unpleasant as this would be, had somehow been taken into the kitchen. 'Where have you left Klara?' asked Mr Pollunder, who did not seem to mind being disturbed, for he promptly changed his position in his armchair and faced Karl head on. Mr Green pretended to be unconcerned, drew out a wallet whose size and thickness made it a monster of its kind, seemed to be searching in its many compartments for a particular document, but while searching also read other papers that he happened to light on. 'I'd like to ask you for a favour, but you mustn't misunderstand me,' said Karl, going hastily to Mr Pollunder and placing, in order to be very close to him, his hand on the arm of his chair. 'What sort of favour?' asked Mr Pollunder, gazing at Karl with an open and frank expression. 'Of course it's already granted.' And he put his arm round Karl and drew him closer, between his legs. Karl tolerated this willingly, though in general he felt too grown-up for such treatment. But of course that made it harder to ask for the favour. 'How do you like it here?' asked Mr Pollunder. 'Don't you feel that in the country one is set free, so to speak, when one comes from the city? As a rule'—and an unambiguous side-glance, partially concealed by Karl, was directed at Mr Green—'as a rule I always have that feeling, every evening.' 'He's talking', thought Karl, 'as if he didn't know about the huge house, the endless corridors, the chapel, the empty rooms, the darkness everywhere.' 'Now!' said Mr Pollunder. 'The favour!' and he gave Karl, who was standing there mute, a friendly shake. 'Please,' said Karl, and however much he lowered his voice, there was no stopping every word being heard by Green, who was sitting close by and from whom Karl would so much have wished to conceal his request for a favour which could be interpreted as an insult to Pollunder—'please let me go home, now, at night.' And now that the worst was out, he said, without telling the slightest lie, things that he hadn't previously thought of at all. 'I'd really like to go home. I'd be glad to come back, for wherever you are, Mr Pollunder, I like being there too. Only today I can't stay here. You know my uncle was reluctant to allow me to pay this visit. I'm sure he had good reasons for that, as he has for everything he does, and I was presumptuous enough to practically demand permission against his better judgement. I have simply abused his love for me. It doesn't matter now what misgivings he had about this visit, I just know for certain that there was nothing in those misgivings, Mr Pollunder, that could hurt your feelings, for you are my uncle's best friend, his very best. None of my uncle's other friends can be remotely compared with you. And that's the only excuse for my disobedience, but not a sufficient one. You may not quite understand the relationship between my uncle and me, I'll just say what's most obvious. Until my English course is finished and I've seen enough of commercial practice, I'm entirely dependent on my uncle's kindness, which, to be sure, I'm entitled to as a blood relative. You mustn't think that I could already earn my living honestly—and God forbid I should try any other way. I'm afraid my education was too impractical for that. I've been through four classes of a European grammar school as an average pupil, and for earning money that means much less than nothing, for the syllabus in our grammar schools is very much behind the times. You'd laugh if I told you what I learnt. If one goes on studying, finishes grammar school, and gets to university, then I daresay everything balances out and you end up with a systematic education that is good for something and makes you determined to earn money. But I'm afraid I was torn out of this coherent course of study, sometimes I think I know nothing at all, and anyway whatever I could know would still be too little for America. Recently reformed schools have been set up in my home country, where you can learn modern languages and perhaps commercial skills as well, but when I left primary school that wasn't yet the case. My father did want to have me taught English, but for one thing I couldn't foresee what a misfortune would befall me and how much I would need English, and for another I had to learn a lot for grammar school, so that I hadn't much time for other pursuits.—I mention all this to show you how dependent I am on my uncle and how deeply I'm indebted to him. I'm sure you'll admit that in these circumstances I mustn't do anything against what I even suspect to be his will. And so, to make good even partly the wrong I did him, I must go home immediately.' During this long speech Mr Pollunder had listened attentively, often, especially when Karl's uncle was mentioned, pressing Karl closer to him, even though imperceptibly, and giving several serious and seemingly expectant glances at Green, who was still busy with his wallet. Karl, however, as his position vis-à-vis his uncle became ever clearer to him in the course of his speech, had become more and more restless, had made involuntary attempts to escape from Pollunder's arm, everything was pressing in on him here, the way to his uncle through the glass door, down the steps, along the avenue, through the country roads, through the suburbs to the big main street, ending at his uncle's house, appeared to him as a firmly structured unit lying there empty, smooth, and prepared for him, and calling for him in a loud voice. Mr Pollunder's kindness and Mr Green's loathsomeness melted together and he wanted nothing more for himself from this smoky room but the permission to take his leave. Admittedly, he felt detached from Mr Pollunder and ready for a fight with Mr Green, and yet he was filled with an indefinite, all-pervasive fear which dimmed his eyes with its jolts.

He took a step back and was now standing equally distant from Mr Pollunder and Mr Green. 'Didn't you want to say something to him?' Mr Pollunder asked Mr Green, taking Mr Green's hand in a pleading manner. 'I'm not aware of anything I have to say to him,' said Mr Green, who had at last pulled a letter out of his wallet and placed it on the table before him. 'It's highly commendable that he wants to go back to his uncle, and in all likelihood one would expect that he will thus give his uncle great pleasure. Unless his disobedience has made his uncle too angry with him, which is also possible. Then of course it would be better for him to stay here. It's hard to say anything definite, we are both friends of his uncle's and it would no doubt be difficult to say whether my friendship or Mr Pollunder's is the more important, but we cannot see into his uncle's mind, especially not over the many kilometres separating us here from New York.' 'Please, Mr Green,' said Karl, forcing himself to approach Mr Green, 'I can tell from your words that you too think it would be best for me to go back immediately.' 'I said nothing of the kind,' observed Mr Green, immersing himself in the contemplation of the letter and running two fingers along its edges. He seemed to be implying that he had been asked a question by Mr Pollunder and had answered it, while Karl was really no concern of his.

Meanwhile Mr Pollunder had gone over to Karl and pulled him gently away from Mr Green to one of the big windows. 'My dear Mr Rossmann,' he said, bending down to Karl's ear and by way of preparation wiping his face with his handkerchief, pausing at his nose and blowing it, 'you can't think that I want to keep you here against your will. That's out of the question. I can't of course place my automobile at your disposal, because it's kept in a public garage a long way from here, since I haven't yet had time, what with everything being changed here, to install a garage of my own. And then the chauffeur doesn't sleep in this house but somewhere near the garage, I really don't know myself where that is. Besides, it isn't part of his job to be here, his job is only to drive here at the right time in the morning. But none of that need be any obstacle to your immediate return, for if you insist I'll accompany you at once to the nearest train station, though to be sure it's so far away that you wouldn't get home much earlier than if you were to drive with me—we'll leave at seven o'clock—in my automobile.'

'Then, Mr Pollunder, I'd rather take the train,' said Karl. 'I never thought of the train. You said yourself that I'd get back sooner with the train than with the automobile.' 'But it's a very small difference.' 'All the same, Mr Pollunder,' said Karl, 'remembering your kindness, I'll always be glad to come here, assuming of course that you want to invite me after the way I've behaved today, and perhaps I'll be better able to explain next time why every minute that lets me see my uncle sooner is so important to me.' And as though he had already received permission to leave, he added: 'But you mustn't on any account accompany me. And there's no need. There's a servant outside who will be willing to accompany me to the station. I must just look for my hat.' And with these last words he was already striding through the room for a last hasty attempt to find his hat after all. 'Couldn't I help you out with a cap,' said Mr Green, pulling a cap out of his pocket, 'it might happen to fit you.' 'I won't deprive you of your cap. I can perfectly well go bare-headed. I don't need anything.' 'It isn't my cap. Take it!' 'Then thank you,' said Karl, not wishing to lose any time, and took the cap. He put it on and first laughed because it fitted perfectly, then he took it off and examined it but could not discover anything special about it, it was a brand new cap. 'It fits so well!' he said. 'So it fits!' exclaimed Mr Green, striking the table.

Karl was already going towards the door to fetch the servant, when Mr Green rose to his feet, stretched himself after his hearty meal and his lengthy repose, struck himself firmly on the chest, and said in a tone between advice and command: 'Before you go, you must say goodbye to Miss Klara.' 'Yes, you must,' said Mr Pollunder, who had likewise got up. One could tell that his words did not come from the heart, he was feebly touching the seams of his trousers and repeatedly buttoning and unbuttoning his jacket, which in line with current fashion was very short, hardly reaching to his hips, which did not suit fat people like Mr Pollunder. Moreover, one had the strong impression, when he thus stood next to Mr Green, that Mr Pollunder's fatness was unhealthy, his massive back was somewhat bowed, his stomach looked soft and flabby, a real burden, and his face appeared pale and worried. By contrast, there stood Mr Green, perhaps even fatter than Mr Pollunder, but his fatness was well balanced and well supported, his feet were close together in a military manner, his head was erect and swaying, he seemed to be a great gymnast, a champion gymnast.

'Go first of all', went on Mr Green, 'to Miss Klara. I'm sure you'll enjoy that and it also fits into my timetable. You see, before you leave here I do have something interesting to tell you, which will probably also settle the question of your return. Unfortunately a higher command forbids me to tell you anything before midnight. You may imagine that I regret this myself, for it keeps me from my night's rest, but I am obeying my instructions. It's now quarter past eleven, so I can finish discussing business with Mr Pollunder, where you'd only be in the way, and you can have a nice time with Miss Klara. On the stroke of twelve you'll be back here and learn what you need to know.'

Could Karl refuse this demand, which really only required him to show Mr Pollunder the minimum of politeness and gratitude and besides was made by a vulgar man with no interest in the matter, while Mr Pollunder, whom it did concern, was as restrained as possible in his words and expressions? And what was the interesting thing that he could learn only at midnight? If it didn't speed up his return at least by cancelling out the present three-quarters of an hour's delay, then he wasn't interested. But his greatest doubt was whether he could go to see Klara, who after all was his enemy. If only he'd brought along the iron bar that his uncle had given him as a paperweight. Klara's room must surely be a dangerous den. But it was completely impossible for him to voice the slightest criticism of Klara here, since she was not only Pollunder's daughter but also, as he had now heard, Mack's fiancée. If she'd only behaved a little bit differently to him, he'd have admired her openly for her connections. He was still thinking all this over when he noticed that nobody wanted him to think, for Green was opening the door and saying to the servant, who jumped down from the pedestal: 'Take this young man to Miss Klara.'

'That's how to obey orders,' thought Karl, as the servant, groaning with age and feebleness, took him almost at a run by an extremely short route to Klara's room. As Karl passed his own room, the door of which was still open, he felt like going in for a moment, perhaps to reassure himself. But the servant would not allow it. 'No,' he said, 'you've got to go to Miss Klara. You heard it yourself.' 'I'd only stay inside for a moment,' said Karl, thinking about throwing himself onto the sofa for a change and to make the time pass more quickly before midnight. 'Don't make it harder for me to carry out my instructions,' said the servant. 'He seems to think I'm being sent to Miss Klara as a punishment,' thought Karl, taking a few steps but then stopping defiantly. 'Come along, young sir,' said the servant, 'now that you're here anyway. I know you wanted to leave during the night, but one can't have everything one wants, I did tell you that it would hardly be possible.' 'Yes, I want to leave and I'm going to leave,' said Karl, 'and I just want to say goodbye to Miss Klara.' 'All right,' said the servant, who Karl could clearly see didn't believe a word of all this, 'why are you hesitating to say goodbye, come along.'

'Who's in the corridor?' came Klara's voice, and she could be seen leaning out of a nearby door, holding a big table-lamp with a red shade in her hand. The servant hurried up to her and delivered his message, Karl followed slowly. 'It's very late,' said Klara. Without answering her for the moment, Karl said to the servant in low voice, but, as he already knew his nature, in a severe tone of command: 'Wait for me just outside this door!' 'I was about to go to bed,' said Klara, putting the lamp on the table. Here, as he had done down in the dining-room, the servant again carefully closed the door. 'Why, it's after half-past eleven.' 'After half-past eleven,' repeated Karl in a questioning tone, as though alarmed by the figure.

'Then I must say goodbye right away,' said Karl, 'because on the stroke of twelve I have to be down in the dining-room.' 'What urgent business you have,' said Klara, tidying the folds of her loose night-dress in a preoccupied fashion, her face was glowing and she kept smiling. Karl thought he could tell that there was no danger of getting into another fight with Klara. 'Couldn't you play the piano a bit, as Papa promised yesterday and as you promised today?' 'But isn't it too late?' asked Karl. He would have been glad to oblige her, for she was quite different now, as though she had somehow ascended into Pollunder's circles and further into Mack's. 'Yes, it is late,' she said, seeming already to have lost the desire for music. 'And every note echoes all through the house, I'm sure that if you play the servants in the attics will wake up.' 'Then I won't play, after all I hope to come back here, besides, if it doesn't cause you any trouble, visit my uncle some time and then take a look at my room. I've got a magnificent piano. My uncle gave it to me. Then, if you like, I'll play you all my pieces, I'm afraid there aren't many of them, and they aren't at all suitable for such a big instrument, which should only be played by virtuosos. But you can have that pleasure as well, for my uncle wants soon to engage a famous teacher for me—you can imagine how much I'm looking forward to it—and his playing, to be sure, will make it worth your while to call on me during a lesson. I'm glad, to be honest, that it's too late for me to play, for I really can't do anything, you'd be amazed how little I can do. And now allow me to say goodbye, it's high time you were asleep.' And because Klara was looking at him kindly and didn't seem to bear him any grudge because of their scrap, he added with a smile, holding out his hand to her: 'In my homeland they say "Have a good sleep and sweet dreams".'

'Wait,' she said, without taking his hand, 'perhaps you should play after all.' And she disappeared through a small side door, beside which stood the piano. 'What's up?' thought Karl, 'I can't wait long, however nice she is.' There was a knock at the door giving onto the corridor, and the servant, not daring to open the door completely, whispered: 'I'm sorry, but I've just been called away and can't wait any longer.' 'Off you go,' said Karl, who was now sure he could find the way to the dining-room by himself, 'just leave the lantern outside the door. What's the time, anyway?' 'Almost quarter to twelve,' said the servant. 'How slowly the time passes,' said Karl. The servant was about to close the door when Karl remembered that he hadn't given him a tip, took a shilling* from his trouser pocket—he now always carried small change jingling in his trouser pocket, in the American fashion, but banknotes in his waistcoat pocket—and gave it to the servant with the words: 'For your good service.'

Klara had already returned, her hands on her well-groomed hair, when it occurred to Karl that he should not have sent the servant away, for who would now take him to the train station? Well, Mr Pollunder would surely be able to find a servant, and anyway perhaps this servant had been summoned to the dining-room and would be available. 'Do play a little, please. One hears music so seldom that one doesn't want to miss any opportunity to hear some.' 'Then I'd better not lose any time,' said Karl without further reflection and sat down immediately at the piano. 'Do you want a score?' 'No thanks, I can't read a score very well,' answered Karl, already playing. It was a little song that as Karl knew should have been played quite slowly so that foreigners in particular could appreciate it, but he dashed it off like a military march. When he had finished, the silence of the house which he had disturbed returned to its place as though in a great throng. They sat there as though dazed without stirring. 'Very nice,' said Klara, but there was no polite remark that could have flattered Karl after such playing. 'What's the time?' he asked. 'Quarter to twelve.'

'Then I've got a little time left,' he said, thinking to himself: 'It's one or the other. I don't have to play all the ten songs I know, but I can play one of them as well as I possibly can.' And he began the soldiers' song that he was fond of. So slowly, that the listener's desire, once aroused, strained after the next note, which Karl kept back and yielded only with reluctance. He actually had, as with every song, to look for the necessary keys with his eyes, but in addition he felt a sorrow growing inside himself that was seeking beyond the end of the song for another end and could not find it. 'I'm no good,' said Karl after finishing the song, looking at Klara with tears in his eyes.

Then loud clapping was heard from the next room. 'Someone else is listening!' exclaimed Karl, shaken out of his mood. 'Mack,' said Klara softly. And Mack could already be heard calling: 'Karl Rossmann, Karl Rossmann!'

Karl swung himself off the piano stool with both feet at once and opened the door. He saw Mack half reclining in a large four-poster bed, the blanket thrown loosely over his legs. The blue silk canopy was the only bit of rather girlish luxury in what was otherwise a simple bed fashioned with sharp corners from heavy timber. There was only one candle burning on the bedside table, but the bedclothes and Mack's shirt were so white that the candle-light falling on them radiated from them in an almost dazzling reflection; but the canopy was shining too, at least at its edges, with its undulating, rather loose silk. Just behind Mack, however, the bed and everything sank into complete darkness. Klara was leaning on the bedpost with eyes only for Mack.

'Hi,'* said Mack, giving Karl his hand. 'You play very well, till now I only knew how good you were at riding.' 'I'm as bad at one as at the other,' said Karl. 'If I'd known you were listening, I certainly wouldn't have played. But your'—he stopped, unwilling to say 'fiancée', as Mack and Klara were obviously already sleeping together. 'I suspected it,' said Mack, 'that's why Klara had to tempt you here from New York, otherwise I'd never have heard your playing. You're a complete beginner, and even in these songs, which you've practised and which are set in a very elementary way, you made some mistakes, but all the same I enjoyed it, quite apart from the fact that I don't despise anyone's playing. But wouldn't you like to sit down and spend some time with us? Klara, give him a chair.' 'Thank you,' said Karl hesitantly. 'I can't stay, much as I'd like to. I'd no idea there were such comfortable rooms in this house.' 'I'm having everything rebuilt in this way,' said Mack.

At that moment bells rang twelve times in rapid succession, each ring breaking into the noise of the previous one. Karl felt the wind from these bells' mighty motion against his cheeks. What kind of village was it that had such bells!

'I've got to go,' said Karl, stretched out his hands to Mack and Klara without taking theirs, and ran out into the corridor. There he could not find the lantern and wished he hadn't been in such a hurry to tip the servant. He wanted to feel his way along the wall to the open door of his room, but had hardly got halfway when he saw Mr Green rolling along with a candle held aloft. In the hand in which he was holding a candle he was also carrying a letter.

'Rossmann, why haven't you come? Why are you keeping me waiting? What have you been up to with Miss Klara?' 'A lot of questions,' thought Karl, 'and now he's pressing me against the wall', for indeed he was standing right in front of Karl, whose back was leaning against the wall. Green assumed an absurdly huge size in this corridor and Karl asked himself in jest whether he mightn't have eaten good Mr Pollunder up.

'You really aren't a man of your word. Promised to come down at twelve o'clock, and instead you prowl around Miss Klara's door. I, on the other hand, promised to give you something interesting at midnight, and I've brought it.'

And with these words he handed Karl the letter. On the envelope was written: 'For Karl Rossmann. To be given to him in person at midnight, wherever he may be found.' 'After all,' said Mr Green, as Karl opened the letter, 'I think I deserve gratitude for coming all the way from New York on your behalf, so you really shouldn't have made me chase you along the corridors.'

'From my uncle!' said Karl, as soon as he had glanced into the letter. 'I was expecting it,' he said, turning to Mr Green.

'I couldn't give two hoots whether you were expecting it or not. Just read it,' said the latter, holding out the candle for Karl.

In its light Karl read:

My dear nephew! As you will have realized during the regrettably short period we spent together, I am through and through a man of principle. That is very sad and unpleasant, not only for those around me but also for me, but I owe to my principles everything I am, and nobody can ask me to remove myself from the face of the earth, not even you, my dear nephew, even though you would have the foremost place if it ever entered my head to allow such a universal attack on my person. You of all people are the one whom I would dearly like, with these two hands with which I am holding this paper and writing on it, to catch and hold aloft. Since, however, there is at present no sign that this could ever happen, I have no choice after today's incident but to send you away, and I beg you neither to seek me out yourself, nor to attempt any communication with me, whether by letter or through intermediaries. You decided this evening, against my will, to leave me, so abide by this decision for the rest of your life, that alone will make it a manly decision. I chose as the bearer of this message Mr Green, my best friend, who is sure to find enough kind words for you, since at this moment I am at a loss for any. He is a man of influence who, if only for my sake, will stand by you with help and good counsel in your first steps as an independent person. To make sense of our parting, which as I conclude this letter again seems beyond my understanding, I must again remind myself: from your family, Karl, no good ever comes. If Mr Green should forget to hand over your suitcase and your umbrella, remind him to do so. With best wishes for your future welfare,

Your faithful Uncle Jakob.

'Have you finished?' asked Mr Green. 'Yes,' said Karl, 'have you brought me my suitcase and my umbrella?' 'Here it is,' said Mr Green, placing Karl's old suitcase, which he had hitherto kept hidden behind his back with his left hand, on the floor in front of him. 'And the umbrella?' asked Karl. 'It's all here,' said Green, producing the umbrella too, which he had hanging from a coat pocket. 'These things were delivered by one Schubal, a chief engineer on the Hamburg–America Line, who claimed to have found them aboard the ship. You can thank him when you get the chance.' 'Well, at least I've got my old belongings back,' said Karl, placing the umbrella on top of the suitcase. 'You should take better care of them in future, that's the Senator's advice to you,' remarked Mr Green, and then asked, evidently to satisfy his own curiosity, 'What sort of funny-looking suitcase is that?' 'It's the kind of suitcase which soldiers in my homeland take when they join the army,' answered Karl, 'it's my father's old army suitcase.

It's very useful.' He added with a smile: 'Provided you don't leave it about anywhere.' 'Well, you've had your lesson,' said Mr Green, 'and I don't suppose you've got another uncle in America. Here is a third-class ticket to San Francisco. I decided to send you there because for one thing your chances of making a living are much better in the East,* and because for another, everything here that might concern you involves your uncle in some way, and a meeting between the two of you must be avoided at all costs. In Frisco you can work without any trouble, just begin at the bottom and try gradually to work your way up.'

Karl could discern no malice in these words, the bad news that had been lurking in Green all evening had now been delivered and henceforth Green seemed a harmless man to whom one could perhaps speak more frankly than to anyone else. Even the best person who, through no fault of his own, is chosen as the messenger for such a private and painful decision must, as long as he keeps it to himself, appear suspicious. 'I shall leave this house at once,' said Karl, expecting agreement from an experienced man, 'for I have been received here only as my uncle's nephew, whereas as a stranger I have no business here. Would you be kind enough to show me the way out and then point me in the direction of the nearest hotel.' 'Hurry up, then,' said Green. 'You're giving me a lot of hassle.' On seeing the enormous stride that Green had immediately taken, Karl hesitated, such haste was surely suspicious, and he seized Green by the hem of his jacket and said, suddenly grasping the true state of affairs: 'There's one thing you still have to explain. On the envelope of the letter you had to give me it just says that I have to get it at midnight, wherever I am to be found. So why did you hold me back by mentioning this letter when I wanted to leave here at quarter past eleven? You were going beyond your instructions.' Green prefaced his answer with a gesture showing how pointless Karl's observation was, and then said: 'Does it say on the envelope that I should run myself ragged for your sake, and do the contents of the letter suggest that the directions are to be understood that way? If I hadn't held you back, I'd have had to give you the letter at midnight on the highway.' 'No,' said Karl doggedly, 'it isn't quite like that. On the envelope it says "to be given to him at midnight". If you'd been too tired, you might not have been able to go after me at all, or I might, though Mr Pollunder himself denied this, to be sure, already have been back at my uncle's by midnight, or it would have been your duty to take me back to my uncle in your automobile, which you suddenly stopped mentioning, since I was so keen to return. Doesn't the direction say quite clearly that midnight is my last deadline? And it's your fault that I missed it.'

Karl, looking intently at Green, could see clearly how Green's shame at being thus unmasked was struggling with his pleasure in the success of his plan. Finally he pulled himself together, said in a tone as though he were interrupting Karl, who however had been silent for a while, 'Not another word!' and pushed him, now that he had again picked up his suitcase and umbrella, out through a little door that he shoved open in front of him.

Karl was standing, astonished, in the open air. A flight of steps without a banister, built onto the house, led downwards. He had only to descend and then turn right towards the avenue leading to the highway. In the bright moonlight it was impossible to miss the way. Down in the garden he could hear the barking of many dogs that had been let loose and were running around in the darkness of the trees. As everything else was silent, they could clearly be heard landing in the grass as they bounded along.

Karl got safely out of the garden without being molested by these dogs. He could not make out for certain in which direction New York lay, on the way here he had paid so little attention to the details that might now have been useful for him. Finally he said to himself that he didn't actually need to go to New York, where nobody was expecting him and one person certainly wasn't expecting him. So he chose a direction at random and set off.

4

*Walking to Ramses**

IN the little inn that Karl reached after a short walk, and that was really only a last station for trucks headed for New York and was therefore scarcely used for overnight accommodation, Karl asked for the cheapest bed they had, since he thought he should start economizing immediately. To satisfy his request, the landlord pointed him with a jerk of his finger, as though he had been an employee, up the stairs, where a tousled old woman, annoyed at having her sleep disturbed, received him and, hardly listening to him, but continually telling him to step quietly, took him into a room, the door of which, not without breathing on him with a 'Ssh!', she closed.

Karl at first could not tell whether the window curtains had been lowered or whether the room had no windows at all, it was so dark; finally he noticed a small air-vent and drew back the sheet covering it, thus admitting some light. The room had two beds, but both were already occupied. Karl saw in them two young men who were sound asleep and looked far from trustworthy, especially as for no apparent reason they were sleeping in their clothes, one of them even had his boots on.

At the very moment when Karl uncovered the air-vent, one of the sleepers slightly raised his arms and legs, which offered such a sight that Karl, despite his worries, laughed silently.

He soon realized that, quite apart from the fact that there was nowhere else to sleep, neither a couch nor a sofa, he would not get any sleep, for he could not put his newly recovered suitcase and the money he had on him at any risk. But he didn't want to go away either, for he dared not leave the house immediately since it meant passing the old woman and the landlord. After all, this place probably wasn't any more dangerous than the highway. It was certainly remarkable that in the whole room, so far as one could tell in the dim light, there wasn't a single piece of luggage to be seen. But perhaps, indeed very likely, the two young men were servants, who would soon have to get up and look after the guests and were sleeping in their clothes for that reason. Then, to be sure, it wasn't very honourable to sleep in the same room with them, but it was that much safer. Only, at least until this was established beyond doubt, he must on no account lie down and go to sleep.

On the floor beside one of the beds were a candle and matches, which Karl fetched with stealthy steps. He had no scruples about striking a light, since the room which the landlord had assigned to him belonged to him just as much as to the other two, who besides had already enjoyed half a night's sleep and were incomparably better off than he was in having the beds. For the rest, he of course took pains, by walking and moving carefully, not to wake them.

First of all he wanted to inspect his suitcase and make an inventory of his things, for he could remember them only vaguely and the most valuable items were sure to be lost. For if Schubal gets his hands on anything, there's little hope of getting it back undamaged. To be sure, he could have expected a large tip from Karl's uncle, but then if individual objects had been missing he could have blamed it on Mr Butterbaum, who was supposed to be guarding the suitcase.

On opening his suitcase, Karl was initially horrified at the sight. How many hours he had spent during the crossing arranging and rearranging its contents, and now everything was crammed together so messily that when he opened the lock the lid sprang up by itself. Soon, however, Karl realized to his joy that the untidiness was only because the suit he had worn during the voyage, for which of course the suitcase had not been intended, had been packed in afterwards. Not the slightest thing was missing. In the concealed pocket of his jacket there was not only his passport but also the money he had brought from home, so that Karl, if he added what he had on him, was for the moment amply provided with money. The underwear he had worn on his arrival was also there, washed and ironed. He immediately put his watch and money in the tried and tested secret pocket. The only regrettable thing was that the Veronese salami, which was still there too, had imparted its smell to everything else. If that couldn't be removed in some way, Karl had the prospect of walking around for months swathed in this smell.

As he was looking for some objects that lay at the bottom, a pocket bible, writing-paper, and his parents' photographs, his cap fell off his head and into the suitcase. In its old surroundings he recognized it immediately, it was his cap, the cap his mother had given him as a travelling cap. He had, however, been careful not to wear this cap aboard the ship, for he knew that in America people generally wore caps instead of hats, for which reason he didn't want to wear his out before his arrival. Now, to be sure, Mr Green had used it in order to amuse himself at Karl's expense. Had that also been part of his uncle's instructions? And in his fury he involuntarily seized the lid of the suitcase, which fell shut with a loud noise.

Now there was no help for it, the two sleepers had been woken. First one of them stretched and yawned, then the other followed. Meanwhile almost the entire contents of the suitcase were spread out on the table, if they were thieves they had only to approach and take their pick. Not only in order to anticipate this possibility, but also to make everything clear, Karl went to their beds with the candle in his hand and explained his right to be there. They seemed not to have expected this explanation, for, still far too sleepy to speak, they just looked at him without any astonishment. They were both very young men, but hard work or poverty had made their faces prematurely thin and bony, untidy beards hung from their chins, their hair, which had not been cut for a long time, was unkempt, and they were still so sleepy that they were rubbing and squeezing their deep-set eyes with their knuckles.

Karl wanted to take advantage of their momentary state of weakness, so he said: 'My name's Karl Rossmann and I'm a German.* As we're sharing a room, please tell me your names and your nationality. I'll just explain right away that I'm making no claim to a bed, as I've come here so late and don't intend to sleep anyway. Besides, you mustn't mind my good clothes, I'm completely poor and without prospects.'

The smaller of the two—he was the one with his boots on—indicated with arms, legs, and facial expression that none of this interested him in the least and that anyway this wasn't the time for such polite phrases, lay down, and went straight back to sleep; the other, a swarthy man, also lay down but said, before going to sleep, with his hand carelessly outstretched: 'He's called Robinson and is an Irishman, my name's Delamarche, I'm a Frenchman,* and now I want some quiet.' No sooner had he said this when he blew out Karl's candle with a big puff and fell back onto his pillow.

'Well, that danger is averted for the time being,' said Karl to himself, returning to the table. Provided they weren't just pretending to be sleepy, everything was all right. It was only unfortunate that one of them was an Irishman. Karl could no longer remember in which book at home he had once read that in America you had to be on your guard against Irishmen.* While staying with his uncle, of course, he had had the best opportunity of getting to the bottom of the question about Irishmen being dangerous, but, thinking himself safe for ever, he had entirely neglected to do so. Now at least he wanted to use the candle, which he had lit again, to take a closer look at this Irishman, and on doing so he found that this individual actually looked more congenial than the Frenchman. There was still some plumpness in his cheeks and he was smiling quite pleasantly in his sleep, so far as Karl, standing on tiptoe at some distance, could make out.

Firmly resolved, nonetheless, not to sleep, Karl sat down on the room's only chair, put off packing the suitcase for the time being, since he had the whole night in which to do so, and leafed through the bible a little without reading anything. Then he picked up his parents' photograph,* in which his little father was standing upright, while his mother sat leaning back a bit in the armchair in front of him. His father was holding the back of the armchair with one hand, while the other, clenched to form a fist, was placed on an illustrated book which was lying open on a fragile ornamental table beside him. There was also a photograph on which Karl was portrayed with his parents, his father and mother were looking at him intently, while he, following the instructions of the photographer, had had to look at the camera. That photograph, however, had not been given to him for his journey.

He looked all the more carefully at the one in front of him and tried to meet his father's gaze from various angles. But his father, however much he changed his view by holding the candle in different positions, wouldn't come to life, and his thick horizontal moustache didn't at all resemble the reality, it was not a good picture. His mother, though, was portrayed much better, her lips were twisted as though she had been hurt and were trying to smile. Karl felt that anyone looking at the picture must find this so obvious that the next moment he felt this impression was too powerful and almost absurd. How could a picture impart so strongly the unshakeable conviction that the person portrayed was concealing their emotion? And he looked away from the picture for a while. When his gaze returned to it, he noticed his mother's hand hanging down from the front of the arm of the chair, close enough to kiss. He wondered whether it might be good to write to his parents, as they had both asked him in Hamburg to do, his father being very strict about it. He had of course, when his mother one terrible evening had told him at the window that he must go to America, sworn an unalterable oath never to write, but what did such an oath, sworn by an inexperienced boy, matter here in his new circumstances. He might just as well have sworn at that time that after two months' stay in America he would be a general* in the American army, whereas in fact he was in a garret alongside two tramps, in an inn near New York, and had to admit too that it was the right place for him. And he examined his parents' faces with a smile, as though they could tell him whether they still wanted to hear news from their son.

While thus gazing, he soon noticed that he was very tired and would hardly be able to stay awake all night. The picture dropped from his hands, then he laid his face on the picture, the coolness of which did his cheek good, and with a pleasant feeling he went to sleep.

He was woken early by somebody tickling him under his arm. It was the Frenchman who allowed himself this impertinence. But the Irishman, too, was standing in front of Karl's table, and both were looking at him with no less interest than Karl had looked at them that night. Karl was not surprised that they had not woken him when getting up; there was no need for them to have stepped softly for a wicked purpose, for he had been in a deep sleep, and anyway getting dressed hadn't cost them much effort and evidently neither had washing.

Now they greeted one another properly and with a certain formality, and Karl learnt that the two were locksmiths who had been unable to find any work in New York for a long time and were therefore pretty much down on their luck. Robinson, to demonstrate this, opened his jacket, and one could see that he had no shirt, which to be sure was apparent anyway from the loose fit of his collar, which was attached to the back of his jacket. They intended to walk to the small town of Butterford, two days' march from New York, where there were said to be jobs available. They had no objection to Karl accompanying them and promised firstly to carry his suitcase part of the time and secondly, if they got jobs, to get him an apprenticeship, which would be easy so long as there were any jobs at all. Karl had no sooner agreed than they gave him the friendly advice to take off his good suit, as it would be an obstacle whenever he applied for a post. In this very house there was a good opportunity for disposing of such a suit, because the housekeeper traded in clothes. They helped Karl, who had not quite made up his mind, out of the suit and took it away.

As Karl, left on his own and still a little drowsy, slowly put on his old travelling outfit, he reproached himself for selling the suit, which might have reduced his chances of an apprenticeship but could only be useful in getting a better post, but he immediately bumped into them as they placed half-a-dollar on the table as the price, looking so cheerful that it was impossible to believe that they had not also taken their cut from the profits, and probably an annoyingly large one.

Anyway, there was no time to have this out, for the housekeeper came in, just as sleepy as she had been at night, and drove all three into the corridor, explaining that the room had to be made ready for new guests. Of course there was no question of this, she was just acting out of malice. Karl, who had just been about to arrange his suitcase, had to watch the woman grabbing his things with both hands and throwing them into the suitcase with as much force as if they had been some kind of animal that had to be brought to heel. The two locksmiths hung around her, tugging at her skirt and clapping her on the back, but if they meant to help Karl by doing so they were going the wrong way about it. When the woman had shut the suitcase she pressed the handle into Karl's hand, shook off the locksmiths, and chased all three out of the room, threatening that if they didn't obey they would get no coffee. The woman must have completely forgotten that Karl hadn't been with the locksmiths all along, for she treated them as a single gang. To be sure, the locksmiths had sold her Karl's suit and thus demonstrated a certain solidarity.

In the corridor they had to spend a long time pacing to and fro, and the Frenchman in particular, who had taken Karl's arm, never stopped grumbling, threatened to knock the landlord out if he should show his face, and seemed to be preparing to do so by rubbing his clenched fists together furiously. At last an innocent little boy came along, who had to reach up to hand the Frenchman the coffee-pot. Unfortunately there was only a pot and they could not get the boy to understand that they needed glasses as well. So only one of them could drink at a time, and the others stood before him waiting, Karl did not feel like drinking, but he didn't want to hurt the others' feelings, so when it was his turn he stood there and merely held the pot to his lips.

By way of leave-taking the Irishman threw the pot onto the stone floor, they left the house, seen by nobody, and stepped into the thick, yellowish morning fog. They marched in silence for the most part, side by side, at the edge of the road, Karl had to carry his suitcase, the others would probably take their turn only when asked, every now and then an automobile would dart out of the fog and the three would turn their heads towards the cars, which were mostly gigantic and were so curiously built and appeared so briefly that there was no time to see who was inside them. Later the columns of carts began bringing foodstuffs to New York, passing by in five lines that took up the whole breadth of the road and in such an unbroken flow that nobody could have crossed the road. From time to time the road broadened out to form a square, in the centre of which a policeman was striding up and down on a tower-like elevation in order to survey what was happening and to direct with his small cane the traffic on the main road and the traffic emerging from the side-roads, which then remained unsupervised till the next square and the next policeman, but was kept voluntarily in sufficient order by the silent and attentive carters and chauffeurs. The universal calm astonished Karl the most. If it hadn't been for the bellowing of the animals being unwittingly led to slaughter, nothing might have been audible but the clattering of hooves and the whooshing of tyres. And of course not all the vehicles travelled at the same speed. When on some squares the excessive pressure from the sides made large diversions necessary, all the lines slowed down and travelled only a step at a time, then again everything raced past like lightning for a little while, until, as though governed by a single set of brakes, it calmed down again. Meanwhile no dust at all rose from the road, everything moved through completely clear air. There were no pedestrians, market-women did not walk to the town as they did in Karl's home, but every now and then large flat automobiles would appear with some twenty women carrying baskets on their backs, so perhaps they were market-women after all, standing and craning their necks to see how heavy the traffic was and to nourish hopes of a quicker journey. Then one could see similar automobiles with men strolling about on them, their hands in their pockets. On one of these automobiles, which had various names written on them, Karl with a little cry read: 'Dock-workers wanted for Jakob's Deliveries.' This car happened to be moving very slowly and a lively little man, standing with bent back on its step, invited the three travellers to get on board. Karl took refuge behind the locksmiths, as though his uncle might be on the car and see him. He was glad that the two of them refused the invitation, though he was hurt by the arrogant expressions with which they did so. They certainly needn't think themselves too good to enter his uncle's service. He immediately told them so, though not in so many words. Thereupon Delamarche told him to kindly mind his own business, taking on people in this way was a disgraceful fraud and the firm of Jakob & Co. was notorious throughout the United States. Karl made no answer, but henceforth stuck more closely to the Irishman, also asking him now to carry his suitcase for a bit, and the latter, after Karl had repeated his request several times, did so. Only he never stopped complaining about the weight of the suitcase, until it turned out that he only wanted to lighten it by taking out the Veronese salami, which must have aroused his appetite back in the hotel. Karl had to unpack it, and the Frenchman laid hold of it in order to cut it up with his dagger-like knife and eat almost all of it himself. Robinson only got the occasional slice, but Karl, who had to carry his suitcase again if he didn't want to leave it on the highway, got nothing, as though he had had his share already. He felt that to beg for a piece was too petty, but his irritation mounted.

By now all the fog had vanished, in the distance gleamed a range of high mountains whose undulating crest led into a yet more distant sunny haze. Beside the road there lay badly cultivated fields surrounding large, smoke-blackened factories that stood in the open country. In the tenement blocks located here and there at random the many windows were trembling with manifold movement and shades of light, and on all the small, flimsy balconies women and children were busy, while around them, concealing and revealing them, sheets and laundry, hung up to dry, fluttered and billowed mightily. When one's gaze slipped from the buildings, one could see larks flying high in the sky and, further down, swallows not far above the travellers' heads.

Many things reminded Karl of his home, and he was not sure if he was acting wisely by leaving New York and going into the interior of the country. New York was on the sea and offered the possibility of returning home at any time. And so he stopped and said to his two companions that he felt like staying in New York after all. And when Delamarche simply tried to drive him onwards, he refused to be driven and said that he surely had the right to decide his own actions. The Irishman, obliged to mediate, explained that Butterford was much nicer than New York, and both had to plead with him before he would go any further. And even then he wouldn't have gone on if he hadn't told himself that it might be better for him to reach a place where it wasn't so easy to return home. He was sure to work better there and make more progress without being hampered by futile ideas.

And now it was he who drew the other two along, and they were so pleased at his enthusiasm that, without needing to be asked, they took it in turn to carry the suitcase, and Karl could not understand how he had given them so much pleasure. They reached a stretch of rising ground, and when they stopped from time to time they could see on looking back how the panorama of New York and its port kept extending further. The bridge connecting New York with Boston* hung delicately over the Hudson, trembling when you screwed up your eyes. It seemed to be free from traffic, and the smooth ribbon of water stretched beneath it with no sign of life. Everything in the two giant cities seemed empty and useless. Among the houses there was hardly any distinction between big ones and small ones. Down in the invisible streets life probably went on in its usual way, but above them there was nothing to be seen but a light vapour which, though it did not move, seemed easy to dissipate. Even the port, the biggest in the world, was at peace, and only here and there did the onlooker, no doubt influenced by having seen it earlier at close quarters, notice a ship making its way for a short stretch. But one could not follow it for long, it eluded one's gaze and could not be found again.

But Delamarche and Robinson could obviously see a great deal more, they pointed to right and left and stretched out their hands over squares and gardens which they identified by name, They could not grasp how Karl could have been in New York for over two months and yet had seen hardly anything of the city except a single street. And they promised that once they had earned enough in Butterford, they would go with him to New York and show him all the sights, especially of course the establishments where you could have a whale of a time. And upon this Robinson, with his mouth full, began singing a song which Delamarche accompanied by clapping his hands and which Karl recognized as an operetta tune from his home, though he liked it much better with English words. So there was a little open-air performance in which they all took part, only the city down below, which was said to enjoy a good time to this tune, seemed completely unaware of it.

At one point Karl asked where Jakob's delivery company was situated, and instantly he saw Delamarche's and Robinson's outstretched fingers pointing, perhaps at the same point, perhaps at two points miles apart. When they went on, Karl asked what was the soonest they could return to New York with sufficient earnings. Delamarche said it might well be in a month, for in Butterford there was a shortage of labour and the wages were high. Of course they'd put their money in a kitty, as comrades, to even out any differences in their earnings. Karl did not like the kitty, although as an apprentice he would of course earn less than trained workers. Moreover, Robinson mentioned that if there was no work in Butterford they would of course have to travel further, either to get taken on somewhere as farm labourers or perhaps to go to the goldfields in California, which to judge from his lengthy accounts was his favourite plan. 'Why did you become a locksmith if you want to go to the gold-diggings?' asked Karl, who disliked hearing that such uncertain journeys might be necessary. 'Why did I become a locksmith?' said Robinson, 'well, certainly not in order to starve to death. You can make good money in the gold-diggings.' 'You could once,' said Delamarche. 'You still can,' said Robinson, and talked about various people he knew who had become rich there and had stayed, who of course never lifted a finger now, but for old times' sake would help him and naturally also his comrades to get rich. 'We'll get jobs in Butterford by hook or by crook,' said Delamarche, saying what Karl wanted to hear, but not in words that inspired much confidence.

During the day they stopped only once at an inn, where, at what Karl thought was an iron table in the open air outside it, they ate almost raw meat that you could not cut up with a knife and fork but only tear apart. The bread was cylindrical in shape, and each loaf had a long knife sticking in it. This meal was accompanied by a black liquid* that burned your throat. Delamarche and Robinson, however, liked it, they often raised their glasses to toast their future, clinking them together and holding them aloft for a bit. At the neighbouring tables sat workmen in blouses streaked with lime, all drinking the same liquid. Automobiles passing in large numbers threw swathes of dust over the tables. Big newspapers were handed round, the builders' strike was discussed with excitement, Mack's name was often mentioned, Karl asked about it and learned that this was the father of the Mack he knew and the head of the biggest building firm in New York. The strike was costing him millions and might threaten his business. Karl did not believe a single word of this gossip uttered by ill-informed and ill-natured people.

The meal was further spoiled for Karl by the uncertainty about who was going to pay for it. The obvious thing would have been for each to pay his share, but both Delamarche and Robinson had remarked several times that the last of their money had been spent on their night's lodging. Neither seemed to have a watch, a ring, or anything else saleable. And Karl couldn't very well point out that they had made some money by selling his clothes, that would have been an insult which would have meant parting for ever. Yet the astonishing thing was that neither Delamarche nor Robinson seemed at all worried about paying, instead they were cheerful enough to try repeatedly to flirt with the waitress, who walked proudly and with a heavy tread to and fro between the tables. Her hair was coming loose at the sides and falling over her forehead and cheeks, and she kept pushing it back by passing her hands over it. At last, when one might have expected the first friendly word from her, she stepped over to the table, placed both hands on it, and asked: 'Who's paying?' Never did hands shoot up more quickly than those of Delamarche and Robinson did now, pointing to Karl. Karl was not alarmed, for he had seen it coming and saw no harm if his comrades, from whom he was expecting some benefits, let him pay for a few small items, even though it would have been more decent to discuss the matter explicitly before the decisive moment. It was only embarrassing that he had to extract the money from his secret pocket. His original intention had been to keep the money for a dire emergency and thus for the time being to place himself on the same level, as it were, with his comrades. His advantage over his comrades in having this money, and above all in concealing it from them, was outweighed by the fact that they had been in America since their childhood, had plenty of knowledge and experience when it came to earning money, and anyway weren't used to any way of life better than their present one. These plans concerning his money that Karl had had till now weren't necessarily frustrated by paying for the meal, for after all he could spare a quarter of a pound* and could therefore put a quarter-pound coin on the table and say it was all he had and he was ready to sacrifice it for their journey to Butterford. But he didn't know if he had enough change, and anyway the money and the folded-up banknotes were somewhere in the depths of his secret pocket, in which the easiest way to find

something was to spread all its contents on the table. Besides, there
was not the slightest need for his comrades to know of the existence
of this secret pocket. Now, fortunately, his comrades still seemed
more interested in the waitress than in how Karl was going to find the
money to pay with. By asking her to draw up the bill, Delamarche
induced the waitress to stand between him and Robinson, and she
could only fend off their advances by covering the face of one or the
other with her hand and pushing him away. Meanwhile Karl, flushed
with the effort, collected his money in one hand under the table,
hunting for each coin in the secret pocket and pulling it out. At last he
thought that, although he was not yet quite familiar with American
money, at least judging by the number of coins he had a sufficient
sum, and placed it on the table. The chinking of money immediately
brought the flirting to a halt. To Karl's annoyance and to the general
astonishment it turned it that there was nearly a whole pound there.
At least nobody asked why Karl had said nothing earlier about the
money, which would have sufficed for a comfortable train ride to
Butterford, but Karl still felt very embarrassed. After the meal had
been paid for, he slowly gathered up the money again, Delamarche
actually took from his hand a coin required as a tip for the waitress,
whom he embraced and hugged, in order then to give her the money
from the other side.

Karl was also grateful to them for making no comments on his
money during their onward march, and he even thought for a while of
admitting to them how much he had, but he refrained, since no suitable opportunity presented itself. Towards evening they reached a
more rural, fertile district. All around could be seen open fields in the
first green of spring stretching over gentle hills, the road was lined
with prosperous country estates and for hours they walked between
the gilded railings of the gardens, several times they crossed the same
slowly flowing river, and often they heard railway trains thundering
over their heads on the lofty curved viaducts.

The sun was just sinking over distant forests on the horizon when,
having climbed a small hill, they threw themselves down on the grass
amid a cluster of trees in order to rest from their exertions. Delamarche
and Robinson lay there stretched out at full length, Karl sat upright
and looked at the road a few metres below, where automobiles, as they
had done all day, were rushing past one another, as though a precise
number of them were continually being sent from a distant point and

awaited at another distant point in the opposite direction. All day, ever since early in the morning, Karl had not seen a single automobile stop nor a single passenger get out.

Robinson suggested spending the night here, as they were all pretty tired, would then be able to set off all the earlier, and anyway would hardly be able to find a cheaper and better-located place to spend the night before it became completely dark. Delamarche agreed, and only Karl felt obliged to observe that he had enough money to pay for all three to spend the night in a hotel. Delamarche said they would need the money later and Karl should take good care of it. Delamarche made not the least secret of the fact that they regarded Karl's money as theirs. As his first suggestion had been accepted, Robinson further explained that before going to sleep, in order to strengthen themselves for the next day, they should have a good meal, and one of them should fetch a meal for everyone from the hotel whose sign, Hotel Occidental, was gleaming on the nearby highway. As the youngest, and since nobody else offered, Karl did not hesitate to volunteer for this errand, and after receiving an order for bacon, bread, and beer, he went across into the hotel.

There must be a big city nearby, for the very first room of the hotel that Karl entered was filled with a noisy crowd, and at the buffet, which stretched along the whole length of the room and two side walls as well, many waiters with white aprons over their chests were continually running about and yet could not satisfy the impatient guests, for from various directions one kept hearing curses being uttered and fists being banged on the tables. Nobody paid any heed to Karl, and there was no service in the room itself, the guests, seated at tiny tables which vanished from sight if three people sat round them, fetched all they wanted from the buffet. On each of the little tables was a large bottle of oil, vinegar, or the like, and all the food fetched from the buffet had the contents of this bottle poured over it. If Karl was ever to reach the buffet, where probably, especially with such a big order, his difficulties would only begin, he had to squeeze between many tables, which of course, however careful he was, could not be done without rudely incommoding the guests, who, however, ignored him as though they were insensible, even when Karl was shoved, by another guest to be sure, against a table and almost knocked it over. He did apologize but was evidently not understood, and anyway he did not understand a word of what was shouted at him.

At the buffet he found, with some effort, a tiny free space, where his view was blocked for a long time by his neighbours' elbows planted on the counter. It seemed the usual custom here to lean on your elbows and press your fists against your temples; Karl could not help remembering how his Latin teacher, Dr Krumpal, had hated this very posture, and how he would always creep up unexpectedly, suddenly produce a ruler, and sweep one's elbows off the desk with a painful jerk.

Karl was standing pressed right against the buffet, for he had no sooner taken his place when a table had been set up just behind him, and one of the guests who had sat down there, if he leaned back only slightly while talking, touched Karl's back with his big hat. And then there was so little hope of ever getting anything from the waiter, even when Karl's two coarse neighbours had gone away satisfied. A few times Karl had grabbed a waiter by his apron across the table, but each time the waiter had torn himself free with contorted features. There was no stopping any of them, they just kept running and running. If at least there had been anything near Karl that was suitable to eat and drink he would have taken it, asked the price, put down the money, and gone away gladly. But in front of him there were only dishes with herring-like fish whose black scales shone golden at the edges. These might be very expensive and would probably not satisfy anyone's appetite. Apart from that, there were small barrels of rum within reach, but he didn't want to bring his comrades rum, they already seemed to look for the most concentrated alcohol at every opportunity, and he wasn't going to encourage them.

So Karl had no alternative but to look for another place and start his efforts all over again. But by now it was getting very late. The clock at the other end of the room, whose hands were just about visible through the smoke if you looked hard, already showed that it was after nine o'clock. But elsewhere at the buffet the crowd was even thicker than at the somewhat remote place where Karl was. Besides, the room was getting fuller as the evening wore on. New guests kept streaming through the main entrance with loud cries. At many places guests were clearing the buffet without asking leave, sitting on the counter and drinking one another's health; these were the best seats, giving a view of the whole room.

Karl did squeeze further through the crowd, but no longer had any real hope of obtaining anything. He reproached himself for offering to run this errand when he did not know the local circumstances.

His comrades would give him a well-deserved telling-off and even think that he had brought nothing in order to save money. Now he was standing in an area where hot meat dishes and fine yellow potatoes were being eaten at the tables all round, he could not understand how people had got hold of such food.

Then he saw, a few steps in front of him, a middle-aged woman, obviously one of the hotel staff, who was talking and laughing with a guest. She kept fiddling with a hair-pin in her well-groomed hair. Karl immediately resolved to place his order with this woman, if only because as the sole woman in the room she stood out amid the general hubbub and tumult, and also for the simple reason that she was the only hotel employee within his reach, assuming, to be sure, that she wouldn't rush off on her business at the first word he addressed to her. But the exact opposite happened. Karl had not even spoken to her, only watched her a little, when, as one sometimes glances aside during a conversation, she looked at Karl, broke off what she was saying, and asked him kindly and in an English as clear as the grammar-book if he was looking for something. 'To be sure,' said Karl, 'I can't get anything here.' 'Then come with me, my boy,' she said, took leave of her acquaintance, who removed his hat, which here seemed like an incredible degree of politeness, seized Karl by the hand, went to the buffet, pushed a guest aside, opened a hinged door in the counter, took Karl across the corridor behind the counter, where you had to watch for the waiters tirelessly running about, opened a concealed double door, and there they were in large, cool larders. 'You just have to know the mechanism,' said Karl to himself.

'So what do you want?' she asked, bending down to him in her readiness to help. She was very fat, her body was swaying, but her features, in proportion of course, were almost delicate. Karl was tempted, on seeing the various foodstuffs carefully piled on shelves and tables here, to quickly devise and order a choicer supper, especially as he could expect to be served cheaply by this influential woman, but in the end, as he could think of nothing more suitable, he said only bacon, bread, and beer. 'Nothing else?' asked the woman. 'No thank you,' said Karl, 'but for three people.' When the woman asked him about the two others, Karl told her in a few brief words about his comrades, it gave him pleasure to be asked a few questions.

'But that's a meal for convicts,' said the woman, obviously expecting Karl to ask for something more. He, however, was afraid she would want to give him a present and not take any money, and therefore said nothing. 'We'll soon get that together,' said the woman, went with an agility that was admirable considering her fatness to a table, cut off a big piece of bacon with plenty of meat on it with a long, thin knife resembling a saw-blade, took a loaf of bread from a shelf, picked up three bottles of beer from the floor, and put everything in a light straw basket which she handed to Karl. While doing so she explained to Karl that she had brought him here because the foodstuffs out on the buffet, though they were used up quickly, always lost their freshness in the smoke and the smells. But it was quite good enough for the people out there. Karl said nothing at all, for he did not know how he had deserved this special treatment. He thought of his comrades, who, however well they knew America, wouldn't have found their way to these larders and would have had to make do with the spoiled food-stuffs on the buffet. Not a sound from the room could be heard here, the walls must be very thick to keep this vault cool enough. Karl had already had the straw basket in his hand for some time, but wasn't thinking about payment and did not stir. Only when the woman wanted to add a bottle, similar to those on the table outside, to the contents of the basket, did he refuse politely with a shudder.

'Have you still got a long way to go?' asked the woman. 'As far as Butterford,' answered Karl. 'That's a long way,' said the woman. 'Another day's walk,' said Karl. 'No more than that?' asked the woman. 'Oh, no,' said Karl.

The woman tidied some things on the table, a waiter came in, looked round in search of something, was shown by the woman a large dish containing a pile of sardines with a little parsley strewn on them, and then carried this dish in his upraised hands out to the dining-room.

'Why on earth do you want to spend the night in the open air?' asked the woman. 'We've plenty of room here. Sleep in this hotel.' This was very tempting for Karl, especially as he had spent the previous night so uncomfortably. 'My luggage is out there,' he said hesitantly and not quite without vanity. 'Just bring it here,' said the woman, 'that's no problem.' 'But my comrades!' said Karl, realizing immediately that they indeed were a problem. 'Of course they can spend the night here too,' said the woman. 'Just come along! Don't be so awkward.' 'My comrades are fine people on the whole,' said Karl, 'but they aren't clean.' 'Didn't you see the dirt in the dining-room?' asked the woman, pulling a face. 'Anyone can come here, however bad they are. So I'll have three beds made ready right away. Only in the attic, though, the hotel is full, I've moved to the attic as well, but it's still better than the open air.' 'I can't bring my comrades,' said Karl. He imagined the uproar the two would make in the corridors of this smart hotel, and Robinson would make everything filthy and Delamarche was sure to harass even this woman. 'I don't see why that shouldn't be possible,' said the woman, 'but if you want, leave your comrades outside and come here by yourself.' 'That won't do, that won't do,' said Karl, 'they're my comrades and I must stay with them.' 'You are stubborn,' said the woman, looking away from him, 'one does one's best for you, one would really like to help you, and you resist as hard as you can.' Karl understood all this, but he saw no way out, so he only said: 'Thank you very much for your kindness,' then he remembered that he hadn't yet paid, and asked how much he owed. 'Just pay when you bring back the straw basket,' said the woman. 'I must have it tomorrow morning at the latest.' 'Thanks,' said Karl. She opened a door that led straight into the open air and added, as he stepped out with a bow: 'Good night. But you aren't doing the right thing.' He had already taken a few steps when she called after him: 'See you tomorrow!'

No sooner was he outside than he again heard the noise from the dining-room, as loud as ever and now including the sound of a wind orchestra. He was glad that he had not had to go out through the dining-room. All five storeys of the hotel were now lit up, casting light over the whole width of the road in front of it. Automobiles were still passing outside, though now with gaps in their sequence, growing larger more rapidly as they approached than by day, illuminating the road in front of them with the white beams of their lamps, growing dimmer as they crossed the zone of light from the hotel, and growing brighter as they hastened into the distant darkness.

Karl found his comrades fast asleep, but then he'd stayed away too long. He was about to arrange the food he had brought appetizingly on pieces of paper he found in the basket, when to his horror he saw that his suitcase, which he had left locked and whose key he carried in his pocket, was gaping open, while half its contents were scattered in the grass around it. 'Get up!' he called. 'You're asleep, and meanwhile thieves have been here.' 'Is anything wrong?' asked Delamarche. Robinson, not yet fully awake, was already reaching for the beer. 'I don't know,' cried Karl, 'but my suitcase is open. It's very careless to fall asleep and leave my suitcase standing unprotected.' Delamarche and Robinson laughed, and the former said: 'Well, another time don't stay away so long. The hotel is only ten steps away, and it takes you three hours to go there and back. We were hungry, thought you might have something to eat in your suitcase, and we tickled the lock till it opened. Anyway, there was nothing inside, so you may as well pack everything up again.' 'All right,' said Karl, staring into the basket that was rapidly being emptied, and listening to the peculiar noise that Robinson produced when drinking, as the liquid first flowed to the back of his throat and then shot back with a kind of whistle in order to roll into the depths of his body in a great flood. 'Have you finished eating?' he asked, as the two paused for a moment's breath. 'Haven't you already eaten in the hotel?' asked Delamarche, thinking Karl was demanding his share. 'If you want to eat any more, then get a move on,' said Karl, going to his suitcase. 'He's in a funny mood,' said Delamarche to Robinson. 'I'm not in a funny mood,' said Karl, 'but do you think it's right to break open my suitcase in my absence and throw my things out of it? I know one has to put up with a lot among comrades, and I was prepared for it, but this is too much. I shall spend the night in the hotel and I'm not going to Butterford. Eat up quickly, I must give the basket back.' 'You see, Robinson, that's the way to speak,' said Delamarche, 'that's the grand way of talking. Well, after all, he's a German. You warned me about him, but I was a sucker and let him come with us all the same. We trusted him, we dragged him with us for a whole day, wasting at least half a day in the process, and now—because somebody or other in the hotel has tempted him—he's taking his leave, simply taking his leave. But because he's a sneaky German, he isn't doing this openly, he uses the suitcase as an excuse, and because he's a rude German, he can't go without insulting our honour and calling us thieves because we played a little prank with his suitcase.' Karl, who was packing his things, said without turning round: 'Go on talking like that, you're making it easier for me to go away. I know quite well what comradeship is. I had friends in Europe too, and nobody can say that I behaved dishonestly or meanly towards him. Of course we've lost touch, but if I should ever come back to Europe they will all welcome me and promptly acknowledge me as their friend. And you Delamarche, and you Robinson, you say I betrayed you when, and this is something I'll never deny, you were kind enough to look after me and offer me the chance of an apprenticeship in Butterford. But this is something else. You've got nothing, and I don't think any the worse of you for that, but you grudge me the little I own and you're trying to humiliate me, that's more than I can stand. And now after you've broken open my suitcase, you don't say a single word by way of apology, you just insult me and what's more you insult my nation—that means I can't possibly stay with you. Anyway, all that doesn't really apply to you, Robinson. My only complaint about your character is that you're too dependent on Delamarche.' 'Now we see,' said Delamarche, going over to Karl and striking him a slight blow as though to attract his attention, 'now we see your true nature. You followed us all day, you hung onto my coat-tails, you imitated my every movement, and otherwise you were as quiet as a mouse. But now, when you think you've found some support in the hotel, you start talking big. You're a little slyboots, and I'm not at all sure that we're going to take this lying down. We might ask you to pay for the lessons you've learned from us during the day. Hey, Robinson, he says we envy him his possessions. One day's work in Butterford—never mind California—and we'll have ten times as much as what you showed us and more than you have hidden in the lining of your coat. So mind your language!' Karl had got up from his suitcase and could see Robinson, who was sleepy but somewhat animated by the beer, approaching. 'If I stay here any longer,' he said, 'I might get more surprises. You seem to want to beat me up.' 'There's a limit to patience,' said Robinson. 'You'd better be quiet, Robinson,' said Karl, without taking his eyes off Delamarche, 'in your heart you know I'm right, but for appearances' sake you've got to stand by Delamarche.' 'Want to bribe him, do you?' asked Delamarche. 'Certainly not,' said Karl. 'I'm glad to be going and I don't want anything more to do with either of you. I'll just say one thing, you criticized me for having money and concealing it from you. Assuming that was true, wasn't it right to behave that way towards people I'd only known for a couple of hours, and doesn't your behaviour now prove I was right to act that way?' 'Keep calm,' said Delamarche to Robinson, although the latter wasn't stirring. Then he asked Karl: 'As you're so shamelessly frank, be a bit franker and admit why you really want to go to the hotel.' Karl had to take a step back over his suitcase, Delamarche had come so close to him. But Delamarche wasn't to be discouraged, he pushed the suitcase aside, took a step forwards, placing his foot on a white shirt-front left in the grass, and repeated his question.

As though in answer, a man with a powerful torch climbed up from the road to meet the group. It was a waiter from the hotel. No sooner had he caught sight of Karl than he said: 'I've been looking for you for nearly half an hour. I've already searched all the embankments on either side of the road. The Head Cook has asked me to say that she needs to have the straw basket she lent you back right away.' 'Here it is,' said Karl, his voice trembling with exertion. Delamarche and Robinson had stepped aside in seeming modesty, as they always did in the presence of highly placed strangers. The waiter took the basket and said: 'And then the Head Cook wants to know if you haven't changed your mind and would rather stay in the hotel overnight. The other two gentlemen would be welcome too, if you want to bring them. The beds are already prepared. It's a warm night, but it can be dangerous to sleep on this slope, there are often snakes about.' 'As the Head Cook is so kind, I'll accept her invitation', said Karl, waiting for his comrades to say something. But Robinson was standing there like a lump of wood, and Delamarche had his hands in his trouser pockets and was gazing up at the stars. Both were obviously expecting Karl to take them along without further ado. 'If you want to come,' said the waiter, 'my instructions are to guide you to the hotel and to carry your luggage.' 'Just wait a minute, please,' said Karl, bending down to put the few things that were still lying about into the suitcase.

Suddenly he stood up. The photograph was missing,* it had been right at the top in the suitcase and was nowhere to be found. 'I can't find the photograph,' he said pleadingly to Delamarche. 'What photograph?' asked the latter. 'The photograph of my parents,' said Karl. 'We didn't see any photograph,' said Delamarche. 'There was no photograph in there, Mr Rossmann,' confirmed Robinson for his part. 'But that's impossible,' said Karl, looking around for help and thus drawing the waiter closer. 'It was on top, and now it's gone. I wish you hadn't played that joke with the suitcase.' 'There can't be any mistake,' said Delamarche, 'there was no photograph in the suitcase.' 'It mattered more to me than anything else in the suitcase,' said Karl to the waiter, who was walking around and searching in the grass. 'You see, it's irreplaceable, I can't get another.' And as the waiter gave up the futile search, he added: 'It was the only picture of my parents that I have.' Thereupon the waiter said quite bluntly: 'Perhaps we could investigate the gentlemen's pockets.' 'Yes,' said Karl immediately, 'I must find the photograph. But before searching their pockets,

I'll say also that whoever returns the photograph of his own accord can have the suitcase and everything in it.' After a moment of general silence Karl said to the waiter: 'So my comrades evidently want to have their pockets searched. But even now I promise the person in whose pocket the photograph is found the whole suitcase. I can't do more.' The waiter promptly began searching Delamarche, who struck him as harder to handle than Robinson, whom he left to Karl. He pointed out to Karl that both had to be searched at the same time, so that neither could dispose of the photograph without being noticed. The moment he put his hand in Robinson's pocket, Karl found a tie belonging to him, but he did not reclaim it and called to the waiter: 'Whatever you may find on Delamarche, please leave it with him. All I want is the photograph, only the photograph.' In searching Robinson's breast pockets, Karl's hand came in contact with his warm, greasy chest, and he realized that he might be doing his comrades a great injustice. He went on as quickly as he possibly could. However, it was all in vain, neither on Robinson nor on Delamarche was the photograph to be found.

'It's no use,' said the waiter. 'They probably tore the photograph up and threw away the pieces,' said Karl, 'I thought they were my friends, but secretly they wanted to do me down. Not so much Robinson, it would never have occurred to him that I set so much store by the photograph, but Delamarche all the more.' Karl could see only the waiter in front of him, in the small circle of light from the latter's lantern, while everything else, including Delamarche and Robinson, was in deep darkness.

There was of course no longer any question of taking the two of them to the hotel. The waiter swung the suitcase onto his shoulder, Karl took the straw basket, and off they went. Karl was already on the road when, interrupting his reflections, he stopped and called up into the darkness: 'Listen! If either of you has the photograph after all, and brings it to me in the hotel—he'll still get the suitcase and— I swear—won't be reported.' No proper answer came back, only a fragmentary word, the beginning of a shout from Robinson, who obviously had his mouth stopped right away by Delamarche. Karl waited a while longer in case they changed their minds. He called twice at intervals: 'I'm still here.' But there was no sound in answer, only a stone rolled down the slope, perhaps by accident, perhaps because someone had thrown it and missed.

5

In the Hotel Occidental

IN the hotel Karl was immediately taken into a kind of office in which the Head Cook, a notebook in her hand, was dictating a letter to a young typist. The extremely precise dictation, the controlled and elastic touch on the keys, raced past the intermittently audible ticking of the clock on the wall, which already showed almost half-past eleven. 'Right!' said the Head Cook, clapping the notebook shut, the typist leapt to her feet and put the wooden cover over the machine, doing this mechanical task without taking her eyes off Karl. She still looked like a schoolgirl, her apron was very carefully ironed, ruffled at the shoulders, her hair was piled high on her head, and it was somewhat surprising after these details to see her serious face. After curtseying first to the Head Cook then to Karl, she went away, and Karl involuntarily gave the Head Cook a questioning glance.

'It's nice that you've come after all,' said the Head Cook. 'And your comrades?' 'I didn't bring them,' said Karl. 'They must be setting off very early,' said the Head Cook, as though to explain the matter to herself. 'Mustn't she be thinking that I'll be setting off too?' wondered Karl, and said, to leave no room for doubt: 'We parted on bad terms.' The Head Cook seemed pleased by this news. 'So you're free?' she asked. 'Yes, I'm free,' said Karl, and nothing seemed more worthless. 'Listen, wouldn't you like to take a job here in the hotel?' asked the Head Cook. 'I'd love to,' said Karl, 'but I know terribly little. For example, I can't even type.' 'That doesn't really matter,' said the Head Cook. 'I'd give you a very small job for the time being, and you'd have to get ahead by working hard and paying attention. But at all events I think it would be better for you to settle somewhere than to tramp from place to place. I don't think you're made for that.' 'My uncle would second all of that,' said Karl to himself, nodding in agreement. At the same time he remembered that though he was the object of so much concern, he hadn't yet introduced himself. 'Please excuse me', he said, 'for not having introduced myself, my name's Karl Rossmann.' 'You're a German, aren't you?' 'Yes,' said Karl, 'I haven't been long in America.' 'Where are you from?' 'From Prague in Bohemia,' said Karl. 'Well I never,' cried the Head Cook in German with a strong English accent, almost raising her arms, 'then we're compatriots, my name's Grete Mitzelbach and I'm from Vienna.* And I know Prague perfectly, I worked for six months in the Golden Goose on Wenceslas Square.* Just think!' 'When was that?' asked Karl. 'That was many, many years ago.' 'The old Golden Goose', said Karl, 'was demolished two years ago.' 'Yes, of course,' said the Head Cook, lost in thoughts of the past.

Suddenly coming back to life, however, she exclaimed, seizing Karl's hands: 'Now you've turned out to be my fellow-countryman, you mustn't leave here at any price. You mustn't do that to me. Would you fancy being a lift-boy, for example? Say yes and the job's yours. If you've been around a bit, you'll know that it isn't particularly easy to get such jobs, for they're the best start you can imagine. You'll meet all the guests, they'll see you every day, they'll give you little errands, in short, you'll get a chance every day to rise to something better. Let me take care of everything else!' 'I'd really like to be a lift-boy,' said Karl after a short pause. It would have been absurd, just because of his five years at grammar-school, to have doubts about a lift-boy's job. If anything, he had reason, here in America, to be ashamed of the five years at grammar-school. Anyway, Karl had always liked the look of the lift-boys, they seemed to him like an ornament of the hotel. 'Wouldn't I need to know languages?' he asked. 'You speak German and beautiful English, that's quite enough.' 'I learned English only in America, in two-and-a-half months,' said Karl, thinking he shouldn't conceal the one thing he had going for him. 'That says enough in your favour,' said the Head Cook. 'When I think how much difficulty I had with English. To be sure, that's all of thirty years ago. I was talking about it only yesterday. You see, yesterday was my fiftieth birthday.' And she tried, smiling, to gather from Karl's expression what he felt about this dignified age. 'Then I wish you every happiness,' said Karl. 'That never goes amiss,' she said, shaking Karl's hand and growing a little sad again at this phrase from the old country that had occurred to her as she was speaking German.

'But I'm detaining you here,' she then exclaimed. 'And you must be very tired, and we can talk everything over much better by day. I'm so pleased to have met a fellow-countryman that I don't know what I'm doing. Come along, I'll take you to your room.' 'I'd just like to ask you one more thing, ma'am,' said Karl, noticing a table with a telephone on it. 'It's possible that tomorrow, perhaps very early, my former comrades may bring me a photograph that I urgently need. Could you be kind enough to telephone the porter and say he should send these people to me or else have me fetched?' 'Certainly,' said the Head Cook, 'but wouldn't it be enough if he took the photograph from them? What sort of photograph is it, if I may ask?' 'It's the photograph of my parents,' said Karl, 'no, I must speak to these people myself.' The Head Cook said no more and telephoned the appropriate orders to the porter's lodge, giving 536 as the number of Karl's room.

They then went through a small door opposite the main entrance into a small corridor, where a little lift-boy was leaning, fast asleep, against the balustrade of a lift. 'We can look after ourselves,' said the Head Cook softly, ushering Karl into the lift. 'A working day of ten to twelve hours is a bit too much for a boy like that,' she said as they ascended. 'But it's strange in America. Take that little boy for example, he arrived here with his parents only six months ago, he's an Italian. Now he looks as if he couldn't possibly stand the work, his face is very thin, he falls asleep on duty, although he's very obliging by nature—but he only has to work for another six months here or anywhere else in America, and he'll stand everything easily and in five years he'll be a big strong man. I could spend hours telling you about such instances. And I'm not thinking of you, for you're a sturdy boy. You're seventeen, aren't you?' 'I'll be sixteen next month,' answered Karl. 'Only sixteen!' said the Head Cook. 'Well, be brave!'

When they reached the top floor she took Karl to a room which, as a garret, had one sloping wall, but otherwise, being lit by two electric bulbs, looked quite comfortable. 'Don't be alarmed by the furnishings,' said the Head Cook, 'it isn't a hotel room but a room in my flat, which consists of three rooms, so that you won't disturb me in the slightest. I'll lock the connecting door so that you can feel quite at ease. Tomorrow, of course, as a new hotel employee, you'll get a little room of your own. If you had arrived with your comrades, then I'd have had beds prepared for you in the servants' dormitory, but as you're on your own, I think it will suit you better here, even if you have only a sofa to sleep on. And now sleep well so that you get your strength up for your work. It won't be too hard tomorrow.' 'Thank you very much for your kindness.' 'Wait,' she said, stopping in the doorway, 'you'd have been woken up too soon.' And she went to one of the room's side doors, knocked, and called: 'Therese!' 'Yes, ma'am,' replied the voice of the little typist. 'When you wake me early in the morning, you must go through the corridor, there's a guest sleeping in this room. He's dead tired.' She smiled at Karl as she said this. 'Do you understand?' 'Yes, ma'am.' 'Well then, good night!' 'Good night to you.'

'You see,' said the Head Cook by way of explanation, 'for some years I've been a very bad sleeper. Now of course I can be content with my position and have nothing to worry about. But it must be the effect of my former worries that causes this insomnia. If I get to sleep at three, I can think myself lucky. But as I've got to be back at work by five, or half-past five at the latest, I need to be woken, and with particular care, so that I don't get any more nervous than I am already. And so Therese wakes me up. But now you really do know all you need to, and I'm not moving. Good night!' And despite her bulk she almost pattered out of the room.

Karl was looking forward to his sleep, for the day had taken a lot out of him. And he couldn't have wished for more comfortable surroundings for a long, undisturbed sleep. The room was of course not intended as a bedroom, it was more a sitting-room or rather drawing-room belonging to the Head Cook, and a wash-stand had been brought for his sake just for tonight, but all the same Karl did not feel like an intruder, but very well looked after. His suitcase had been fetched here and was probably safer than it had been for a long time. On a low chest of drawers, with a loosely woven woollen blanket spread over it, there were various photographs, framed and behind glass, while inspecting the room Karl paused there and looked at them. They were mostly old photographs, the majority showing girls in outdated uncomfortable clothes, with small but high hats placed loosely on their heads, their right hands resting on parasols, facing the viewer and yet avoiding his gaze. Among the likenesses of men, Karl noticed especially the picture of a young soldier who had put his cap on a small table and was standing to attention with his wild black hair and was filled with proud but suppressed laughter. The buttons on his uniform had been gilded after the photograph was taken. All these photographs must come from Europe, as one could probably have read on their backs, but Karl did not want to pick any of them up. The way the photographs were standing here was the way he would have liked to put the photograph of his parents in the room he was going to have.

He was just stretching out on the sofa, after giving his whole body a thorough wash as quietly as possible in order not to wake the girl in the next room, and anticipating the pleasure of sleep, when he thought he heard a faint knocking at a door. It was impossible to be sure right away which door it was, and it might be a mere accidental noise. It did not recur right away, and Karl was almost asleep when it happened again. But now there was no longer any doubt that it was the sound of knocking and that it came from the typist's door. Karl ran on tiptoe to the door and asked, so softly that if the person next door were asleep after all he couldn't have woken anyone: 'Do you want something?' At once, and just as softly, came the answer: 'Won't you open the door? The key's in the lock on your side.' 'Excuse me,' said Karl, 'I must put my clothes on first.' There was a short pause, then the words: 'That isn't necessary. Open the door and get into bed, I'll wait for a bit.' 'All right,' said Karl, and did so, also turning on the electric light. 'I'm in bed now,' he said, slightly louder. Then out of her dark room came the little typist, dressed exactly as she had been down in the office, she probably hadn't thought of going to bed the whole time.

'I'm very, very sorry,' she said, standing slightly bent in front of Karl's bed, 'and please don't give me away. I won't bother you for long, I know you're dead tired.' 'It's not that bad,' said Karl, 'but it might have been better if I had put my clothes on.' He had to lie stretched out in order to be covered up to the throat, for he had no night-shirt. 'I'll only stay for a moment,' she said, reaching for a chair, 'can I sit beside the sofa?' Karl nodded. She sat down so close to the sofa that Karl had to move over to the wall in order to look up at her. She had a round, evenly shaped face, only her forehead was unusually high, but that might only be due to her hairdo, which did not really suit her. She was very cleanly and carefully dressed. In her left hand she was squeezing a handkerchief.

'Will you stay here long?' she asked. 'It's not certain yet,' answered Karl, 'but I think I'll stay.' 'That would be very good,' she said, drawing her handkerchief across her face, 'you see, I'm so alone here.' 'That surprises me,' said Karl, 'after all, the Head Cook is very kind to you, she doesn't treat you at all like an employee. I thought you must be related.' 'Oh no,' she said, 'my name's Therese Berchtold, I'm from Pomerania.'* Karl introduced himself too. Thereupon she looked straight at him for the first time, as though by giving his name he had become more of a stranger. They were silent for a while.

Then she said: 'You mustn't think I'm ungrateful. Without the Head Cook I'd be much worse off. I used to be a kitchen-maid here in the hotel, and I was in great danger of being sacked because I couldn't do the heavy work. They demand a lot here. A month ago a kitchen-maid collapsed just from overwork and was in hospital for a fortnight. And I'm not very strong, I used to be ill a lot and that has hindered my development, you'd never guess that I'm already eighteen. But now I'm getting stronger.' 'The work here must really be very hard,' said Karl. 'Down below I saw a lift-boy standing fast asleep.' 'All the same, the lift-boys are the best off,' she said, 'they make good money in tips and in the end they don't have to slave like the people in the kitchen. But I was really lucky, the Head Cook needed a girl to prepare the napkins for a banquet, she sent down to us kitchen-maids, there are about fifty such girls, I happened to be on the spot and I did the job just as she wanted, for I've always known how to fold napkins. And so from then on she kept me close to her and gradually trained me to be her secretary. I learned a lot that way.' 'Is there so much writing to be done?' asked Karl. 'Oh, a great deal,' she answered, 'you probably can't imagine it. After all, you saw that today I worked till half-past eleven, and this isn't a special day. To be sure, I don't write all the time, I also have to run many errands in the city.' 'What's the name of the city?' asked Karl. 'Don't you know that?' she said, 'Ramses.' 'Is it a big city?' asked Karl. 'Very big,' she answered, 'I don't like going there. But don't you want to go to sleep?' 'No, no,' said Karl, 'I still have no idea why you came in.' 'Because I've got nobody to talk to. I'm not sorry for myself, but when you've got nobody, you're happy if anyone will listen to you. I saw you earlier down in the dining-room, I was just coming to fetch the Head Cook as she took you into the larders.' 'That's a terrible room,' said Karl. 'I don't notice it any more,' she answered. 'But I just wanted to say that the Head Cook is as kind to me as my late mother used to be. But the difference between our positions is too great for me to be able to talk freely to her. I used to have good friends among the kitchen-maids, but they left ages ago and I hardly know the new girls. After all, I sometimes feel that my present work is harder than what I used to do, but that I don't do it so well, and that the Head Cook keeps me in my job out of compassion. After all, one needs to have had a good education to be a secretary. It's a sin to say so, but again and again I'm afraid of going mad. For heaven's sake,' she suddenly said, speaking much faster and reaching momentarily for Karl's shoulder, as his hands were under the blanket, 'you mustn't say a word of this to the Head Cook, or else I really shall be lost. If I were to cause her pain, on top of the trouble I give her through my work, that would really be the limit.' 'Of course I won't say anything to her,' answered Karl. 'Then that's all right,' she said, 'and stay here. I'd be glad if you'd stay here and we could, if that suits you, stick together. The very first time I saw you I felt I could trust you. And yet—just think, that's how bad I am—I was afraid the Head Cook might make you secretary in my place and give me the sack. I sat by myself for a long time, while you were down in the office, before I came to the conclusion that it might even be good if you would take over my work, for you'd be sure to understand it better. If you didn't want to run the errands in the city, I'd keep that job. But otherwise I'm sure I'd be much more useful in the kitchen, especially now I've got a bit stronger.' 'The matter is already arranged,' said Karl, 'I'm going to be a lift-boy and you'll stay a secretary. But if you give the Head Cook the slightest hint of your plans, I'll reveal everything else you said to me, though I'd be sorry to do so.' This tone upset Therese so much that she threw herself down beside the bed, whimpering and pressing her face into the bedclothes. 'I won't give anything away,' said Karl, 'but you mustn't say anything either.' Now he could no longer remain completely concealed under his blanket, stroked her arm a little, could not think what to say to her, and only thought that life here was bitter. Finally she calmed down enough to be ashamed of weeping, gave Karl a grateful look, urged him to sleep late the next morning, and promised, if she could find time, to come up towards eight o'clock and wake him. 'You're very good at waking people,' said Karl. 'Yes, there are some things I can do,' she said, ran her hand gently over his blanket by way of farewell, and ran into her room.

The next day Karl insisted on starting work immediately, although the Head Cook wanted to give him the day off to look round Ramses. But Karl declared frankly that he'd have the chance to do that later, the important thing for him now was to start work, for in Europe he had been working towards a different goal and had broken it off without achieving anything, and he was starting as a lift-boy at an age when at least the more capable boys were naturally moving on to a higher level of work. It was quite right for him to start as a lift-boy, but it was equally right for him to be in a particular hurry. Under these circumstances he wouldn't get any enjoyment from looking

round the city. He would not even take a short walk when asked by
Therese. He kept thinking that if he didn't work hard he might end
up the same way as Delamarche and Robinson.

At the hotel tailor's he tried on the lift-boy's uniform, which to
outward appearance was magnificently equipped with gold buttons
and gold braid, but while putting it on Karl shuddered a little, for
under the arms the jacket was cold, hard, and irreparably damp from
the sweat of the lift-boys who had worn it before him. The uniform
also had to be altered for Karl, especially across the chest, for none of
the ten available would even approximately fit him. Despite the sewing that was required, and although the master tailor seemed very
hard to please—he twice threw a uniform that was presented to him
back into the workshop—it took barely five minutes to sort everything out, and Karl left the studio as a lift-boy in close-fitting trousers
and a little jacket which, despite the tailor's assurances to the contrary, was very tight and constantly tempted him to do breathing
exercises in order to see if breathing was still possible.

Then he reported to the Head Waiter under whose command he
was to serve, a slim, handsome man with a big nose, who might already
be in his forties. He had no time for even the briefest conversation
and merely rang for a lift-boy, the very same one, as it happened,
whom Karl had seen yesterday. The Head Waiter called him only by
his Christian name, Giacomo, but Karl learned it only later, as its
English pronunciation made the name unrecognizable. This boy was
now given the task of showing Karl what he needed to know in order
to work the lift, but he was so shy and in so much of a hurry that Karl,
however little there was basically to show him, could hardly learn that
little. Giacomo must also be annoyed because he had to give up working his lift to make way for Karl and was assigned to help the cham-
bermaids, which, on the basis of certain experiences which he kept
to himself, he considered dishonourable. Karl was especially disappointed to find that a lift-boy had nothing to do with the machinery
of the elevator except to set it in motion by simply pressing a button,
while repairs to the engine were assigned so exclusively to the hotel
mechanics that Giacomo, for example, despite working the lift for six
months, had seen neither the engine in the basement nor the machinery inside the lift with his own eyes, although, as he expressly said, he
would very much have liked to. In general it was monotonous work,
and the twelve-hour shift, alternately by day and by night, made it so

laborious that according to Giacomo one could only endure it by snatching a few minutes' sleep while standing. Karl said nothing in reply, but he was well aware that this feat had cost Giacomo his job.

It was welcome news for Karl that the elevator he had to take care of was intended only for the upper floors, so that he would have no contact with the most demanding rich people. To be sure, one could not learn so much here as elsewhere and it was good only as a start.

After the first week it was already clear to Karl that he was fully up to the job. The brass on his elevator was the best-polished, none of the other thirty lifts could compare with it, and it might have gleamed even more brightly if the boy working in the same elevator had been anything like so industrious and had not felt that Karl's industriousness allowed him to be idle. He was a born American, named Rennel,* a vain boy with dark eyes and smooth, rather hollow cheeks. He owned an elegant suit in which, on his evenings off, he would hurry, lightly perfumed, into the city; now and again he would ask Karl to take his place for an evening, saying he had family affairs to see to, and he was unconcerned by the fact that his appearance contradicted any such excuses. All the same Karl got on well with him and liked it when on such evenings Rennel, before going out, stopped beside the lift, wearing his suit, made a few more apologies while pulling his gloves over his fingers, and then went away down the corridor. For the rest, Karl was happy to stand in for him just as a favour, which seemed to him a natural thing to do for an older colleague while starting his job, but did not want it to become a regular routine. For this incessant travelling in the lift was tiring enough, to be sure, and in the evenings it went on with hardly a break.

Karl soon also learned to make the short, low bows that were expected of the lift-boys, and he caught tips as they were thrown to him. They vanished into his waistcoat pocket, and no one could have told from his expression whether they were large or small. For ladies he would open the door with a little touch of gallantry, swinging himself slowly into the elevator behind them, since in their concern for their coats, hats, and ornaments they tended to enter more hesitantly than men. While the elevator was moving he would stand, this being the most inconspicuous position, close to the door with his back to the guests, holding the door-handle so that at the moment of arrival he could push it sideways suddenly and yet without causing alarm. Only rarely did someone tap him on the shoulder during the journey to get some small piece of information, and then he would turn round quickly, as though he had been expecting it, and give the answer in a loud voice. Often, although there were so many lifts, there would be such a crush, especially after the theatres closed or after the arrival of certain express trains, that as soon as the guests had been let out on an upper floor he would have to shoot down again in order to collect those waiting below. He could also increase the usual speed by pulling on a cable that ran through the elevator, though this to be sure was forbidden in the elevator regulations and was said also to be dangerous. Karl never did it when he had passengers, but when he had let them out on an upper floor and others were waiting down below, he threw caution to the winds and worked the cable with strong, regular tugs, like a sailor. He knew, anyway, that the other lift-boys did this too, and he did not want to lose his passengers to other boys. Individual guests who had been staying in the hotel for a long time, which incidentally was quite common here, would show now and again by smiling at him that they recognized Karl as their lift-boy, Karl accepted this kindness with a serious expression but with pleasure. Sometimes, when traffic was a little quieter, he could take on small tasks such as fetching some little item that had been left in a room by a guest who didn't want the trouble of going to his room, then he would fly up alone in his elevator, which at such moments felt especially familiar, go into the room, where there were usually strange things, such as he had never seen, lying around or hanging on clothes-hangers, breathe in the characteristic scent of someone else's soap, perfume, or mouthwash, and hurry, without lingering in the slightest, back again with the object, which he usually found despite receiving only vague instructions. He often regretted that he could not take on bigger jobs, as these were assigned to servants and messenger-boys who ran their errands on bicycles, even on motor-cycles, it was only errands from the rooms to the dining-rooms or gaming-rooms that he could undertake when there was a favourable opportunity.

When he left his work after the twelve-hour shift at six in the evening on three days, then at six in the morning on the following three days, he would be so tired that he would go straight to bed without bothering about anyone. His bed was in the dormitory shared by all the lift-boys, the Head Cook, whose influence was perhaps not so great as he had thought on his first evening, had tried to get him a little room to himself, and she might well have succeeded, but when

Karl saw how much trouble it cost and how often the Head Cook had to telephone his boss, the hard-worked Head Waiter, about this matter, he declined the room and managed to persuade the Head Cook that he was serious by pointing out that he didn't want the other boys to envy him for an advantage that he had not actually earned for himself.

This dormitory, to be sure, was not a quiet place to sleep in. For since everyone divided his twelve hours of free time in different ways among eating, sleeping, enjoying himself, and extra work, the dormitory was always in commotion. Some would be sleeping with the blankets over their ears in order not to hear anything; if one of them was wakened nevertheless, then he would yell with such fury at the yelling of the others that the others, however good sleepers they might be, could not stand it either. Almost every boy had his pipe, this was a kind of luxury, Karl too had got himself one and soon enjoyed it. Now it was forbidden to smoke on duty, the consequence being that everyone in the dormitory who was not actually sleeping would smoke. Consequently each bed was swathed in its own cloud of smoke and everything in a general fog. It was impossible, although the majority was basically in agreement, to enforce the principle that at night there should be a light at only one end of the room. If this suggestion had been put into practice, then those who wanted to sleep could have done so in peace in the darkness of one half of the room—it was a big room with forty beds—while the others could have played dice or cards in the lighted part and done everything else for which light was needed. If someone whose bed was in the lighted half of the room had wanted to sleep, he could have lain down in one of the unoccupied beds in the dark, for there were always enough beds unoccupied and nobody minded his bed being used temporarily by someone else. But there was never a night when the room was thus divided. Again and again there would be a couple of people who, when they had used the darkness to get some sleep, felt like playing cards in bed on a table placed between them, and of course they turned on a suitable electric lamp whose piercing light, when turned towards those who were sleeping, made them start up. You might toss and turn for a bit longer, but in the end you found nothing better to do than to turn on more light and begin another game with your neighbour who had likewise been wakened. And of course all were puffing at their pipes. There were, to be sure, some who wanted to sleep at all costs—Karl was usually among them—and who, instead of laying their heads on their pillows, covered it with their pillows or wrapped it in them, but how could you remain asleep when your nearest neighbour got up in the middle of the night to have some fun in the city before starting work, when he washed noisily, scattering water all round him, in the wash-stand at the head of his bed, when he not only pulled on his boots noisily but stamped his feet in order to get into them—almost everyone, despite the shape of American boots, had boots that were too tight—and then finally, as he was missing some small part of his outfit, lifted the pillow of the sleeper, who, long since awakened, to be sure, was simply waiting under it to lay into him. Besides, they were all sportsmen and for the most part young, strong lads who didn't want to miss any chance of sporting exercises. And you could be sure that if you jumped up, awakened from sleep by uproar during the night, you would find two wrestlers on the floor beside your bed and expert onlookers, in their shirts and underpants, standing on all the surrounding beds under a glaring light. Once, during such a nocturnal boxing-match, one of the combatants fell on top of the sleeping Karl, and the first thing Karl saw on opening his eyes was the blood which was running from the boy's nose and, before anything could be done about it, flowing over all the bedclothes. Often Karl spent almost the whole twelve hours trying to get a few hours' sleep, though he would have liked very much to take part in the others' conversations, but he always thought that the others' lives had given them an advantage over him, which he must compensate for by working harder and doing without some things. So although he very much wanted to sleep, mainly because of his work, he complained neither to the Head Cook nor to Therese about conditions in the dormitory, because for one thing all the boys suffered from it, generally speaking, without seriously complaining, and for another the irritations in the dormitory were a necessary part of his job as lift-boy, which, after all, he had gratefully accepted from the hands of the Head Cook.

Once a week, after finishing his shift, he had twenty-four hours off, which he used partly to pay one or two visits to the Head Cook and to exchange with Therese, whose scanty free time he awaited eagerly, a few hasty words somewhere in a corner, on a corridor, or, though rarely, in her room. Sometimes he would accompany her on her errands in the city, which all had to be done in a tremendous hurry. Then they would almost run, Karl with her shopping-bag in his hand, to the nearest subway station, the journey would pass in a flash, as though the train were swept along without resistance, they'd already jumped out, instead of waiting for the elevator, which took too long, they'd clatter up the stairs, the great squares from which the streets radiated would appear with the tumult of the traffic streaming in a straight line from all sides, but Karl and Therese would hurry, close together, into various offices, laundries, warehouses, and shops, in which orders or complaints that could not easily be made by telephone and anyway were not specially important had to be registered. Therese soon noticed that Karl's help was not to be despised, in fact in many ways it speeded things up a great deal. In his company she never had to wait, as she often had before, for the overworked shop assistants to listen to her. He would go up to the counter and rap on it with his knuckles till someone came, he would shout across human barriers in his still rather over-precise English, distinguishable amid a hundred voices, he would go up to people without hesitation even if they had retreated arrogantly into the depths of the longest rooms in the shop. He was not acting from high spirits and respected their resistance, but he felt he was in a secure position that gave him certain rights, the Hotel Occidental was a customer not to be taken lightly, and after all Therese, despite her commercial experience, still needed a lot of help. 'You ought to come with me every time,' she would sometimes say, smiling happily, when they returned from an expedition that had gone particularly well.

Only three times during the six weeks that Karl spent in Ramses did he spend more than a couple of hours in Therese's room. It was of course smaller than any of the Head Cook's rooms, the few things in it were really only arranged round the window, but Karl, after his experiences in the dormitory, knew the value of a relatively quiet room of one's own, and even if he did not say so in so many words, Therese still noticed how much he liked her room. She had no secrets from him and it would hardly have been possible, after her visit on that first evening, to have any secrets from him. She was an illegitimate child, her father was a foreman on a building site and had sent for mother and child from Pomerania, but as though he had thus done his duty or had expected someone different from the toil-worn woman and the weak child whom he met at the quay, soon after their arrival and without much by way of explanation he had emigrated to Canada, and those he left behind had received neither a letter nor any other news of him, which was not really to be wondered at, since they were lost without trace in the crowded slums of New York's East Side.

Once Therese recounted—Karl was standing beside her at the window and looking down into the street—the death of her mother. How her mother and she, one winter evening—she might have been five or so—were hurrying through the streets, each with her bundle, in search of a bed for the night. How her mother at first led her by the hand, it was a blizzard and hard to get along, until her hand became numb and without looking round she let go of Therese, who now had to make an effort to keep hold of her mother's skirts. Therese often stumbled and even fell, but her mother seemed to be obsessed and wouldn't stop. And the blizzards in those long, straight New York streets! Karl hadn't yet been through a winter in New York. If you're walking into the wind, and it moves in a circle, you can't open your eyes for a moment, the wind never stops dashing the snow into your face, you run but don't make any progress, it's desperate. A child is of course better off than an adult, it can run under the wind and even enjoy it a little. So Therese hadn't quite been able to understand her mother, and she was convinced that if she'd been a bit smarter—she was still such a little child—in her behaviour towards her mother that evening, the latter wouldn't have suffered such a miserable death. At that time her mother had been without work for two days, not even the smallest coin was left, the day had been spent in the open air without a bite to eat and in their bundles they were only lugging useless scraps of cloth which perhaps only superstition prevented them from throwing away. Now her mother had been promised work on a building site the next day, but she was afraid, as she spent the whole day trying to explain to Therese, that she wouldn't be able to make use of this lucky chance, for she was feeling dead tired, that morning she'd alarmed the passers-by by coughing up a lot of blood in the street, and her only yearning was to get somewhere warm and have a rest. And on that very evening it was impossible to find anywhere. In buildings where the porter didn't tell them to leave the gateway in which they could at least have sheltered from the weather, they hurried through the narrow, icy corridors, climbed to the highest floors, went all round the narrow terraces of the courtyards, knocked on doors at random, didn't dare speak to anyone, but then pleaded with whoever approached them, and once or twice her mother, out of breath, crouched down on a quiet staircase, hugged the almost reluctant

Therese close to her, and kissed her with a painful pressure on the lips. Knowing now that these were the last kisses, you can't understand how, even if you were just tiny, you could be so blind as not to realize that. In many of the rooms they passed the doors were open to let out the stifling air, and from the smoky fog which filled the rooms, as though caused by a fire, there would emerge the shape of someone standing in the doorway and telling them, either by his mute presence or by a curt word, that it was impossible for them to find accommodation in that room. Therese now thought in retrospect that it was only in the first few hours that her mother was seriously looking for a place to sleep, for after midnight or so she didn't speak to anyone else, although apart from a few pauses she didn't stop hurrying on till daybreak and although in these buildings, where neither the front door nor the doors of the apartments are ever shut, there's always activity and you meet people at every step. Of course it wasn't running, but only the utmost exertion of which they were capable, that got them along, and in reality they may have been crawling. And Therese couldn't tell whether between midnight and five in the morning they'd been in twenty buildings or in two or just in one. The corridors of these buildings are cunningly planned to make the best use of space but with no consideration for finding one's way, how often they must have come through the same corridors! Therese could dimly remember leaving the gateway of a building where they'd spent ages searching, but she also had the impression that once in the street they had promptly turned round and plunged back into the same building. For the child it was of course incomprehensible and painful to be dragged along, sometimes held by her mother, sometimes holding her tightly, without a single word of comfort, and in her ignorance she could only explain it all by thinking that her mother was trying to run away from her. Accordingly Therese, to be on the safe side, even when her mother was holding her by one hand, held onto her mother's skirts all the tighter with her other hand, weeping at intervals. She didn't want to be left behind here, among the people who were stamping up the stairs ahead of them, approaching, still out of sight behind a turning in the stairs behind them, quarrelling in front of a door in the corridors and pushing each other into the room. Drunks, singing tunelessly, were wandering about in the building, and her mother just managed to slip with Therese through a group of them as they crowded together. Late at night, when people were not paying much attention and nobody was insisting on his rights, they could certainly have squeezed into one of the general dormitories hired by sub-tenants, of which they passed several, but Therese didn't understand that and her mother no longer wanted to rest. In the morning, at the beginning of a fine winter day, they both leaned against the wall of a house and might have snatched a little sleep there, or perhaps just stared around with open eyes. It turned out that Therese had lost her bundle, and her mother was getting ready to hit her as punishment for her carelessness, but Therese didn't hear any blow and didn't feel any. Then they went on through the back streets which were gradually coming alive, her mother close to the wall, crossed a bridge where her mother swept the frost off the parapet with her hand, and finally arrived, Therese just accepted it, now she couldn't understand it, at the very building site where her mother was to work that morning. She didn't tell Therese either to wait or to go away, and Therese took this as an order to wait, as that was what she wanted. So she sat down on a pile of bricks and watched her mother untie her bundle, take out a brightly coloured scrap of cloth, and tie it round the headscarf which she had been wearing the whole night. Therese was too tired to think of helping her mother. Without reporting for duty in the shed, as was customary, and without asking anyone, her mother climbed a ladder as though she already knew which task had been assigned to her. Therese was surprised, as the female assistants were usually employed on the ground, slaking lime, handing up bricks, and in similar simple jobs. She therefore thought her mother wanted to do some better-paid work, and smiled sleepily up at her. The building was not yet high, the ground floor was scarcely complete, although the lofty scaffolding poles for the next stage of building, but without planks between them, were already projecting into the blue sky. At the top her mother skilfully avoided the masons who were putting one brick on top of another and, astonishingly, didn't ask her what she was doing, with her delicate hand she carefully held onto a wooden parti-tion that served as a banister, and the drowsy Therese down below was astonished at her skill and thought she'd received a kind look from her mother. But now her mother's walk took her to a small pile of bricks where the banister, and probably also the walkway, came to an end, but she did not stop, went straight up to the pile of bricks, her skill seemed to have deserted her, she knocked over the pile of bricks and fell over it to the ground. Many bricks rolled after her and finally, quite a while later, a heavy plank came loose somewhere and crashed down onto her. Therese's last memory of her mother was of how she lay there with her legs apart in the checked skirt that had come from Pomerania, how the rough plank lying on her almost covered her, how people came running from all sides, and how some man or other shouted down angrily from the top of the building.

It was late by the time Therese had finished her story. She had told it in great detail, which was not usual for her, and at unimportant points, like the description of the scaffolding poles that each projected separately into the sky, she had had to break off with tears in her eyes. Even after ten years she knew every detail of what had happened, and because the sight of her mother on top of the half-finished ground floor was her last memory of her mother's life and she could not entrust it to her friend clearly enough, she wanted to come back to it after finishing her story, but stopped, put her hands over her face, and said not another word.

But sometimes there was more fun in Therese's room. On his very first visit Karl had seen a textbook of commercial correspondence lying there and had asked to borrow it. At the same time it was agreed that Karl should do the exercises in the book and show them to Therese, who had already worked her way through as much of the book as was necessary for her small jobs. Now Karl would spend whole nights, cotton wool in his ears, lying on his bed in the dormitory, in all sorts of positions for the sake of variety, reading in the book and scribbling the exercises into an exercise book with a fountain pen that the Head Cook had given him as a reward for designing and neatly compiling a large inventory for her. He managed to get some benefit from most of the other boys' interruptions by asking them for advice about the English language, until they got tired of it and left him in peace. Often he was astonished at how the others were perfectly reconciled to their present situation, weren't conscious— lift-boys aged more than twenty weren't tolerated—of its temporary character, didn't realize that they needed to decide on their future careers, and, despite Karl's example, read nothing but detective stories, which, dirty and dog-eared, were passed from bed to bed.

When they met, Therese corrected the exercises with excessive fussiness, they ended up at loggerheads, Karl cited his great New York professor as a witness, but Therese respected him no more than she did the grammatical opinions of the lift-boys. She took the fountain pen from his hand and stroked out the passage that she was sure was wrong, but in such dubious cases, although no authority higher than Therese would set eyes on the book, Karl, being very precise, would strike out Therese's strokes again. Sometimes, to be sure, the Head Cook would come and would always decide in Therese's favour, but that proved nothing, for Therese was her secretary. At the same time, however, she brought general reconciliation, for tea would be made, cakes fetched, and Karl would have to talk about Europe, with many interruptions, to be sure, on the part of the Head Cook, who kept asking questions and expressing astonishment, thus making Karl conscious how much over there had changed entirely in a relatively short time and how much must have changed even since his departure and would keep on changing.

Karl might have been in Ramses for a month when one evening Renell told him in passing that he had been accosted outside the hotel and questioned about Karl by a man called Delamarche. Renell had had no reason to conceal anything and had told him truthfully that Karl was a lift-boy, but had prospects, thanks to the patronage of the Head Cook, of getting quite different jobs. Karl noticed how carefully Renell had been treated by Delamarche, who had even invited him to have dinner that evening. 'I have nothing more to do with Delamarche,' said Karl. 'You watch out for him too!' 'Me?' said Renell, stretching and hurrying off. He was the most elegant boy in the hotel, and among the other boys, though no one knew who had started it, there was a rumour that a grand lady, who had been staying in the hotel for a while, had, at least in the lift, covered him with kisses. For anyone who knew the rumour it was quite delightful to see this self-assured lady, nothing in whose outward appearance suggested the remotest possibility of such behaviour, passing by with her light, calm steps, her delicate veils, her tightly corseted waist. She lived on the first floor, and Renell's lift was not the one she used, but of course if the other lifts happened to be occupied one could not prevent such guests from entering another lift. So it was that this lady now and again used Karl's and Renell's lift, and, indeed, only when Renell was on duty. It might be chance, but nobody believed that, and when the lift went off with the two of them, there was such ill-suppressed restlessness among the whole team of lift-boys that a head waiter had already had to intervene. Whether the lady or the rumour were the cause, at any rate Renell had changed, had become much more self-assured, left the cleaning entirely to Karl, who was already waiting for the next opportunity to have it out with him, and was no longer to be seen at all in the dormitory. Nobody else had so completely abandoned the community of lift-boys, for in general, at least in questions of work, they all stuck close together and had an organization which was recognized by the hotel management.

Karl pondered all this, thought also about Delamarche, and otherwise did his duty as usual. Towards midnight he had a little diversion, for Therese, who often surprised him with little presents, brought him a big apple and a bar of chocolate. They chatted for a bit, scarcely disturbed by the interruptions caused by trips in the elevator. The conversation turned to Delamarche, and Karl noticed that he had actually been influenced by Therese in considering him, as he had for some time, a dangerous person, for that to be sure was how he seemed to Therese from Karl's stories. Karl however considered him basically a poor wretch who had been corrupted by misfortune and with whom one could get on all right. But Therese sharply contradicted this view and demanded volubly that Karl should promise never to speak another word to Delamarche. Instead of giving this promise, Karl repeatedly urged her to go to sleep, as it was already past midnight, and when she refused, he threatened to leave his post and take her to her room. When at last she was ready to go, he said: 'Why do you worry so unnecessarily, Therese? If it helps you sleep better, I'm willing to promise to speak to Delamarche only if it can't be avoided.' Then a large number of guests came along, for the boy at the next lift had been called away for some other task and Karl had to take care of both lifts. There were guests who spoke of disorder, and one gentleman, accompanying a lady, even prodded Karl gently with his walking-stick in order to make him hurry, an admonition that was quite uncalled-for. If only the guests who could see that there was no boy at one of the lifts had at once stepped over to Karl's lift, but they did not do that, instead they went to the next lift and stood there with their hands on the latch or even entered the lift themselves, which according to the strictest articles in the elevator regulations the lift-boys were supposed to prevent at all costs. So Karl had to run to and fro exhaustingly, without feeling that he was quite fulfilling his duty. Towards three in the morning, moreover, a porter, an old man with whom he was friendly, wanted some help from him, but Karl was quite unable to provide it, for there were guests standing in front of both his lifts and it took presence of mind to decide which group to serve and to go over to them with big strides. He was therefore happy when the other boy returned, and shouted over to him a few words of rebuke because of his long absence, although it was probably not his fault. After four in the morning things quietened down, and for Karl it was high time. He leaned heavily against the balustrade beside his elevator, slowly ate the apple, which gave off a strong scent after the very first bite, and looked down a lighted shaft surrounded by the big windows of the larders, behind which masses of hanging bananas could just be made out shimmering in the darkness.

6

The Robinson Affair

THEN someone tapped him on the shoulder. Karl, thinking of course that it was a guest, hurriedly put the apple in his pocket and hurried, scarcely looking at the man, over to the lift. But: 'Good evening, Mr Rossmann,' said the man, 'it's me, Robinson.' 'You've changed a lot,' said Karl, shaking his head. 'Yes, things are going well,' said Robinson, looking down at his clothes, which might consist of high-quality items but were so oddly assorted that they looked positively shabby. The most conspicuous item was a white waistcoat, obviously being worn for the first time, with four small, black-edged pockets to which Robinson tried to draw attention by puffing out his chest. 'You've got expensive clothes,' said Karl, thinking briefly of his own nice simple suit in which he could have held his own even alongside Renell and which his two false friends had sold. 'Yes,' said Robinson, 'I buy myself something nearly every day. How do you like my waistcoat?' 'Very much,' said Karl. 'These aren't real pockets, though, it's just made that way,' said Robinson, taking Karl's hand so that the latter could establish this for himself. But Karl drew back, for out of Robinson's mouth came an intolerable smell of brandy. 'You're drinking a lot again,' said Karl, standing at the balustrade again. 'No,' said Robinson, 'not a lot,' and added, contradicting his earlier expression of contentment: 'What else is there to do in the world.' A trip in the lift interrupted their conversation, and no sooner was Karl down again than there came a telephone call telling Karl to fetch the hotel doctor as a lady on the seventh floor* had had a fainting fit. On the way Karl secretly hoped that Robinson would in the meantime have left, for he did not want to be seen with him, nor, with Therese's warning in mind, to hear anything about Delamarche. But Robinson was still waiting in the stiff posture of somebody completely drunk, and just then a high-up hotel official in black frock-coat and top hat went past, fortunately, as it seemed, without paying Robinson any particular attention. 'Don't you want to come and see us, Rossmann, we're living in style,' said Robinson, giving Karl a tempting look. 'Are you inviting me or is Delamarche?' asked Karl. 'Me and Delamarche.

We're in agreement,' said Robinson. 'Then let me tell you, and I'll ask you to give Delamarche the same message: When we parted, in case that wasn't clear at the time, it was for good and all. The two of you did me more harm than anyone else. Have you decided not to leave me in peace, even now?' 'But we're your comrades,' said Robinson, his eyes brimming with disgusting drunken tears. 'Delamarche asked me to tell you that he'll make up for everything in the past. We're now living with Brunelda,* a wonderful singer.' And thereupon he was on the point of singing a song in a loud voice, if Karl hadn't hissed at him in the nick of time: 'Be quiet this minute, don't you know where you are.' 'Rossmann,' said Robinson, restrained only from singing, 'I'm still your comrade, say what you like. And now you've such a fine position here, couldn't you let me have some money.' 'You'll just drink it,' said Karl, 'I can even see some kind of brandy bottle in your pocket, and you must have drunk out of it while I was away, for at first you were more or less in your senses.' 'That's just to keep up my strength when I'm running an errand,' said Robinson apologetically. 'I don't want to reform you,' said Karl. 'But the money!' said Robinson, opening his eyes wide. 'I dare say Delamarche told you to fetch some money. All right, I'll give you money, but only on condition that you leave here at once and never come to see me here again. If you have anything to tell me, write to me. Karl Rossmann, lift-boy, Hotel Occidental, will suffice as an address. But here, I repeat, you mustn't come to see me again. Here I'm on duty and have no time for visitors. So do you want the money on that condition?' asked Karl, reaching into his waistcoat pocket, for he was resolved to sacrifice that night's tips. Robinson simply nodded in response to the question and breathed heavily. Karl misinterpreted this and asked again: 'Yes or no?'

Then Robinson beckoned him over and whispered, with gulping movements whose meaning was unmistakable, 'Rossmann, I'm feeling very ill.' 'Damnation,' Karl couldn't help saying, and he dragged him over to the balustrade with both hands.

And already Robinson's mouth was emptying itself into the depths below. In the pauses between his vomiting fits he pawed helplessly at Karl. 'You really are a good boy,' he'd say then, or 'it's stopping', which was far from the truth, or 'those bastards, what sort of stuff did they pour down my throat!' Karl felt such unease and disgust that he couldn't stand being with him and began to walk up and down.

Here in the corner beside the elevator Robinson was partly hidden, but what if anyone did notice him, one of those nervous rich guests who are only waiting to register a complaint with a subservient hotel official, for which the latter then takes a furious revenge against the whole establishment, or if one of those constantly changing hotel detectives came along, whom nobody knows except the hotel management and whom one suspects in every person who casts sharp glances, even if he is only short-sighted. And in the basement, since the restaurant stayed open all night, someone only had to go into the larders, observe with astonishment the filthy mess in the shaft, and ask Karl by telephone what in heaven's name was happening up above. Could Karl pretend not to know Robinson? And if he did, wouldn't the stupid and desperate Robinson, instead of apologizing, appeal precisely to Karl? And wouldn't Karl then be sacked on the spot, given the unheard-of fact that a lift-boy, the lowest and most dispensable employee in the immense hierarchy of staff in this hotel, had let his friend befoul the hotel and frighten the guests or even drive them away? Could a lift-boy be tolerated who had such friends and even received visits from them when he was on duty? Didn't it look as though such a lift-boy must himself be a drunkard or worse, for wasn't it the obvious conclusion that he overfed his friends from the hotel's supplies until they did what Robinson had just done at whatever place they liked in this same hotel that was kept so meticulously clean? And why should such a boy confine himself to stealing foodstuffs, when the well-known carelessness of the guests, the wardrobes left open everywhere, the valuables left lying on the tables, the open jewel-cases, the keys thrown down thoughtlessly, provided absolutely innumerable opportunities for stealing?

At that very moment Karl could see in the distance guests ascending from a basement bar where a vaudeville performance had just ended. Karl took his place beside his elevator, not daring to turn round to look at Robinson for fear of what he might see. He was scarcely reassured by hearing not a sound, not even a groan, from there. He attended to his guests and travelled up and down with them, but he could not completely conceal his distraction and every time he descended he was prepared to find an embarrassing surprise down below.

At last he again had time to look for Robinson, who was huddled in his corner in a little ball, with his face pressed against his knees.

He had pushed his round, hard hat well away from his forehead. 'Now off you go,' said Karl softly and firmly, 'here's the money. If you hurry, I can show you the quickest way.' 'I won't be able to go,' said Robinson, wiping his brow with a tiny handkerchief, 'I shall die here. You can't imagine how ill I feel. Delamarche takes me into all the high-class bars, but that dainty stuff doesn't agree with me, as I tell Delamarche daily.' 'You simply can't stay here,' said Karl, 'just think where you are. If anyone finds you here, you'll be punished and I'll lose my job. Is that what you want to happen?' 'I can't go,' said Robinson, 'I'd rather jump down there,' and he pointed between the railings into the shaft. 'When I sit here like this, I can just about bear it, but I can't stand up, I tried to when you were away.' 'Then I'll fetch an automobile and you can go to the hospital,' said Karl, shaking Robinson's legs a little, as he threatened to collapse any moment into complete unawareness of his surroundings. But no sooner had Robinson heard the word hospital, which seemed to awaken dreadful memories, than he began to weep loudly and stretched out his hands towards Karl, begging for mercy.

'Quiet,' said Karl, beating his hands down with a slap, and ran to the lift-boy whose place he'd taken that night, asked him for the same favour for a little while, hurried back to Robinson, who was still sobbing, pulled him upright with all his strength, and whispered to him: 'Robinson, if you want me to take care of you, then make the effort to walk just a little way. I'll take you to my bed, and you can stay there until you feel better. You'll be surprised how quickly you'll recover. But now behave sensibly, for there are lots of people in the corridors and my bed is in a general dormitory. If you attract anyone's attention, even a little, then I can do nothing more for you. And you must keep your eyes open, I can't lead you around as if you were at death's door.' 'I'll do whatever you think best,' said Robinson, 'but you can't lead me all by yourself. Couldn't you get Renell to help you?' 'Renell isn't here,' said Karl. 'Oh, yes,' said Robinson, 'Renell is with Delamarche. The two of them sent me to you. I'm getting everything mixed up.' Karl took advantage of this and other unintelligible monologues by Robinson to push him forwards, and managed to get him to a corner from which a more dimly lit corridor led to the lift-boys' dormitory. At that moment a lift-boy raced towards them and past them at full speed. For the rest, they only had harmless encounters; after all, between four and five was the quietest period, and Karl had been well aware that if he didn't manage to get rid of Robinson now, the early morning and the beginning of the day's business would put it out of the question.

In the dormitory, at the far end of the room, a big fight or some other performance was in full swing, one could heard rhythmic clapping, excited stamping, and sporting cries. In the half of the room near the door only a few determined sleepers could be seen in the beds, most people were lying on their backs and staring into space, while here and there somebody, dressed or undressed as the case might be, jumped out of bed in order to see how things were shaping up at the other end of the room. Thus Karl got Robinson, who by now had got a little used to walking, to Renell's bed without attracting much attention, as it was very near the door and fortunately unoccupied, while in his own bed, as he could see from the distance, another boy, whom he didn't know at all, was sleeping quietly. No sooner did Robinson feel the bed beneath him than he immediately—one leg was still dangling out of the bed—fell asleep. Karl pulled the blanket right over his face and thought that for the time being at least he had nothing to worry about, since Robinson certainly wouldn't wake up before six, and by then he'd be back here and might manage, together with Renell, to find a way of getting rid of Robinson. An inspection of the dormitory by some higher authority occurred only in extraordinary cases, the lift-boys had years ago secured the abolition of the general inspections that had once been customary, so from this side too there was nothing to fear.

When Karl had got back to his elevator, he saw that both his elevator and that of his neighbour were just ascending. He waited uneasily to see what the explanation would be. His elevator was the first to descend, and out of it stepped the boy who had run along the corridor a while ago. 'Hey, wherever have you been, Rossmann?' asked the latter. 'Why did you go away? Why didn't you report it?' 'But I asked him to take my place for a little,' answered Karl, pointing to the boy from the neighbouring lift, who was just arriving. 'After all, I took his place for two hours when things were busiest.' 'That's all very well,' said the boy he had spoken to, 'but it isn't enough. Don't you know that even the slightest absence from duty has to be reported in the Head Waiter's office? That's what you've got the telephone for. I wouldn't have minded taking your place, but you know that isn't so easy. There were new guests in front of both lifts, just off the four-thirty express.

I could hardly run to your lift first and keep my own guests waiting, so I went up first in my own lift.' 'Well?' asked Karl tensely, as both boys were silent. 'Well,' said the boy from the neighbouring lift, 'the Head Waiter happens to walk past, sees the people in front of your lift with nobody attending to them, flies into a fury, I run up and he asks me what's happened to you, I haven't the least idea, for you didn't tell me where you were going, and so he immediately telephones the dormitory to say that another boy is to come right away.' 'I even met you in the corridor,' said Karl's replacement. Karl nodded. 'Of course,' affirmed the other boy, 'I said right away that you'd asked me to take your place, but do you think he listens to such excuses? You probably don't know him yet. And we've got to inform you that you must go to the office straight away. So you'd better not hang about, but run there. Perhaps he'll forgive you, after all, you were only away for two minutes. You can certainly tell them that you asked me to take your place. I'd rather you didn't say that you took my place, take my advice, of course nothing can happen to me, I had permission, but it isn't good to talk about a thing like that and to mix it up with this affair, which it has nothing to do with.' 'It was the first time I left my post,' said Karl. 'That's always the way, but they don't believe it,' said the boy, running to his lift, as people were approaching. Karl's stand-in, a boy of about fourteen who was obviously sorry for Karl, said: 'There have been lots of cases in which people have been forgiven for a thing like that. Usually one is transferred to different work. I only know of one person who was sacked for a thing like that. You just have to think up a good excuse. Don't on any account say that you were suddenly taken ill, he'll laugh at you. You'd better say that a guest gave you some urgent message for another guest and you've forgotten who the first guest was and you couldn't find the second.' 'Oh, well,' said Karl, 'it won't be so bad,' from all that he had heard he no longer believed that things would turn out all right. And even if his neglect of duty were forgiven, Robinson was still lying in the dormitory as the living proof of his guilt, and given the Head Waiter's choleric temper, it was only too likely that they wouldn't be content with a superficial investigation but would end up unearthing Robinson. There was no explicit rule against bringing strangers into the dormitory, but that was only because unthinkable things are not forbidden.

When Karl entered the Head Waiter's office the latter was having his morning coffee, he would take a gulp and then look at a list which the hotel's Head Porter, who was likewise present, had evidently brought for his inspection. This was a big man whose splendidly ornamented uniform—golden chains and ribbons twined over its shoulders and down its arms—made him seem even more broad-shouldered than he was by nature. A gleaming black moustache, drawn into points as Hungarians wear them, never budged, however quickly he turned his head. For the rest, his burdensome clothes made it difficult for the man to move, and he only ever stood with his legs wide apart, in order to distribute his weight properly.

Karl had hurried in without knocking, as he had become used to doing here in the hotel, for the measured and careful behaviour which signifies politeness among private individuals is considered laziness with lift-boys. Besides, his guilt shouldn't be apparent as soon as he entered. The Head Waiter had indeed glanced up briefly as the door opened, but had then returned immediately to his coffee and his reading, without bothering any further about Karl. The Porter, however, might have felt incommoded by Karl's presence, or perhaps he had some confidential news or request to convey, at any rate he looked over at Karl every minute, nastily and with stiffly bowed head, and then, when, as he obviously intended, he had met Karl's gaze, turned back to the Head Waiter. Karl thought it would not look good if, now that he was here, he left the office again without the Head Waiter having ordered him to do so. The latter, however, went on studying the list, taking occasional bites from a piece of cake from which, without pausing in his reading, he now and then shook the sugar. Once a page of the list fell to the ground, the Porter did not even attempt to pick it up, knowing that he wouldn't be able to, nor was it necessary, for Karl was already on the spot and handed the page to the Head Waiter, who took it from him with a gesture as though it had flown up from the floor by itself. This little service had not helped, for the Porter still did not stop giving him nasty looks.

All the same, Karl was more composed than he had been. Even the fact that his business seemed to matter so little to the Head Waiter could be considered a good sign. After all, it was perfectly understandable. Of course a lift-boy counts for nothing and may therefore not take any liberties, but precisely because he counts for nothing he cannot get up to anything extraordinary. Anyway, the Head Waiter himself had been a lift-boy in his youth—which was the pride even of this generation of lift-boys—it was he who had first organized the lift-boys and he must surely once have left his post without permission, even if nobody could now force him to remember it and if it could not be ignored that, precisely because he had been a lift-boy, he saw it as his duty to keep this profession in order by sometimes inflexible severity. But Karl was also placing his hopes in the steadily advancing time. According to the office clock it was already after a quarter past six, Renell could return at any moment, he might even be there already, for he must have noticed that Robinson hadn't come back, and anyway, it now struck Karl, Delamarche and Renell couldn't have been far from the Hotel Occidental, for otherwise Robinson in his wretched condition couldn't have found the way here. If Renell now found Robinson in his bed, which must happen, everything would be all right. For, practical as Renell was, especially where his own interests were concerned, he would find some way of immediately getting Robinson out of the hotel, since Robinson had gained some strength in the meantime and anyway Delamarche was probably waiting outside the hotel to collect him. But once Robinson was out of the way, Karl could face the Head Waiter much more calmly and perhaps get off this time with a reprimand, albeit a harsh one. Then he would consult Therese about whether he could tell the truth to the Head Cook—he for his part saw no obstacle—and if that was possible, the matter would be disposed of without doing any particular damage.

Karl had just calmed himself a little by such reflections and was beginning inconspicuously to count the tips he had received that night, for he felt it had been a specially good haul, when the Head Waiter, with the words 'Please wait a moment, Feodor', put the list on the table, leapt elastically to his feet, and yelled at Karl so loudly that at first the latter could only stare in terror into his great black open mouth.

'You left your post without permission. Do you know what that means? It means the sack. I won't listen to any apologies. You can keep your made-up excuses to yourself, the fact that you weren't there is quite enough for me. If I put up with that and overlook it once, the next thing you know all forty lift-boys will run away while on duty and I can carry my five thousand guests upstairs by myself.'

Karl was silent. The Porter had come closer and was pulling down Karl's jacket, which was slightly crumpled, no doubt to draw the Head Waiter's attention to this slight untidiness in Karl's outfit.

'Were you suddenly taken ill?' asked the Head Waiter cunningly.

Karl scrutinized him and answered: 'No.' 'So you weren't even taken ill!' yelled the Head Waiter all the louder. 'So then you must have made up some first-class lie. Let's have it. What sort of excuse have you got?' 'I didn't know that one had to telephone for permission,' said Karl. 'That's rich, to be sure,' said the Head Waiter, seizing Karl by his jacket collar and placing him, his feet barely touching the ground, in front of a copy of the elevator regulations which was nailed to the wall. 'There! Read it!' said the Head Waiter, pointing to one article. Karl thought he was meant to read it silently. 'Out loud!' commanded the Head Waiter. Instead of reading out loud, Karl said, hoping to appease the Head Waiter better that way: 'I know that article, I got a copy of the regulations and read it carefully. But that sort of rule that you never actually need is the sort you forget. I've been working for two months* and have never left my post.' 'You'll leave it now, all right,' said the Head Waiter, went over to the table, picked up the list as though to continue reading it but knocked it against the table as though it were a worthless rag, and walked, forehead and cheeks bright red, hither and thither in the room. 'I don't need this from such a brat. Such disruption on the night shift!' he spat out several times. 'Do you know who wanted to ascend just as this fellow ran away from the lift?' he turned to the Porter. And he mentioned a name at which the Porter, who undoubtedly knew all the guests and could judge their importance, gave such a shudder that he looked quickly at Karl as though his mere existence were a proof that the bearer of that name had had to wait futilely for a while beside a lift whose boy had run away. 'That's terrible!' said the Porter, slowly and in boundless disquiet shaking his head at Karl, who looked sadly at him, thinking that he would also have to pay for this man's slow-wittedness. 'Anyway, I know you already,' said the Porter, stretching out his big, fat, stiff index finger. 'You're the only boy who makes a point of not bidding me good day. Who do you think you are! Everyone who passes the porters' lodge has to bid me good day. With the other porters you can behave as you please, but I demand that people bid me good day. I may sometimes pretend not to notice, but don't you worry, I know very well who bids me good day and who doesn't, you lout.' And he turned away from Karl and strode, bolt upright, over to the Head Waiter, who, however, instead of commenting on the Porter's business, finished his breakfast and skimmed through a morning paper which a servant had just handed into the room.

'Sir,' said Karl, wanting, while the Head Waiter was otherwise engaged, at least to settle the matter with the Porter, and realizing that while a scolding from the Porter might not harm him, his enmity certainly would, 'I'm sure I do bid you good day. After all, I haven't been long in America and I come from Europe, where everyone knows people say good day much more often than they need to. Of course I haven't yet been able to lose the habit, and only two months ago, in New York, where I happened to move in better social circles, people urged me at every opportunity to give up my excessive politeness. And how could I not say good day to you of all people. I've said good day to you several times every day. But of course not every time I saw you, for I pass you hundreds of times a day.' 'You're to bid me good day every time, every time without exception. You're to hold your cap in your hand the whole time you're speaking to me. You're always to call me "Sir", not just "you". And all that every single time.' 'Every time?' repeated Karl in a low, questioning tone, he now remembered how throughout his stay here the Porter had always given him severe and reproachful looks, even on that first morning when, not yet quite adjusted to his subordinate position, he had been rather too bold in questioning this Porter urgently and minutely about whether two men might have been asking for him and have left a photograph for him. 'Now you see what such behaviour leads to,' said the Porter, again coming very close to Karl and pointing to the Head Waiter, who was still reading, as though the latter were the agent of his revenge. 'In your next job you'll know how to bid the porter good day, even if it's only in a wretched low dive.'

Karl realized that he had in effect already lost his job, for the Head Waiter had already said so, the Head Porter had repeated it as an established fact, and it was hardly necessary for the dismissal of a lift-boy to be confirmed by the hotel management. To be sure, it had happened quicker than he expected, for after all he'd been working here for two months and undoubtedly better than many other boys. But evidently no account is taken of such things in the decisive moment, not in any continent, neither in Europe nor in America, but the decision is taken just as one utters a judgement in one's initial fit of rage. Perhaps it would have been best if he had taken his leave and gone away at once, the Head Cook and Therese might still be asleep, he could have spared them disappointment and sorrow at his behaviour, at least on bidding them a personal farewell, by saying farewell in a letter, could have packed his suitcase quickly and gone away quietly. But if he stayed even one more day—and to be sure, he could have done with some sleep—there was nothing in store for him but to have his affair blown up into a scandal, reproaches from all sides, the unbearable sight of Therese's tears and perhaps even the Head Cook's, and possibly, on top of everything else, a punishment as well. On the other hand, however, he was confused by facing two enemies, knowing that every word he uttered would be criticized, if not by one then by the other, and interpreted in the most unfavourable way. Therefore he was silent and enjoyed for the time being the peace that reigned in the room, for the Head Waiter was still reading the paper and the Head Porter was arranging the pages of his list, which were scattered over the table, by their numbers, which because of his evident short-sightedness he found very difficult.

At last the Head Waiter laid down his paper with a yawn, assured himself by glancing at Karl that the latter was still present, and turned on the bell of the telephone on the table. He called 'Hallo' several times, but nobody answered. 'Nobody's answering,' he said to the Head Porter. The latter, who seemed to Karl to be watching the tele-phoning with particular interest, said: 'It's already a quarter to seven. She must be awake by now. Just ring more loudly.' At the moment the telephone rang without further dialling. 'Head Waiter Isbary* here,' said the Head Waiter. 'Good morning, Cook. I hope I haven't woken you. Oh, I'm very sorry. Yes, yes, it's already a quarter to seven. But I'm truly sorry I gave you a fright. You should turn off the telephone when you go to sleep. No, no, I assure you, there's no excuse, espe-cially as the matter I want to speak to you about is so trivial. But of course I've got time, I beg your pardon, I'll stay by the telephone if you don't mind.' 'She must have run to the telephone in her night-dress,' said the Head Waiter, smiling, to the Head Porter, who had the whole time been bending down towards the telephone with an expect-ant expression. 'Yes, I did wake her, you see she's usually woken by the little girl who does her typing, and who must have failed to do so today for once. I'm sorry I gave her a fright, she's nervous enough anyway.' 'Why isn't she continuing the conversation?' 'She's gone to see what's up with the girl,' answered the Head Waiter with the receiver already at his ear, for it was ringing again. 'She'll turn up all right,' he continued speaking into the telephone. 'You mustn't be so frightened at everything, you really need a thorough break. Yes, my little inquiry. There's a lift-boy called'—he turned round questioningly to Karl, who, as he was paying close attention, promptly supplied his name—'called Karl Rossmann, if I recall correctly, you took some interest in him; I'm afraid he's made a poor return for your kindness, he left his post without permission, thus causing me grave difficulties which may get much worse, so I've just sacked him. I hope you won't be too upset. What did you say? Sacked, yes, sacked. But I just told you he left his post. No, I really can't give way to you, my dear Cook. It's a matter of my authority, there's a lot at stake, a boy like that will spoil the lot of them. The lift-boys are the very ones I need to keep an eagle eye on. No, no, in this case I can't do you a favour, however anxious I always am to oblige you. And even if I let him stay here, despite everything, for no other reason than to keep myself in a rage, for your sake, yes, for your sake, ma'am, he can't stay here. You feel a concern for him that he doesn't deserve in the least, and as I know not only him, but also you, I know that would lead to bitter disappointments for you, which I want to spare you at all costs. I'm telling you that quite frankly, although the obdurate boy is standing only two steps from me. He's getting the sack, no, no, ma'am, he's getting sacked for good, no, no, he won't be transferred to a different job, he's completely useless. Anyway, there are other complaints being made against him. The Head Porter for example, yes, what was it, Feodor, yes, he complains about this boy's rudeness and impertinence. What, isn't that enough? Really, my dear ma'am, you're betraying your character for the sake of this boy. No, you mustn't speak to me like that.'

At that moment the Porter bent down to the Head Waiter's ear and whispered something. The Head Waiter first looked at him in astonishment and then talked into the telephone so quickly that Karl at first couldn't quite understand him and took two steps closer on tiptoe.

'My dear ma'am,' he went on, 'quite frankly, I wouldn't have thought you were such a bad judge of character. I've just learnt something about your angelic boy which will completely change your opinion of him, and I'm almost sorry to be the one to tell you. This well-bred boy, who you say is a model of good behaviour, never lets a free night pass without running into the city, and doesn't come back till the morning. Yes, yes, ma'am, there are witnesses to prove it, unimpeachable witnesses, yes. Now can you tell me where he gets the money for these dissipations? How he is supposed to have any attention left for his work? And do you want me to describe what he gets up to in the city? I intend to get rid of this boy as quickly as possible. And please take this as a warning about how careful one has to be with vagrant boys.'

'But sir,' Karl now exclaimed, positively relieved by the gross error that seemed to have intruded and that might lead to an unexpected change for the better, 'there must be some mix-up. I think the Head Porter told you that I go out every night. But that's not true at all, I spend every night in the dormitory, all the boys can confirm that. When I'm not sleeping I study commercial correspondence, but I never leave the dormitory on any night. That's easy to prove. The Head Porter is obviously mixing me up with someone else, and now I understand why he thinks I don't bid him good day.'

'Be quiet this instant,' yelled the Head Porter, shaking his fist where anyone else would have pointed a finger, 'how can you say I mix you up with someone else. I couldn't be Head Porter if I got people mixed up. Listen, Mr Isbary, I couldn't be Head Porter, could I, if I got people mixed up. In my thirty years of work I have never mixed anyone up, as the hundreds of Head Waiters we've had during that time must confirm, but with you, you wretched boy, I'm supposed to have started mixing people up. You, with your unnaturally smooth mug. How can that be mixed up? You could have run into the city every night behind my back and I can still confirm, just by looking at your face, that you're a hardened rascal.'

'Calm down, Feodor!' said the Head Waiter, whose telephone conversation with the Head Cook seemed suddenly to have been broken off. 'The matter is quite simple. His night-time amusements aren't really the point. Before he leaves, he might want to instigate some big investigation of his night-time activities. I dare say he'd like that. All forty lift-boys would have to be summoned and interrogated as witnesses, of course they'd all have mixed him up with someone else, so eventually the entire staff would have to give evidence, the hotel would of course have to be closed down for a while, and in the end, when he got thrown out all the same, he'd at least have had some fun. So let's not do that. He's already made a fool of the Head Cook, that good woman, and it's got to stop at that. I won't listen to anything more, you're dismissed on the spot for neglecting your duty. Here's a note for the cashier so that you can be paid your wages up to today. What's more, considering how you've behaved, that, between ourselves, is simply a present, and I'm only giving it to you to please the Head Cook.'

A telephone call prevented the Head Waiter from signing the note right away. 'The lift-boys are giving me a hard time today!' he exclaimed as soon as he had heard the first few words. 'That's incredible!' he exclaimed after a little while. And turning away from the telephone towards the Head Porter, he said: 'Hold on to this lad for a bit, please, Feodor, we'll have more to say to him.' And into the telephone he issued the order: 'Come up at once!'

Now the Head Porter could give free rein to his fury, which he hadn't been able to do in speaking. He held Karl firmly by his upper arm, but not with a steady grip, which after all would have been bearable, instead he slackened his grip now and again and then made it by stages firmer and firmer, which, given his great physical strength, seemed a never-ending process and made everything go dark in front of Karl's eyes. However, he didn't just hold Karl, but, as though he had also been ordered simultaneously to stretch him out, he also pulled him upright now and again and shook him, repeatedly saying to the Head Waiter in a somewhat questioning tone: 'I'm not mixing him up now, I'm not mixing him up now.'

It was a deliverance for Karl when the chief lift-boy, a certain Bess, a fat boy who was always puffing, entered and attracted some of the Head Porter's attention. Karl was so worn out that he could hardly utter a greeting when, to his astonishment, he saw Therese, as pale as a corpse, untidily dressed, with her hair loosely pinned up, slipping in after the boy. In a moment she was beside him, whispering: 'Does the Head Cook know?' 'The Head Waiter telephoned to tell her,' answered Karl. 'Then it's all right, then it's all right,' she said quickly with her eyes lighting up. 'No,' said Karl, 'you don't know what they've got against me. I have to go, the Head Cook is convinced of that as well by now. Please don't stay here, go upstairs, I'll be able to say goodbye to you later.' 'But Rossmann, what are you thinking of. You'll stay with us as long as you like. The Head Waiter does whatever the Head Cook wants, he loves her, I recently found that out by accident. Just be calm.' 'Please, Therese, go away. I can't defend myself so well if you're here. And I've got to defend myself with great care, because lies are being produced against me. But the better I can pay attention and defend myself, the more hope there is that I can stay. So, Therese—' Unfortunately, in a sudden burst of pain, he couldn't refrain from adding softly: 'If only this Head Porter would let me go! I'd no idea he was my enemy. But how he keeps squeezing and pulling me.'

'Why on earth am I saying that!' he thought simultaneously, 'no woman can hear that unmoved,' and indeed Therese turned, without his being able to restrain her with his free hand, to the Head Porter. 'Sir, please let Rossmann go at once. You're hurting him. The Head Cook will be here in person any minute and then we'll see that he's being treated unfairly in every way. Let him go, what sort of pleasure can it give you to torment him?' And she even reached for the Head Porter's hand. 'Orders, little miss, orders,' said the Head Porter, pulling Therese kindly towards him with his free hand, while with the other he squeezed Karl very hard, as though, having got hold of this arm, he wanted to do something special with it but was still far from achieving his purpose.

It took Therese some time to extract herself from the Head Porter's embrace, and she was about to start pleading Karl's cause with the Head Waiter, who was still listening to the very circumstantial story told by Bess, when the Head Cook entered with rapid steps. 'Thank goodness,' exclaimed Therese, and for a moment nothing was audible in the room except these loud words. The Head Waiter promptly jumped up and pushed Bess aside: 'You've come yourself, Cook? Just for a trifle like this? After our telephone conversation I suspected you might, but I couldn't quite believe it. And meanwhile things are getting worse and worse for your protégé. I'm afraid I'll have not just to sack him but to have him locked up. Listen for yourself!' And he beckoned to Bess. 'I'd like first to have a few words with Rossmann,' said the Head Cook, sitting down on a chair which the Head Waiter pressed on her. 'Karl, come closer, please,' she said. Karl followed or rather was dragged closer by the Head Porter. 'Do let him go,' said the Head Cook crossly, 'he isn't a murderer.' The Head Porter did let him go, but first squeezed him so hard that the effort brought tears into his own eyes.

'Karl,' said the Head Cook, placing her hands calmly in her lap and looking at Karl with bowed head—it wasn't at all like an interrogation— 'I want first of all to tell you that I still have complete confidence in you. And the Head Waiter is a just man, I guarantee. We both want basically to keep you here.'—Here she glanced across at the Head Waiter as though begging him not to interrupt. Nor did he—'So forget what people may have told you up till now. Especially what the Head Porter may have said, you mustn't take it too hard. He's a bit excited, which is no wonder considering the work he does, but he's got a wife and children and knows that a boy who's on his own mustn't be unnecessarily harassed, the rest of the world will soon see to that.'

The room was completely silent. The Head Porter was looking at the Head Waiter, demanding an explanation, the latter was looking at the Head Cook and shaking his head. The lift-boy Bess was grinning senselessly behind the Head Waiter's back. Therese was sobbing to herself with joy and sorrow, and having great difficulty in preventing anyone else from hearing her.

Karl, however, was looking, although this could only be interpreted as a bad sign, not at the Head Cook, who surely wanted him to look her in the eye, but at the floor in front of him. Pain was shooting through his arm in every direction, his shirt was sticking to his bruise, and he should really have taken off his jacket and inspected the matter. What the Head Cook had said was of course kindly meant, but unfortunately he felt that it was the Head Cook's conduct that would reveal that he didn't deserve any kindness, that he had enjoyed her favour for two months without deserving it, indeed that he deserved nothing better than to be handed over to the Head Porter.

'I'm saying this,' went on the Head Cook, 'so that you can answer frankly, which you would probably have done anyway, if I know you as I think I do.'

'Please may I fetch the doctor, you see the man might bleed to death,' the lift-boy Bess suddenly put in, very politely but very inopportunely.

'Go,' said the Head Waiter to Bess, who promptly ran off. 'It's like this. The Head Porter wasn't holding onto the boy for fun. You see, down in the lift-boys' dormitory, carefully covered up in a bed, a complete stranger, drunk out of his mind, has been discovered. Of course people woke him and tried to get rid of him. Then the man started to kick up a row and kept shouting that the dormitory belonged to Karl Rossmann, whose guest he was, who had brought him there and who would punish anyone who dared touch him. Besides, he also had to wait for Karl Rossmann because the latter had promised him money and had just gone to fetch it. Please note that, Cook: had promised him money and gone to fetch it. You pay attention too, Rossmann,' said the Head Waiter casually to Karl, who had just turned round to Therese, who was staring fixedly at the Head Waiter and constantly either trying to push some hair from her forehead or making this gesture for its own sake. 'But perhaps I can remind you of certain obligations. The man down below also went on to say that after your return the two of you would pay a nocturnal visit to some singer, though nobody, to be sure, could make out her name, as the man could only utter it while singing.'

Here the Head Waiter paused, for the Head Cook, visibly pale, rose from the chair, pushing it back a little. 'I'll spare you the rest,' said the Head Waiter. 'No, please, no,' said the Head Cook, seizing his hand, 'go on, I want to hear everything, that's why I'm here.' The Head Porter, who stepped forward and as a sign that he had seen through everything from the outset, slapped himself on the chest, was told by the Head Waiter: 'Yes, you were quite right, Feodor', which simultaneously appeased and restrained him.

'There's not much more to tell,' said the Head Waiter. 'You know what boys are like, they first laughed at the man, then quarrelled with him, and as there are always good boxers to hand, he was simply knocked to the floor, and I haven't dared to ask where and at how many places he's bleeding, for those boys are terrible boxers and of course a drunk gives them an easy job.'

'All right,' said the Head Cook, holding the arm of the chair and looking at the spot she had just left. 'Well, do say something, Rossmann!' she then said. Therese had run from the place where she had previously been standing across to the Head Cook and—something Karl had never before seen her do—taken the Head Cook's arm. The Head Waiter was standing just behind the Head Cook, slowly smoothing a modest little lace collar of the Head Cook's, which had got a little crumpled. The Head Porter, beside Karl, said: 'Well then?' but only to disguise a blow with which he struck Karl in the back.

'It's true', said Karl, made more hesitant by the blow than he would have liked, 'that I brought the man into the dormitory.'

'We don't need to know any more,' said the Porter on behalf of everyone else. The Head Cook turned mutely to the Head Waiter and then to Therese.

'I couldn't do anything else,' went on Karl. 'The man is my comrade from earlier, he came here, after we hadn't seen each other for two months, to pay me a visit, but he was so drunk that he couldn't go away on his own.'

The Head Waiter, standing beside the Head Cook, said to himself in an undertone: 'So he came on a visit and afterwards he was so drunk that he couldn't go away.' The Head Cook whispered something over his shoulder to the Head Waiter, who seemed to be objecting, though with a smile that was evidently unconnected with this matter. Therese—Karl was looking only at her—was pressing her face, entirely helpless, against the Head Cook and didn't want to see anything more. The only person who was completely satisfied with Karl's explanation was the Head Porter, who repeated several times: 'Quite right, one must help one's boozing companion', and tried to impress this explanation by looks and gestures on all those present.

'So I am to blame,' said Karl, pausing as though waiting for a kind word from his judges that would encourage him to go on defending himself, but it did not come, 'I am to blame only for bringing this man, he's called Robinson, he's an Irishman, into the dormitory. Everything else he said was just the drink talking and it isn't true.'

'So you didn't promise him any money?' asked the Head Waiter.

'Yes,' said Karl, sorry that he had forgotten about that, he had, whether rashly or absent-mindedly, described himself as guiltless in too definite terms, 'I promised him money because he asked me for some. I wasn't going to fetch it, though, but to give him the tips that I earned last night.' And by way of proof he pulled the money out of his pocket and displayed a few small coins on the palm of his hand.

'You're painting yourself into a corner,' said the Head Waiter. 'If anyone is to believe you, they have to keep forgetting what you just said. First of all you brought the man—I don't even believe his name is Robinson, no Irishman in Ireland's whole existence has ever been called that—so first you brought him into the dormitory, for which alone, by the way, you could be thrown out on your ear—but at first you didn't promise him any money, then, when you're taken off guard, it turns out you did promise him money. But this isn't a game of Twenty Questions, we want to hear what you can say to justify yourself. At first, though, you didn't want to fetch the money, but to give him today's tips, but then it turns out that you still have this money on you, so you obviously wanted to fetch some different money, and the fact that you were away so long proves it. After all, it wouldn't really matter if you had wanted to fetch him money from your suitcase, but the fact that you're denying it as hard as you can really does matter. Just as you keep concealing the fact that you got the man drunk here in the hotel, of which there isn't the slightest doubt, for you yourself admitted that he got here on his own but couldn't go away on his own and he himself yelled to everyone in the dormitory that he was your guest. So there are only two things left to be cleared up, which, if you want to simplify matters, you can explain yourself, but which we'll be able to establish anyway without your help. First, how did you get access to the larders, and second, how did you collect money to give away?'

'It's impossible to defend oneself when people aren't well disposed,' said Karl to himself, giving the Head Waiter no further answer, however painful this probably was to Therese. He knew that whatever he could say would be made to look quite different from the way he meant it, and that a good or bad outcome depended solely on his judges' attitude.

'He isn't answering,' said the Head Cook.

'That's the most sensible thing he can do,' said the Head Waiter.

'He'll soon think up something,' said the Head Porter, carefully stroking his beard with the hand that had previously exercised such cruelty.

'Be quiet,' said the Head Cook to Therese, who was beginning to sob at her side, 'you see he isn't answering, so how can I do anything for him? After all, I'm the one who is placed in the wrong before the Head Waiter. Just tell me, Therese, do you think there's anything I neglected to do for him?' How could Therese know that or what use was it for the Head Cook to weaken her position in relation to the two gentlemen by publicly addressing the little girl with this question and request?

'Ma'am,' said Karl, pulling himself together once more, but only to spare Therese the answer, for no other reason, 'I don't believe I have disgraced you in any way, and that must be the conclusion anyone else would reach after a thorough investigation.'

'Anyone else,' said the Head Porter, pointing his finger at the Head Waiter, 'that's a dig at you, Mr Isbary.'

'Now, ma'am,' said the latter, 'it's half past six, and time is getting short. I think you'd better let me have the last word in this matter, which has been treated only too patiently.'

Little Giacomo had come in, wanting to go over to Karl, but, frightened by the general silence, he refrained and waited.

The Head Cook, since Karl's last words, had not turned her gaze from him, and there was nothing to indicate that she had heard the Head Waiter's remark, her eyes were fixed on Karl, they were big and blue but slightly faded by her age and her many labours. The way she stood there, feebly rocking the chair in front of her, you could well have expected her to say at the next moment: 'Well, Karl, now I think about it, the matter hasn't yet been clarified and needs, as you rightly say, a thorough investigation. And let's start that now, never mind whether others agree or not, for justice must be done.'

Instead, however, the Head Cook said after a short pause that no one dared to interrupt—only the clock, confirming what the Head Waiter had said, struck half past six and at the same time, as everyone knew, so did all the clocks in the whole hotel, to the ear and the imagination it sounded like the double throbbing of a single huge impatience: 'No, Karl, no, no! Let's not try to believe that. Honest things have a particular appearance and I must admit that your affair doesn't. I can say that and what's more I must say it, for I'm the one who came here predisposed in your favour. You see, Therese is silent too.' (But she wasn't silent, she was crying.)

The Head Cook stopped, overtaken by a sudden decision, and said: 'Karl, come here,' and when he had come to her—the Head Waiter and the Head Porter promptly joined in a lively conversation behind his back—she clasped him with her left hand, went with him and Therese, who followed automatically, to the back of the room, and walked up and down a few times with the two of them, saying: 'It's possible, Karl, and you seem confident of it, otherwise I couldn't understand you at all, that an investigation would prove you right in a few details. Why not? Perhaps you did bid the Head Porter good day. In fact I'm sure of it, I know what to think of the Head Porter. You see, even now I'm talking frankly to you. But being justified in such small things wouldn't help you at all. The Head Waiter, whose judgement of people I've learnt to value over many years and who is the most reliable person of any I know, has stated the matter clearly and to be sure it seems to me irrefutable. Perhaps you just acted thoughtlessly, but perhaps you aren't the person I took you for. And yet,' she said, interrupting herself as it were and casting only a quick glance back at the two gentlemen, 'I still can't stop myself from thinking that at bottom you're a decent boy.'

'Ma'am, ma'am,' admonished the Head Waiter, who had caught her eye.

'We're nearly done,' said the Head Cook, addressing Karl more rapidly: 'Listen, Karl, as I view the matter, I'm at least glad the Head Waiter isn't going to start an investigation, for if he did, I'd have to prevent it in your own interests. Nobody's going to find out how you entertained the man and with what, and anyway he can't be one of your former comrades, as you pretend, because when you left them you had a big quarrel, so you aren't going to stand one of them drinks now. So it can only be an acquaintance with whom you struck up a friendship in some city bar at night. How could you, Karl, keep all these things from me? If you couldn't stand the dormitory and began going out on the town at night for this innocent reason, why didn't you say a word to me, you know I wanted to get you a room of your own and only gave up because you asked me to. Now it seems you preferred the general dormitory because you felt under less restraint. And you kept your money in my safe and brought me your tips every week, so for heaven's sake, boy, where did you get the money for your amusements and where were you going to get the money for your friend? Of course these are all things that I mustn't even hint to the Head Waiter, for then an investigation might be unavoidable. So you've got to leave the hotel, and as quickly as possible. Go straight to Brenner's Hotel—you've already been there several times with Therese—they'll give you a room for free at my recommendation'— and the Head Cook wrote some lines on a visiting-card with a golden pencil she took out of her blouse, but without pausing in her speech— 'I'll send your suitcase after you straight away, Therese, run to the lift-boys' cloakroom and pack his suitcase' (but Therese did not move, wanting, as she had endured all the suffering, also to share in the turn for the better that Karl's affair was taking thanks to the Head Cook's kindness).

Somebody opened the door a little without showing himself and promptly closed it again. It must have been intended for Giacomo, for the latter stepped forward and said: 'Rossmann, I've got a message for you.' 'Just a moment,' said the Head Cook, putting the visiting-card into Karl's pocket as he listened to her with head bowed, 'I'll keep your money for the time being, you know you can trust me with it. Stay indoors today and think over your situation, tomorrow— I haven't time today, and anyway I've stayed here much too long—I'll go to Brenner's and we'll see what else we can do for you. I won't abandon you, I want you to know that for certain today. You mustn't worry about your future, but rather about the time that's just passed.' Thereupon she patted him on the shoulder and went over to the Head Waiter, Karl raised his head and followed with his eyes the big, stately woman as she moved away from him with quiet steps and a relaxed attitude.

'Aren't you glad', said Therese, who had stayed behind with him, 'that everything has turned out so well?' 'Oh yes,' said Karl, smiling at her without knowing why he should be glad to be dismissed as a thief. Therese's eyes were beaming with joy, as though she didn't care whether Karl had done something wrong or not, whether he had been judged fairly or not, so long as he was allowed to escape, in disgrace or with honour. And Therese was behaving like that, she of all people, who was so meticulous in her own affairs and could spend weeks worrying obsessively about an ambiguous word from the Head Cook. He asked pointedly: 'Will you pack my suitcase and send it off right away?' Despite himself he could not help shaking his head with astonishment at the speed with which Therese reacted to the question, and, convinced that there were things in the suitcase that must be kept secret from everybody, she didn't even look at Karl or give him her hand, but only whispered: 'Of course, Karl, right away, I'll pack the suitcase right away.' And she was already gone.

But now Giacomo couldn't hold back any longer and shouted, excited by his long wait: 'Rossmann, the man's rolling about down in the corridor and won't let anyone remove him. They wanted to send him to hospital, but he won't let them and keeps saying you'd never put up with him being taken to hospital. He wants them to fetch an automobile and send him home, and says you'll pay for the automobile. Will you?'

'The man trusts you,' said the Head Waiter. Karl shrugged his shoulders and paid his money into Giacomo's hand: 'That's all I've got,' he said.

'And I'm to ask you whether you'll come too,' asked Giacomo, jingling the money.

'He won't come,' said the Head Cook.

'Well, Rossmann,' said the Head Waiter quickly, not waiting till Giacomo had left, 'you're dismissed on the spot.'

The Head Porter nodded several times as though these were his own words which the Head Waiter was merely repeating.

'I can't say out loud the reasons why you're being dismissed, because otherwise I'd have to have you locked up.'

The Head Porter looked across at the Head Cook with notable severity, for he must have realized that she was the cause of this unduly lenient treatment.

'Now go to Bess, change your clothes, give Bess your uniform, and leave the building at once, and I mean at once.'

The Head Cook closed her eyes, wanting thereby to reassure Karl. As he bowed by way of leave-taking, he glimpsed the Head Waiter clasping the Head Cook's hand as though secretly and playing with it. The Head Porter accompanied Karl with heavy steps as far as the door, which he did not let him close, instead holding it open himself so that he could yell after Karl: 'I want to see you go past me at the main entrance in a quarter of a minute, don't forget that.'

Karl hurried as best he could in order to avoid any harassment at the main entrance, but it all went much more slowly than he wished. First of all Bess wasn't to be found right away and now at breakfast-time the place was full of people, then it turned out that a boy had borrowed Karl's old trousers and Karl had to search the clothes-racks at almost all the beds until he found these trousers, so that a good five minutes had passed before he reached the main entrance. Just in front of him a lady was walking with four gentlemen. They were all going towards a big automobile which was waiting for them and whose door was already being held open by a lackey while he stretched out his free left arm stiffly and horizontally to the side, which looked extremely solemn. But it was in vain that Karl had hoped to get out unnoticed behind this smart group. The Head Porter had already seized him by the hand and was pulling him between two gentlemen, whose pardon he asked, closer to himself. 'You call that a quarter of a minute,' he said, looking at Karl from the side as though inspecting a defective clock. 'Just come here,' he then said, leading him into the big porters' lodge, which Karl had long wanted to take a look at, but which he now entered, shoved by the Porter, only with mistrust. He was already in the doorway when he turned round and tried to push the Head Porter away and get away. 'No, no, this is the way in,' said the Head Porter, turning Karl round. 'But they've let me go,' said Karl, meaning that no one in the hotel could give him any more orders. 'You can't go as long as I'm holding you,' said the Porter, which to be sure was true.

In the end Karl could find no reason for resisting the Porter. After all, what more could happen to him? Anyway, the walls of the porters' lodge consisted entirely of enormous glass panes through which the crowd of people streaming through the vestibule could be seen as clearly as though one were among them. In fact the whole porters' lodge didn't seem to have a single corner where one could hide from people's eyes. However much of a hurry the people outside seemed to be in, for they were making their way with outstretched arms, bent heads, watchful eyes, and luggage held aloft, hardly any of them failed to cast a glance into the porters' lodge, for behind its panes there were always announcements and notices hanging which were important for the guests as well as the hotel staff. In addition, however, the porters' lodge was in direct contact with the vestibule, for two assistant porters were sitting at two big sliding windows and were incessantly occupied in dispensing information about various matters. These people were really overburdened, and Karl was certain that the Head Porter, judging from his knowledge of him, had in the course of his career managed to dodge these jobs. These two information givers— one couldn't imagine this properly when seeing them from outside— always confronted at least ten enquiring faces. Among these ten enquirers, who were constantly changing, there was often a confusion of languages, as though each had been sent from a different country. Some were always asking questions simultaneously, and others were always talking among themselves. Most of them wanted to collect something from the porters' lodge or leave something there, so one could also see impatiently gesturing hands projecting from the crowd. One had a request connected with some newspaper or other which was unexpectedly unfolded and for a moment concealed all the faces. The two assistant porters had to cope with all this. Mere speaking would not have sufficed for their task, they rattled away, one of them in particular, a gloomy man with a dark beard surrounding his entire face, gave information without the slightest interruption. He looked neither at the counter, where he had constant little tasks to do, nor at the face of this or that enquirer, but only straight ahead, obviously in order to husband and concentrate his energies. His beard, moreover, prevented his speech from being wholly intelligible, and Karl, in the short time he spent standing beside him, could pick up very little of what he said, though besides his English accent he might have had to use foreign languages. It was further confusing that one piece of information followed so closely on another and faded into it, so that often an enquirer would be listening intently, thinking his question was still being answered, and would notice only after a short time that it had already been dealt with. One also had to get used to the fact that the assistant porter never asked for a question to be repeated, even if it was mostly intelligible and had been asked in a slightly unclear way,

a barely perceptible shake of his head would then convey that he was
not going to answer the question and it was up to the enquirer to realize his mistake and formulate the question better. This especially
made many people spend a long time in front of the window. To help
the assistant porters, each was assigned a messenger-boy, who, running at full speed, had to fetch from a bookshelf and from various
boxes everything the assistant porter happened to need. These were
the best-paid jobs, though also the most demanding, available for
young people in the hotel, in some ways they had a harder time than
the assistant porters, for these had only to think and speak, whereas
these young people had to think and run simultaneously. If they ever
brought the wrong thing, the assistant porter was of course in too
much of a hurry to give them lengthy instructions, instead he simply
took whatever they put on his counter and pushed it off the counter
with a sudden jerk. It was very interesting how one assistant porter
replaced another, which happened just after Karl's arrival. Such a
changeover must of course happen quite often, at least during the
day, for there could hardly be anyone capable of enduring more than
an hour at the counter. When the changeover was due a bell would
ring and simultaneously the two assistant porters whose turn it was
entered from a side door, each followed by his messenger-boy. They
first stood at the window without doing anything, watching the people
outside for a while in order to establish what stage the answering of
questions had reached. When the moment seemed suitable for them
to intervene, they tapped the assistant porter who was going off duty
on the shoulder, and he, though he had previously paid no attention
to anything happening behind his back, understood immediately and
left his place. All this took place so fast that the people outside were
often taken by surprise and almost shrank back in alarm at the new
face popping up in front of them so suddenly. The two men relieved
of their duty stretched themselves and then splashed their hot heads
with water from two wash-stands, but the messenger-boys relieved of
their duty were not yet allowed to stretch themselves but were kept
busy a while longer picking up the objects that had been thrown on
the floor and putting them back in their places.

Karl had taken all this in, watching intently, within a few moments,
and with a slight headache he silently followed the Head Porter who
was leading him further. Evidently the Head Porter too had noticed
the strong impression that this way of dispensing information had

made on Karl, and he suddenly tugged Karl's hand and said: 'You see, that's how work is done here.' Karl, to be sure, had not been idle here in the hotel, but he had had no conception of work like that, and, almost completely forgetting that the Head Porter was his great enemy, he looked up at him and nodded his head in mute appreciation. That, however, again struck the Head Porter as an overestimation of the assistant porters and perhaps as a discourtesy towards his own person, for, as though he had been making a fool of Karl, he shouted without worrying about being overheard: 'Of course this is the most mindless work in the whole hotel; when you've been listening for an hour, you know pretty well all the questions that get asked, the rest don't need to be answered. If you hadn't been cheeky and ill-behaved, if you hadn't been a liar, loafer, drunkard, and thief, I might have put you at one of those windows, for I only need blockheads for that.' Karl completely ignored the insults directed at him, so indignant was he that the honest and demanding work of the assistant porters, instead of being acknowledged, was being mocked, and moreover mocked by a man who, if he had ever dared to sit at such a counter, would certainly have had to relinquish his place after a few minutes amid the laughter of all the enquirers. 'Leave me alone,' said Karl, his curiosity regarding the porters' lodge was more than satisfied, 'I want nothing more to do with you.' 'That's not enough to get away,' said the Head Porter, squeezing Karl's arms so hard that the latter could not move them, and positively carrying him to the other end of the porters' lodge. Didn't the people outside see the Head Porter's violence? Or if they saw it, what did they think of it, that nobody at least knocked on the glass pane to show the Head Porter that he was being watched and could not treat Karl just as he thought fit.

But soon Karl no longer had any hope of getting help from the vestibule, for the Head Porter pulled a cord and half the panes of the porters' lodge were swiftly covered at their full height by black curtains. There were people also in this part of the porters' lodge, but all hard at work and with no eyes or ears for anything unconnected with their work. Besides, they were completely dependent on the Head Porter, and instead of helping Karl, they would sooner have helped to conceal anything that the Head Porter might take it into his head to do. There were, for example, six assistant porters at six telephones. The arrangement, as one saw immediately, was such that one of them only took notes of conversations, while his neighbour, using the notes received from the first, passed the messages on. They were the most up-to-date telephones which did not require booths, for the ringing was no louder than a chirping, one could speak into the telephone in a whisper and yet the words, thanks to a special electric amplification, would reach their destination in a thunderous tone. Hence the three speakers at their telephones could scarcely be heard, and one might have thought they were simply murmuring as they watched something going on inside the receivers, while the others, as if stunned by the noise that was pressing on them though inaudible to anyone else, let their heads droop onto the paper that it was their job to write on. Here too each of the three speakers had a boy standing by to help him; these three boys did nothing but take turns to incline their heads towards their masters, listening carefully, and then, as hurriedly as though they had been stung, open gigantic yellow books—the rustling of the massive pages as they were turned over was far louder than the sound of the telephones—to look for telephone numbers.

Karl indeed could not restrain himself from following all this closely, although the Head Porter, who had sat down, was holding him in a kind of lock. 'It is my duty,' said the Head Porter, shaking Karl as though only to make the latter turn his face towards him, 'in the name of the hotel management, to make up, at least a little, for what the Head Waiter, for whatever reason, neglected to do. That's how one person always helps another out. Otherwise such a big organization would be unthinkable. Perhaps you want to say that I'm not your immediate superior, well, that just shows how nice it is of me to take care of this matter when nobody else would. Anyway, as Head Porter I'm above everyone else in a sense, for I'm in charge of all the entrances to the hotel, that is, this main entrance, the three middle entrances, and the ten side entrances, to say nothing of the innumerable small doors and exits without doors. Of course all the relevant service teams have to obey me absolutely. In return for this great honour, on the other hand, I of course have the duty towards the hotel management to let nobody out who is in the least suspicious. But you in particular, because that's what I feel like, strike me as highly suspicious.' And in his pleasure at this he raised his hands and lowered them with a smack that was painful. 'It's possible,' he added, enjoying himself royally, 'that you might have got out unnoticed by another exit, for of course you weren't important enough for me to have received any particular instructions concerning you. But now you're here, I'm going to enjoy you. Anyway

I never doubted that you'd keep the appointment we arranged at the main entrance, because it's always the case that a cheeky and disobedient person gives up his vices at the very moment when it hurts him most to reform. You're sure to encounter many more examples in your own life.'

'You needn't think,' said Karl, breathing in the strangely stale smell emitted by the Head Porter, which he only noticed here, standing close to him for so long, 'you needn't think', he said, 'that I'm completely in your power, after all I can scream.' 'And I can stop your mouth,' said the Head Porter just as quietly and quickly as he no doubt meant to do it if necessary. 'And do you really think that if anyone were to come in here on your account, they would take your side against me, the Head Porter? So you see how absurd your hopes are. You know, when you were still in uniform you really did look a bit respectable, but in this suit, which is really possible only in Europe.' And he tugged at various parts of the suit, which now, to be sure, although it had been almost new five months ago, was worn-out, crumpled, and above all stained, which was mainly due to the carelessness of the lift-boys, who were under orders to keep the dormitory floor clean and free of dust, but were too lazy to clean it properly and instead sprinkled some kind of oil on the floor, thus simultaneously covering all the clothes on the clothes-racks with lamentable stains. Now you might keep your clothes wherever you wanted, there was always somebody who didn't have his clothes to hand but had no trouble in finding and borrowing the clothes somebody else had hidden. And quite possibly this was the very person who was supposed to clean the room on that day and not only stained the clothes with oil, but poured it all over them. Only Renell had hidden his expensive clothes in some secret place from which they had hardly ever been taken, especially as nobody borrowed another's clothes from malice or greed, but simply from hurry and carelessness took whatever he could find. But even Renell's suit had a circular reddish oil-stain on the back, and in the city this stain would have enabled a sharp-witted person to identify even this elegant young man as a lift-boy.

And Karl said to himself as he recalled these things that even as a lift-boy he had suffered a great deal and that it had still been all in vain, for the lift-boy's job had not been, as he had hoped, a prelude to a better position, but instead he had been pushed further down and was even close to being sent to prison. Moreover, he was now being held tight by the Head Porter who was probably thinking how he could disgrace Karl yet further. And entirely forgetting that the Head Porter was not at all the man to be persuaded, Karl exclaimed, striking his forehead several times with his free hand, 'And even if I didn't bid you good day, how can a grown-up person be so vindictive because of a missed greeting!'

'I'm not vindictive,' said the Head Porter, 'I only want to search your pockets. I'm convinced, it's true, that I won't find anything, because you'll have been careful enough to let your friend remove everything, a little each day. But you need to have been searched.' And already he was reaching into one of Karl's jacket pockets with such force that the seams at its side burst. 'Nothing there,' he said, rummaging through the contents of the pocket, a calendar advertising the hotel, a page with an exercise in commercial correspondence on it, a few jacket- and trouser-buttons, the Head Cook's visiting-card, a nail-file which a guest had once thrown to him when packing his suitcase, an old pocket-mirror which Rennel had given him in gratitude for replacing him some ten times, and a few other odds and ends. 'Nothing there,' repeated the Head Porter, throwing everything under the seat as though it went without saying that Karl's property, so far as it was not stolen, belonged under the seat. 'That's enough,' said Karl to himself—his face must have been blushing bright red—and as the Head Porter, rendered careless by his greed, was poking about in Karl's second pocket, Karl slipped out of his sleeves with a jerk, took a first, wild leap which shoved an assistant porter quite hard against his telephone, ran through the clammy air more slowly than he had intended to the door, but happily was outside before the Head Porter in his heavy coat had even been able to stand up. The security organization couldn't be faultless after all, bells were ringing in a few places, but heaven only knew why, hotel employees were going hither and thither in the entrance-way in such numbers that one might almost have thought they were trying inconspicuously to cut off his escape, for otherwise little sense could be made of this movement to and fro—anyway Karl soon got into the open air, but still had to walk along the pavement beside the hotel, for one could not reach the street, as an unbroken series of automobiles was moving past the main entrance and stopping for passengers. These automobiles, in order to reach the passengers as soon as possible, practically ran into one another, each was being pushed forward by the one behind. Pedestrians who were in a special hurry to get to the street sometimes climbed right through an individual automobile as though it were a public thoroughfare, and they did not care whether only the chauffeur and the servants were sitting in the automobile or the smart people as well. Karl thought such behaviour was going too far, and anyway one had to know one's way around in order to venture it, for how easily he might find an automobile whose occupants would take it amiss, throw him out, and cause a scandal, and there was nothing that a runaway, suspicious-looking hotel employee in his shirt-sleeves had to dread more. Anyway, the series of automobiles couldn't stretch out for ever and he would look least suspicious so long as he stayed close to the hotel. In fact Karl finally got to a place where the series of automobiles didn't stop, but curved towards the street and left some spaces. He was just going to slip into the traffic on the street, in which people who probably looked much more suspicious than he did could run about freely, when he heard his name being called from somewhere close by. He turned round and saw two lift-boys whom he knew well coming out of a small, low door, which looked like the entrance to a burial-vault, and pulling, with the utmost effort, a stretcher, on which, as Karl now realized, none other than Robinson was lying, his head, face, and arms thickly covered with bandages. It was horrid to see how he put his arms to his eyes in order to use the bandages to wipe away the tears that he was shedding, either from pain or from some other suffering or even for joy at seeing Karl again. 'Rossmann,' he exclaimed reproach-fully, 'why did you keep me waiting so long. I've spent a whole hour fighting people off so that I shouldn't be carried away before you came. These fellows'—and he struck one of the lift-boys on the head as though he were protected against blows by his bandages—'they're absolute devils. Oh, Rossmann, my visit to you has cost me dear.' 'What have they done to you?' said Karl, stepping closer to the stretcher, which the lift-boys, in order to rest, had put down, laugh-ing. 'How can you ask,' groaned Robinson, 'when you can see how I look. Just think! I've probably been crippled for the rest of my life. I've got awful pains from here to here'—and he pointed first at his head and then at his toes—. 'I wish you'd seen how my nose bled. My waistcoat is completely ruined, I just left it there, my trousers are in rags, I'm in my underpants'—and he lifted the blanket a little, inviting Karl to look under it. 'What's going to become of me! I'll have to stay in bed for several months at least, and let me tell you now,

I've got nobody but you who could look after me. Delamarche is much too impatient. Rossmann, little Rossmann!' And Robinson stretched out his hand in order to conciliate Karl, who took a step backwards, by stroking him. 'Why on earth did I have to go and see you!' he repeated several times, in order not to let Karl forget the latter's share in the responsibility for his misfortune. Now Karl did of course realize at once that Robinson's laments were not due to his wounds, but to his monstrous hangover, since he had no sooner fallen into a drunken stupor than he had been awakened and attacked, to his surprise, till he bled, so he had no idea where he was in the waking world. How slight his wounds were was evident from the shapeless bandages, consisting of old rags in which the lift-boys had obviously swathed him for a joke. And even the two lift-boys at the end of the stretcher kept snorting with laughter. But this was not the place to bring Robinson to his senses, for passers-by were racing along without troubling about the group round the stretcher, quite often people jumped right over Robinson with the agility of gymnasts, the chauffeur, paid with Karl's money, was shouting 'Let's go, let's go,' the lift-boys raised the stretcher with the last of their strength, Robinson took Karl's hand and said coaxingly, 'Now do come along,' wasn't Karl in his present outfit best concealed in the darkness of the automobile? And so he sat down beside Robinson, who leant his head against him, the lift-boys waited to shake his hand heartily through the window, since he was their ex-colleague, and the automobile turned sharply towards the street, an accident seemed unavoidable, but at once the all-embracing traffic quietly enveloped even the dead-straight course of this automobile.

IT must have been a remote suburban street in which the automobile stopped, for silence prevailed all around, children were crouching and playing at the edge of the pavement, a man with a lot of old clothes over his shoulders was calling watchfully up to the windows of the houses, in his exhaustion Karl felt uncomfortable as he stepped out of the automobile onto the asphalt on which the morning sun was shining brightly and warmly. 'Do you really live here?' he shouted into the automobile. Robinson, who had been sleeping peacefully throughout the journey, muttered some indistinct assent and seemed to be waiting for Karl to carry him out. 'Then I've nothing more to do here. Goodbye,' said Karl, preparing to walk down the slightly sloping street. 'But Karl, what are you thinking of?' cried Robinson, standing almost upright with alarm, though with shaking knees, in the car. 'I've got to go,' said Karl, who had been watching Robinson's rapid recovery. 'In your shirt-sleeves?' asked the latter. 'I'll soon earn enough money to buy a jacket,' answered Karl, gave Robinson a confident nod, raised his hand to wave goodbye, and would indeed have gone away, if the chauffeur hadn't called: 'Just wait a minute, sir.' It turned out, disagreeably enough, that the chauffeur was claiming some additional payment, because he had not yet been paid for the time spent waiting outside the hotel. 'Oh yes,' shouted Robinson from the automobile, confirming the correctness of this demand, 'I had to wait for you for such a long time. You've got to give him something.' 'Yes indeed,' said the chauffeur. 'Yes, if only I had anything,' said Karl, reaching into his trouser pockets although he knew it was pointless. 'I can only rely on you,' said the chauffeur, planting himself squarely in position, 'I can't ask that sick man there for anything.' From the gateway a young lad with his nose partly eaten away* approached and listened from a few paces' distance. Just then a policeman, going on his rounds through the street, looked down, caught sight of the man in shirt-sleeves, and stopped. Robinson, who had also noticed the policeman, was stupid enough to shout to him from the other window: 'It's nothing, it's nothing,' as though one could drive a policeman away like a fly. The children who had been watching the policeman, now that he had stopped, started paying attention to

Karl and the chauffeur, and came up at a trot. In the opposite gateway stood an old woman, staring across.

'Rossmann,' shouted a voice from high up. It was Delamarche, shouting from the balcony of the top storey. He himself could be made out only indistinctly against the whitish-blue sky, was evidently wearing a dressing-gown, and was watching the street through an opera-glass. Beside him a red sunshade was spread out and there seemed to be a woman sitting under it. 'Hallo,' he shouted with the utmost effort in order to make himself understood, 'is Robinson there too?' 'Yes,' answered Karl, strongly supported by a second and much louder 'Yes' from Robinson in the car. 'Hallo,' came the answering shout, 'I'll be down right away.' Robinson bent out of the car. 'That's a real man,' he said, directing this praise of Delamarche at Karl, at the chauffeur, at the policeman, and at anyone who wanted to hear it. Up on the balcony, which everyone was still distractedly gazing at although Delamarche had already left it, a powerful woman in a red dress did indeed get up under the sunshade, took the opera-glass from the ledge, and looked through it at the people below, who only slowly turned their gaze away from her. Karl, waiting for Delamarche, looked into the gateway and into the courtyard beyond, which was being traversed by an almost unbroken series of servants, each carrying a small but evidently very heavy chest on his shoulder. The chauffeur had gone over to his car, and in order to use the time was polishing its lamps with a rag. Robinson was feeling his limbs, seeming astonished at experiencing so little pain despite the utmost attention, and began, with lowered face, carefully unwrapping one of the thick bandages from his leg. The policeman was holding his black truncheon out in front of him and was waiting silently with the great patience that policemen need to have, whether they are doing their normal duty or are on the watch. The lad whose nose was eaten away sat down on a gatepost and stretched out his legs. The children tiptoed slowly closer to Karl, for because of his blue shirt-sleeves they thought him, although he paid them no heed, the most important person of all.

The length of time before Delamarche's arrival let one judge the great height of this house. And Delamarche actually came in a great hurry, with his dressing-gown barely tied together. 'So there you are!' he cried, pleased and severe at the same time. With each stride he took his coloured underclothes became visible for a moment. Karl could not quite understand why Delamarche, here in the city, in the gigantic tenement, on the open street, went about so comfortably dressed, as though he were in his private villa. Like Robinson, Delamarche too had changed a great deal. His swarthy, smooth-shaven, scrupulously clean, coarsely muscular face looked proud and imposing. The harsh glint of his eyes, which were always somewhat puckered up, took one by surprise. Although his violet dressing-gown was old, stained, and too big for him, this ugly garment revealed at the top a massive dark cravat of heavy silk. 'Well?' he asked of all and sundry. The policeman stepped a little closer and leaned on the bonnet of the automobile. Karl gave a brief explanation. 'Robinson is a bit off colour, but if he makes an effort he'll be able to get up the stairs all right; the chauffeur here wants some more money on top of the fare I already paid him. And now I'm off. Goodbye.' 'You're not going,' said Delamarche. 'That's what I already told him,' piped up Robinson from the car. 'I'm going all right,' said Karl, taking a few steps. But Delamarche was right behind him and pushed him back forcibly. 'I said you're staying,' he shouted. 'Let go of me, will you,' said Karl, getting ready to win his freedom with his fists if necessary, however little chance of success he had against a man like Delamarche. But after all, there was the policeman, there was the chauffeur, occasional groups of workmen went through the otherwise quiet street, would people allow Delamarche to do him wrong? He wouldn't have liked to be alone with him in a room, but here? Delamarche was now quietly paying the chauffeur, who with many bows put the unduly large sum of money in his pocket and from gratitude went over to Robinson and was obviously talking with the latter about how to get him out. Karl saw himself unobserved, perhaps Delamarche would allow him to go away quietly, naturally it would be best to avoid a quarrel, and so Karl simply walked into the roadway in order to get away as quickly as possible. The children crowded to Delamarche in order to draw his attention to Karl's flight, but he had no need to intervene himself, for the policeman stretched out his truncheon and said: 'Stop!'

'What's your name?' he asked, putting his truncheon under his arm and slowly pulling out a book. Karl now looked at him closely for the first time, he was a powerful man but his hair was already almost completely white. 'Karl Rossmann,' he said. 'Rossmann,' repeated the policeman, doubtless only because he was a quiet and conscientious person, but Karl, who was now having his first contact with American officialdom, saw even in this repetition the expression of a certain suspicion. And in fact things couldn't look good for him, for even Robinson, who was so preoccupied with his own concerns, was making silent gestures from the car to ask Delamarche to help Karl. But Delamarche was shaking his head hastily by way of refusal and was looking on passively, his hands in his over-large pockets. The lad on the doorpost was explaining the whole state of affairs from the very beginning to a woman who had just stepped out of the gateway. The children were standing in a semicircle behind Karl and looking silently up at the policeman.

'Show me your identity papers,' said the policeman. That was probably only a formal question, for if you haven't got a jacket you aren't likely to have any identity papers on you. Karl therefore kept quiet so that he could answer the next question fully and thus gloss over his lack of identity papers as far as possible. But the next question was: 'So you haven't got any identity papers?' and Karl now had to answer: 'Not with me.' 'That's bad,' said the policeman, looking pensively round in a circle and tapping the cover of his book with two fingers. 'Have you any kind of job?' asked the policeman finally. 'I used to be a lift-boy,' said Karl. 'You used to be a lift-boy, so you aren't one any longer and how do you live now?' 'I'm going to look for a new job.' 'Were you sacked?' 'Yes, an hour ago.' 'On the spot?' 'Yes,' said Karl, raising his hand as though by way of apology. He couldn't tell the whole story here, and even if it had been possible, it seemed futile to try to forestall an injustice that was threatening him by recounting an injustice that had already happened to him. And if he hadn't received justice from the kindness of the Head Cook and the intelligence of the Head Waiter, he certainly couldn't expect any from the company here on the street.

'And you were sacked without a jacket?' asked the policeman. 'Well yes,' said Karl, so in America too it was the officials' habit to ask questions about what they could see for themselves. (How annoyed his father had been about the pointless questions asked by the officials when he was obtaining his passport.) Karl felt a strong desire to run away, hide somewhere, and not have to listen to any more questions. And now the policeman asked the very question that Karl had most dreaded, in fact his uneasy anticipation of it had probably made him behave more incautiously than he would otherwise: 'In which hotel were you employed?' He bowed his head and did not answer, he was determined not to answer this question. He simply could not return to the Hotel Occidental escorted by a policeman, so that interrogations could take place attended by his friends and enemies, the Head Cook would completely abandon her good opinion of Karl, which had already been much weakened, since she thought he was already in Brenner's Hotel but would see him returning, picked up by a policeman, in his shirt-sleeves, without her visiting-card, while the Head Waiter might only nod sympathetically, but the Head Porter would talk about the hand of God that had at last found the rascal.

'He was employed in the Hotel Occidental,' said Delamarche, stepping over beside the policeman. 'No,' cried Karl, stamping his foot, 'it isn't true.' Delamarche looked at him, mockingly pursing his lips, as though he could reveal lots of other things. Karl's unexpected excitement produced much movement among the children, who went over to Delamarche in order to scrutinize Karl from there. Robinson had stuck his head right out of the car and was so excited that he kept quite still; the occasional blinking of his eyes was his only movement. The lad in the gateway clapped his hands with pleasure, the woman beside him nudged him with her elbow to make him be quiet. The porters were having their breakfast break and all appeared with large pots of black coffee which they stirred with bread-sticks. A few sat down on the edge of the pavement, all slurped their coffee very loudly.

'I expect you know the boy,' said the policeman to Delamarche. 'Only too well,' said the latter. 'I once did him many good turns, but he gave me no thanks, which I expect, after the little interrogation you gave him, you can well understand.' 'Yes,' said the policeman, 'he seems to be an obdurate boy.' 'He is,' said Delamarche, 'but that isn't his worst quality.' 'Really?' said the policeman. 'Yes,' said Delamarche, who was now in full flow and was swinging his dressing-gown to and fro by moving his hands in his pockets, 'he's a rough customer. My friend in the car there and I, we happened to pick him up when he was destitute, he'd no idea at that time of conditions in America, he'd come straight from Europe, where they had no use for him either, well, we dragged him along with us, let him live with us, explained everything to him, tried to get him a job, thought that despite all the signs to the contrary we could make him into a useful person, then one night he disappeared, he was simply gone, under circumstances that I'd rather not mention. Was it like that or wasn't it?' asked

Delamarche finally, plucking Karl by the shirt-sleeve. 'Back, you children,' shouted the policeman, for they had pressed so far forward that Delamarche nearly stumbled over one of them. Meanwhile the porters, only now realizing how interesting the interrogation was, had started paying attention and gathered in a close circle round Karl, who couldn't have taken a single step back and moreover had constantly in his ears the confused voices of these porters, who were bellowing rather than talking in a completely unintelligible English, perhaps mingled with Slav words.

'Thanks for the information,' said the policeman, saluting Delamarche. 'At any rate, I'll take him with me and have him returned to the Hotel Occidental.' But Delamarche said: 'Might I ask you to hand the boy over to me for the time being, I need to sort out some things with him. I promise to take him back to the hotel afterwards.' 'I can't do that,' said the policeman. Delamarche said: 'Here's my visiting-card,' and handed him a card. The policeman looked at it appreciatively but said with a polite smile: 'No, it's no use.'

However much Karl had hitherto been on his guard with Delamarche, he now saw in him his only possible rescue. It was certainly suspicious the way the latter kept asking the policeman to give him Karl, but at any rate it would be easier to persuade Delamarche than the policeman not to take him back to the hotel. And even if Karl were to return to the hotel in Delamarche's custody, that would be much less bad than doing it accompanied by the policeman. For the moment, however, Karl of course couldn't show that he did want to join Delamarche, otherwise all would be lost. And he looked uneasily at the policeman's hand, which might at any moment be raised to seize him.

'I ought at least to find out why he was sacked on the spot,' said the policeman finally, while Delamarche looked sourly to one side and crushed the visiting-card between his fingers. 'But he hasn't been sacked at all,' shouted Robinson to the general amazement, bending as far out of the car as he could with the chauffeur's support. 'On the contrary, he's got a good job there. He's the boss in the dormitory and can take in whoever he likes. Only he's incredibly busy, and if you want anything from him, you have a long wait. He's always with the Head Waiter and the Head Cook and is in their confidence. He certainly hasn't been sacked. I don't know why he said that. How can he have been sacked? I did myself a severe injury in the hotel and he got the job of getting me home, and because he happened not to have a jacket on, that's why he came without a jacket. I couldn't wait till he fetched his jacket.' 'You see,' said Delamarche, spreading out his arms, in a tone as though he were rebuking the policeman's deficient knowledge of human nature, and these two words of his seemed to give Robinson's vague statement a clarity that brooked no contradiction.

'Is that really true?' asked the policeman more weakly. 'And if it is true, why does the boy claim he was sacked?' 'Answer him,' said Delamarche. Karl looked at the policeman, who was supposed to sort things out among strangers each of whom was thinking only of himself, and something of his general worry transmitted itself to Karl. He did not want to tell a lie, and kept his hands firmly clasped behind his back.

A supervisor appeared in the gateway and clapped his hands as a sign that the porters should return to their work. They shook the dregs out of their coffee-pots, fell silent, and paraded into the house with uncertain steps. 'We'll never get to the end of this,' said the policeman, trying to seize Karl's arm. Karl involuntarily drew back a little, felt the empty space opened by the retreat of the porters, turned round, and with a few initial bounds set off at a run. The children screamed in unison and ran a few steps after him with their little arms outstretched. 'Stop him!' shouted the policeman down the long, almost empty alleyway, repeating this cry regularly as he ran after Karl in a noiseless run that revealed great strength and practice. It was lucky for Karl that the chase occurred in a working-class district. Workmen don't side with officials. Karl ran down the middle of the roadway, because it offered the fewest obstacles, occasionally seeing workmen standing on the pavement and quietly watching him, while the policeman shouted to them his 'Stop him!' and as he ran, prudently staying on the smooth pavement, constantly stretched out his truncheon towards Karl. Karl had not much hope, and almost lost it altogether when the policeman, as they reached intersecting streets which doubtless also held police patrols, uttered positively deafening whistles. Karl's only advantage lay in being lightly dressed, he flew or rather plunged down the increasing gradient of the street, only, distracted by lack of sleep, he sometimes took excessively high, useless, and time-consuming bounds. Moreover, the policeman had his object always before his eyes without having to think, whereas for Karl running was a minor concern, he had to think, choose among various possibilities, constantly take a fresh decision. His rather desperate plan was to avoid the intersections for the time being, since there was no knowing what might be hidden in them, he might run straight into a police station; as long as he could, he wanted to stay in this street where the view was clear, ending far below at a bridge which, hardly begun, disappeared into water and haze. After this decision he was just preparing to run faster in order to pass the first intersection as fast as possible, when not far ahead he saw a policeman lurking beside the dark wall of a house in shadow, ready to jump out at Karl at the right moment. Now there was nothing for it but the intersecting street, and when his name was even shouted quite inoffensively from this alley—at first he thought it was an illusion, for he had had a rushing sound in his ears the whole time—he hesitated no longer and turned, in order to surprise the policemen as much as he could, on one foot at a right angle into this alley.

Hardly had he taken two bounds—he had already forgotten that someone had shouted his name, the second policeman was now whistling too, his strength was obviously fresh, distant passers-by in this intersecting street seemed to quicken their pace—when from a small door a hand seized Karl and pulled him, with the words 'Keep quiet', into a dark hallway. It was Delamarche, quite out of breath, with flushed cheeks, his hair was plastered against his head. He was carrying his dressing-gown under his arm and was dressed only in his shirt and underpants. As for the door, which was not the actual front door but formed only an inconspicuous side entrance, he had already shut and locked it. 'One moment,' he said, leaned against the wall with his head held high, and breathed heavily. Karl was almost lying in his arms, half-unconsciously pressing his face against his chest. 'There are the gentlemen running,' said Delamarche, pricking up his ears and pointing his finger at the door. Indeed, the two policemen were now running past, the running sounded in the empty alleyway like the striking of steel against stone. 'But you're all in,' said Delamarche to Karl, who was still gasping for breath and unable to utter a word. Delamarche seated him carefully on the floor, knelt down beside him, stroked his forehead several times and looked closely at him. 'It's all right,' said Karl at last, getting to his feet with difficulty. 'Then off we go,' said Delamarche, who had put on his dressing-gown again, and he pushed Karl, whose head was still bowed from weakness, in front of him. From time to time he shook Karl in order to make him more alert. 'You're tired, are you?' he said. 'In the open air you could run like a horse, but I had to creep through the damned corridors and courtyards. Fortunately I'm a runner too.' In his pride he slapped Karl hard on the back. 'From time to time a race like that with the police can be a good exercise.' 'I was already tired when I started running,' said Karl. 'There's no excuse for bad running,' said Delamarche. 'If it hadn't been for me, they'd have caught you by now.' 'I think so too,' said Karl. 'I'm very much obliged to you.' 'You sure are,' said Delamarche.

They went through a long, narrow hallway paved with dark, smooth stones. Now and again a stairway opened up to the right or the left or one caught a glimpse of another large hall. There were hardly any adults to be seen, only children lying on the empty stairs. Beside a banister a little girl was standing and crying so hard that her whole face was shining with tears. No sooner had she seen Delamarche than she ran up the stairs, panting for breath with her mouth open, and calmed down only at the top, when she had reassured herself by frequent backward glances that nobody was following her or intending to. 'I ran her down a moment ago,' said Delamarche, laughing, and shook his fist at her, whereupon she screamed and ran further upstairs.

The courtyards* they passed through were also almost completely abandoned. Only now and again a messenger pushed a two-wheeled barrow along, a woman filled a jug with water at the pump, a postman crossed the whole courtyard with quiet steps, an old man with a white moustache sat at a glass door with his legs crossed, smoking a pipe, crates were being unloaded outside a delivery office, the unoccupied horses turned their heads equably, a man in a work-coat was supervising the work with a sheet of paper in his hand, in one office the window was open and a clerk sitting at his desk had turned away and was looking pensively out just as Karl and Delamarche went past.

'You couldn't wish for anywhere quieter,' said Delamarche. 'In the evening there's a lot of noise for a couple of hours, but during the day it couldn't be better.' Karl nodded, he thought it was too quiet. 'I couldn't live anywhere else,' said Delamarche, 'because Brunelda can't stand the slightest noise. Do you know Brunelda? Well, you'll soon see her. Anyway, I advise you to stay as silent as you can.'

When they reached the staircase that led to Delamarche's flat, the automobile was already gone, and the lad whose nose had been eaten away reported, without showing any astonishment at Karl's reappearance, that he had carried Robinson upstairs. Delamarche merely nodded at him as though he were a servant who had done what was obviously his duty, and pulled Karl, who was hesitating and looking at the sunny street, up the stairs with him. 'We'll soon be at the top,' said Delamarche several times as they climbed the stairs, but his prediction was slow to be fulfilled, again and again a staircase would lead to a new one heading in an imperceptibly different direction. At one point Karl stopped, not really because he was tired, but because the length of the staircase made him feel defenceless. 'Yes, the flat's very high up,' said Delamarche as they went on, 'but that has its good sides. You rarely go out, you wear your dressing-gown all day, it's very cosy. Of course nobody comes to call on us at this height.' 'Who's going to call on you,' thought Karl.

Finally Robinson appeared on a landing in front of the closed door of a flat, and now they'd arrived; the staircase was not even now at an end, but led further in semi-darkness, with no sign that it was about to terminate. 'I thought so,' said Robinson softly, as though still oppressed by pain, 'Delamarche will bring him! Rossmann, where would you be without Delamarche?' Robinson was standing there in his underclothes, trying to wrap himself as much as possible in the small blanket that he had been given in the Hotel Occidental, it was not clear why he didn't go into the flat instead of making a fool of himself here in front of anyone who might pass by. 'Is she asleep?' asked Delamarche. 'I don't think so,' said Robinson, 'but I thought it better to wait till you came.' 'We must first see if she's asleep,' said Delamarche, bending down to the keyhole. After he had peered through for a long time and turned his head various ways, he stood up and said: 'You can't see her clearly, the blind is down. She's sitting on the sofa, she may be asleep.' 'Is she sick?' asked Karl, for Delamarche was standing there as though seeking advice. But he returned the question sharply: 'Sick?' 'He doesn't know her,' said Robinson apologetically.

A couple of doors further on two women had come out into the corridor, they were wiping their hands clean on their aprons and looking at Delamarche and Robinson and seemed to be talking about them. A very young girl with shining blonde hair* sprang out of another door and nestled between the two women by joining arms with them.

'These are disgusting women,' said Delamarche softly, but obviously only from concern for the sleeping Brunelda, 'some day soon I'll report them to the police and then I'll have peace from them for years. Don't look,' he hissed at Karl who found nothing wrong in looking at the women since they had to wait in the corridor anyway for Brunelda to wake up. And he shook his head crossly as though Delamarche had no business to admonish him, and was about to show this even more clearly by going up to the women, but Robinson held him back by the sleeve with the words, 'Rossmann, don't you dare,' and Delamarche, already irritated by Karl, became so enraged by the girl's loud laughter that he took a run at the women, waving his arms and legs, so rapidly that each vanished into her door as though blown away. 'I often have to clean the corridors like that,' said Delamarche, returning with slow steps; then he remembered Karl's resistance and said: 'But I expect quite different behaviour from you, otherwise you'll have a bad time with me.'

Then a questioning voice, in a gentle, weary tone, called from inside the room: 'Delamarche?' 'Yes,' answered Delamarche, looking kindly at the door, 'can we come in?' 'Oh yes,' came the reply, and Delamarche, after casting another glance at the two waiting behind him, slowly opened the door.

They went into complete darkness. The curtain of the door leading to the balcony—there was no window—had been lowered to the floor and let little light through, but in addition the room was filled with furniture and clothes hanging up everywhere, which made it even darker. The air was stale and you could positively smell the dust which had accumulated in corners that obviously no hand could reach. The first thing Karl noticed on entering was three chests of drawers, each close behind the other.

On the sofa lay the woman who had earlier looked down from the balcony. Her red dress was rucked up at the front and a long stretch of it hung down to the floor, her legs were visible almost to the knees, she was wearing thick white woollen stockings, and had no shoes on. 'How hot it is, Delamarche,' she said, turning her face from the wall and holding her hand negligently in front of Delamarche, who seized and kissed it. Karl was looking only at her double chin, which rolled whenever she turned her head. 'Shall I pull up the curtain?' asked Delamarche. 'Oh, don't do that,' she said, closing her eyes as though in despair, 'that will make it even worse.' Karl had gone to the foot of the sofa in order to look at the woman more closely, he was surprised at her complaints, since the heat was by no means extraordinary. 'Wait, I'll make it a bit more comfortable for you,' said Delamarche anxiously, undoing a couple of buttons at her neck and pulling her dress to either side, so that her throat and the top of her chest were exposed and the delicate yellowish lace fringe of her blouse became visible. 'Who's that,' said the woman suddenly, pointing at Karl, 'why is he staring at me like that?' 'You'd better start making yourself useful,' said Delamarche, pushing Karl aside while he reassured the woman with the words: 'It's only the boy I've brought to serve you.' 'But I don't want anyone,' she exclaimed, 'why do you bring strangers into the flat?' 'But you've always wanted a servant,' said Delamarche, kneeling down; although the sofa was very broad, there was not the slightest room beside Brunelda. 'Oh Delamarche,' she said, 'you just don't understand me.' 'Then I really don't understand you,' said Delamarche, taking her face in both hands. 'But it doesn't matter, if you want he can go this minute.' 'Now he's here, he may as well stay,' she said, and the weary Karl was so grateful to her for these words, which might not have been kindly meant at all, that, thinking vaguely about that endless staircase that he might have had to descend straight away, he stepped over Robinson, who was sleeping peacefully on his blanket, and said, ignoring Delamarche's irritated gestures, 'Thank you anyway for letting me stay here a little. I haven't slept for a good twenty-four hours, and during that time I've done plenty of work and had a lot of excitement. I'm terribly tired. I don't quite know where I am. But after I've had a few hours' sleep you can send me away without any further consideration and I'll be glad to go.' 'You can stay here as long as you like,' said the woman, adding ironically: 'We've got more than enough room, as you can see.' 'So you've got to go,' said Delamarche, 'we've no use for you.' 'No, he must stay,' said the woman, again in earnest. And Delamarche said to Karl, as though fulfilling this desire: 'Well, find somewhere to lie down.' 'He can lie on the curtains, but he must take his boots off so he doesn't tear anything.' Delamarche showed Karl the spot she meant. Between the door and the three chests of drawers a great variety of window curtains had been thrown down in a big pile. If they had all been regularly folded, the heaviest placed at the bottom and the lighter ones on top, and if finally the various planks and wooden rings that were stuck in the pile had been removed, it would have been a tolerable place to sleep, but at present it was only an unstable, slippery mass on which Karl nevertheless lay down immediately, for he was too tired to make any special preparations for sleep and consideration for his hosts also forbade him to make any fuss.

He was almost asleep when he heard a loud scream, rose, and saw Brunelda sitting upright on the sofa, spreading her arms wide and embracing Delamarche as he knelt before her. Karl, embarrassed by this sight, leant back again and sank down into the curtains in order to continue sleeping. He was sure he wouldn't be able to stand it here even for two days, but that made it all the more necessary to have a good sleep, in order then to take quick and sensible decisions with full presence of mind.

But Brunelda had already noticed Karl's eyes, wide open with tiredness, which had already frightened her, and exclaimed: 'Delamarche, I can't stand this heat, I'm burning, I must take my clothes off, I must have a bath, send those two out of the room, wherever you want, into the corridor, onto the balcony, just so long as I don't see them any longer. One doesn't get any peace in one's own flat. If only I were alone with you, Delamarche. Heavens, they're still there! That shameless Robinson is stretching himself out in his underclothes in the presence of a lady. And this strange boy, who was looking at me quite wildly a moment ago, has lain down again just to deceive me. Just get rid of them, Delamarche, they're a nuisance, they stop me breathing, if I die, it'll be because of them.'

'They'll be out of here right away, just start taking your clothes off,' said Delamarche, going over to Robinson, putting his foot on his chest, and shaking him. At the same time he shouted to Karl: 'Rossmann, get up! You must both go onto the balcony! And it'll be the worse for you if you come in before you're called! And now look sharp, Robinson'—he shook Robinson harder—'and you, Rossmann, mind I don't get my hands on you as well'—he clapped his hands loudly twice. 'How long it's taking!' exclaimed Brunelda on the sofa, she had spread her legs wide as she sat in order to give her enormously fat body more room, with much panting and many pauses for rest she could bend down far enough to take hold of her stockings at their upper end and pull them down a little, she could not pull them off completely, that had to be done by Delamarche, for whom she was waiting impatiently.

Numb with tiredness, Karl had crawled down from the pile of curtains and was going slowly towards the balcony door, a piece of curtain material had wrapped itself round his foot and he dragged it uncaringly after him. He was so absent-minded that he even said as he passed Brunelda: 'I wish you good night,' and then wandered past Delamarche, who pulled the curtain on the balcony door a little aside, onto the balcony. Right after Karl came Robinson, probably no less sleepy, for he was murmuring to himself: 'I get maltreated all the time! I'm not going onto the balcony unless Brunelda comes too.' But despite this assertion he went out without offering any resistance, and as Karl had already sunk into the armchair, he lay down on the stone floor.

When Karl awoke it was already evening, the stars were already in the sky, behind the high houses on the other side of the street the light of the moon was rising. Only after gazing about in this unknown district and breathing in some of the cool, refreshing air did Karl become conscious of where he was. How careless he had been, he had ignored all the Head Cook's advice, all Therese's warnings, all his own fears, was sitting quietly here on Delamarche's balcony and had slept through half the day, as if Delamarche, his great enemy, weren't just behind the curtain. The lazy Robinson was wriggling on the floor and pulling Karl by the foot, he seemed also to have wakened him in this way, for he was saying: 'You don't half sleep, Rossmann! That's care-free youth for you. How much longer are you going to sleep. I'd have let you go on sleeping, but for one thing I'm bored with lying on the floor and for another I'm very hungry. Please stand up for a moment, I've got something to eat stored inside the chair, I'd like to get it out. You'll get something too.' And Karl, standing up, then watched as Robinson, without standing up, rolled across on his belly, stretched out his hands under the chair, and pulled out a silver salver, such as is used to hold visiting-cards. On this salver, however, lay half a sausage, all blackened, some thin cigarettes, an open tin of sardines, still almost full and overflowing with oil, and a lot of sweets, which were mostly so squashed that they formed a single lump. Then came a large piece of bread and a kind of perfume bottle which, however, seemed to contain something other than perfume, for Robinson pointed to it with particular satisfaction and smacked his lips as he looked up at Karl. 'You see, Rossmann,' said Robinson, gulping down one sardine after another and occasionally wiping the oil from his hands with a woollen towel which Brunelda had evidently left on the balcony, 'you see, Rossmann, that's how to store your food if you don't want to starve.

I tell you, I count for nothing here. And if you keep being treated like a dog you end up thinking you are one. It's good that you're here, Rossmann, I at least have someone to talk to. Nobody in the building speaks to me. They hate us. And all because of Brunelda. Of course she's a magnificent woman. Listen'—and he beckoned Karl down so that he could whisper to him—'I once saw her naked. Oh!'—and at this delightful memory he began to squeeze and slap Karl's legs, till Karl, exclaiming: 'Robinson, you're out of your mind,' seized his hands and pushed them back.

'You're still a child, Rossmann,' said Robinson, pulling a dagger, which he carried on a string round his neck, from under his shirt, removing its sheath and cutting up the hard sausage. 'You've still got a lot to learn. But with us you've come to the right place. Do sit down. Don't you want something to eat too? Well, perhaps you'll get an appetite from watching me. Don't you want anything to drink either? You just don't want anything at all. And you're not specially talkative either. But I couldn't care less who's on the balcony with me, so long as someone's there. You see, I spend a lot of time on the balcony. Brunelda enjoys that so much. Whatever comes into her head, one minute she feels cold, the next she feels hot, then she wants to sleep, then she wants to comb her hair, then she wants to undo her bodice, then she wants to put it on, and I'm sent onto the balcony. Sometimes she actually does what she says she's going to do, but mostly she just keeps lying on the sofa without stirring. I used often to pull the curtain aside a little and peep through, but since Delamarche on one such occasion—I know he didn't want to, he only did it because Brunelda asked him—struck me several times in the face with his whip—do you see the marks?—I no longer dare to peep through. And so I lie here on the balcony and my only pleasure is eating. The day before yesterday, when I was lying here all by myself in the evening, I was still wearing my elegant clothes which I unfortunately lost in your hotel—those brutes! tearing the expensive clothes off one's body!—so as I was lying all by myself and looking down through the railings of the balustrade, I felt so sad and I began to cry. Then, as it happened, though I didn't notice at first, Brunelda came out to me in her red dress—that's the one that suits her best of all—looked at me for a bit, and finally said: "Robinson, darling, why are you weeping?" Then she lifted her dress and wiped my eyes with the hem. Who knows what else she might have done if Delamarche hadn't called her and she hadn't had to go straight back into the room. Of course I thought it was my turn and I asked through the curtain if I could come into the room. And what do you think Brunelda said? "No!" she said and "Whatever are you thinking of?" she said.'

'Why on earth do you stay here if you get treated like that?' asked Karl.

'Sorry, Rossmann, but that isn't a very smart question,' answered Robinson. 'You'll stay here too, even if you're treated even worse. Anyway I don't get treated that badly.'

'No,' said Karl, 'I'm definitely going, this very evening if possible. I'm not staying with you.'

'How are you going to manage, for example, to go away this evening?' asked Robinson, who had cut the soft interior out of his loaf and was carefully dipping it in the oil from the sardine tin. 'How are you going to go away when you can't even go into the room?'

'Why can't we go in?'

'Well, until the bell has rung, we can't go in,' said Robinson, consuming the greasy bread with his mouth as wide open as it would go, while with one hand he caught the oil dripping from the bread in order to dip the remaining bread from time to time into the palm of this hand, which served as a reservoir. 'Everything here has become stricter. There used to be only a thin curtain there, you couldn't quite see through, but in the evening you could make out shadows. Brunelda didn't like that, so I had to turn one of her theatre gowns into a curtain and hang it up here instead of the old curtain. Now you can't see anything. Then I used always to be allowed to ask if I could go in and I got the answer "yes" or "no" depending on circumstances, but I probably overdid it and asked too often, Brunelda couldn't stand it—despite being so fat she's got very delicate health, she often has headaches and she has rheumatism in her legs almost all the time— and so it was settled that I couldn't ask any more but that when I can go in they press the bell on the table. It rings so loudly that it wakes even me from sleep—I used to have a cat here to keep me amused, it was so frightened by this ringing that it ran away and didn't come back. Anyway, it hasn't rung yet today—when it rings, you see, I'm not just allowed to go in, I've got to—and if it hasn't rung for so long, then it may be a very long time until it does.'

'Yes,' said Karl, 'but what applies to you needn't apply to me. Anyway, something like that only applies to a person who puts up with it.'

'But,' exclaimed Robinson, 'why ever shouldn't it apply to you as well? Of course it applies to you as well. Just wait here quietly with me until the bell rings. Then you can see if you can get away.'

'Why don't you go away from here? Just because Delamarche is your friend, or rather was? Is this a life? Wouldn't it be better in Butterford, where you originally wanted to go? Or even in California, where you've got friends.'

'Yes,' said Robinson, 'nobody could see it coming.' And before going on, he added: 'Cheers, Rossmann, old man,' and took a long draught from the perfume bottle. 'When you left us in that nasty way, we were in very bad shape. We couldn't get any work in the first few days, anyway Delamarche didn't want any work, he could have got some, but he always sent me in search of it, and I don't have any luck. He just drifted around, but it was already almost evening, he had only brought a lady's purse, it was very beautiful, made of pearls, he's now given it to Brunelda, but there was hardly anything in it. Then he said we should go round the flats begging, if you do that of course you can find lots of useful things, so we went begging, and to make it look better I sang outside the doors of the flats. And as Delamarche is always lucky, we were only standing in front of the second flat, a very expensive ground-floor flat, singing something at the door for the cook and the servant, when the lady who owns the flat, Brunelda, comes up the stairs. She must have been too tightly laced and couldn't get up those few steps. But how beautiful she looked, Rossmann! She was wearing a completely white dress and had a red parasol. You wanted to lick her all over. You wanted to drink her up. Oh God, oh God, she was beautiful. What a woman! Just tell me, how can there be such a woman? Of course the girl and the servant immediately ran towards her and almost carried her up the stairs. We were standing right and left of the door, saluting, that's the way they do it here. She stopped for a bit, because she was still out of breath, and now I don't quite know how it happened, I was so hungry I wasn't quite in my right mind and she was even more beautiful close to and enormously broad and because of a special bodice, I can show it to you in the chest of drawers, so firm everywhere—in short, I touched her a little on her bottom, but very gently you know, just touched her. Of course it's impossible for a beggar to touch a rich lady. I hardly touched her, but after all in the end I did touch her. Who knows how badly it might have ended if Delamarche hadn't given me a slap in the face, and such a slap that I immediately needed both my hands for my cheek.'

'What a lot you've been up to,' said Karl, quite entranced by the story, sitting on the floor. 'So that was Brunelda?'

'Why, yes,' said Robinson, 'that was Brunelda.'

'Didn't you once say she was a singer?' asked Karl.

'She's a singer all right and a great singer,' answered Robinson, rolling a great lump of sweets on his tongue and occasionally pushing a piece that was squeezed out of his mouth back with his fingers. 'But of course we didn't yet know that then, we only saw that she was a rich and very fine lady. She behaved as if nothing had happened and perhaps she hadn't felt anything, for I really had only tapped her with my fingertips. But she never took her eyes off Delamarche, who looked— he can do that—straight back into her eyes. Thereupon she said to him: "Come inside for a bit," and pointed into the flat with her parasol to show how Delamarche was to walk in front of her. Then they both went in and the servants locked the door behind them. They forgot all about me waiting outside and so I thought it wouldn't take long and sat down on the staircase to wait for Delamarche. But instead of Delamarche the servant came out and brought me a whole plate of soup, "that's Delamarche being thoughtful!" I said to myself. The servant stayed with me for a bit while I ate and told me something about Brunelda and I saw how important the visit to Brunelda might be for us. For Brunelda was a divorcée, she was very rich and was completely independent. Her former husband, a cocoa-manufacturer, still loved her, but she didn't want to hear anything from him. He often came into her flat, always dressed very elegantly, as though for a wedding—every word of this is true, I know him myself—but although the servant got a big bribe, he didn't dare ask Brunelda if she would receive him, for he had asked several times already, and every time Brunelda had thrown whatever she had to hand into his face. Once even her big hot-water-bottle which had just been filled, and it had knocked out one of his front teeth. Yes, Rossmann, just think!'

'How do you know the man?' asked Karl.

'He sometimes comes up here too,' said Robinson.

'Up here?' Karl was so astonished that he struck the floor gently with his hand.

'You may well be astonished,' continued Robinson, 'I was astonished myself when the servant told me that. Just think, when Brunelda wasn't at home, her husband got the servant to take him into her rooms and he always removed some small thing as a memento and always left something very expensive and fine for Brunelda and strictly forbade the servant to say who it was from. But once when he had brought something—this is what the servant told me and I believe it—positively priceless made of china, Brunelda must somehow have recognized it, and immediately threw it on the floor, stamped on it, spat on it, and did something else so that the servant was almost too disgusted to take it away.'

'What did her husband do to her?' asked Karl.

'I don't actually know,' said Robinson. 'But I don't think it was anything much, at least he himself doesn't know what it was. I've sometimes talked about it with him. He waits for me every day there at the street corner, when I come I have to tell him news, if I can't come he waits for half an hour and then goes away again. It was a good way for me to earn money on the side, for he pays for the news very handsomely, but since Delamarche has found out about it I've had to hand it all over to him, so I don't go there so often.'

'But what does her husband want?' asked Karl, 'What on earth can he want? He knows she doesn't want him.'

'Yes,' sighed Robinson, lighting a cigarette and blowing the smoke aloft while swinging his arms. Then he seemed to change his mind and said: 'What's that to me? All I know is he'd give a lot of money to lie here on the balcony like us.'

Karl stood up, leaned on the balustrade, and looked down at the street. The moon was already visible, but its light didn't penetrate to the depths of the alley. The alley, so empty by day, was thronged with people, especially in front of the gateways, they were all in slow, heavy motion, the men's shirt-sleeves and the women's bright dresses stood out faintly against the darkness, all their heads were uncovered. The many balconies all around were all occupied, families were sitting in the light of an electric lamp, depending on the size of the balcony, round a little table or just in a row of chairs, or at least they were poking their heads out of the rooms. The men were planted on their seats with their legs stretched out between the rails of the balustrades, reading newspapers that reached almost to the floor, or playing cards, apparently mute but striking the table hard, the women had their laps full of sewing and could only occasionally spare a quick glance for their surroundings or for the street, a weak blonde woman on the next balcony kept yawning and turning up her eyes while holding up in front of her mouth a piece of clothing that she was patching, even on the smallest balconies the children were managing to chase one another, which was very annoying for their parents. Inside many of the rooms there were gramophones emitting songs or orchestral music, nobody bothered much about this music, but occasionally the father of a family would give a sign and somebody would hurry into the room to put on a new record. At many windows one could see loving couples completely motionless, at one window opposite Karl such a couple were standing upright, the young man had put his arm round the girl and was squeezing her breast with his hand.

'Do you know any of the people next door?' Karl asked Robinson, who had got up too and, because he was shivering, had wrapped not only the sheet but also Brunelda's blanket round himself.

'Hardly anyone. That's the bad thing about my position,' said Robinson, pulling Karl closer in order to whisper in his ear, 'otherwise I wouldn't have much to complain of at the moment. Brunelda sold everything she had for Delamarche's sake and moved with all her wealth into this suburban flat, so that she can devote herself entirely to him without anyone disturbing her, and besides that was what Delamarche wanted too.'

'And she's dismissed her servants?' asked Karl.

'That's right,' said Robinson. 'How could the servants fit in here? Those servants are very demanding gentlemen. Once when Delamarche was with Brunelda he drove one such servant out of the room by slapping him in the face, one slap came after the next until the man was outside. Of course the other servants joined together with him and made a noise outside the door, then Delamarche came out (I wasn't a servant then but a guest, but I was with the servants) and asked: "What do you want?" The oldest servant, one Isidor, said in reply: "You've no right to speak to us, Madame is our mistress." As you can probably tell, they had a great respect for Brunelda. But Brunelda ran over to Delamarche without bothering about them, at that time she wasn't as heavy as she is now, and in front of all of them she hugged him, kissed him, and called him "dearest Delamarche". "And send those apes away," she said finally. Apes—that meant the servants, imagine how they looked. Then Brunelda pulled Delamarche's hand to the purse she wore on her belt, Delamarche put his hand inside it and began to pay the servants off, all Brunelda did to pay them was to stand there

with the purse open on her belt. Delamarche had to reach into it a lot,
for he handed out the money without counting and without checking
their demands. Finally he said: "Since you don't want to speak to me,
I'll just say to you in Brunelda's name: Get lost, this minute." So they
were dismissed, it led to a few court cases. Delamarche even once had
to appear in court, but I don't know the details. Only just after the
servants had gone, Delamarche said to Brunelda: "So you've got no
servants now?" She said: "But there's Robinson." Thereupon
Delamarche said, hitting me on the shoulder: "All right, you'll be our
servant." And Brunelda patted me on the cheek, if you get the chance,
Rossmann, let her pat you on the cheek, you'll be astonished at how
nice that is.'

'So you've become Delamarche's servant?' said Karl, summing up.

Robinson heard the pity implicit in Karl's question and answered:
'I'm a servant, but very few people notice. You yourself didn't know,
even though you've been with us for some time now. Why, you saw
how I was dressed when I was with you in the hotel last night. I was
wearing the best of the best, is that how servants dress? Only it's like
this, I'm not allowed out much, I always have to be on hand, there's
always something to do in the household. One person is simply not
enough for all the work. As you may have noticed, we have an awful
lot of things lying around in the room, whatever we couldn't sell when
we made our big move, we just took with us. Of course we could have
given it away, but Brunelda doesn't give anything away. Just think
how much work it took to get these things up the stairs.'

'Robinson, did you carry all that up here?' exclaimed Karl.

'Who else?' said Robinson. 'There was also an assistant, a lazy
brute, I had to do most of the work by myself. Brunelda stood down
below beside the car, Delamarche was up here saying where to put
things, and I kept on running between the two. It took two days, a
very long time, don't you think? But then you've no idea how many
things there are here in the room, the chests of drawers are full and all
the space behind the chests of drawers is crammed full, right up to
the ceiling. If they'd employed a couple of people to help transporting
them, it would all have been finished quite soon, but Brunelda
wouldn't entrust the job to anyone but me. That was very nice, but
I ruined my health for the rest of my life and what had I but my health.
If I exert myself even a little, I feel stabbing pains here and here and
here. Do you think those boys in the hotel, those little toads—what

else are they?—could ever have overcome me if I'd had my health? But no matter what may be wrong with me, I won't say a word to Delamarche and Brunelda, I shall work as long as I can, and when I can't work any more I shall lie down and die and only then, when it's too late, will they see that I was ill and that I worked myself to death in their service. Oh, Rossmann,' he said finally, drying his eyes on Karl's shirt-sleeve. After a while he said: 'Aren't you cold, you're only wearing your shirt.'

'Honestly, Robinson,' said Karl, 'you're always crying. I don't believe you're all that ill. You look perfectly healthy, but because you spend all your time lying on the balcony, you've imagined all sorts of things. You may sometimes have a stabbing pain in your chest, I have that too, so has everyone. If everyone were to cry at every trifle, the way you do, people would be crying on all the balconies.'

'I know better,' said Robinson, wiping his eyes now with the end of his blanket. 'The student living next door with our landlady who also cooked for us said to me the last time I brought back the crockery, "Listen, Robinson, aren't you ill?" I'm not allowed to talk to people, so I just put down the crockery and was about to go away. Then he came over to me and said: "Listen man, don't take things to extremes, you're ill." "Well, please tell me, what can I do," I asked. "That's your problem," he said, turning his back. The others sitting at the table laughed, we've got enemies everywhere here, so I chose to go away.'

'So you believe people who want to make a fool of you, and you don't believe people who mean well by you.'

'But I must know the state I'm in,' shouted Robinson indignantly, but immediately resumed crying.

'No, you don't know what's wrong with you. You ought to look for some proper work instead of being Delamarche's servant. For so far as I can tell from your stories and from what I've seen for myself, this isn't service but slavery. Nobody can stand that, there I believe you. But you think that because you're Delamarche's friend, you can't leave him. That's wrong, if he doesn't see what a miserable life you lead, you haven't got the slightest obligation towards him.'

'So you really think, Rossmann, that I'd get better if I gave up serving here.'

'Certainly,' said Karl.

'Certainly?' asked Robinson once more.

'Quite certainly,' said Karl, smiling.

'Then I could start getting better right away,' said Robinson, looking at Karl.

'How do you mean?' asked the latter.

'Well, because you're supposed to take over my work here,' answered Robinson.

'Who told you that?' asked Karl.

'It's an old plan. We've been talking about it for several days. It started when Brunelda bawled me out for not keeping the flat clean enough. Of course I promised to tidy everything up right away. But that's very hard. In my state, for example, I can't crawl everywhere to wipe away the dust, even in the middle of the room you can't move, so what's it like among the furniture and the stores. And if you want to clean everything carefully, then you have to push the bits of furniture away from their places, and how am I supposed to do that by myself? What's more, it would all have to be done very quietly, because Brunelda, who hardly ever leaves the room, mustn't be disturbed. So I did promise to clean everything, but in fact I didn't clean it. When Brunelda noticed that, she said to Delamarche that things couldn't go on that way and they'd have to take on an assistant. "I don't ever want you, Delamarche," she said, "to reproach me for not running the household properly. I'm not strong enough to do it myself, you do realize that, and Robinson isn't enough, when we started he was fresh and attended to everything, but now he's always tired and mostly sits in a corner. But a room with so many things in it as ours has doesn't keep itself tidy." Thereupon Delamarche thought about what could be done, because of course you can't take just anyone into such a household, not even on trial, because we're being watched from all sides. But as I'm a good friend of yours and had heard from Renell how hard you had to work in the hotel, I suggested you. Delamarche agreed right away, even though you'd been so cheeky to him that time, and of course I was very pleased at being able to do you such a good turn. You see, this job is just tailor-made for you. You're young, strong, and skilful, whereas I'm no longer good for anything. Only let me tell you that you haven't yet been taken on by any means, if Brunelda doesn't like you we've got no use for you. So do your best to please her, I'll take care of everything else.'

'And what will you do if I'm the servant here?' asked Karl, he felt quite free, the first alarm caused by Robinson's information was past. So Delamarche had nothing worse in mind than to make him his servant—if he had had anything worse in mind, the loose-mouthed Robinson would have been sure to give it away—but if things were like that, Karl was confident he could make his escape this very night. Nobody can be forced to take a job, And while Karl had previously been worried, after his dismissal from the hotel, about finding a suitable and if possible no humbler job soon enough to avoid starvation, he now felt that compared to the job intended for him here, which revolted him, any other job would be good enough, and even unemployment and hardship would be preferable to this job. But he didn't even try to explain this to Robinson, especially as Robinson's judgement was completely clouded by the hope that Karl would relieve him of his burden.

'Well,' said Robinson, accompanying his words with comfortable gestures—he had propped his elbows on the balustrade—'first I'll explain everything to you and show you the stores. You're educated and I'm sure you write a good hand. So you could begin by drawing up a list of all the things we've got. Brunelda's wanted that for a long time. If the weather's nice tomorrow morning, we'll ask Brunelda to sit on the balcony and meanwhile we'll be able to work in the room in peace and without disturbing her. For that, Rossmann, is the main thing you must keep in mind. On no account disturb Brunelda. She hears everything, probably it's because she's a singer that she has such sensitive ears. Say for example you roll the barrel of schnapps from behind the chests of drawers, it makes a noise because it's heavy and there are all sorts of things lying around so that you can't roll it out in a single movement. Say Brunelda is lying quietly on the sofa, catching flies, which bother her a great deal. So you think she isn't paying you any attention and you keep on rolling your barrel. She's still lying quietly. But at the moment when you least expect it and you're making less noise than before, she suddenly sits upright, strikes the sofa with both hands so you can't see her for dust—since we've been here I haven't dusted the sofa, I can't, she's always lying on it—and starts yelling frightfully, like a man, and goes on yelling like that for hours. The neighbours have forbidden her to sing, but nobody can forbid her to yell, she can't help yelling, besides it now happens only rarely, Delamarche and I have become very careful. It's done her a lot of harm, too. Once she fainted, and I—Delamarche happened to be away—had to fetch the student from next door, he sprinkled some liquid on her from a big bottle, and it worked, but this liquid had an unbearable smell, even now if you put your nose against the sofa, you can smell it. I'm sure the student is our enemy, like everyone else here, you must be on your guard against everybody and not get involved with anyone.'

'Why, Robinson,' said Karl, 'that's a hard service. A fine job you've recommended me for.'

'Don't worry,' said Robinson, shutting his eyes and shaking his head to dispel all possible worries on Karl's part, 'the job has advantages too that no other job can offer you. You're constantly close to a lady like Brunelda, you sometimes sleep in the same room with her, that offers you all sorts of extra amenities, as you can imagine. You'll be well paid, there's plenty of money around, I didn't get anything as a friend of Delamarche, it was only when I went out that Brunelda always gave me something, but of course you'll be paid, like any other servant. Anyway, that's all you are. But the most important thing for you is that I'll make your job a lot easier. At first, of course, I won't do anything, so that I get better, but as soon as I'm even a little better, you can count on me. I'll keep the personal attendance on Brunelda for myself, doing her hair and helping her dress, except when Delamarche does it, So you'll only have to take care of cleaning the room, going shopping, and doing the hard domestic jobs.'

'No, Robinson,' said Karl, 'all that doesn't tempt me.'

'Don't be a fool, Rossmann,' said Robinson, very close to Karl's face, 'don't throw away this fine opportunity. Where else are you going to get a job? Who knows you? Who do you know? The two of us, two men who've been through a lot and have plenty of experience, spent weeks running around without finding work. It isn't easy, in fact it's desperately hard.'

Karl nodded, surprised at how sensibly Robinson could talk. For him, to be sure, this advice didn't count, he couldn't stay here, in the big city there was sure to be a niche for him, throughout the night, as he knew, all the hotels were filled to bursting, services were needed for the guests, he now had experience in that area, he would fit quickly and inconspicuously into some concern. On the ground floor of the building right opposite there was a small hotel, from which noisy music could be heard. The main entrance was covered only by a big yellow curtain that sometimes, moved by a breeze, fluttered far out into the street. Otherwise the street had become much quieter. Most of the balconies were dark, only in the distance could the occasional light be seen here or there, but no sooner did you rest your gaze on it than the people there got up, and as they crowded back into their flats a man seized the electric lamp and, as the last person remaining behind on the balcony, took a quick look at the street and turned out the light.

'Now the night is beginning,' said Karl to himself, 'if I stay here any longer, I'll belong to them.' He turned round in order to pull aside the curtain in front of the door into the flat. 'What do you want?' said Robinson, placing himself between Karl and the flat. 'I want to go,' said Karl, 'leave me alone, leave me alone!' 'You're not going to disturb them,' exclaimed Robinson, 'what on earth are you thinking of.' And he put his arms round Karl's neck, hung on him with his entire weight, enfolded Karl's legs in his own, and thus in a moment pulled him down to the ground. But Karl had learnt a bit of fighting among the lift-boys, and so he shoved his fist under Robinson's chin, but gently so as not to hurt him. Robinson quickly and ruthlessly thrust his knee into Karl's stomach, but then, both hands on his chin, began to howl so loudly that a man on the next-door balcony clapped his hands wildly and ordered 'Quiet'. Karl lay still for a little in order to get over the pain caused by Robinson's blow. He only turned his face towards the curtain, which was hanging quietly and heavily in front of the evidently darkened room. There no longer seemed to be anyone in the room, perhaps Delamarche had gone out with Brunelda and Karl already had complete freedom. Robinson, who was really behaving like a watchdog, had finally been shaken off.

Then, from the street, distant drum-beats and trumpet-calls became audible. Many people's separate shouts soon gathered into a general yelling. Karl turned his head and saw all the balconies coming back to life. Slowly he got to his feet, he could not quite stand upright and had to lean heavily against the balustrade. Down below on the pavements young lads were marching with big strides, arms outstretched, caps in their raised hands, their faces turned backward. The roadway was still free. Some people were waving lanterns attached to long poles and swathed in yellowish smoke. The drummers and trumpeters in broad ranks were just coming into the light, astonishing Karl by their number, when he heard voices behind him, turned round, and saw Delamarche lifting the heavy curtain and then Brunelda emerging from the darkness of the room, in her red dress, with a lace shawl over her shoulders, a black cap over her hair which had probably not been groomed but merely piled up with its ends visible here and there. In her hand she was holding a small fan unfolded, but pressing it closely against herself instead of moving it.

Karl squeezed sideways along the balustrade to make room for the two. Surely nobody would force him to stay here, and even if Delamarche were to try, Brunelda would let him go as soon as he asked. After all, she couldn't stand him, his eyes frightened her. But when he took a step towards the door, she noticed it all the same and said: 'Where are you off to, my boy?' Karl paused under the stern gaze of Delamarche and Brunelda pulled him towards her. 'Don't you want to watch the procession down there?' she said, pushing him in front of her towards the balustrade. 'Do you know what it's about?' Karl heard her say behind him, as he tried involuntarily and unsuccessfully to escape from her pressure. He looked sorrowfully down at the street, as though it held the cause of his sorrow.

Delamarche at first stood behind Brunelda with his arms folded, then he ran into the room and brought Brunelda the opera-glasses. Down below, behind the musicians, the main part of the procession had appeared. On the shoulders of a gigantic man sat a gentleman of whom, at this height, nothing could be seen but his dully shimmering bald pate, above which he was holding his top hat raised high as he constantly waved to the crowd. All round him wooden placards were evidently being carried, which, seen from the balcony, appeared completely white; they were so arranged that they seemed to lean from all sides against the gentleman who towered in their midst. As everything was in motion, this wall of placards kept disintegrating and then resuming its shape. In a further circle round the gentleman, the whole breadth of the street, although, so far as one could tell in the darkness, only an insignificant length, was filled with the gentleman's supporters, who were all clapping their hands and proclaiming what was probably the gentleman's name, a very short but unintelligible name, in a long-drawn-out chant. Some people, skilfully distributed throughout the crowd, had automobile headlamps with an extremely powerful light, which they slowly shone up and down the houses on either side of the street. At Karl's height the light was not a nuisance, but on the lower balconies the people it shone on could be seen hastily putting their hands over their eyes.

Delamarche, at Brunelda's request, asked the people on the next-door balcony what the event was all about. Karl was a little curious to see whether and how they would answer him. And in fact Delamarche had to ask three times without getting an answer. He was already bending dangerously far over the balustrade, Brunelda was stamping her foot slightly in her annoyance at the neighbours, Karl could feel her knee. At last some kind of answer was given, but at the same time everyone on these balconies, which were crammed full of people, burst into loud laughter. Thereupon Delamarche yelled something across, so loudly that if there hadn't been so much noise at that moment in the entire street, everyone all round would have pricked up their ears in astonishment. At any rate it had the effect of putting an unnaturally sudden end to the laughter.

'A new judge is being elected tomorrow in our district, and the man they're carrying down there is a candidate,' said Delamarche, returning to Brunelda in complete calm. 'No!' he exclaimed, patting Brunelda caressingly on the back, 'we no longer have any idea what's going on in the world.'

'Delamarche,' said Brunelda, coming back to the behaviour of the neighbours, 'how I'd like to move, if it weren't such an effort. But I'm afraid it's beyond my strength.' And with great sighs, restlessly and absent-mindedly, she fiddled with Karl's shirt, while he kept trying as unobtrusively as possible to push away those fat little hands, which he easily managed, for Brunelda was not thinking about him, she was preoccupied with quite different thoughts.

But Karl too soon forgot about Brunelda and tolerated the burden of her arms on his shoulders, for the proceedings in the street claimed too much of his attention. On the orders of a small group of gesticulating men who marched just in front of the candidate and whose conversations must have had a special significance, for from all sides faces could be seen inclined towards them and listening intently, an unexpected halt was made in front of the hotel. One of these men in charge raised his hand and made a sign intended for both the crowd and the candidate. The crowd fell silent and the candidate, who made several attempts to stand upright on his bearer's shoulders but always fell back into his seat, delivered a little speech, during which he waved his top hat to and fro at immense speed. This could be seen quite clearly, for during his speech all the headlamps had been directed towards him, so that he was in the midst of a bright star.

Now one could also discern the interest that the whole street was taking in the affair. On the balconies occupied by the candidate's supporters, people joined in chanting his name while stretching their hands far out over the balustrades and clapping with machine-like regularity. On the rest of the balconies, which were actually the majority, a powerful counter-chant began, but it was not uniform, since the supporters of various candidates were involved. Accordingly all the opponents of the candidate present joined in a general whistling, and even gramophones were started up again. Between the individual balconies political disputes were fought out with an excitement intensified by the late hour of the night. Most people were already in their pyjamas and had only thrown on overcoats, the women were wrapped in big, dark shawls, the neglected children clambered about alarmingly on the protective railings of the balconies and emerged in ever greater numbers from the dark rooms in which they had been sleeping. Here and there unidentifiable objects were thrown by particularly enraged people at their opponents, sometimes reaching their object but mostly falling down into the street, where they often provoked howls of fury. Whenever the noise got too much for the leading men down below, the drummers and trumpeters would be ordered to intervene, and their interminable din, produced with their full strength, would drown out all the human voices right up to the rooftops. And they always stopped quite suddenly—you could hardly believe it—whereupon the crowd in the street, who had obviously been drilled, would bawl their party chant into the sudden universal silence—in the light of the headlamps each person's wide-open mouth was visible—until their opponents, having now regained their presence of mind, would yell ten times as loudly as before from all the balconies and windows, reducing the party below, after its brief victory, to a silence which, at least at this height, seemed total.

'How do you like it, my boy?' asked Brunelda, who was turning from side to side just behind Karl in order to see as much as possible through the opera-glass. Karl answered only by nodding. In passing he noticed Robinson eagerly telling Delamarche various things, obviously about Karl's conduct, to which Delamarche, however, seemed to attach little importance, for he kept trying to push Robinson aside with his left hand, while embracing Brunelda with his right. 'Don't you want to look through the glass?' asked Brunelda, tapping Karl on the chest to show that she meant him.

'I can see enough,' said Karl.

'Do try,' she said, 'you'll see better.'

'I have good eyes,' answered Karl, 'I can see everything.' He felt it was not kindness but a nuisance when she put the glass close to his eyes, and indeed she now said nothing but the one word 'You!', melodiously but menacingly. And Karl now had the glass in front of his eyes and could indeed see nothing.

'I can't see anything,' he said, trying to get rid of the glass, but she held onto the glass tightly, and now that his head was embedded on her bosom he could move it neither back nor sideways.

'Now you'll see all right,' she said, turning the screw of the glass.

'No, I still can't see anything,' said Karl, reflecting that without wanting to he had indeed freed Robinson from his burden, for Brunelda's insufferable whims were now being inflicted on him.

'Whenever will you see anything?' she said, continuing—Karl's whole face was now within her heavy breathing—to turn the screw. 'Now?' she asked.

'No, no, no!' exclaimed Karl, though now he could indeed, though only very indistinctly, make out everything. But just then Brunelda had some business with Delamarche, she held the glass only loosely before Karl's face and Karl was able, without her paying much attention, to look down under the glass at the street. Later she stopped insisting on having her own way and used the glass herself.

From the hotel down below a waiter had emerged and, hurrying to and fro on the threshold, was taking orders from the leaders. One could see him stretching out in order to survey the interior of the hotel and summon as many servants as possible. During these preparations, evidently for a great round of free drinks, the candidate never stopped speaking. His bearer, the gigantic man who served him alone, turned slightly after every few sentences, so that the speech should be audible to every part of the crowd. The candidate stayed for the most part in a crouching position, trying by means of jerky movements with his free hand and with the top hat in the other to give his words the greatest possible impact. Sometimes, however, at almost regular intervals an impulse would flash through him, he would rise to his feet with arms outspread, no longer addressing a group but everyone present, he would speak to the inhabitants of the houses right up to the top floors, and yet it was perfectly clear that even on the lowest floors nobody could hear him, indeed that, if they had had a choice, nobody would have wanted to listen, for every window and every balcony was occupied by at least one yelling speaker. Meanwhile some waiters brought from the hotel a board, the size of a billiard-table, covered with full, gleaming glasses. The leaders organized the distribution, which took the form of a march past the hotel door. But although the glasses on the board kept being refilled, they were not sufficient for the crowd, and two rows of bartenders, to right and left of the board, had to slip through and supply the crowd with additional drinks. The candidate had of course stopped speaking and was using the pause to restore his strength. At a distance from the crowd and the harsh light his bearer was slowly carrying him to and fro, and only a few of his closest supporters were accompanying him and calling up to him.

'Just look at the boy,' said Brunelda, 'he's so busy looking, he's forgotten where he is.' And taking Karl by surprise, she turned his face with both hands towards her, so that she was looking into his eyes. But it lasted only a moment, for Karl immediately shook off her hands, and, annoyed at not being left in peace even for a short time and simultaneously anxious to go onto the street and see everything at close quarters, he now tried with all his strength to free himself from Brunelda's pressure and said:

'Please let me go.'

'You're staying with us,' said Delamarche, without taking his gaze from the street, only stretching out a hand to prevent Karl from going.

'Just leave him,' said Brunelda, warding off Delamarche's hand, 'he'll stay all right.' And she pressed Karl still harder against the balustrade, he would have had to fight with her in order to free himself from her. And even if he had managed that, what would he have achieved? Delamarche was standing on his left, Robinson had taken up a position on his right, he was a regular prisoner.

'Just be glad we don't throw you out,' said Robinson, tapping Karl with the hand he had inserted under Brunelda's arm.

'Throw him out?' said Delamarche. 'You don't throw out a runaway thief, you hand him over to the police. And that can be done first thing tomorrow morning, if he isn't quiet.'

From that moment on Karl no longer took any pleasure in the spectacle below. Only under compulsion, because Brunelda was stopping him from standing upright, did he bend a little over the balustrade. Full of his own worries, he looked absent-mindedly at the people below, who were walking up to the hotel door in groups of about twenty, seizing glasses, turning round, and brandishing these glasses in the direction of the candidate, who was now left to himself; they shouted a party slogan, emptied the glasses, and put them back on the board with a noise that must have been deafening but was inaudible at this height, in order to make room for another impatient and noisy group. At the leaders' orders the band which had hitherto been playing in the hotel had now come into the street, their big wind instruments shone amid the dark crowd, but their playing was almost drowned in the universal uproar. The street, at least on the side where the hotel was situated, was now filled with people far and wide. From the upper end, from which Karl had come that morning in the automobile, they were streaming down, from the lower end, from the bridge, they were running up, and even the people in the houses had been unable to resist the temptation to intervene directly in these affairs, on the balconies and at the windows there was almost nobody left but women and children, while the men were thronging out of the doorways down below. Now, however, the music and the hospitality had achieved their purpose, the assembly was sufficiently large, a leader flanked by two headlamps waved for the music to stop, uttered a loud whistle, and now the bearer, who had slightly lost his way, could be seen hurriedly bringing the candidate along a path lined by supporters.

No sooner had he reached the hotel door than the candidate, in the light of the headlamps which were now being held in a tight circle round him, began his new speech. But now everything was much more difficult than before, his bearer no longer had the slightest freedom of movement, the throng was too great. His nearest supporters, who had previously tried to strengthen the effect of the candidate's speech by all possible means, now had trouble keeping close to him, about twenty managed with their utmost efforts to hold onto his bearer. But even this strong man could no longer take a single step as he wished, to influence the crowd by definite movements or by advancing or retreating was now unthinkable. The crowd was drifting without a plan, one person was leaning on the next, nobody could stand upright any more, the opponents seemed to have greatly increased their number through reinforcements, the bearer had been standing for a long time near the hotel door but now, apparently without resistance, he allowed himself to be driven up and down the street, the candidate was continually speaking, but it was no longer clear whether he was expounding his programme or calling for help, and unless all

the signs were deceptive an opposing candidate had also turned up, if
not several, for here and there in a sudden flare of light one could see
a man lifted by the crowd, with pale face and clenched fists, giving a
speech that was greeted by shouts from many voices.

'What's happening there?' asked Karl, turning in breathless
confusion to his guards.

'How excited the boy is,' said Brunelda to Delamarche, taking Karl
by the chin in order to pull his head towards her. But Karl hadn't
wanted that and he shook himself, rendered quite ruthless by the proceedings in the street, so hard that Brunelda not only let go of him
but drew back and set him completely free. 'Now you've seen enough,'
she said, evidently annoyed by Karl's behaviour, 'go into the room,
make the beds, and get everything ready for the night.' She stretched
out her hand towards the room. That was the direction that Karl had
been wanting to take for several hours, he uttered not a word of contradiction. Then the crash of much shattered glass was heard from
the street. Karl could not control himself and jumped quickly to the
balustrade for one more glimpse. An attack by the opposing side, perhaps a decisive one, had been successful, the supporters' headlamps,
whose powerful light had made at least the main proceedings visible
to the public and thus kept things within certain bounds, had all been
smashed simultaneously, the candidate and his bearer were now enveloped by the general dim light which, being diffused so suddenly, had
the effect of total darkness. Nobody could have said even approximately where the candidate now was, and the deceptive effect of the
darkness was further increased by the sudden beginning of a broad,
uniform chanting that was approaching from the lower end, from the
bridge.

'Didn't I tell you what you've got to do,' said Brunelda, 'hurry up.
I'm tired,' she added, stretching her arms aloft so that her bosom
bulged out even more than usual. Delamarche, who still had his arms
round her, pulled her with him into a corner of the balcony. Robinson
followed them in order to push to one side the remains of his meal
which were still lying there.

Karl had to make use of this favourable opportunity, this was no
time to gaze down, he'd see quite enough of the proceedings on the
street from down below, and more than from up here. In two bounds
he had hurried through the room with its reddish lighting, but the
door was locked and the key had been removed. It had to be found,

but who could find a key in this mess, let alone in the short spell of precious time available to Karl. He should have been on the stairs by now, running and running. And now he was looking for the key! Looking for it in all the drawers within reach, rummaging on the table where all sorts of crockery, napkins, and a piece of embroidery that had barely been begun were lying around, he was tempted by an armchair on which there was a tangled heap of old articles of clothing in which the key might be lurking but could never be found, and finally threw himself onto the sofa, which did indeed have a nasty smell, in order to feel for the key in all its corners and folds. Then he gave up searching and paused in the middle of the room. Brunelda was sure to have fastened the key to her belt, he said to himself, there were so many things hanging there, searching was pointless.

And Karl blindly seized two knives and inserted them between the wings of the door, one above, one below, in order to attack it at two points distant from each other. No sooner had he tugged at the knives than of course the blades broke. That was just what he wanted, the stumps that he could now force in harder would stick all the more firmly. And now he tugged with all his might, his arms spread out wide, his legs braced far apart, groaning but keeping a close eye on the door. In the long run it wouldn't be able to resist, he could tell that to his pleasure from the clearly audible loosening of the bolts, the longer it took the better it was, after all the lock shouldn't leap open or else people on the balcony would notice, instead the lock should slacken very slowly, and that was what Karl was working towards with the utmost care, his eyes coming ever closer to the lock.

'Just look,' he heard the voice of Delamarche. All three were standing in the room, the curtain was already closed behind them, Karl must have failed to hear them coming, on seeing them his hands fell from the knives. But he had no time to say a word of explanation or apology, for in an outburst of rage that far exceeded the present occasion Delamarche—his loose dressing-gown formed a wide outline in the air—leapt at Karl. Karl evaded the attack at the last moment, he could have pulled the knives out of the door and used them to defend himself, but he didn't, instead, bending down and jumping up, he reached for the broad collar of Delamarche's dressing-gown, struck it upwards, then pulled it still further up—the dressing-gown was much too big for Delamarche—and was now successfully holding Delamarche by his head, who, taken by surprise, first blindly waved his hands and only after a while, but without the full effect, struck Karl's back with his fists, Karl having, to protect his face, thrown himself onto Delamarche's chest. Karl could stand the blows from his fists, even though he writhed in pain and even though the blows kept getting harder, but why wouldn't he have stood them, for he had the prospect of victory in sight. His hands on Delamarche's head, his thumbs probably right over his eyes, he was pulling him into the most chaotic pile of furniture and was also trying with his toes to twine the dressing-gown cord round Delamarche's feet and thus trip him up.

However, as he was obliged to concentrate entirely on Delamarche, especially as he could feel his resistance constantly growing and this hostile body was opposing him with ever greater sinewy strength, he quite forgot that he and Delamarche were not alone. But he was reminded of it only too soon, for suddenly his feet gave way, because Robinson, who had flung himself down on the floor behind him, was forcing them apart while yelling. Groaning, Karl let go of Delamarche, who took another step back. Brunelda was standing with legs apart and knees bent in her full bulk in the middle of the room and following the proceedings with shining eyes. As though she were actually taking part in the fight, she breathed deeply, took aim with her eyes, and gradually raised her fists. Delamarche pushed his collar down, had his sight unimpeded, and now of course there was no longer a fight, only a punishment. He seized Karl by the front of his collar, almost lifted him off the floor, and hurled him, not even looking at him out of contempt, so hard against a chest of drawers a couple of steps away, that in the first moment Karl thought the stabbing pains in his back and head caused by crashing against the chest of drawers were the direct effect of Delamarche's hand. 'You ruffian,' he heard Delamarche shouting loudly in the darkness that arose before his shuddering eyes. And in the exhaustion in which he sank down in front of the chest of drawers, the words 'Just you wait' rang only faintly in his ears.

When he regained his senses, everything around him was dark, it must be late at night, from the balcony a faint shimmer of moonlight penetrated under the curtain into the room. The calm breathing of the three sleepers was audible, much the loudest was Brunelda's, she was panting in her sleep as she sometimes did while talking; it was not easy, however, to tell exactly where the individual sleepers were, the whole room was filled with the sound of their breathing. Only after he had examined his surroundings a little did Karl think about himself and then he got a bad fright, for although he felt bent and stiff with pain, he still hadn't thought of receiving a severe injury with loss of blood. Now, however, he felt a weight on his head, and his whole face, his throat, his chest under his shirt, were wet as though with blood. He must get to the light to see exactly what state he was in, perhaps the beating had crippled him for life, in that case Delamarche would no doubt be willing to let him go, but what was he to do then, for then he really would have no prospects left. The lad in the gateway whose nose had been eaten away came to his mind and for a moment he put his hands over his face.

He then turned automatically towards the door and groped his way to it on all fours. Soon he managed with his fingertips to feel a boot and then a leg. That was Robinson, who else would sleep in his boots? He had been ordered to lie across the door in order to prevent Karl from escaping. But didn't people know the state Karl was in? For the time being he had no intention of escaping, he just wanted to get to the light. So if he couldn't get out the door, he must go onto the balcony.

He found the table evidently at a quite different place from where it had been that evening, the sofa, which Karl of course approached very cautiously, was, surprisingly enough, empty, whereas in the middle of the room he came upon clothes, blankets, curtains, cushions, and carpets, squashed together but piled high. At first he thought it was only a small heap such as he had found that evening on the sofa, and it might have rolled to the ground, but to his astonishment he noticed as he crawled further that there was a whole cartload of such things, which had probably been removed for the night from the chests of drawers where they were kept during the day. He crawled round the heap and soon realized that the whole thing formed a kind of bed, with Delamarche and Brunelda, as he established by extremely cautious groping, reposing on its summit.

Now that he knew where everyone was sleeping, he hurried to get onto the balcony. It was a quite different world in which, beyond the curtain, he now quickly rose to his feet. In the fresh night air, in the light of the full moon, he walked several times up and down the balcony. He looked at the street, which was quite silent, music was still audible from the hotel, but only quietly, outside the door a man was sweeping the pavement, in the street, where that evening amid the universal wild uproar the yelling of an electoral candidate could not be distinguished from a thousand other voices, one could now distinctly hear the scraping of the broom on the paving-stones.

The sound of a table being moved on the next-door balcony caught Karl's attention, somebody was sitting there and studying. It was a young man with a small goatee beard which, as he read, accompanying his reading with rapid lip movements, he kept twisting. He was sitting, his face towards Karl, at a small table covered with books, he had taken the electric lamp from the wall, wedged it between two big books, and was now all lit up by its harsh light.

'Good evening,' said Karl, as he thought he had noticed the young man looking across at him.

But that must have been a mistake, for the young man seemed not to have noticed him at all, put his hand over his eyes to screen off the light and establish who had suddenly spoken to him, and then, as he could still see nothing, raised the electric lamp in order to throw some light also on the next-door balcony.

'Good evening,' he too said, looked sharply across for a moment, and then added: 'and what else?'

'Am I disturbing you?' asked Karl.

'Sure, sure,' said the man, putting the electric lamp back in its previous place.

These words were certainly a rejection of any contact, but Karl still did not leave the corner of the balcony in which he was closest to the man. He watched silently as the man read his book, turned the pages, occasionally looked something up in another book, which he seized with lightning speed, and often made notes in an exercise-book, always lowering his face surprisingly close to it.

Could this man be a student? He looked just as if he were studying. In much the same way—it was a long time ago now—Karl had sat at his parents' table at home and done his homework, while his father read the paper or made ledger entries and answered letters for a club and his mother occupied herself with sewing, pulling the thread high up out of the fabric. In order not to bother his father, Karl had placed only his exercise-book and his writing materials on the table, while he had arranged the books he needed on chairs to his right and left. How silent it had been there! How rarely did strangers enter that room! Even as a small child Karl had always enjoyed watching his mother, as evening approached, lock the door of their flat with her key. She had no idea that Karl had now reached the point of trying to break open other people's doors with knives.

And what had been the point of all his studying! He'd forgotten everything; if there had been any question of continuing his studies here, he'd have found it very hard. He remembered how he had once been ill at home for a month—what effort it had cost him to find his way back into his interrupted course of learning. And now, apart from the textbook of English business correspondence, it was so long since he'd read a book.

'You, young man,' Karl heard himself suddenly being addressed, 'couldn't you stand somewhere else? The way you stare across is terribly distracting. At two in the morning one can surely expect to be able to work on the balcony without being disturbed. Do you want something from me?'

'Are you studying?' asked Karl.

'Yes, yes,' said the man, using the short time lost for learning to arrange his books in a new order.

'Then I won't disturb you,' said Karl, 'I'm going back into the room anyway. Good night.'

The man did not even answer, after the removal of this distraction he had, with a sudden decision, resumed studying and was resting his heavy forehead in his right hand.

Then Karl, just in front of the curtain, remembered why he had actually come out here, he didn't know what state he was in. What was weighing so heavily on his head? He reached up and was astonished, it was not a blood-stained injury, as he had feared in the darkness of the room, it was only a turban-like bandage that was still damp. Judging from the remnants of lace hanging down here and there, it had been torn from an old piece of Brunelda's underclothes, and Robinson must have wrapped it hastily round Karl's head. Only he had forgotten to wring it out, and so while Karl had been unconscious all the water had run down his face and under his shirt and had given Karl such a fright.

'Are you still there?' asked the man, blinking across.

'Now I really am going,' said Karl, 'I just wanted to look at something here, inside the room it's completely dark.'

'Who on earth are you?' said the man, putting his pen-holder in the book open in front of him and coming over to the balustrade. 'What's your name? How do you come to be with those people?

Have you been here long? What do you want to look at? Turn on your electric lamp so that I can see you.'

Karl did so, but, before he answered, pulled the curtains over the door more closely together, so that those inside could not notice anything. 'Forgive me,' he then said in a whisper, 'for speaking so softly. If those people inside hear me, there will be another row.'

'Another?' asked the man.

'Yes,' said Karl, 'only this evening I had a big fight with them. I must have a frightful bruise.' And he felt the back of his head.

'What kind of fight was that?' asked the man, adding, as Karl did not answer immediately: 'You needn't worry about confiding in me whatever you've got against those gentry. I hate all three of them, you see, and especially your Madame. Besides, I'd be surprised if they hadn't already set you against me. My name's Josef Mendel and I'm a student.'

'Yes,' said Karl, 'they have already told me about you, but they didn't say anything bad. You once treated Madame Brunelda, didn't you?'

'That's right,' said the student with a laugh, 'does the sofa still smell of it?'

'Oh yes,' said Karl.

'I'm glad,' said the student, running his hand through his hair. 'And why do they give you bruises?'

'It was a quarrel,' said Karl, pondering how to explain it to the student. Then he interrupted himself and said: 'But aren't I disturbing you?'

'First of all,' said the student, 'you've already disturbed me, and unfortunately I'm so nervous that it takes me a long time to find my place again. Since you started your walks on the balcony, I haven't been able to get on with studying. Second of all, I always take a break around three o'clock. So just tell me your story. I'm interested, too.'

'It's quite simple,' said Karl. 'Delamarche wants me to be his servant. But I don't want to. I'd sooner have gone away this very evening. He wouldn't let me, locked the door, I wanted to break it open, and that started the scuffle. I'm unhappy at still being here.'

'Have you got another job?' asked the student.

'No,' said Karl, 'but I don't care about that, if only I were out of here.'

'Just listen,' said the student, 'you don't care about that?' And both were silent for a while.

'Why don't you want to stay with these people?' the student then asked.

'Delamarche is a bad man,' said Karl, 'I know him from the past. I once spent a day tramping alongside him and I was glad when I was no longer with him. And now I'm supposed to become his servant?'

'If all servants were as picky about their masters as you!' said the student, apparently smiling. 'Look, during the day I'm a salesman, the lowest grade of salesman, more a messenger-boy in Montly's department store. There's no doubt this Montly is a scoundrel, but that doesn't trouble me, I'm only angry at being so badly paid. So learn from my example.'

'What?' said Karl. 'You're a salesman by day and at night you study?'

'Yes,' said the student, 'there's no other way. I've already tried everything, but this way of life is still the best. Years ago I was only a student, by day and night, you know, but I almost starved to death, I slept in a dirty old hovel and in the suit I had then I didn't venture into the lecture-halls. But that's past.'

'But when do you sleep?' asked Karl, looking at the student in amazement.

'Ah, sleep!' said the student, 'I'll sleep when I've finished my studies. For the time being I drink black coffee.' And he turned round, pulled out a big flask from under his table, poured black coffee from it into a small cup, and gulped it down as one hurriedly gulps medicine, in order to taste it as little as possible.

'A fine thing, black coffee,' said the student, 'a pity you're so far away that I can't give you a little.'

'I don't like black coffee,' said Karl.

'Me neither,' said the student, with a laugh. 'But what could I do without it? If it wasn't for the black coffee, Montly wouldn't keep me on for a moment. I always say Montly, though of course he has no idea that I even exist. To be exact, I've no idea how I would behave in the shop if I didn't have a flask as big as this one always ready in my counter, for I've never dared to stop drinking coffee, but believe you me, I'd soon lie down behind the counter and sleep. Unfortunately people have an inkling of that, they call me "Black Coffee" there, which is a stupid joke and has undoubtedly hindered my progress.'

'And when will you finish your studies?' asked Karl.

'It's a slow business,' said the student, bowing his head. He left the balustrade and sat down again at his table; propping his elbows on his open book, running his hands through his hair, he then said: 'It could take one or two more years.'

'I wanted to study as well,' said Karl, as though this fact entitled him to even greater confidence than the student, now silent, had shown towards him.

'Well,' said the student, and it wasn't clear whether he was again reading his book or only looking into it absent-mindedly, 'be glad you've given up studying. For years now I've really only been studying because, having started, I won't stop. It gives me little satisfaction and even less in the way of future prospects. What sort of prospects could I expect! America is full of phoney doctors.'

'I wanted to become an engineer,' said Karl hurriedly to the student, who now seemed completely inattentive.

'And now you're to be these people's servant,' said the student, glancing up, 'of course you find that painful.'

This conclusion drawn by the student was, to be sure, a misunderstanding but perhaps Karl could use it to get the student's help. He therefore asked: 'Couldn't I also get a job in a department store?'

This question drew the student completely away from his book; the idea that he could help Karl in applying for a job did not occur to him. 'Try,' he said, 'or better, don't try. Getting my job with Montly's is the biggest achievement of my life so far. If I had to choose between studying and my job, of course I'd choose the job. All my efforts are directed at not having to face such a choice.'

'It's so difficult to get a job there,' said Karl, mainly to himself.

'What are you thinking of,' said the student, 'it's easier to become a district judge here than a doorkeeper at Montly's.'

Karl was silent. This student, who was so much more experienced than he was, who hated Delamarche for some reason unknown to Karl, yet who certainly wished Karl no harm, couldn't say a word to encourage Karl to leave Delamarche. And he had no idea of the threat to Karl from the police, from which only Delamarche offered him any protection.

'You saw the demonstration down there this evening? Didn't you? If one didn't know the situation, one would think this candidate, his name's Lobter, had some chance or was at least a possibility, wouldn't one?'

'I don't know anything about politics,' said Karl.

'That's a mistake,' said the student. 'But apart from that, you've got eyes and ears. The man certainly had friends and enemies, that can't have escaped you. And now just think, the man has in my opinion not the remotest chance of being elected. I happen to know all about him, somebody who lives with us knows him. He's not incompetent, and his political views and his political past would make him just the right judge for the district. But nobody imagines that he could be elected, he'll be defeated as spectacularly as anyone could be, he'll have thrown away his dollars on his election campaign, that will be all.'

Karl and the student looked at each other for a while in silence. The student nodded, smiled, and pressed a hand against his tired eyes.

'Well, aren't you going to bed?' he asked, 'I must get back to my studies. Look how much I still have to work through.' And he leafed quickly through half of a book, to give Karl an idea of the amount of work still awaiting him.

'Well then, good night,' said Karl, bowing.

'Come over and see us some time,' said the student, already sitting at his table again, 'of course, only if you feel like it. You'll always find a lot of people here. I've got time for you between nine and ten in the evenings.'

'So you advise me to stay with Delamarche?' asked Karl.

'Absolutely,' said the student, lowering his head to his books. It seemed as though it wasn't he who had said the word; it rang in Karl's ears as though uttered by a voice that was deeper than the student's. He went slowly to the curtain, threw one more glance at the student, who was now sitting quite motionless, enveloped by the immense darkness, in his pool of light, and slipped into the room. The united breathing of the three sleepers received him. He groped along the wall for the sofa, and when he had found it, he stretched out quietly on it as though it were his usual sleeping-place. As the student, who knew all about Delamarche and the situation here and was moreover an educated man, had advised him to stay here, he had for the time being no misgivings. He had no such lofty ambitions as the student, who knows if even at home he would have managed to complete his studies, and if it hardly seemed possible at home, nobody could expect him to do it here in a foreign country. However, his hopes of finding a job in which he could achieve something and have his achievement acknowledged were undoubtedly greater if for the time being he accepted the job as Delamarche's servant and in this secure position awaited a favourable opportunity. This street seemed to have many offices of the middling and lower order, which, in case of need, might not be too picky in choosing their staff. He would be glad, if necessary, to become a shop assistant, but after all it wasn't impossible that he might be employed for pure office work and would one day be an office worker sitting at his desk and gazing for a while, free from worries, through the open window, like the official he had seen this morning while marching through the courtyards. The consoling thought occurred to him as he closed his eyes that he was young and that Delamarche would one day set him free; this household didn't look as though it were designed to last for ever. But if Karl once had such an office job, he would attend to nothing but his office work, and not divide his energies like the student. If it should be necessary, he would also use the night for the office, which, in view of his scanty commercial experience, he would initially be expected to do anyway. He would think only of the interests of the company he had to serve, even those that other office employees would reject as unworthy of them. Good intentions crowded together in his head, as though his future boss were standing in front of the sofa and reading them from his face.

Amid such thoughts Karl fell asleep, disturbed only in his first drowsiness by a mighty groan from Brunelda, who was tossing and turning on her sleeping-place, seemingly tormented by uneasy dreams.

'GET up! Get up!' cried Robinson, almost before Karl had opened his eyes. The curtain over the door had not yet been pulled away, but the sunlight falling evenly through the gaps showed how late in the morning it already was. Robinson was dashing to and fro with worried looks, now he was carrying a towel, now a bucket of water, now items of underwear and clothing, and whenever he passed Karl he tried to encourage him to get up by nodding his head and showed by raising whatever he happened to be holding in his hand that this was the last time he would take any trouble on behalf of Karl, who of course on his very first morning could not understand the details of his duties.

But Karl soon saw whom Robinson was really serving. In a space that Karl had not yet seen, separated from the rest of the room by two chests of drawers, a great washing was in progress. Brunelda's head, her bare throat—her hair was over her face—and the nape of her neck could be seen over the chest of drawers, and Delamarche's hand was raised from time to time holding a bath-sponge which sprayed water all round and with which Brunelda was being washed and scrubbed. One could hear the brief orders Delamarche was giving to Robinson, who, the normal means of access being blocked, was obliged to hand things through a small aperture between a chest of drawers and a screen, and moreover, each time he handed something over, had to stretch his arm out fully and keep his face averted. 'The towel! The towel!' cried Delamarche. And no sooner had Robinson, alarmed by this order just as he was looking under the table for something else, put his head out from under the table, than it was: 'Where's the water, damn it,' and above the chest of drawers appeared Delamarche's furious face. Everything that, in Karl's opinion, was normally needed just once for getting washed and dressed, was here demanded and fetched many times in every possible sequence. On a small electric stove there was always a basin of water being heated, and Robinson repeatedly carried this heavy burden between his legs, which he kept far apart, over to the washing-room. With so much work to do it was understandable that he did not always strictly obey his orders and once, when another towel was demanded, simply took a shirt from the great sleeping-place in the middle of the room and threw it over the chest of drawers in a great ball.

But Delamarche too had to work hard, and perhaps that was why he was so irritated with Robinson—in his irritation he ignored Karl completely—because he himself could not satisfy Brunelda. 'Oh,' she screamed, and even the uninvolved Karl shuddered in fright, 'how you're hurting me! Go away! I'd rather wash myself than suffer like this! Now I can't raise my arm again. I feel quite ill, the way you squeeze me. I must have blue marks all over my back. Of course you won't tell me. Wait, I'll get Robinson or our boy to look at me. No, I won't, but do be a bit gentler. Be considerate, Delamarche, but I can repeat that every morning, you just aren't the least bit considerate. Robinson,' she then called suddenly, waving some lacy knickers above her head, 'come to my aid, look how I'm suffering, this torture is what he calls washing, that Delamarche. Robinson, Robinson, where are you, haven't you got a heart either?' Karl silently signalled with his finger to tell Robinson to go across, but Robinson shook his head with lowered eyes and a superior expression, he knew better. 'What are you thinking of?' said Robinson, bending down to Karl's ear, 'she doesn't mean it. I went across to her once, but never again. They both grabbed me and plunged me into the tub so that I nearly drowned. And Brunelda spent days reproaching me for being shameless and she kept saying: "It's a long time since you were in the bath with me" or "When are you coming to see me in my bath again?" It wasn't till I'd begged her several times on my knees that she finally stopped. I won't forget that.' And while Robinson was telling this story, Brunelda kept calling: 'Robinson! Robinson! Where on earth is that Robinson?'

Still, although nobody came to her aid and there was not even an answer—Robinson had sat down beside Karl and both were gazing silently at the chests of drawers, above which Brunelda's or Delamarche's head would appear from time to time—Brunelda still would not stop complaining loudly about Delamarche. 'But Delamarche,' she cried, 'I can't feel you washing me at all. Where have you put the sponge? Well, grab it! If only I could bend down, if only I could move! I'd soon show you how to wash somebody. Where are the days of my girlhood, when on my parents' estate I used to swim every morning in the Colorado, the most agile of all my girlfriends. And now! Whenever will you learn to wash me, Delamarche, you wave the sponge around, you try your hardest and I don't feel a thing.

When I said you shouldn't squeeze me till I was sore, I didn't mean I wanted to stand here and catch cold. I've a good mind to jump out of the tub and run away just as I am.'

But then she did not carry out this threat—which in any case she wouldn't have been capable of—Delamarche, fearing she might catch cold, seemed to have seized her and forced her into the tub, for there was a mighty splash in the water.

'That's what you're good at, Delamarche,' said Brunelda in a slightly lower voice, 'you keep sweet-talking me when you've made a mess of something.' Then she was quiet for a while. 'Now he's kissing her,' said Robinson, raising his eyebrows.

'What's the next job?' asked Karl. As he had now resolved to stay here, he wanted to attend to his duties immediately. He left Robinson, who did not answer, alone on the sofa and began to dismantle the bed which was still crushed by the weight of the sleepers during the long night, so that he could neatly fold up every item forming this mass, which had probably not been done for weeks.

'Take a look, Delamarche,' said Brunelda, 'I think they're destroying our bed. One has to think of everything, one never has any peace. You must be much stricter with these two, or else they'll do whatever they like.' 'That must be the boy who's so damned devoted to his work,' exclaimed Delamarche, probably trying to dive out of the washing-room, Karl let go of everything, but fortunately Brunelda said: 'Don't go away, Delamarche, don't go away. Oh, how hot the water is, one gets so tired. Stay with me, Delamarche.' Only now did Karl actually notice how the steam was continually rising from behind the chests of drawers.

Robinson put his hand to his cheek in alarm, as though Karl had done some mischief. 'Leave everything the way it was,' rang out Delamarche's voice, 'don't you know that Brunelda always rests for an hour after her bath? What a wretched household! Wait till I get my hands on you. Robinson, I expect you're dreaming again. You, you're the one I blame for everything that happens. You've got to restrain the boy, this household isn't run according to his fancies. When one wants something, one can't get anything from you, when there's nothing to be done, you're hard at work. Crawl into some corner and wait till you're needed.'

But in a moment all was forgotten, for Brunelda was whispering in a weary voice as though she were being deluged by the hot

water: 'The perfume! Bring the perfume!' 'The perfume!' yelled
Delamarche. 'Get moving.' Yes, but where was the perfume? Karl
looked at Robinson, Robinson looked at Karl. Karl saw that he had to
take charge of everything himself, Robinson had no idea where the
perfume was, he simply lay down on the floor and kept reaching with
both arms under the sofa, but brought out nothing but tangles of dust
and women's hair. Karl first hurried to the chest of drawers right next
to the door, but found nothing in its drawers except old novels in
English, magazines, and musical scores, and everything was crammed
so full that the drawers could not be closed once they had been
opened. 'The perfume!' Brunelda was meanwhile groaning. 'How
long it's taking! I wonder if I'll get my perfume today!' Given
Brunelda's impatience, Karl of course could not make a thorough
search anywhere, he had to rely on his first superficial impression.
The bottle wasn't in the washstand, on top of the washstand there
were only old bottles with medicines and ointments, everything else
must already have been taken into the washing-room. Perhaps the
bottle was in the drawer of the dinner-table. On the way to the dinner-
table, however—Karl was thinking only of the perfume, nothing
else—he collided violently with Robinson, who had finally given up
searching under the sofa and, beginning to suspect where the perfume might be, was running as though blindly towards Karl. Their
heads could be distinctly heard knocking together, Karl remained
mute, but Robinson, though without ceasing to run, screamed, in
order to ease his pain, incessantly and at an exaggerated volume.

'Instead of looking for the perfume, they're fighting,' said Brunelda.
'This household is making me ill, Delamarche, I'm quite sure I shall
die in your arms. I've got to have the perfume,' she then called, rous-
ing herself, 'I've absolutely got to have it. I'm not getting out of the
tub till someone brings it to me, even if I have to stay here till night-
time.' And she struck the water with her fist, one could hear the
splash.

But the perfume wasn't in the drawer of the dinner-table either, it
contained lots of old articles of toiletry belonging to Brunelda, such
as old powder-puffs, jars of make-up, hairbrushes, curlers, and many
small objects that were matted and stuck together, but the perfume
wasn't there. And Robinson, who, still screaming, was in a corner
opening and rummaging through about a hundred boxes and cases
piled up there, one after the other, always dropping half the contents,

mostly sewing-things and letters, on the floor and leaving it there, couldn't find anything, as he occasionally indicated to Karl by shaking his head and shrugging his shoulders.

Then Delamarche jumped out of the washing-room in his under-clothes, while Brunelda could be heard weeping convulsively. Karl and Robinson paused in their search and looked at Delamarche, who, completely soaked, with water dripping even from his face and hair, shouted: 'Now start searching, if you don't mind.' 'Here!' he first ordered Karl to search, and then 'There!' to Robinson. Karl did indeed search, checking even the places where Robinson had been commanded to look, but he no more found the perfume than did Robinson, who put less energy into searching than into keeping an eye on Delamarche, who, as far as space allowed, was going up and down in the room stamping his feet and would undoubtedly have liked best to give both Karl and Robinson a good thrashing.

'Delamarche,' cried Brunelda, 'come and dry me at least. Those two aren't going to find the perfume and they're just messing everything up. Tell them to stop searching at once. Right now! And let go of everything! And not touch anything else! I expect they'd like to turn the flat into a pig-sty. Take them by the collar, Delamarche, if they won't stop! But they're still working, I just heard a box falling. Tell them not to pick it up, they should leave everything lying and get out of the room! Bolt the door behind them and come to me. I've been in the water for far too long, my legs are already quite cold.'

'Right away, Brunelda, right away,' called Delamarche, hurrying with Karl and Robinson to the door. But before he let them out, he gave them orders to fetch breakfast and if possible borrow from some-one a good perfume for Brunelda.

'Your place is so untidy and dirty,' said Karl outside in the corri-dor, 'as soon as we come back with breakfast we must start tidying it up.'

'If only I weren't so ill,' said Robinson. 'And such treatment!' Robinson must be hurt that Brunelda didn't make the slightest dis-tinction between him, who had after all been serving her for months, and Karl, who had only arrived yesterday. But he deserved nothing better, and Karl said: 'You must pull yourself together a bit.' But in order not to abandon him entirely to his despair, he added: 'After all, it will only need to be done once. I'll make a bed for you behind the chests of drawers, and once things have been tidied up a bit, you'll be able to lie there the whole day, not bother about anything, and soon recover your health.'

'Now even you can see what sort of state I'm in,' said Robinson, turning his face away from Karl in order to be alone with himself and his suffering. 'But will they ever let me lie in peace?'

'If you want, I'll talk about that myself with Delamarche and Brunelda.'

'Has Brunelda any consideration?' shouted Robinson, and, without giving Karl any warning, he knocked open with his fist a door they had just come to.

They entered a kitchen, from whose oven, which seemed in need of repair, small black clouds were rising. In front of the oven door one of the women whom Karl had seen yesterday in the corridor was kneeling and with her bare hands putting large lumps of coal into the fire, which she was examining from every angle. As she did so, in a posture that was uncomfortable for an old woman, she was groaning.

'Of course, here comes this nuisance,' she said on seeing Robinson, rose laboriously to her feet with one hand on the coal-scuttle, and closed the oven door, the handle of which she had wrapped in her apron. 'Now at four in the afternoon'—Karl looked in astonishment at the kitchen clock—'you still want your breakfast? What a shower!'

'Sit down,' she said then, 'and wait till I have time for you.'

Robinson drew Karl down onto a low bench near the door and whispered to him: 'We must do what she says. You see, we depend on her. We rented our room from her and of course she can give us notice at any moment. But we can't change flats, how would we move all the stuff again, and above all Brunelda isn't transportable.'

'And isn't there another room to be found on this corridor?' asked Karl.

'Nobody will take us in,' answered Robinson, 'nobody in the whole building will take us in.'

So they sat silently on their bench and waited. The woman kept running between two tables, a tub of washing, and the oven. From her exclamations it appeared that her daughter was ill, so she had to do all the work of attending to and providing for thirty lodgers on her own. On top of this, the oven was damaged, she couldn't prepare the food, a thick soup was cooking in two gigantic pots, and however often the woman tested it with ladles and poured it down from high up, she couldn't get it right, it must be the fault of the inadequate fire, and so she sat down in front of the oven door, almost on the floor, and raked about in the glowing coals with the poker. The smoke which filled the kitchen gave her a cough which at times was so violent that she would reach for a chair and for several minutes do nothing but cough. She often observed that today she wouldn't be able to supply any breakfast at all, because she had neither time nor inclination. As Karl and Robinson had on the one hand been ordered to fetch breakfast, but on the other had no way of forcing her to provide it, they made no answer to such observations, but remained sitting silently as before.

All around, on chairs and footstools, on and under the tables, even on the ground, squashed in a corner, the lodgers' unwashed breakfast crockery was still lying. There were jugs in which a little coffee or milk was still to be found, many of the plates still had remnants of butter, a large tin box had fallen over and cakes had rolled out of it. It was certainly possible to use all this to make a breakfast with which Brunelda, provided she didn't know where it had come from, couldn't have found the slightest fault. Just as Karl was thinking this and a glance at the clock showed him that they had already been waiting for half an hour and Brunelda might be in a rage and urging Delamarche to punish their servants, the woman called in the midst of a coughing fit—during which she stared at Karl—'You can sit here all right, but you won't get any breakfast. But in two hours you can get supper.'

'Come on, Robinson,' said Karl, 'we'll make breakfast ourselves.' 'What?' exclaimed the woman, bending her head. 'Do please be reasonable,' said Karl, 'why won't you give us breakfast? We've been waiting for half an hour, that's long enough. You get paid for everything, and I'm sure we pay you better prices than anyone else. I know it's a nuisance for you that we have breakfast so late, but we're your lodgers, we're in the habit of breakfasting late and you've got to adjust to us a bit. Of course this is a particularly difficult day for you because your daughter is ill, but to make up for that we're prepared to put breakfast together from the leftovers, if there's no alternative and you won't give us a fresh breakfast.'

But the woman wouldn't enter into an amicable discussion with anyone, she felt that for these lodgers even the leftovers from the other breakfasts were too good; but on the other hand she was already fed up with the impertinence of the two servants, so she seized a tray and thrust it against Robinson, who only gradually realized, with a self-pitying expression, that he was supposed to hold the tray and receive the food that the woman was going to choose. She now loaded the tray in a great hurry with a lot of things, but it all looked more like a pile of dirty crockery than like a breakfast ready to be served. Even as the woman was forcing them out and they, hunched as though fearing insults or blows, were hurrying to the door, Karl took the tray from Robinson's hands, for with Robinson he didn't think it was safe enough.

In the corridor, once they were far enough from the landlady's door, Karl sat down on the floor with the tray, in order especially to clean the tray, collect the things that belonged together, pouring the milk into one jug and scraping the various scraps of butter onto one plate, then to remove all signs of previous use, cleaning the knives and spoons, trimming the pieces of bread from which bites had been taken, and thus giving the whole thing a better appearance. Robinson thought this work unnecessary and claimed that breakfast had often looked much worse, but Karl remained impervious and was only glad that Robinson with his dirty fingers didn't try to help with the work. To keep him quiet, Karl had immediately given him—to be sure, for this occasion only, as he told him—some cakes and the thick dregs of a pot that had been filled with hot chocolate.

When they reached their flat and Robinson without more ado put his hand on the latch, Karl held him back, since it was not certain whether they would be allowed to enter. 'But of course,' said Robinson, 'he's only doing her hair.' And indeed, in the room, which had not been aired and where the curtains had not been opened, Brunelda was sitting in the armchair, her legs wide apart, and Delamarche, standing behind her, was bending low down and combing her short, probably very matted hair. Brunelda was again wearing a very loose-fitting dress, this time, however, pale pink in colour, it might be a little shorter than yesterday's, at any rate her white, coarsely knitted stockings were visible almost to the knees. Impatient at the length of time it was taking to comb her hair, Brunelda was moving her fat red tongue to and fro between her lips, sometimes she even tore herself completely away from Delamarche with the exclamation 'But Delamarche!' while he waited calmly, comb upraised, until she again reclined her head.

'It took a long time,' said Brunelda to all present, and to Karl in particular she said: 'You'll need to be a bit quicker if you want people to be satisfied with you. Robinson is so lazy and greedy, you mustn't follow his example. I expect you've had breakfast somewhere along the way, I tell you, I won't stand for that the next time.'

That was very unjust, and Robinson too shook his head and moved his lips, silently to be sure, Karl however realized that these masters could only be influenced if one gave clear proof of one's work. So he pulled a low Japanese table from a corner, covered it with a cloth, and put on it the things they had brought. Anyone who had seen where the breakfast came from would have been pleased on the whole, but otherwise, as Karl had to admit to himself, there was a lot wrong with it.

Fortunately Brunelda was hungry. She nodded complacently to Karl as he got things ready, and she often got in his way by hastily putting out her soft fat hand, ready to squash everything if given a chance, and grabbing some titbit for herself. 'He's done a good job,' she said, smacking her lips, and pulling Delamarche, who left the comb in her hair so as to continue his work later, down onto a chair beside her. Delamarche too became friendly at the sight of the meal, both were very hungry, their hands hurried hither and thither over the little table. Karl realized that the way to satisfy them was always to bring as much as possible, and recalling that in the kitchen he had left various still eatable foodstuffs lying on the floor, he said: 'As this was the first time, I didn't know how to arrange everything, next time I'll do it better.' But even as he spoke he remembered who he was talking to, he was too much caught up in his work. Brunelda nodded to Delamarche with satisfaction and gave Karl a handful of biscuits by way of reward.

FRAGMENTS

(1)

Brunelda's Departure

ONE morning Karl pushed the invalid carriage in which Brunelda was sitting out of the gateway. It was no longer so early as he had hoped. They had agreed to undertake their migration* during the night in order not to attract the attention in the streets that would have been unavoidable by day, even though Brunelda wanted to cover herself modestly with a big grey blanket. But transporting her down the stairs had taken too long, despite the very ready assistance of the student, who turned out to be much weaker than Karl. Brunelda was very brave, scarcely groaned at all, and tried to make her bearers' work easier in every way. But there was nothing for it but to put her down on every fifth step in order to give themselves and her the time for the bare minimum of rest. It was a chilly morning, the air in the corridors was as cold as in cellars, but Karl and the student were bathed in sweat and whenever they paused to rest they had to take a corner of Brunelda's blanket, which she kindly held out to them, in order to wipe their faces. Hence it took them two hours to get to the bottom, where the carriage had been standing since the night before. Lifting Brunelda into it cost some labour, but then they could feel that they had done the job successfully, for pushing the carriage, thanks to its high wheels, could not be hard, and their only fear was that the carriage might fall apart under Brunelda's weight. This danger, to be sure, just had to be accepted, they couldn't bring along a spare carriage, though the student had half-jokingly offered to get one ready and pull it along. They now took their leave of the student, very cordially. All the disagreements between Brunelda and the student seemed to be forgotten, he even apologized for insulting Brunelda during her illness, but Brunelda said all that had long been forgotten and more than made up for. Finally, as a memento of her, she asked the student to be kind enough to accept a dollar, which she laboriously brought out from among her many petticoats. Given Brunelda's well-known meanness, this present meant a great deal, the student was genuinely very pleased and from pleasure threw the coin high into the air. Then, to be sure, he had to look for it on the ground and Karl had to help him, finally Karl found it under Brunelda's carriage. The leave-taking between the student and Karl was of course much simpler, they merely shook hands and said they were sure that they would meet again and that by that time at least one of them—the student said it would be Karl, Karl that it would be the student— would have achieved something brilliant, which as yet, unfortunately, was not the case. Then Karl cheerfully grasped the handle of the carriage and pushed it out of the gateway. The student watched them till they were out of sight, waving a handkerchief. Karl often turned back to nod and wave, Brunelda too would have liked to turn round, but such movements cost her too much effort. To let her bid a final farewell all the same, at the end of the street Karl turned the carriage round in a circle so that Brunelda too could see the student, who took advantage of this opportunity to wave his handkerchief with particular zeal.

But then Karl said that now they couldn't afford to pause any longer, they had a long way to go and had set out much later than they intended. Indeed carts were already to be seen here and there and also, though only occasionally, people going to work. By his remark Karl had meant to imply nothing more than he had actually said, but the sensitive Brunelda understood it differently and covered herself completely in her grey blanket. Karl made no objection; the carriage covered with a grey blanket was certainly very conspicuous, but incomparably less conspicuous than the uncovered Brunelda would have been. He went very cautiously; before turning a corner he would scrutinize the next street, would even, if it seemed necessary, leave the carriage and take a few steps ahead by himself, if he foresaw what could be a disagreeable encounter he would wait till it could be avoided or would even choose a route through a quite different street. Even then, as he had carefully studied all the possible routes in advance, he never ran the risk of making a substantial detour. There were, to be sure, obstacles which might have been feared but could not have been foreseen in detail. Thus in a street which rose slightly, so that its whole length was visible, and happily was completely empty, an advantage that Karl sought to exploit by particular haste, from the dark corner of a gateway there suddenly emerged a policeman who asked Karl what was in the carriage that he had covered up so carefully.

However severely he had looked at Karl, he still had to smile when he raised the blanket and caught sight of Brunelda's flushed and frightened face. 'What?' he said. 'I thought you had ten sacks of potatoes here and now it's just one woman? Where are you going? Who are you?' Brunelda dared not even look at the policeman, but only gazed at Karl, clearly doubting whether even he would be able to save her. But Karl had enough experience of policemen by now, he didn't think there was much risk in all this. 'Show the document that you were given, Miss,' he said. 'Oh yes,' said Brunelda, beginning to search in such a hopeless manner that she could not help seeming highly suspicious. 'The lady', said the policeman with unmistakable irony, 'won't be able to find the document.' 'Oh yes,' said Karl calmly, 'she's got it all right, only she's mislaid it.' He now began searching himself and did indeed pull it out from behind Brunelda's back. 'So that's it,' said the policeman, smiling, 'the lady is that kind of lady?* And you, my boy, are in charge of making contacts and transporting her? Can you really not find a better job?' Karl merely shrugged his shoulders, here were the police interfering again in their well-known way. 'Well, have a good trip,' said the policeman, on receiving no answer. The policeman's words probably implied contempt, so Karl went on his way without saying goodbye, contempt from the police was better than their attention.

Shortly afterwards he had an, if anything, even more unpleasant encounter. A man came up to him, pushing a cart with big jugs of milk, and extremely anxious to know what was under the grey blanket on Karl's carriage. It was not likely that he was taking the same route as Karl, yet he stayed at his side, whatever unexpected changes of direction Karl might make. At first he confined himself to exclamations such as 'You must have a heavy load!' or 'You've loaded that badly, something's going to fall out.' Later, however, he asked outright: 'What have you got under the blanket?' Karl said: 'What's that to you?' But as this only made the man more inquisitive, Karl said finally: 'It's apples.' 'What a lot of apples!' said the man in astonishment, and wouldn't stop repeating this exclamation. 'That's a whole harvest,' he said then. 'Sure,' said Karl. But whether he didn't believe Karl, or whether he wanted to annoy him, he went further, beginning—all this while pushing his cart—to stretch out his hand towards the blanket as though in fun, and finally venturing to give a tug at the blanket. What must Brunelda be going through! Out of consideration

for her Karl didn't want to get into a quarrel with the man and pushed
the carriage into the nearest open gateway, as though that had been
his destination. 'This is where I live,' he said, 'thanks for your company.' The man stopped outside the gateway in astonishment and
gazed after Karl, who was quite prepared if necessary to cross the
whole of the first courtyard. The man could no longer be in any doubt,
but to satisfy his malice one last time he left his cart, ran after Karl on
tiptoe, and tugged at the blanket so hard that he almost exposed
Brunelda's face. 'To give your apples some air,' he said, running back.
Karl took even this in his stride, as it finally freed him from the man.
He then pushed the carriage into a corner of the courtyard where
there were some big empty crates, wanting to say some soothing
words to Brunelda under their cover. But he had to spend a long time
reassuring her, for she was bathed in tears and begged him in all seriousness to stay here behind the crates all day and only continue their
journey at night. On his own he might not have been able to convince
her of how mistaken that would have been, but when somebody at the
other end of the pile of crates threw an empty crate to the ground
with a monstrous crash that echoed all through the empty courtyard,
she got such a fright that without daring to say another word she
pulled the blanket over herself and was probably only too glad when
Karl, without further ado, promptly continued their journey.

The streets were now filling up with people, but the attention the
carriage aroused was not so great as Karl had feared. Perhaps, all
things considered, it would have been wiser to choose a different time
to transport Brunelda. If such a journey should be necessary again,
Karl would venture to undertake it at midday. Without any more serious hold-ups, he at last turned into the narrow dark alley where
Enterprise No. 25 was situated. The wall-eyed manager was standing
outside the door with his watch in his hand. 'Are you always so
unpunctual?' he asked. 'There were all sorts of obstacles,' said Karl.
'There always are, as we all know,' said the manager. 'But in this house
they don't count. Mind that!' Karl hardly listened to such utterances
any longer, everyone exploited his power to insult the lowly. Once you
were used to it, it didn't sound any different from the regular striking
of a clock. He was alarmed, however, as he now pushed the carriage
into the hallway, by the dirt that prevailed here and which he had, to
be sure, expected. It was, when you looked more closely, not dirt that
you could put your hand on. The stone floor of the hallway had been

swept almost clean, the painting on the walls was not old, the artificial palm-trees had only a little dust on them, and yet everything was greasy and repulsive, it was as though everything had been put to a bad use and as if no amount of cleanliness could ever set that right. Karl, whenever he arrived at a new place, liked thinking about what could be improved and what a pleasure it must be to get started straight away, without considering the perhaps endless work it would cause. Here, however, he did not know what was to be done. He slowly took the blanket off Brunelda. 'Welcome, Miss,' said the manager in an affected tone, there was no doubt that Brunelda was making a good impression on him. As soon as Brunelda noticed this, she knew, as Karl saw with satisfaction, how to turn it to her advantage. All the fear of the last few hours disappeared. She

(2)

KARL saw at a street corner a poster with the following announcement: 'Today on the Clayton* racecourse, from six a.m. till midnight, staff will be recruited for the theatre in Oklahama!* The great theatre of Oklahoma is calling you! It is calling only today, only once! Anyone who misses the opportunity now, misses it for ever! Anyone who is thinking about his future belongs to us! Everyone is welcome! If you want to be an artist, come along! We are the theatre that can use everyone, each in his place! Anyone who decides to join us gets our congratulations right now! But hurry so that you can be admitted before midnight! At twelve everything will close down and not be opened again! A curse on anyone who doesn't believe us! Off to Clayton!'

A lot of people were standing in front of the poster, but it did not seem to find much favour. There were so many posters, nobody believed in posters any more. And this poster was even more implausible than posters usually are. Above all it had one great fault: it contained not a word about payment. If that had been remotely worth mentioning, the poster would surely have specified it; it would not have forgotten the thing most likely to tempt people. Nobody wanted to be an artist, but everybody wanted to be paid for his work.

For Karl, however, the poster contained something very tempting. 'Everyone is welcome,' it said. Everyone, so that meant Karl as well.

Everything he had done hitherto was forgotten, nobody would criticize him for it. He could report for a job that was not shameful, but to which, instead, a public invitation was issued! And the promise was given just as publicly that he too would be accepted. He asked for nothing better, he wanted to find the beginning of a respectable career at last, and here perhaps it showed itself. Even if all the bombast in the poster was a lie, even if the great theatre of Oklahama were a small travelling circus, it was seeking to employ people, that was sufficient. Karl did not read the poster a second time, but he did once again seek out the sentence: 'Everyone is welcome'.

First he thought of going to Clayton on foot, but that would have meant three hours' brisk walk, and he might arrive just in time to learn that all the available jobs had been taken. According to the poster, to be sure, the number of people to be taken on was unlimited, but all such job offers were always written like that. Karl realized that he must either give up on the job or travel by train. He counted up his money, without this journey it would have lasted for a week, he pushed the small change to and fro on the palm of his hand. A gentleman who had been watching him tapped him on the shoulder and said: 'Have a good journey to Clayton.' Karl nodded mutely and went on counting. But he soon made up his mind, set aside the money he needed for the journey, and ran to the subway.

As soon as he got out in Clayton, he heard the noise of many trumpets. It was a confused noise, the trumpets were not in tune with one another, they were being blown quite heedlessly. But that did not bother Karl, instead it confirmed for him that the Theatre of Oklahoma was a big enterprise. But as he came out of the station and saw the whole set-up in front of him, he saw that it was all much bigger than he could possibly have imagined, and he did not understand how an enterprise could go to such lengths just in order to recruit staff. In front of the entrance to the racecourse a long, low stage had been erected, on which a hundred women, dressed as angels in white sheets with big wings on their backs, were blowing on long gleaming golden trumpets. They were not directly on the stage though, but each was standing on a pedestal, which, however, could not be seen, for the long flowing sheets of the angel costume covered it completely. As the pedestals were very high, probably as much as two metres high, the women's forms looked gigantic, only their small heads rather spoiled the impression of great size, and their loose hair hung down, too short and almost ridiculous, between their big wings and at their sides. In order to avoid monotony, pedestals of very different sizes had been used, some women were quite low down and seemed not much taller than they were naturally, but alongside them others had mounted to such a height that one feared the slightest gust of wind might put them in danger. And now all these women were blowing trumpets.

There were not many people listening. Ten or so lads, small by comparison with those big figures, were walking to and fro in front of the stage and looking up at the women. They pointed out this or that one to each other, but they seemed to have no intention of going in and getting taken on. Only a single older man was to be seen, he was standing a little apart. He had also brought his wife and a baby in a pram. His wife was holding the pram with one hand and supporting herself with the other on the man's shoulder. They were admiring the spectacle, but one could tell that they were disappointed. They had no doubt expected to find the chance of work, but this trumpet-blowing perplexed them.

Karl was in the same position. He went close to the man, listened to the trumpets for a little, and then said: 'This is the place where people are being taken on for the Theatre of Oklahoma, isn't it?' 'That's what I thought,' said the man, 'but we've been waiting here for an hour and we've heard nothing but the trumpets. There's no poster to be seen anywhere, nobody giving instructions, nobody who could provide any information.' Karl said: 'Perhaps they're waiting till more people have gathered. There are really very few here as yet.' 'Possibly,' said the man, and they were silent again. It was difficult to make out anything amid the noise of the trumpets. But then the woman whispered something to her husband, he nodded and she promptly called to Karl: 'Couldn't you go into the racetrack and ask where people are taken on.' 'Yes,' said Karl, 'but I'd have to go over the stage, amid all the angels.' 'Is that so difficult?' asked the woman. She thought it was easy for Karl to go, but she didn't want to send her husband. 'All right,' said Karl, 'I'll go.' 'You're very kind,' said the woman, and both she and her husband shook Karl's hand. The lads gathered in a group to watch Karl climbing onto the stage. The women seemed to blow harder in order to welcome the first job-seeker. But those whose pedestals Karl happened to pass even removed the trumpets from their mouths and bent sideways to follow his path.

Karl saw at the other end of the stage a man walking up and down uneasily, obviously just waiting for people so that he could provide all the information anyone could wish for. Karl was about to go straight up to him when he heard his name being called above his head. 'Karl,' called an angel. Karl looked up and began to laugh from surprise and pleasure; it was Fanny. 'Fanny,' he called, waving to her. 'Do come here,' called Fanny, 'you surely aren't going to pass me by.' And she parted her sheets so that the pedestal and a small flight of steps leading up it were exposed. 'Am I allowed to come up?' asked Karl. 'Who's going to stop us from shaking hands,' cried Fanny, looking round angrily in case anyone were coming to issue such a prohibition. But Karl was already running up the steps. 'Not so fast,' cried Fanny, 'the pedestal will fall over, and so will both of us.' But nothing happened, Karl got safely to the highest step. 'Just look,' said Fanny after they had welcomed each other, 'just look what sort of job I've got.' 'It's lovely,' said Karl, looking round. All the women nearby had noticed Karl and were giggling. 'You're almost the highest,' said Karl, stretching out his hand to estimate how high the others were. 'I saw you right away,' said Fanny, 'when you came out of the station, but unfortunately I'm in the back row here, I can't be seen and I couldn't call either. I did blow specially loud, but you didn't recognize me.' 'All of you play badly,' said Karl. 'Let me have a go.' 'Of course,' said Fanny, handing him the trumpet, 'but don't spoil the chorus, or I'll lose my job.' Karl began to blow, he had imagined that it was a crudely made trumpet, just intended to make a noise, but now it appeared that it was an instrument capable of almost any subtlety. If all the instruments were of the same design, they were being used very badly. Karl, without letting himself be distracted by the others' noise, used all his strength to play a song that he had once heard in a pub somewhere. He was glad to have met an old friend, to have the special privilege of playing the trumpet here, and possibly to get a good job soon. Many women stopped blowing and listened; when he suddenly broke off, barely half the trumpets were being played, only gradually did the complete noise resume. 'You're an artist,' said Fanny, when Karl handed her back the trumpet. 'Are men taken on as well?' asked Karl. 'Yes,' said Fanny, 'we play for two hours. Then our place is taken by men dressed as devils. One half plays the trumpet, the other half beats the drum. It's very beautiful, and all the equipment is very expensive. Aren't our dresses lovely too? And our wings?' She looked down at herself. 'Do you think,' asked Karl, 'that I'll get a job as well?' 'Of course you will,' said Fanny, 'after all, it's the biggest theatre in the world. How lucky it is that we'll be together again. To be sure, it depends what kind of job you get. You see, even if we're both employed here, we might never see each other.' 'Is the whole thing really that big?' asked Karl. 'It's the biggest theatre in the world,' said Fanny once more, 'to be sure, I haven't seen it yet myself, but many of my colleagues who've been in Oklahama say it's almost limitless.' 'But not many people are coming forward,' said Karl, pointing down to the lads and the little family. 'That's true,' said Fanny. 'But remember that we take people on in every city, that our troop of recruiters is always on the move, and that there are many more such troops.' 'Hasn't the theatre been opened yet?' asked Karl. 'Oh yes,' said Fanny, 'it's an old theatre, but it keeps being enlarged.' 'I'm surprised', said Karl, 'that more people aren't crowding into it.' 'Yes,' said Fanny, 'it is odd.' 'Perhaps,' said Karl, 'the display of angels and devils frightens more people off than it attracts.' 'Fancy thinking of that,' said Fanny. 'Still, it's possible. Tell that to our director, you might be doing him a service.' 'Where is he?' asked Karl. 'In the racetrack,' said Fanny, 'on the judges' platform.' 'That surprises me too,' said Karl, 'why on earth are people taken on in the racetrack?' 'Yes,' said Fanny, 'everywhere we go, we make enormous preparations for an enormous influx of people. In the racetrack there's plenty of room. And in all the stands, where normally people place bets, the employment offices have been installed. There are said to be two hundred different offices.' 'But,' exclaimed Karl, 'does the Theatre of Oklahama earn such huge amounts that it can maintain such troops of recruiters?' 'What do we care about that,' said Fanny, 'but now, Karl, go, so you don't miss anything, I must start playing again. Try to get a job with this troop, at any rate, and come straight back to tell me. Remember, I'll be waiting anxiously for your news.' She shook his hand, told him to take care going down the steps, put the trumpet to her lips once more, but did not start blowing it until she saw that Karl had reached the ground in safety. Karl replaced her sheets over the steps as they had been before. Fanny thanked him with a nod of her head, and Karl, pondering what he had just heard from various angles, went up to the man, who had already seen Karl aloft with Fanny and had approached the pedestal in order to wait for him.

'You want to join us?' asked the man. 'As the head of personnel with this troop, I bid you welcome.' He constantly bent forward a little, as though from politeness, skipped up and down, though without moving from the spot, and played with his watch-chain. 'Thank you,' said Karl, 'I read your company's poster and I'm reporting for duty as requested.' 'Quite correct,' said the man approvingly, 'unfortunately not everyone here behaves so correctly.' Karl thought of drawing the man's attention to the possibility that the recruiting troop's advertising methods failed precisely because they were so grandiose. But he did not say it, because this man was not the director of the troop, and anyway it would not have been much of a recommendation if he had started suggesting improvements before he had even been taken on. So he only said: 'There's somebody else waiting outside who wants to report for duty and sent me on ahead. May I fetch him now?' 'Of course,' said the man, 'the more the merrier.' 'He's got a woman with him and a baby in a pram. Are they to come as well?' 'Of course,' said the man, seeming to smile at Karl's uncertainty. 'We can use everyone.' 'I'll be right back,' said Karl, and ran back again to the edge of the stage. He waved to the couple and called out that everyone could come. He helped to lift the pram onto the stage and they now went together. The lads, watching this, discussed what to do, then climbed slowly onto the stage, hesitating till the last moment, their hands in their pockets, and finally followed Karl and the family. New passengers were just emerging from the subway station, raising their arms in astonishment at the sight of the stage. Applications for jobs did seem to be livening up. Karl was very glad to have come so early, perhaps as the very first, the couple were nervous and asked all sorts of questions about whether great demands would be made of them. Karl said he didn't yet know anything for certain, but he had definitely got the impression that everyone would be taken without exception. He thought one could be confident.

The Head of Personnel came to meet them, was very pleased that so many had showed up, rubbed his hands, welcomed everyone individually with a little bow, and made them all stand in a row. Karl was the first, then came the couple, and only then the others. When they were all standing in line—the lads began jostling for positions and it took a while for them to settle down—the Head of Personnel said, as the trumpets fell silent: 'I bid you welcome in the name of the Theatre of Oklahoma. You have arrived early (though it was nearly midday), the crowd isn't yet very large, so the formalities of your reception can be dealt with quickly. Of course you all have your personal documents with you.' The lads promptly pulled papers of some kind out of their pockets and brandished them at the Head of Personnel, the husband nudged his wife, who drew a whole bundle of papers from under the mattress of the pram, only Karl didn't have any. Would that be an obstacle to his acceptance? It was not unlikely. Still, Karl knew from experience that such rules, provided one shows some determination, can easily be got round. The Head of Personnel surveyed the line, assured himself that they all had papers, and as Karl too raised his hand, his empty hand to be sure, assumed that everything was in order with him as well. 'That's fine,' said the Head of Personnel, waving his hand to quieten the lads who wanted to have their papers examined there and then, 'your papers will now be checked in the reception offices. As you have seen from our poster, we can use everyone. But of course we have to know what kind of job each has had before, so that we can put him in the right place to make use of his expertise.' 'It's a theatre, after all,' thought Karl doubtfully, listening with close attention. 'Therefore,' continued the Head of Personnel, 'we have set up reception offices in the betting booths, one office for each job. Each of you must now tell me your job, the family as a whole should go to the husband's reception office, then I'll take you to the offices, where first your papers and then your professional knowledge will be examined by experts—it will only be a very short examination, nobody need worry. Then you will be accepted on the spot and will receive further instructions. So let's begin. Here the first office is intended, as the sign says, for engineers. Is there by any chance an engineer among you?' Karl raised his hand. He thought that, precisely because he had no papers, he should try to get through all the formalities as quickly as possible, and he was in a way justified in raising his hand, because he had wanted to become an engineer. But when the lads saw Karl raising his hand, they became envious and raised their hands too, everybody raised his hand. The Head of Personnel stood up straight and said to the lads: 'Are you engineers?' Then they all slowly lowered their hands, whereas Karl persisted in identifying himself. The Head of Personnel did look disbelievingly at him, for Karl seemed to him too shabbily dressed and also too young to be an engineer, but he said nothing more, perhaps from gratitude, because Karl, at least in his opinion, had brought the applicants in. He simply pointed invitingly towards the office and Karl went there, while the Head of Personnel turned to the others.

In the office for engineers two gentlemen were sitting at either side of a rectangular desk, comparing two large lists that were lying in front of them. One read aloud, the other ticked off the names in his list as they were read out. When Karl came up to them with a greeting, they immediately put away their lists, took out some other big books, and opened them. One, evidently only a clerk, said: 'Please give me your personal papers.' 'I'm afraid I haven't got them with me,' said Karl. 'He hasn't got them with him,' said the clerk to the other gentleman, promptly writing the answer in his book. 'You are an engineer?' asked the other, who seemed to be in charge of the office. 'Not yet,' said Karl quickly, 'but—' 'That's enough,' said the gentleman much more quickly, 'then you don't belong to us. Please pay attention to the sign.' Karl gritted his teeth, the gentleman must have noticed this, for he said: 'There's no reason to worry. We can use everyone.' And he waved to one of the servants who were going to and fro between the barriers with nothing to do: 'Take this gentleman to the office for people with technical knowledge.' The servant interpreted the order literally and took Karl by the hand. They went past many booths, in one of them Karl saw one of the lads who had already been accepted and was gratefully shaking hands with the gentlemen there. In the office to which Karl was now taken the procedure, as Karl had foreseen, was similar to that in the first office. But when people heard that he had attended a secondary school, he was sent to the office for former secondary-school pupils. However, when Karl said there that he had attended a European secondary school, he was told he was again in the wrong place and was sent to the office for European secondary-school pupils. It was a booth on the outer edge, not only smaller but also lower than any of the others. The servant who had brought him here was furious at having to take Karl such a distance and at being turned away so many times, which, in his opinion, was entirely Karl's fault. He did not wait for the questioning but ran off immediately. This office must be the last refuge. When Karl caught sight of the manager, he was almost frightened by the latter's resemblance to a teacher who was probably still teaching in the school at home. The resemblance, as immediately became apparent, consisted only in details, but the spectacles resting on the broad nose, the full beard cared for as though it were an item on display, the gently stooping back, and the loud voice, always bursting out unexpectedly, caused Karl an astonishment from which he did not recover for some time.

Fortunately he did not have to pay close attention, for things were simpler here than in the other offices. Certainly the fact that his papers were missing was noted down, and the manager called it an incomprehensible piece of carelessness, but the clerk, who had the upper hand here, quickly passed over the matter and after the manager had asked a few short questions and was preparing to ask a bigger question, declared that Karl had been accepted. The manager turned open-mouthed to the clerk, but the latter made a decisive gesture, said: 'Accepted,' and promptly entered the decision in his book. Evidently the clerk thought that to have been a European secondary-school pupil was something so shameful that anyone who claimed to have been one must immediately be believed. Karl for his part had no objection to make, he went up to him and was about to thank him. However, there was another small delay when he was asked his name. He did not answer immediately, he was shy of giving his real name and having it written down. Once he had been given a job, however tiny, and done it satisfactorily, then people could learn his name, but not now, he had concealed it for so long that he wasn't going to reveal it now. So, as no other name occurred to him at that moment, he gave the name by which he had been called in his last few posts: 'Negro.'* 'Negro?' asked the manager, turning his head and pulling a face as though Karl's untrustworthiness had reached its limit. The clerk too looked searchingly at Karl for a while, but then he repeated 'Negro' and wrote the name down. 'You haven't written down Negro, have you,' roared the manager. 'Yes, Negro,' said the clerk calmly, with a gesture as though the manager now had to take the next steps. The manager controlled himself, stood up, and said: 'So you and the Theatre of Oklahama—' But he couldn't say any more, he could not defy his own conscience, he sat down and said: 'His name isn't Negro.' The clerk raised his eyebrows, stood up himself, and said: 'Then I inform you that you have been accepted by the Theatre of Oklahama and will now be introduced to our director.' Another servant was summoned and took Karl to the judges' platform.

At the foot of the stairs Karl saw the pram, and the married couple were just coming down, the woman holding the baby in her arms. 'Have you been taken on?' asked the man, he was much livelier than before, and his wife was laughing as she looked over his shoulder. When Karl answered that he had just been taken on and was going to be introduced, the man said: 'Then I congratulate you. We've been taken on too, it seems to be a good enterprise, to be sure it takes a while to learn your way around, but it's like that everywhere.' They said 'goodbye' to each other, and Karl climbed up to the platform. He walked slowly, for the small space up above seemed to be crammed with people, and he did not want to thrust his way in. He even paused to survey the great racecourse, which on all sides stretched as far as the distant forests. He felt like seeing a horse-race, he hadn't yet had any chance to do so in America. In Europe he had once been taken to a race as a small child, but could remember nothing except that his mother had dragged him through a crowd of people who didn't want to make room. So he had really not yet seen a race at all. Behind him some machinery started creaking, he turned round and saw the apparatus that displays the names of the winners in a race now showing the following inscription: 'Kalla, merchant, with wife and child.' So here the names of those who had been accepted were notified to the offices.

Some gentlemen in animated conversation, with pencils and notebooks in their hands, were just then running down the stairs, Karl pressed himself against the balustrade to let them past and went, as there was now room, up to the top. The platform was surrounded by wooden balustrades—the whole thing looked like the flat roof of a narrow tower—and in a corner, his arms outstretched along the balustrades, sat a man with a wide, white silk ribbon, bearing the inscription: 'Director of the 10th Recruiting Troop for the Theatre of Oklahama' diagonally across his chest. On a small table beside him was a telephone, doubtless also used for the races, by which the Director evidently learnt all the necessary details about the individual applicants even before their introductions, for at first he did not ask Karl any questions, but said to a gentleman leaning beside him with legs crossed and one hand on his chin: 'Negro, a European secondary-school pupil.' And as though he took no further interest in Karl, who was bowing deeply, he looked down the stairs in case anyone else was coming. But as nobody came, he sometimes listened to the conversation that the other gentleman carried on with Karl, but mostly gazed across the racecourse and tapped his fingers on the balustrade. These delicate yet strong, long, rapidly moving fingers often attracted Karl's attention, although the other gentleman was giving him enough to do.

'You've been unemployed?' asked this gentleman first of all. This question and almost all the other questions he asked were quite simple, not at all tricky, and moreover the answers were not tested by additional questions, yet the gentleman managed, by the way in which he asked them with wide-open eyes, accentuated their effect by leaning forward, received the answers with his head lowered to his chest, and occasionally repeated them aloud, to give them a special significance which one did not understand but which one suspected enough to make one cautious and inhibited. Often Karl felt impelled to take back an answer he had given and substitute another that might have found more approval, yet he restrained himself, for he knew what a bad impression such wavering must make and, moreover, how impossible it was to assess the effect of most of his answers. But anyway his acceptance seemed to be certain, and the awareness of this gave him strength.

To the question whether he had been unemployed he answered with a simple 'Yes'. 'Where were you employed most recently?' asked the gentleman then. Karl was about to answer when the gentleman raised his index finger and said once more: 'Most recently!' Karl had understood the initial question correctly, he involuntarily shook his head to show that the last remark was confusing and answered: 'In an office.' That was still true, but if the gentleman asked for more detail about the kind of office it was, he would have to lie. However, the gentleman did not do so, but asked a question to which it was exceedingly easy to give a truthful answer: 'Were you happy there?' 'No,' cried Karl, almost interrupting him. Glancing sideways, Karl noticed the Director smiling slightly. Karl regretted that his last answer had been so spontaneous, but it was too tempting to yell out this No, for through his last period of employment he had wished intensely that some other employer might come in and put this question to him. But his answer might have a further bad consequence, for the gentleman could now ask why he hadn't been happy. Instead, however, he asked: 'What kind of job do you feel suited for?' This question might contain a real trap, for what was the point of asking it, as Karl had already been taken on as an actor; although he realized this, however, he could not bring himself to declare that he felt particularly suited for the acting profession. He therefore evaded the question and said, at the risk of sounding rebellious: 'I read the poster in the city and as it said that everyone could be used, I presented myself.' 'We know that,' said the gentleman, falling silent and thus showing that he still wanted an answer to his earlier question. 'I've been taken on as an actor,' said

Karl hesitantly, in order to make the gentleman understand the perplexity caused by the last question. 'That's right,' said the gentleman, relapsing into silence. 'Well,' said Karl, all his hopes of having found a job beginning to crumble, 'I don't know if I'm suited to acting in the theatre. But I'll work hard and try to perform all the tasks given to me.' The gentleman turned to the Director, both nodded, Karl seemed to have given the right answer, he plucked up courage and sat upright awaiting the next question. This ran: 'What did you originally want to study?' To make the question precise—precision mattered a great deal to the gentleman—he added: 'In Europe, I mean.' As he spoke he took his hand from his chin and made a feeble gesture as though trying simultaneously to indicate how far away Europe was and how insignificant the plans were that had once been made there. Karl said: 'I wanted to be an engineer.' He gave this answer reluctantly, it was ridiculous when he was fully conscious of his career hitherto in America to recall the old memory of wanting to be an engineer—would he ever have managed that, even in Europe?— but he could think of no other answer and therefore gave this one. But the gentleman took it seriously, as he took everything seriously. 'Well,' he said, 'I don't think you can become an engineer right away, but for the time being you might like to carry out some basic technical work.' 'Certainly,' said Karl, he was very pleased, of course if he accepted this offer he would be displaced from the rank of actor and join the technical staff, but he thought that in fact he could show his abilities better in such work. Anyway, he repeated to himself again and again, the kind of work he did mattered less than settling somewhere for the long term. 'Are you strong enough for heavy work?' asked the gentleman. 'Oh yes,' said Karl. Hereupon the gentleman made Karl come closer to him and felt his arm. 'He's a strong boy,' he said, drawing Karl by the arm over to the Director. The Director nodded and smiled, gave Karl his hand without rising from his reclining position, and said: 'Then we're through. In Oklahoma everything will be examined once more. Be a credit to our troop of recruiters!' Karl bowed in farewell, then he wanted also to take his leave of the other gentleman, but the latter was already strolling, as though he had finished his work, up and down the platform with his head held high. As Karl descended, the board at the side of the stairs had the inscription displayed on it: 'Negro, technician.' As everything here was following its orderly course, Karl would not have minded all that much if the board had shown his real name. Everything was organized with the utmost care, for at the foot of the stairs Karl was met by a servant who tied a ribbon round his arm. When Karl then raised his arm to see what was written on the ribbon, it had the perfectly correct inscription 'Technician'.

But wherever Karl might now be taken, he wanted first to tell Fanny how happily everything had turned out. To his regret, however, he learnt from the servant that both the angels and the devils had now set off for the recruiting troop's next port of call, in order to announce that the troop would be arriving there the following day. 'Pity,' said Karl, it was the first disappointment he had had in this enterprise, 'I had a friend among the angels.' 'You'll see her again in Oklahoma,' said the servant, 'but now come along, you're the last.' He led Karl along the back of the stage on which the angels had been standing earlier, now only the empty pedestals were there. However, Karl's assumption that more job-seekers would turn up without the angels' music proved not to be correct, for in front of the stage there were no longer any grown-ups at all, only a couple of children were fighting over a long white feather that had probably fallen from one of the angels' wings. A boy was holding it aloft while the other children were trying to pull down his head with one hand and with the other reaching for the feather.

Karl pointed to the children, but the servant said without looking: 'Get a move on, it took a long time for you to be accepted. They must have had doubts.' 'I don't know,' said Karl in astonishment, but he did not think so. Always, even when things were crystal clear, there was somebody who wanted to upset other people. But the friendly sight of the big platform for spectators, to which they now came, soon made Karl forget the servant's remark. On this platform a whole long bench was covered with a white cloth, all those who had been accepted were sitting on the lower bench alongside it with their backs to the racetrack and were being served food and drink. They were all cheerful and excited, just as Karl, without being noticed, took his place as the last on the bench, many got to their feet with glasses raised and one was proposing a toast to the Director of the Tenth Recruiting Troop, whom he called the 'father of the job-seekers'. Somebody pointed out that he could be seen from here, and indeed the judges' platform with the two gentlemen was visible at no great distance. Now they all brandished their glasses in that direction, Karl too seized the

glass standing in front of him, but however loudly they shouted and
however hard they tried to attract attention, there was no sign on the
judges' platform that anyone had noticed or at least wanted to take
notice of the ovation. The Director was leaning in the corner as before
and the other gentleman was standing beside him with his hand on
his chin.

A little disappointed, people sat down again, occasionally someone
would turn round towards the judges' platform, but soon people were
concerned only with the ample meal, large pieces of poultry, such as
Karl had never seen before, with many forks sticking in the crisp
roasted flesh, were handed round, wine was repeatedly poured out by
the servants—one hardly noticed it, one would be bending over one's
plate and the radiance of the red wine would fall into the goblet—and
anyone who did not want to take part in the general conversation
could look at pictures with views of the Theatre of Oklahoma that
were stacked at one end of the table in order to be passed from hand
to hand. But nobody bothered much about the pictures, and so Karl,
who was the last, only got to see one picture. To judge from this picture, however, they must all be well worth seeing. This picture showed
the box of the President of the United States.* At first glance you
might have thought it was not a box but the stage, the curved balustrade projected so far into the free space. This balustrade was made
entirely of gold in all its parts. Between the slender columns which
seemed to have been cut out with the finest scissors, medallions of
earlier presidents were fixed in a row, one had a remarkably straight
nose, thick lips, and eyes staring downwards under their arched lids.
All round the box, from the sides and from above, there came rays of
light; the foreground of the box was revealed in white yet soft light,
while its recesses, behind folds of red velvet in many shades that hung
down all round the sides and could be moved by cords, seemed to be
a dark, reddish, shimmering emptiness. One could hardly imagine
people in the box, it all seemed so autocratic. Though Karl did not
forget to eat, he kept looking at the picture, which he had put beside
his plate.

He would very much have liked to see at least one of the other
pictures, but he did not want to go and get it himself, for a servant
had his hand lying on the pictures and no doubt they had to be kept
in the right sequence, so he tried only to look down the table and
work out whether another picture might be on its way. Then to his

astonishment—at first he couldn't believe it—he noticed among the faces bent lowest over their plates a well-known one—Giacomo. He immediately ran over to him. 'Giacomo,' he cried. The latter, shy as he always was when taken by surprise, rose from his meal, turned round in the confined space between the benches, wiped his mouth with his hand, but was then very glad to see Karl, asked him to sit down beside him or offered to come over to Karl's seat, they wanted to tell each other everything and always stay together. Karl did not want to disturb the others, so suggested that for the time being each should stay in his seat, the meal would soon be over and then of course they should stay together. But Karl remained with Giacomo all the same, just in order to look at him. What memories of past times! Where was the Head Cook? What was Therese doing? Giacomo himself had scarcely changed in his appearance, the Head Cook's prediction that within six months he would be a bony American had not been fulfilled, he was as delicate as before, his cheeks were sunken as before, at the moment to be sure they were round, because he had in his mouth a huge chunk of meat from which he was slowly removing the bones in order to throw them onto his plate. As Karl could read on his armband, Giacomo too had been taken on not as an actor but as a lift-boy, the Theatre of Oklahoma really seemed able to use everybody.

Lost in the sight of Giacomo, Karl stayed too long away from his seat. Just as he was about to return, the Head of Personnel arrived, took his place on one of the higher benches, clapped his hands, and delivered a little address, while most people stood up and those who remained seated, unable to tear themselves away from the meal, were finally compelled by nudges from the others to stand up as well. 'I hope', he said, Karl meanwhile had already run back on tiptoe to his seat, 'that you were pleased with our welcoming meal. On the whole the meals provided by our recruiting troop receive high praise. Unfortunately I must now bring the meal to a close, for the train that is to take you to Oklahoma leaves in five minutes. It is a long journey, but you will see that you are well provided for. I will now introduce you to the gentleman who is in charge of your transportation and whom you have to obey.' A small, skinny gentleman climbed onto the bench on which the Head of Personnel was standing, hardly took the time to make a perfunctory bow, but began at once to show with outstretched nervous hands how they were all supposed to gather, arrange themselves, and set off. But initially his instructions were not followed, for the member of the company who had previously made a speech knocked on the table with his hand and began quite a long speech of thanks, although—Karl grew most uneasy—it had just been said that the train would soon leave. But the speaker did not even take account of the fact that the Head of Personnel, instead of listening, was giving various instructions to the person in charge of their transportation, his speech was on a grand scale, he listed all the dishes that had been served, gave his opinion of each, and then gave his final summing-up with the exclamation: 'Gentlemen, that is how to win us over.' All laughed, except for those being addressed, but it was more truth than jest.

The penalty for this speech, moreover, was that people had to get to the railway at a run. That was not very difficult, however, for—Karl had not noticed it till now—nobody had any luggage—the only piece of luggage was really the pram, which, steered by the father at the head of the troop, jumped up and down as though by itself. What dubious, destitute characters had gathered here, and yet they were so well received and looked after! And the Head of Transportation practically took loving care of them. Now he would seize the handle of the pram with one hand and raise the other to encourage the troop, now he would be behind the last row urging them on, now he would run along the sides, keeping his eye on slower people and trying to show them by swinging his arms how they ought to run.

When they arrived at the station, the train was already about to go. The people in the station showed one another the troop, exclamations were heard such as 'All these belong to the Theatre of Oklahama', the theatre seemed much better known than Karl had thought, to be sure he had never bothered about theatrical matters. A whole carriage had been specially reserved for the troop, the Head of Transportation urged them to get in even more forcefully than the conductor did. He first looked into every single compartment, set right something here and there, and only then did he get in himself. Karl happened to have got a window seat and had pulled Giacomo down beside him. So they sat close together, both basically looking forward to the journey, never before had they travelled in America with such lightness of heart. When the train began to move they waved their hands out of the window, while the lads opposite nudged one another and found it ridiculous.

*

They travelled for two days and two nights. Only now did Karl realize how big America was. He never tired of looking out of the window and Giacomo squeezed up as well until the lads opposite, who spent much of their time playing cards, got tired of him and voluntarily offered him the window seat. Karl thanked them—not everyone could understand Giacomo's English—and in the course of time, as must be the case with people sharing a compartment, they became much friendlier, though their friendliness was often a nuisance, as, for example, when one of them dropped a card on the floor and looked on the floor for it, he would pinch Karl or Giacomo very hard in the leg. Giacomo would then yell, always taken by surprise anew, and pull up his legs, Karl sometimes tried to respond with a kick, but otherwise endured everything in silence. Whatever happened in the small compartment, filled with smoke even when the window was open, was trivial compared with what was to be seen outside.

On the first day they travelled through a high mountain range. Bluish-black masses of stone descended in sharp wedges as far as the train, people leaned out of the window and tried in vain to make out their peaks, dark, narrow, rugged valleys opened up, people described with their fingers the direction in which they vanished, broad mountain rivers hurried in great waves to the lower slopes and plunged, driving along a thousand little flurries of foam, under the bridges along which the train travelled and they were so close that the breath of their cold made one's face shiver.

EXPLANATORY NOTES

5 *seventeen-year-old*: later (p. 89) we learn that Karl is fifteen going on sixteen.

statue of the Goddess of Liberty: Kafka uses this slightly cumbersome formulation, and gives the statue a sword instead of a torch, presumably to draw attention to the goddess as an allegorical figure whose significance is not so much liberating as threatening. Cf. the allegorical figure in *The Trial* (tr. Mike Mitchell, Oxford World's Classics (Oxford: Oxford University Press, 2009), 104–5) who is first identified as the goddess of justice but ends up looking like the goddess of victory and the hunt.

10 *Line*: short for Adeline or Caroline; pronounced as two syllables.

12 *vermin*: the word used here, 'Ungeziefer', is also used in *The Metamorphosis* for the 'kind of monstrous vermin' into which Gregor Samsa finds himself transformed.

17 *Imperial frock-coat*: 'Kaiserrock', a long, close-fitting coat of military cut, worn on formal occasions.

23 *Senator*: this is the first time that the word 'Senator' has been used; previously he has been referred to by the German term 'Staatsrat'.

31 *elevator specially for furniture*: perhaps suggested by František Soukup's description of the lift used for transporting people and goods in the Metropolitan Life Tower, which, when built in 1909, was the world's tallest building.

33 *fire*: this was apparently suggested by Arthur Holitscher's account in *America Today and Tomorrow* (1913) of a visit to a school in Chicago, where the children recited in unison a poem about the notorious Chicago fire of 1871: see Hartmut Binder, *Kafka Kommentar zu den Romanen, Rezensionen, Aphorismen und zum Brief an den Vater* (Munich: Winkler, 1976), 102.

Mak: Kafka inconsistently writes 'Mak' or 'Mack'. Wolfgang Jahn (*Kafkas Roman 'Der Verschollene'* (Stuttgart: Metzler, 1965), 144) relates the name to that of the mysteriously powerful businessman Mack in Knut Hamsun's novel *Benoni* (1908). Hamsun's novels were extremely popular in German translation; Kafka later read his novel *Growth of the Soil* (1917).

48 *till your cheeks swell up*: as 'cheeks' can also imply 'buttocks', Elizabeth Boa comments: 'The *double-entendre* is a narrator's obscene wink to a reader who knows about spanking' ('Karl Rossmann, or the Boy who Wouldn't Grow Up: The Flight from Manhood in Kafka's *Der Verschollene*', in Mary Orr and Lesley Sharpe (eds.), *From Goethe to Gide: Feminism, Aesthetics and the French and German Literary Canon* (Exeter: University of Exeter Press, 2005), 168–83 (p. 175)).

60 *shilling*: a sign of Kafka's vagueness about American currency.

61 *'Hi'*: in the original Mack says 'Servus', a very informal greeting still common in Austria.

64 *the East*: a mistake for the West.

66 *Ramses*: this is the name of one of the cities in Egypt which the exiled Hebrews were compelled to build (Exodus 1: 11). It may have been suggested to Kafka by a Yiddish play he saw in which the servitude of Jewish immigrants in America is compared to that of their ancestors in the Egyptian cities (Evelyn Torton Beck, *Kafka and the Yiddish Theater* (Madison, Wisc.: University of Wisconsin Press, 1971), 128). It underpins the general theme of exile, but does not seem to be part of any sustained pattern of allusion.

68 *a German*: although Karl comes from Prague, in what is now the Czech Republic, he is a 'German', i.e. a member of the shrinking German-speaking minority in Bohemia.

a Frenchman: though comparatively few French people emigrated to America, Kafka's attention may have been caught by Holitscher's account of a powerfully built Frenchman, with erotic tattoos, on his way to a newly discovered goldmine at Porcupine, Ontario.

69 *Irishmen*: Kafka found this warning in Holitscher's *America Today and Tomorrow*, the 'book' alluded to here.

photograph: this is modelled on an actual photograph of Kafka's paternal grandparents, reproduced, with a sensitive commentary, in Carolin Duttlinger, *Kafka and Photography* (Oxford: Oxford University Press, 2007), 88.

70 *general*: this may have been suggested by the historical figure of Friedrich Wilhelm von Steuben (1730–94), a Prussian aristocrat who emigrated to America, became a major-general in the Continental Army during the War of Independence, and served as George Washington's chief of staff.

74 *Boston*: presumably Kafka's mistake for Brooklyn, in which case the bridge over the Hudson is based on Brooklyn Bridge, though that actually spans the East River. Kafka seems to have thought of New York and Boston/ Brooklyn as two adjacent cities of roughly equal size.

75 *black liquid*: perhaps Coca-Cola.

76 *quarter of a pound*: Kafka is uncertain about American currency, sometimes mentioning pounds, sometimes dollars, once shillings.

85 *The photograph was missing*: earlier Karl went to sleep with his face on the photograph (p. 70); the housekeeper who threw his belongings into his suitcase (p. 71) may well have missed it; so Karl's loss is probably his own fault.

88 *Grete Mitzelbach . . . Vienna*: the Head Cook's name, combined with her Viennese origin, recalls the well-known pornographic novel by Felix Salten, *Josefine Mutzenbacher: The Story of a Viennese Whore, told by herself* (1906). The Cook and Karl are compatriots because they come from different provinces of the Austro–Hungarian Empire.

88 *Wenceslas Square*: in the centre of Prague; the Golden Goose, a well-known hotel, was not demolished, but was extensively rebuilt in 1910.

91 *Pomerania*: German province along the coast of the Baltic.

95 *Rennel*: Kafka inconsistently spells the name 'Rennel' or 'Renell'.

107 *seventh floor*: elsewhere the hotel is said to have five floors. Neither is compatible with its having thirty-one lifts (p. 95) or forty lift-boys, implying twenty lifts (pp. 97, 114).

108 *Brunelda*: the name suggests Wagner's operatic heroine Brünnhilde and also recalls Karl's seductress Johanna Brummer.

115 *two months*: previously 'six weeks', but the incident is also said to occur about a month after Karl's arrival.

117 *Isbary*: the Head Waiter's unusual name is that of a nineteenth-century Austrian industrialist, Rudolf Freiherr von Isbary, who had a palatial town-house, the Palais Isbary, built in the fourth district of Vienna.

138 *nose partly eaten away*: presumably from syphilis. In a letter to his sister Elli of autumn 1921, Kafka says that of the two boys who gave him sexual information in his youth, one is now severely disfigured by syphilis, while the other is a professor of medicine specializing in venereal diseases. This boy, whom Karl thinks of later (p. 173), might have played an important role if Kafka had continued the story.

146 *courtyards*: Kafka obviously imagines American tenements as built on the Central European model, with one or more linked courtyards and staircases opening off them.

147 *shining blonde hair*: this girl may be identical with the landlady's daughter who is said to be ill (p. 186). Binder surmises that if Kafka had continued the story, this girl would have come into contact with Karl and perhaps got him into renewed trouble (*Kommentar zu den Romanen*, 137–8).

191 *migration*: this translates 'Auswanderung', which normally means 'emigration' and implies that Karl's enforced emigration to America makes him a migrant within it, while preserving the suggestion of exile; in their translations Mark Harman and Michael Hofmann have 'exodus', perhaps overemphasizing the possible allusion to the exodus of the Israelites from Egypt (for which the usual German word would be 'Auszug').

193 *that kind of lady*: this hint, and the description of Enterprise No. 25, suggest that Karl and Brunelda are involved in prostitution.

195 *Clayton*: Kafka found the name in Holitscher's book, where it appears as a person's forename.

Oklahama: this is the spelling in Kafka's manuscript, evidently suggested by the misprint 'Oklahama' in Holitscher's book.

203 *Negro*: Kafka originally wrote 'Leo'. Hartmut Binder has suggested that he took the name, with several other motifs, from J. V. Jensen's story 'Der kleine Ahasverus' (published in the *Neue Rundschau* ('New Review'), which Kafka read regularly) about a little Jewish boy from Eastern Europe

called Leo who has a hard time surviving in New York (see Binder, *Kafka: Der Schaffensprozeß* (Frankfurt a.M.: Suhrkamp, 1983), 80). As 'Leo' means 'lion', it evokes also the surname of Kafka's friend the Yiddish actor Yitzkhok Löwy (German *Löwe*, lion). The replacement of Leo with Negro finally equates the oppression of Jews and blacks.

208 *President of the United States*: after Abraham Lincoln was assassinated in the Presidential box at Ford's Theatre, Washington, DC, in 1865, photographs of the box were widely disseminated. One such photograph is reproduced in Duttlinger, *Kafka and Photography*, 97.

The Oxford World's Classics Website

www.worldsclassics.co.uk

- Browse the full range of Oxford World's Classics online

- Sign up for our monthly e-alert to receive information on new titles

- Read extracts from the Introductions

- Listen to our editors and translators talk about the world's greatest literature with our Oxford World's Classics audio guides

- Join the conversation, follow us on Twitter at OWC_Oxford

- Teachers and lecturers can order inspection copies quickly and simply via our website

www.worldsclassics.co.uk

American Literature

British and Irish Literature

Children's Literature

Classics and Ancient Literature

Colonial Literature

Eastern Literature

European Literature

Gothic Literature

History

Medieval Literature

Oxford English Drama

Poetry

Philosophy

Politics

Religion

The Oxford Shakespeare

A complete list of Oxford World's Classics, including Authors in Context, Oxford English Drama, and the Oxford Shakespeare, is available in the UK from the Marketing Services Department, Oxford University Press, Great Clarendon Street, Oxford OX2 6DP, or visit the website at www.oup.com/uk/worldsclassics.

In the USA, visit www.oup.com/us/owc for a complete title list.

Oxford World's Classics are available from all good bookshops. In case of difficulty, customers in the UK should contact Oxford University Press Bookshop, 116 High Street, Oxford OX1 4BR.